DAMNATION REEF

'Never hit me again,' Marcus warned.

Instantly, Marina's hand flashed up. He caught it and bent back her arm.

'Oh!' she cried. 'You're hurting me!'

'You deserve it, ma'am. As you deserve this –'

He pulled her close and kissed her. It was different from the other time, Marina thought . . . but then thought became impossible. Her legs felt weak, and when he lifted his head at last, he had to hold her upright.

'Do you see?' he said. 'You cannot fight me, my ward. One way or another I will always win.'

Marina sighed. She lacked the strength to dispute it. For the moment he had tamed her . . .

**Also by the same author,
and available in Coronet Books:**

Shadows Of Castle Foss
Chanter's Chase
Dark At Noon

DAMNATION REEF

Jill Tattersall

CORONET BOOKS
Hodder and Stoughton

Copyright © 1979 by Jill Tattersall

First published in Great Britain 1980
by Hodder & Stoughton Ltd

Coronet edition 1982

British Library C.I.P.

Tattersall, Jill
  Damnation reef. — (Coronet books)
  I. Title
  023'.914[F]   PR6070.A68

ISBN 0 340 27543 X

Printed and bound in Great Britain for
Hodder and Stoughton Paperbacks, a
division of Hodder and Stoughton Ltd.,
Mill Road, Dunton Green, Sevenoaks,
Kent (Editorial Office: 47 Bedford
Square, London, WC1 3DP) by
Hunt Barnard Printing, Aylesbury, Bucks.

TO SIMON,

WHO HELPED

1

The ship lay adrift in the Sargasso Sea.

Overhead the relentless sun was at its height, sucking the life out of the aging *Carib Queen*, shrinking her caulking and opening the seams of her blistered longboats. From time to time a slow swell set her rolling, sending the patched sails slatting idly along the yards and drawing curses from the crew, who were lying wherever they could find shade. The passengers for the most part were in their cabins, portholes set wide; but Marina Derwent had been discovered by her chaperone unconventionally draped along the bowsprit as she gazed down entranced, into the glassy depths between the floating islands of bright sargasso weed.

Mrs. Hungerford recorked her bottle and slid it into the capacious pocket of her black skirts. She sighed as she regarded her young charge, wondering if she would have been so eager to oblige the senior Miss Derwent by chaperoning her niece to the West Indies if she had known how difficult Miss Marina would prove to control. Not that there was a drop of malice in the girl, but she was so lively, and seemed to have no notion of how a properly brought-up young lady should behave.

"I can see your h'ankles, Miss Marina," Mrs. Hungerford remarked in a reproving tone. "H'and more than that," she added darkly, stifling a hiccup. "What would that old Mrs. Winceyman say if she was to see you now—or that straitlaced Mr. Peppard?"

7

Marina sat up reluctantly, wondering why gin alone enabled Mrs. Hungerford to capture the elusive *h*, careless though she was where she inserted it.

"I was looking for sea monsters," she said dreamily. "Have you heard the tales the sailors tell about the frightful creatures that they swear inhabit these strange, unfrequented waters, far from the shipping lanes?"

Mrs. Hungerford glanced fearfully around the empty ocean wastes.

"We should never 'ave come this far off our course, 'tis true, any more than you ought to be 'obnobbing with the crew. If so be as we comes safe to shore, I swear I'll lay a complaint against the captain, that I shall."

Marina pulled off her bonnet and ran her fingers through her sun-streaked hair. "It is hardly his fault, poor man, that a contrary wind blew us so far out of the Trades that we are now becalmed. Besides, he has a wife and eight children to support at home, and is dependent on his career."

Mrs. Hungerford regarded her in amazement. "Bless me if you don't know h'everything about h'everyone on this 'ere vessel!" she exclaimed. "Not that that h'excuses Captain Burge. 'E should 'ave been more careful, if that is the case. If 'e'd shortened sail earlier, doubtless we should have been in Antilla by this time."

Marina stood up. She was tall and had the promise of beauty, but Mrs. Hungerford thought her as awkward and lanky as a colt.

"I suppose we must be almost overdue," she said thoughtfully. "I hope my aunt Derwent is not dreadfully anxious. It is so hard to wait and do nothing. And my future host, Mr. Granville—do you suppose he imagines me to be the property by now of Barbary pirates, like my namesake in *Pericles?*"

"Mr. Granville would care nothing, if 'e did think so," declared Mrs. Hungerford with a sniff. " 'Is 'eart's made of rock, as I have cause to know—and I doubt if

8

'is sister's death 'as done anything to improve 'is disposition, even though 'e may 'ave gained a fortune by it."

A shadow crossed Marina's expressive face. "I cannot yet believe my poor friend Julia is dead—still less a suicide," she murmured. "Her last letter to me was as full of life as ever. As for Mr. Granville, I am sorry to hear you speak of him like that."

Mrs. Hungerford sniffed. Fortified by gin, she was prepared to defend her remarks, but then she saw that Marina had gone off in a daydream and it hardly seemed worth the trouble of disturbing her. Marina was in fact recalling the single glimpse she had had of Mr. Granville the day he came to London to fetch his half-sister from school. She had seen him from above, for after bidding farewell herself to Julia Granville, who was her aunt Derwent's goddaughter and ready now to return to her godmother and Tamarind, her West Indian home, Marina had felt low in spirits and had retired by secret ways onto the roof. Hearing the rattle of hoofs, she paused to watch a strange carriage driving down Hans Place among the blowing autumn leaves, to pull up opposite the school's front door.

Mr. Granville had been instantly recognizable as he stepped down from the chaise, for Julia had described his black eye-patch, his noble figure, his dark-tanned face and his air of authority with a pride barely tempered by her deep resentment of her half-brother's tyranny. Remembering Julia's tales of his skill and daring, Marina had been prepared for a heroic figure, and her first sight of Marcus Granville had not disappointed her. As she was gazing down at him in uncritical admiration, however, he had disconcerted her by glancing upward, meeting her eyes with astonishment, swiftly succeeded by something both arrogant and censorious to which Marina had impulsively responded by putting out her tongue—an act for which she had mentally flayed herself a thousand times.

Mr. Granville had been admitted to the house im-

mediately. Marina had expected him to betray her to
Miss Mandevan, but since no retribution followed, it
seemed that he had kept her secret. She had been in
the habit of vowing that she had no time for young
men, apart from her cousins, who were good fellows,
but something about this West Indian planter had
undoubtedly impressed her. Her feelings about him
were confused, but strong. She began to look for mention of him in the monthly letters from her aunt
Derwent, who had been part of the household at
Tamarind so long. The Derwents had dispersed from
St. Christopher's more than twenty years before, when
a hurricane had destroyed their great plantation, Peace
and Plenty. Jane Derwent, who always had a mind of
her own, had refused to accompany her mother and
brother to England, or to seek asylum with either of
her married sisters. Instead she had agreed to go with
her friend Juliana Fox to Antilla, in order to help her
through her wedding to the somewhat formidable widower Martin Granville, who had lost his heart so
unreservedly to the ravishing Miss Fox while visiting
St. Christopher's. Once ensconced at Tamarind, Miss
Derwent had found herself staying to assist the bride
with her strongwilled little stepson, Marcus, and somehow she had remained through the years as a sort of
unofficial companion-housekeeper, guide and friend,
and godmother to Julia, the only fruit of the ill-fated
marriage. And when the shocking news had come of
Julia's death, not long after her return from school in
England, Marina had reflected that now Miss Derwent
had survived all the Granvilles but Marcus, who was
now master of Tamarind—and who dwelt in Marina's
thoughts like a persistent burr.

"I 'ave nothing against your aunt Derwent, mind
you," Mrs. Hungerford answered her, feeling she had
kept silent long enough. "She's a reasonable lady, is
Miss Derwent, especially considering she's been living
with the Granvilles these twenty years—and she's
never borne a grudge against my Mr. Flete for 'aving
blinded 'er precious young Marcus when they were

both boys. Well, young Granville asked for it really, taunting my Master Brandon for a coward when everybody knows the Fletes 'ave wicked tempers when they're aroused. 'Course my young master threw that stone, but 'e was sorry afterward—but the Granvilles couldn't seem to forgive 'im, father and son, they was both as bad."

"I suppose it is too small an island for such family feuds," Marina suggested, fanning herself and hoping that Antillan society would not prove disagreeably conflicted by such undercurrents.

Mrs. Hungerford seemed to come to a decision.

"I've been wondering whether to tell you, dear. And then I thought, Why would Miss Derwent ask me to chaperone you if she meant me to keep mum? I mean, thrown together like we are, week after week—it stands to reason everything must come out in the end. The fact of the matter is, that Mr. Marcus Granville 'as 'ad 'is revenge on Mr. Flete. Yes, you may stare, miss, but 'e bided 'is time until the older ones on both sides were dead—never mind all that scandal with Julia's mother and Ralph Flete, and 'ow 'e threw 'er over when old Granville died—no, Mr. Marcus Granville waited till my Mr. Brandon Flete inherited Maroon, and then 'e set to work to ruin 'im—set about forcing my Mr. Flete to leave the 'ouse 'e loved and what 'is father built."

Mrs. Hungerford sat down upon a hen coop in the shade of the mainsail. Marina sighed resignedly and leaned back against the rail while Mrs. Hungerford, without the least appearance of reluctance, poured out a saga of treachery and persecution, of debts called in and mortgages foreclosed, which had culminated in her Mr. Flete leaving his fine great house and moving to a shop in Spanish Wells to scrape a living out of trade.

"But are you sure that it was Mr. Granville behind all this?" Marina asked.

"'Oo else could it 'ave been?" Mrs. Hungerford demanded sharply. "My master 'as no other enemy.

11

Well, there it is, then," she summed up, mopping her face and blowing down the front of her dress. " 'E 'ad to leave Maroon in the end—but 'e wouldn't sell, not 'e. Wouldn't part with an inch of 'is land, 'e says, not if 'e starves. But 'e won't starve, ·miss. You'll see. 'E closed up Maroon and started a shop with second'and pieces and such valuables as remained to 'im, and 'e works all the time for the day when 'e can get back to 'is own. And when 'e does get back, 'e won't stop there—not until Maroon is like it used to be—one of the showplaces of the Caribbean, as they say."

"And you are helping him, I suppose," Marina suggested, glad to see the bitterness easing out of Mrs. Hungerford's hot face.

"Ay, and the Trading Company stepped in—don't ask me about business matters, miss—I believe they was something to do with the Inglebrights, what 'ad the warehouse before us. Well, there's them and Crick, of course. Crick was steward to Mr. Ralph, up at Maroon, and Crick and me, we stayed by Mr. Brandon when things went ill. Funny little fellow, Crick is, always peeping and prying into what don't concern 'im—but 'e's loyal to Mr. Flete, I'm sure, and 'e's a good worker, I must own. Well, we all are, and Mr. Flete works 'ardest of all. I'll be 'ousekeeper at Maroon again before we're done, just you wait and see!"

Marina moved from the rail. She felt hotter than ever, and restless and rather unhappy. "Well, I wish you both good fortune in your endeavours," she said with an attempt at lightness. "I hope—"

A shout from the lookout languishing in the crow's nest interrupted her. Marina looked a question at Mrs. Hungerford, but was answered by a whisper of sound like running water under the ship's bow, followed by the creak of ropes tautening and the crack of sails filling and straining.

"Wind!" Marina cried, as her long hair streamed across her face.

"Thank God," added Mrs. Hungerford fervently, thinking of their depleted, spoiling stores.

12

All around, the decks were bustling with unaccustomed activity. The helmsman seized the unattended wheel, the captain appeared upon the poop, the sailors on watch hurried to their stations. Marina grasped one of the shrouds as a stronger gust caught the *Carib Queen*. The ship leaned away from the breeze, sending the water singing under her forefoot and the wake hissing behind her as she took up the long reach again, down to the south-southwest and the far Caribbees.

Over the next days the wind steadily increased and the sailors were kept busy repairing blown-out sails and parted sheets; then came a period of fitful squalls and showers; and finally Captain Burge was able to announce that they had found the northeast Trades. Their troubles, he said buoyantly, for he was an incurable optimist, were virtually over.

"So 'e says." Mrs. Hungerford sniffed, crouching down to stir their unappetizing soup upon the galley fire, which was lit on deck once every day for the use of passengers when conditions permitted. "So 'e says—but 'ow does 'e know as we won't blunder into the midst of an engagement, and become caught in the crossfire between our ships and the Frenchies—or even be attacked by one of them Danish privateers?"

"It sounds exciting," said Marina, with shining eyes. "But I suppose the odds must be very much against it?"

"Very well for you, dear, who can swim like a fish, but what would 'appen to the likes of me if this tub sank beneath us? And it wouldn't take much of a cannonball to 'ole it, I do know that."

"I would rescue you, ma'am," Marina promised. "Certainly you must be preserved for the benefit of your Mr. Flete. Indeed," she added with a smile, "it's hard for me to understand how you could bring yourself to leave him."

"Ay, well, 'tis part of my duty, you see. Every two years or so—and this is the second time I've done

13

it—I'm required to voyage to London, to sell some particular items for Mr. Brandon. You'd think 'e could sell them back to the Trinket Trading Company," she murmured absently, as if puzzled herself. "But no, 'e won't do that—or they don't want them, perhaps. Besides, it stands to reason there's more money about in London Town. And I pays 'alf my passage, for I'm glad enough to see my relatives from time to time. No, I can't say I grudges the effort really, not when I know the profit will be put by for Maroon."

"And did you make a substantial profit on this voyage?" Marina could not refrain from asking.

"Oh, ay, such goods do fetch a 'igh price in London." But Marina noticed that Mrs. Hungerford's crumpled face showed little pleasure at the thought, and her hand crept to the great monogram in silver hanging at her neck, as if seeking some kind of reassurance from it.

It was time to change the subject, thought Marina. She picked up the ladle bravely and tasted the soup, but before she could make any comment, an elderly gentleman had hobbled up to greet them.

"Good day, Mr. Peppard," Marina exclaimed. "Will you join us in some broth?"

"No, no, my dear—I am limiting myself to biscuit, with an occasional bantam's egg as long as the birds continue to lay."

"It's all right, sir. We won't be offended," Mrs. Hungerford assured him. "It's as much as I can do to get it down myself, these days. Let's 'ope this wind 'olds up, that's all."

"Indeed, we cannot be many days off our landfall now, dear ladies. But let us hope that this will prove a good time for all travellers," he added affably. "My old friend Sir Joseph Banks, president of the Royal Society, you know, has sent off an expedition headed by Mr. Mungo Park, who is attempting to discover," he kindly explained to Mrs. Hungerford, "the reason why the Niger seems to flow away from the sea—in

14

direct contrast, of course, to the behaviour of any other river."

"Fancy," said Mrs. Hungerford. "Of course you do know, sir, that Miss Marina's father is an explorer too? Isn't that right, Miss Marina?"

"I suppose in a sense he is," Marina owned. "The Professor—my father, that is—has just set out to look for the remains of a lost city near Baghdad, among other things."

"Has he indeed? Extraordinarily interesting," Mr. Peppard exclaimed.

Marina agreed. "I longed to accompany him—but the Professor would not hear of it, which is why I'm voyaging to Antilla to stay with his sister, my aunt Derwent, whom I have never met."

"Indeed!" Mr. Peppard raised his exuberant white eyebrows. "But have you no relatives in England, Miss Derwent?"

"Oh, plenty!" Marina avowed, with a flashing smile. "But they were very quick to agree with the Professor that it was time they had a rest from me. Mrs. Hungerford will tell you why: it is because I am such a dreadful tomboy, you must know—quite incorrigible—and they fear my influence upon their daughters."

Mr. Peppard looked suitably grave. "I believe you should not say such things, Miss Derwent, even if they are true. I am bound for Jamaica myself, it does not matter what you say to me, but you will not want to offend the matrons of Antilla if you hope to find a husband there."

"But I intend no such thing!" Marina cried in genuine horror at the notion. "I am averse to the whole idea of matrimony, I do assure you!"

Mr. Peppard pursed his lips. "There are few enough young women in the islands, in all conscience," he declared. "You may expect the bachelors to do all they can to persuade you to change your mind."

"Then the sooner I can establish my ineligibility,

the better," cried Marina, with a toss of the head, like a filly refusing to be haltered.

"Lawks! The soup's boiling!" exclaimed Mrs. Hungerford, with diplomatic intentions. Mr. Peppard raised his hat, and took his leave with unconcealed haste.

"There now!" said Mrs. Hungerford reproachfully. "Just see what you've done! Ruined your reputation, you 'ave, even before you've reached Antilla."

"Good," said Marina decisively. "Now let us eat our soup. I do hope my aunt Derwent is not too straitlaced," she added thoughtfully. "My father said she used to run quite wild when they were children together in St. Christopher's. I have always longed to visit the islands," she went on, dropping a piece of rock-hard biscuit into her soup. "Especially since meeting Julia." Her mind wandered to the exotic tales Julia had told about her island home in the Caribbees, remembering the colour those stories had brought to grey weeping London. The very colour that she was now surrounded by, Marina reflected, looking about her at white sails straining against the cobalt sky, wide sapphire seas scattered with shining shoals of flying fish. Julia had had a gift for bringing just such vibrant scenes to life and filling them with action too, spinning stories out of West Indian legends of pirates and jewels and gold and rum; tales of clashing swords, bright with blood and fire, fighting over outlandish cargoes lost in the crash and thunder of that fearsome graveyard where, Julia whispered daringly, the Atlantic Ocean meets the Caribbean in a perpetual wild mating on the living coral of the reef they call Damnation. . . .

"Ay, Miss Julia could weave a spell, right enough," sighed Mrs. Hungerford, "as my poor master found when she came back from England last year, blooming like a rose."

"Mr. Flete?" Marina exclaimed. "Was he interested in Julia?"

"Couldn't take 'is eyes off 'er—and since she died, 'e don't seem able to look at any of the other young ladies. Ay, you're thinking of the feud, I daresay.

16

Well, you knew 'er, miss. You should be able to understand 'ow Miss Julia could make a man forget a family feud, 'owever bitter."

Yes, thought Marina, dipping her bowl in the nearest bucket of seawater and wiping it slowly, she could understand it well enough. She had been fascinated herself by Julia from the first moment of her arrival in Hans Place, and had been proud to claim some connection, however remote, with such a fairy-tale being, with her blue eyes and golden hair, her charm and airy grace. Even the subsequent discovery, in the relentless intimacy of school life, that Julia used her charm ruthlessly to ensure her own comfort and convenience, and that she told lies as easily as the truth, had not entirely alienated Marina's affection for her.

"Yes, Julia would not let a feud stand in her way," Marina agreed. "So it was your Mr. Brandon Flete whom Julia loved? She wrote to me not long before she died, saying she had made up her mind to marry, but she did not name the man."

"Ay, it was Mr. Flete. Granville forbade the match, of course—and the next thing we knew, the poor child had done away with herself."

Marina stared. "Was that the reason? But why did they not elope?" How could Julia, of all people, have killed herself for love when the remedy lay in her own hands?

Or was it, she wondered suddenly, that Mr. Flete had discovered the odd provisions of the Tancred trust, drawn up by Julia's other, and even more eccentric and disillusioned godmother, by which Julia would forfeit her fortune to her brother if she married, as well as if she died? Was it Mr. Flete who had jilted her, and not Mr. Granville who had broken her heart?

Marina felt unusually troubled. She had been so sure she would feel at home in the Caribbees, where her father had been born and where the sea for which she had been named was king—but now she had been made to understand that no special magic protected the islands, which were as imperfect as anywhere

17

else. It was a world after all that even Julia, who had been privileged as a princess in it, had not been able to survive. It was a violent world compounded not only of beauty and adventure, but also of fevers and storms and blood feuds, of sudden shallows and wicked deadly reefs; a world which all at once Marina felt ill equipped to face.

And it was at that moment that the long-awaited cry came from the lookout, high in the crow's nest.

"*Land!*" His call came faintly through the half-open porthole above the creakings of the straining ship. "*Land on the starboard bow!*"

2

Marina and Mrs. Hungerford stared at each other.

Above them, on the deck, they could hear shouts, and then one clearer than the rest.

"Antilla! Ay, down there—over to your right. I know it by the shape—East Mountain at this end. . . ."

"Antilla," repeated Mrs. Hungerford joyously. Then she sat up, narrowing her eyes at the porthole. "But if they can see it from the deck already, we must be close'. . ."

"Wonderful!" Marina cried, but Mrs. Hungerford shook her head.

" 'Tis almost dusk . . . I only 'ope we're easterly enough to give a wide berth to the reefs—"

The lookout's call came then, cutting off her voice and her hopes together.

"Breaking water on the starboard beam!"

"Lord save us!" gasped Mrs. Hungerford, turning sickly grey. "Breaking water! Oh, God save us!"

Marina flung herself at the porthole, expecting to see rocks, whirlpools, inevitable disaster. To her surprise there was no sign of immediate danger, only a glorious evening and the most beautifully coloured sea stretching away to the west.

Mrs. Hungerford pressed against her shoulder. "Bless us," she moaned. "These are shoal waters—do you mark that poison green?"

"Shoal waters? Do you mean—"

"Reefs on the starboard quarter!" cried the lookout, as if in answer.

Marina felt the plunge of fear within. She clenched her fists and forced her brain to concentrate.

"On the quarter," she repeated. "That means we must be past them, ma'am—the reefs are behind us now."

"Damnation Reef runs on for miles—"

"Damnation Reef?" Marina echoed, recalling Julia's tales of all the lost ships whose voyages had ended in those fatal shoals.

"Ay," moaned Mrs. Hungerford, twisting her fingers about the silver monogram at her throat, "and we'll be in darkness soon. It's not like England, 'ere, the darkness comes suddenly. The lookout was late in spying land and late in noticing 'ow close we were to shallow water. Pray God 'e don't be the death of us! I 'aven't forgot the wreck of the *Otaheite* only last year, when poor Mr. Alfred Singleton perished, and so many others."

Marina was aware of shouted commands above, and the vibration of running feet along the decks. The voice of the topmast hand came hoarsely now above the cracking of the sails and the groaning of the ship as she changed course, turning southerly and coming up closer to the wind.

"Reefs fine on the starboard bow!"

"Lord, Lord," Mrs. Hungerford was muttering, gripping Marina's arm like a drowning man. " 'Tis a bad place to be caught in the dark—a terrible, an accursed place!"

Marina could not answer, for it was at that moment she caught her first glimpse of the dreaded Reef. It was a single sun-bleached tooth of coral rearing above the spray of breaking water a few hundred yards west of the *Carib Queen*; but then other submerged brown masses became spasmodically visible in the shallow heaving seas. Staring through the salt-smeared glass, she could now make out faint lines of white surf as far as she could see, etched between steep seas of blue and green so that the whole ocean seemed to be boiling—a boiling froth in a witch's cauldron, thought Marina.

Deaf to Mrs. Hungerford's expostulations, she leaned forward to push the porthole open to its widest extent, staring out in fear and wonder at the wild beauty of racing green water, yellow and grey coral heads, flying incandescent spume turning to rainbows in the sunset glow, the stark white of narrow sandbanks so far from land . . . and away across the miles of turbulent water she could now see the hazy blue shoulder of a mountainous island half obscured by spray.

"Antilla, praise the Lord," cried Mrs. Hungerford, braving the sting of flying water to peer over Marina's shoulder. "But we are too far to the west. Only see 'ow the reefs do draw us in!"

And Marina was bound to agree that though the *Carib Queen* was now sailing on a course parallel with the nearest line of breaking water, she did seem to be pulled ever closer to it, as though the coral heads were inexorably sucking the helpless ship toward their hungry teeth.

"It must be the ocean swell, rolling us to the west," Marina murmured, reflecting that the fetch of three thousand miles of open water would be a mighty force and one which had contributed, no doubt, to the fearsome record of Damnation Reef.

"'Ark to the roaring of it now," Mrs. Hungerford cried out, her voice almost lost in the booming of the great waves thundering down upon the ragged coral shelves. "Why don't the captain turn the ship?"

"Perhaps there are more reefs to windward too," Marina suggested in a small voice, aware that the light was changing rapidly as the sun sank out of sight. The sky, the very air, glowed amethyst, then turned to violet, until with alarming suddenness the colours faded, and the sea heaved featureless and black under the darkening heaven.

"All passengers on deck!"

Mrs. Hungerford cried out and heaved herself to-

21

ward the door, but Marina tore the case off a pillow and began to stuff it with various things as they came to mind.

"Take the water keg," she cried to Mrs. Hungerford, and to herself she muttered, "Here's a knife—our largest bonnets—as much food as we can fit in—"

The cabin door was flung open and a brawny seaman began to drag Mrs. Hungerford out into the passageway.

"On deck at once," he shouted, a frightened man. "If us strikes, you 'on't want to be caught down 'ere!"

"Shipwreck!" Marina muttered to herself, struggling with the pillowcase and a crock of hardtack. Could this disaster really be about to fall upon them? Her heart thumped furiously, her mouth was dry, but her mind seemed calm and she was relieved to find she felt no temptation yet to give way to panic.

By the time she had followed Mrs. Hungerford and the sailor up on deck, it was already dark, but the lanterns had been lit to reveal a scene of utter confusion. Such livestock as remained at the end of a long voyage had been released, and baas, clucks and bleats mingled horribly with the hysterical screams and pungent oaths of the passengers. People were rushing from one side of the ship to the other for no apparent reason, hindering the seamen who were struggling to unfasten the longboats. Only the captain stood immobile on the poop, his arms folded as he strained his eyes into the dark.

"*Ship ahoy!*" cried the lookout, still high in the crow's nest.

A feeling of relief spread through the ship. At least they were not alone in their peril. . . .

Marina peered forward and soon made out a faint but comfortable yellow glow ahead. Then she realized that the other vessel must be altering course, for another light had appeared, nearer to sea level and some way behind the first. Judging by the distance between the lights, she thought it must be a ship not a great deal smaller than their own, though the mainmast seemed shorter, from the occasional glimpses she had of it illuminated by the bowsprit lantern.

The captain called an order to the helmsman, and the *Carib Queen* began to follow the stranger, who clearly knew his way about the reefs, altering his course to pass safely among the coral heads.

For perhaps a quarter of an hour the game of follow-my-leader continued, the *Carib Queen* reducing sail in order not to overtake the lights ahead.

The passengers had fallen silent. All eyes were straining into the impenetrable night. All ears were full of the thunder of breaking waves. It was to be hoped that there was a passage through, Marina thought fearfully, for they must now be fairly in the middle of Damnation Reef.

And at that moment the ship struck.

There was a terrific crunch, redoubled screams from the passengers, most of whom had been thrown off their feet; an ominous cracking from aloft as a topmast splintered under the strain; then a lift with the next wave, a welcome floating sensation—followed by another concussion even more violent than the first.

Marina fought her way to the rail. It was almost impossible to distinguish anything in the busy darkness, but she thought she could see the glimmer of a sandbank not far ahead. She searched for the other vessel and caught sight of the yellow light for an instant, before it flickered and went out. Had she too foundered?

The angle of the listing *Carib Queen* was making it difficult to launch the lifeboats, but at length the ones on the starboard side were lowered and there was a rush for the rail. The sailors tried to hold back some of the men who were scrambling over the side of the ship, calling for women and children to come forward. Mrs. Hungerford seized hold of Marina.

"Hurry, child, or we'll be drowned!"

"You go," Marina cried. "I believe I'd rather swim." She was thinking of the gaping seams she had seen in the longboats while the ship lay becalmed in the Sargasso Sea.

Mrs. Hungerford let out a despairing cry. "Don't leave me! Stay by me—I need you! And the sharks will get you in the water—fish eat at night!"

"Very well," Marina agreed, relieved despite herself. "But be sure to hold on to the water keg whatever befalls—it is only half full and will support you if you need it. Do not lose your grip on it, for our lives may well depend on it." She began to struggle down the Jacob's ladder, hampered by the bulging pillowcase.

Mr. Peppard scrambled after Marina. "Wait for me," he was shouting. "Oh, my stars! I cannot swim!"

"Nor I! Nor I!" echoed half a dozen voices.

A roar from the captain arrested them.

"Hold your places! More boats will be lowered as soon as they can be brought across. At present the ship is safe—it may be days before she's gone."

Perhaps Captain Burge was being optimistic again but at least he had succeeded in quelling the worst of the rush, Marina reflected, as a sailor caught her ankles and guided her feet into the boat below. Seven men were allowed in after her. Mr. Peppard was one of these. He collapsed thankfully on the seat next to Marina and she could see him anxiously fingering, not hardtack and water jars, but his watch, fob chain, and signet ring.

The longboat was pulling for the sandbank, which gleamed elusively in the pale starlight filtering from a sky half obscured by racing clouds. Distances were hard to judge but Marina, conscious of water lapping round her ankles and rising by the minute, hoped the spit was nearer than it looked.

"Bail!" cried one of the sailors. "Bail for your lives!"

"What shall we use?" asked a thin despairing voice—that of the young woman, Marina recalled, who was travelling to Antilla to be a governess.

"Anything! Use your 'ands!"

Marina cupped her hands together and bailed with

24

the rest, but it was useless. Not only was the longboat leaking in every seam but, being overloaded, as it sank lower in the water the waves were beginning to wash in.

Marina leaned closer to Mrs. Hungerford's shaking frame.

"Be sure to hold on to the keg," she reiterated. "I will see that you are safe. You must trust yourself to me, but do not lose the keg. I will get you safely to the shore."

She hoped she sounded more confident than she felt. She knew she was a strong swimmer, at least as good as her cousins Ralph and Rollo, who had taught her in the lake at Grayling Manor; but she had never swum in the sea and suspected it would be wild and rough, a far cry from the slumbering lake. Besides, she would be encumbered, not only by Mrs. Hungerford but by the bulging pillowcase whose contents must be saved if they were to survive more than a day or two upon the sandbank.

"She's going!" The shout went up as the longboat lurched sickeningly, sending Marina's thoughts to prayer.

"Hold on to the boat, ladies!" cried the coxswain. "Stay with the boat! She may capsize but she'll never sink—"

That was true, Marina supposed, but the struggling passengers, terrified of both the water and the unseen predators lurking below, might well drown each other in their efforts to climb up on the hull. She and Mrs. Hungerford would do better to take their chance alone.

The longboat shuddered and began to turn over, slowly at first, and then with an inevitable rush.

The next moments were horrific. Shouts and cries, frantic splashes and ominous gurgles filled the air as the passengers were thrown out of the boat. Mrs. Hungerford seized hold of Marina in a desperate grip, pulling her down into the cool dark depths.

Kicking strongly, Marina brought them both up to the surface. "Leave go!" she shouted. "I will hold you—and you must hold the water keg, it will help you float!"

She pushed herself free, and to her inexpressible relief, Mrs. Hungerford clutched the water keg obediently to her bosom and began to bob away in the darkness, uttering little gasping cries. Marina turned on her back, grasping a fold of Mrs. Hungerford's billowing gown with her right hand, while holding the sodden pillowcase containing the vital stores against her chest.

Almost at once she realized that salt water was more buoyant than fresh, and encouraged by this, she kicked out for the shore, dragging Mrs. Hungerford beside her. Burdened as she was, she tried to shut her ears to the despairing cries that semed to be coming from all directions. Theirs was not the only longboat to be swamped, she surmised; and remembering the relentless heat of the endless days adrift in the Sargasso Sea, she could not wonder at it. There was nothing she could do to help anyone else at the moment, however, so she tried to concentrate only upon the sound of waves breaking on the shore, and on swimming toward it.

After a while, Mrs. Hungerford gasped out that they were almost there. Marina let her feet drift down, and found she could stand. She helped Mrs. Hungerford ashore, set down the keg and the pillowcase in a dry place, and sat down to get her breath until the cries of others begging for deliverance compelled her to go to their aid.

Three times more she returned to the sea, until it seemed no longer warm, or buoyant. Her petticoats began to hamper her when they became saturated, so she left them on the sand. Once something brushed against her—a drowned sailor, his half-open eyes rolling whitely, his pigtail a lank snake coiled about his neck. Her last journey, with a shrieking lad, was much the worst and after it she had no strength for anything but to lie panting on the shore.

She was roused at last by light, the flooding light of

moonrise to the east, beyond the quiet lagoon. Rapidly, it seemed, the great distorted moon, only a few days past the full, swam free of the horizon and gloriously illuminated the ghastly scene. It painted in black and silver the stark shape of the wreck, now half dismasted and gradually shifting higher up onto the coral with every wave. It played disinterestedly over the aimlessly drifting longboats, and the bodies slowly rolling in the shallows; but it revealed nothing of the ship that had led the *Carib Queen* to her destruction.

Marina sat up, her hands to her aching chest, and looked about the sandspit to count the survivors—of whom there would be but few, she feared. Herself, and Mrs. Hungerford; the governess, Miss Smith, who had nearly strangled her; the lawyer's clerk, still sobbing unrestrainedly; a thin woman, Miss Dampier, who had kept mostly to her cabin on the ship, her face disfigured by a dreadful scar; these were the ones she herself had rescued, and she could see only five more people altogether. There were two sailors working to pull bodies out of the sea, and farther away another dark stooped figure doing the same; and a woman sitting hunched up on the sand, still wearing a bonnet, and clutching a child. Ten in all—no sign of Mr. Peppard, or the captain, or— But Marina checked her thoughts. She heaved herself upright. Her limbs felt swollen and heavy. It seemed to take an unconscionable time to drag on her dripping petticoats again, and another age to stumble down the beach toward the sailors, to offer her assistance. Two of the rescued bodies had recovered consciousness by then, and she was able to coax another young sailor back to life; but by dawn it was apparent that the losses had been great, but thirteen saved out of forty or fifty persons.

It was the child, Sairey Roper, who first saw the sloop.

She had been watching one of the sailors trying to fish with a bent pin. Suddenly she darted back into the shade of the upturned longboat and seized her

27

mother's hand, whispering that she must come out-side and look at something at once. Marina heard her and went with them.

"It is a boat, thank God," Marina declared. "Clever girl, Sairey." She strained her eyes toward the distant splinter in the expanse of shining water. "It looks to me as if a man is fishing—setting out a net."

She called to Jem, who was cutting up a little yellowtail for bait. He strode up the dune, stared, exclaimed, and then, rasping his callused hand across his stubbled chin, announced that they had best be thinking how to attract the fisherman's attention. "For them longboats are leaking yet," said he, "and 'tis too far for young Daniel to swim, the state he's in."

Marina doubted that young Daniel, who had so nearly succumbed, would have been able to swim the dis-tance in any state of health, but she said nothing and set to work to help build a larger fire, and to wave a sail to and fro for the best part of an hour.

"Will he never look round?" she cried angrily at last. In fact she was almost sure the fisherman *had* looked in their direction once or twice, but he had not appeared to be influenced by what he had seen, if anything continuing unhurriedly about his business.

"One would suppose the man was blind," she de-clared in exasperation, and for once in sympathy with little Sairey, who was sobbing that she knew the man would never see them. "Deaf too," Marina added crossly, "for though we are a long way off, he is downwind of us and that conch shell Jacky keeps blowing sounds like the last trump to me!"

"Deaf," repeated Mrs. Hungerford in a startled tone. "Why, of course—that's just what 'e is, miss. I should 'ave thought of it at once. Deaf and dumb, 'e is, for that must be Elijah, sure as I stand 'ere!"

"What, you know him?"

"Well—not to say know 'im," said Mrs. Hungerford primly. "I've seen 'im, 'ere and there, 'ad dealings with 'im, if you like, ay, and bought fish off 'im too. 'E knows me, all right—'e'd rescue us, if we could only get to 'im."

Jem shook his head. "Daniel's in no case to swim so far—not till he's rested up another day or so—not then, maybe. That boat's farther off nor you might think. 'Tis the light in these here parts—so clear it is, it makes things seem closer nor what they are."

"I will swim out to him," Marina said flatly. There was an uneasy murmur of protest, but she assured them she was capable of it, and, all too aware that in her lay their strongest hope, the others soon gave up trying to dissuade her.

"Come 'ere a moment, miss," said Mrs. Hungerford. Marina took off her ruined bonnet and went to the woman's side. Mrs. Hungerford had her hands up to her neck. She unclasped and lifted off the silver chain from which hung the large monogram of her initials.

"Chances are, Elijah will recognize this," she muttered. " 'E must know as I'm away—'e'll 'ave missed me in the shop. 'E's not slow, for all 'e's deaf—"

"In the shop?" Marina's eyes widened as she looked down at Mrs. Hungerford. "Does he come there?"

Mrs. Hungerford pursed out her lips. " 'E does come in, from time to time."

Marina raised her eyebrows. "Does Mr. Flete sell fish, then, ma'am?"

"Certainly not!" cried Mrs. Hungerford indignantly. " 'Tis just that Elijah works for the Company—and besides, he brings us odd things 'e's found, on 'is own account sometimes."

"Odd things?" repeated Marina, with a sense of foreboding.

Mrs. Hungerford looked—could it be *frightened*? Marina wondered.

"Yes, well, never mind that, dear. Only I'm pretty sure 'e'll know this necklet, see. When you show it 'im, 'e'll come and pick us up."

"Let us hope so," said Marina. She took the chain and clasped it about her neck. Then, after a wan smile at the company, she turned and began to cross the soft white sand toward the west side of the bar. She was glad to ease the burning soles of her feet in the shallows at the edge, and welcomed the coolness of the deeper waters beyond. Just before she started swimming, she glanced back at the sandbar, to see that the sailors had picked up a pair of oars and were beginning the unpleasant task of pushing the overheated corpses back into the sea on the far side.

Marina swam steadily. Once she thought she saw a dark shape some way below, but whether coral head or devil ray, it did not threaten her and she saw no other sign of life within the water. After a long while she turned over on her back and floated, to rest awhile. Great clouds passed across the sky continually, the Trade Wind clouds that so fortunately tempered the climate of these latitudes. Their shadows fell gratefully upon her sunburnt face. If she lived—and if she did not blister, she thought wryly—her skin would be as unfashionably tanned as a gypsy's and she would surely have to seek no further for a means of protection from the wife-hunters of Antilla.

When she neared the boat, Marina called out. But the fisherman was sitting hunched with his back toward her, and he did not stir. Very likely he was Elijah, then, she thought resignedly, swimming carefully so as not to get herself entangled with his net. She would have to rock the boat in order to attract his attention. She began to swim toward the stern, noting that it was painted with the name *Sea Hawk*. It was a roughly built but serviceable little sloop, with a satisfying curve of hull and a long boom, reminding Marina of sketches her father had drawn for her of the dhows of Arabia.

Putting her feet upon the rudder, she heaved herself up and tumbled into the boat.

The fisherman seemed to stiffen; then he turned with the speed of a Latin drawing a knife. Marina flung up her hands in an instinctive gesture of submission, and cowered back against the tiller. His jaw dropped open and they stared at each other in mutual dismay.

Elijah, suddenly confronted by a tall, pink-skinned girl with large light eyes and a quantity of straight dripping hair, gowned in a sopping rag of once-white muslin, began to shrink away from her with the unmistakable terror of one experiencing a supernatural visitation.

As soon as Marina realized that he thought she was a ghost, she summoned up a reassuring smile and, her knees feeling suddenly weak, sank down abruptly upon a wooden box and laid her arm along the worn curve of the tiller.

Elijah at once rose to his full height. He was tall and stooped, with huge hands swinging half clenched from long arms, and he wore a tattered robe contrived from sacking, which fell shapelessly to midway down his calves. His skin seemed to Marina to be an interesting mixture of mahogany tones. He had a long face, shaded by a battered hat, wide flaring nostrils, and protruding mobile lips; and his eyes were very bright under their hooded lids.

As the pool of water widened at Marina's feet, Elijah seemed to be considering the possibility that she might be real.

Marina, sensing that his first fear was leaving him, pointed to the sandbar, where the black dots of human figures were plainly visible, passing about the blue smoke of their fire. Elijah's eyes followed the direction of her hand, and he grunted. Marina bit her lip, for the sight of the survivors had not seemed to inspire him with any necessity to act. She slapped her hand against the bulwarks, then waved toward the distant wreck. Elijah shrugged—or was it merely that he felt the need to ease the coarse sacking away from his shoulder blades?

Suddenly Marina remembered Mrs. Hungerford's talisman, and pulled the silver monogram out of her gown.

It was clear that Elijah recognized it at once. He

made another unintelligible grunting sound and pointed in his turn to the sandbar, eyebrows raised. Marina nodded. Elijah rolled his eyes, showing their yellowed whites. Then, without more ado, he turned and began to haul in his net.

As the *Sea Hawk* drew closer to the sandbar, Elijah tacked up to the far end, came smartly up into the wind, dropped his sail and the anchor in almost the same instant, and began at once to clear the sloop for action. He lashed everything but the water barrel, one bucket of fish, and some hen coops onto the raft, dropped it over the side into three feet of water, and then dragged it ashore behind him. He ignored the people crowding round him while he fastened the raft to a small clump of mangroves, and when he did acknowledge their presence it was only to wave them curtly toward the sloop. Since they were as anxious to embark as he clearly was to terminate his association with them, their obedience was swift and absolute.

All the survivors were by this time capable of wading out to the boat with some assistance, and once they were there Elijah heaved them over the bulwark without ceremony. As soon as everyone was safely aboard, he took the helm, allowing the sailors Jem and Jacky to raise the gaff and weigh the anchor. Then he set his course to reach down to Antilla, and the *Sea Hawk* leaned merrily to the sparkling waves as if she were as glad as her passengers to be sailing away from the deadly, treacherous embrace of that lover of lost ships, Damnation Reef.

3

Marina gazed back from the stern of the *Sea Hawk* for a last glimpse of the ship which had been her home for over two long months.

It was a sad sight, for the wreck listed horribly upon the coral ledge, most of her masts gone, her spars lying splintered among the tangled rigging, the last remnants of her sails fluttering hopelessly in the northeast wind and her deck shuddering with every wave that hit her.

Mr. Cornelius Hendrie, with his customary weary courtesy, was the first to fill the awkward silence.

"I had never the least intention of visiting the slight dot on the map that calls itself Antilla," he drawled. "But since Fate has seen fit to cast me in her way, as it were, I shall endeavour to support the experience with good grace, just until I can procure a passage to Jamaica. There is a battalion of Militia, I understand, based upon what charity describes as the capital of the Antillan group. When I last had news of him, a Lieutenant Colonel Dawlish had the dubious honour of commanding it—a gentleman with whom I have the pleasure of some slight acquaintance."

"Oh, you know Colonel Dawlish, then?" cried Mrs. Hungerford. "Such a nice gentleman, 'e is—invalided out of the Army when 'e lost 'is arm, and now 'e's a full colonel of Militia. Very civil, 'e is, and not above calling in our shop from time to time. 'E's quite a friend of Mr. Flete's."

"In that case," said Mr. Hendrie dryly, "I shall certainly take the liberty of proposing myself to the colonel as a temporary guest. No doubt the Fort will also be able to accommodate these good seamen, and—" He glanced with a shade of doubt at Mr. Stebbings, a traveller in osnaburg.

"Nay, sir, there's no call for you to be worrying over me," declared the latter, mopping his perspiring forehead with a spotted handkerchief. "There's a merchant in Charlestown, Da Costa by name, I've been corresponding with for years. 'Twould be a queer thing if I couldn't stop with him, after all the business we have put in each other's way, think on."

"That's all settled, then," cried Mrs. Hungerford cheerfully. "Rest and a few good meals of fresh food is what we need . . . bless me, but I'm 'ungry now!"

She rubbed her stomach with a frank explicit gesture, and at once a high humming noise issued from Elijah's lips. He bent without taking his right hand from the helm or his eyes from the gap between the islands ahead and, dipping his long-fingered left hand into the bucket at his feet, deftly caught and withdrew a wriggling silver fish with a yellow tail. He cracked its head against the tiller, and with no change of expression took a crunching bite out of it.

There was a horrified silence, while Elijah continued nonchalantly to eat the fish, spitting out bones and fins as he encountered them.

"Well," breathed Mrs. Hungerford, "fresh food is one thing, but that is 'orrible!"

Marina giggled, as much at the pained expression on Mrs. Roper's face as at Mrs. Hungerford's indignation.

"I think we must give Elijah a present for rescuing us," she suggested, hastily controlling herself, in the hope of diverting the attention of the ladies before Elijah could become aware of their disapproval.

"Quite right, Miss Derwent," Miss Dampier agreed. "It would be most ungracious to leave him with no more than a word of thanks. Has anyone any ideas upon the subject? I am afraid I have not so much as a groat upon me."

After some discussion as to the appropriate form of Elijah's reward, Mr. Hendrie, who had rejected everyone else's suggestions, brought out his handsome watch and chain.

"Elijah is very welcome to have this," he drawled, and when his fellow passengers protested, he added languidly, "My dear people, I put a very high value on my life, I do assure you. I shall miss the ticking of this timepiece a good deal less than I should that of my pulse. And speaking of that," he added, raising his eyebrows at the shallow waters on either side of the *Sea Hawk*, "one would suppose that this channel would be marked. In fact a lighthouse on that nearest rock would surely greatly reduce the hazard to shipping in these parts."

"They did try to put some sort of light on Great St. George's," Mrs. Hungerford informed him, "but first there was the trouble building it—tumbled down, it did, time and time again. And then there was the question of manning it. Folk didn't like to sit out there, day after day, only to keep the lanterns burning. There are places where lighthouses are successful, I daresay, but I shall be surprised if the St. George's channel ever turns out to be one of them. There are too many people with an interest in preventing it."

Elijah was now steering unhesitatingly between the reefs bordering a narrow channel and the turbulence of the ocean was dying away behind them as the sloop drove into calmer waters. To the left rose Great St. George's, with a few houses visible among cultivated fields; and to the right lay the small islet of Little St. George's, overrun with goats and edged with a beach of purest white. Beyond Little St. George's to the west rose the dark hump of Antilla, looming before a sky already beginning to be faintly tinged with the first lavender of twilight.

Elijah leaned forward to loose his mainsheet as Little St. George's passed astern, and the patched sail billowed free as he changed his course from south to run west-southwest. The *Sea Hawk* drew closer to the mysterious blue bulk of Antilla, and the seas became more lively as the sloop neared the high bluff at the island's eastern end. A few minutes later, yellow lights started to spring out of the dusk among the low foothills that fringed the water's edge down the south coast of Antilla.

"That is East Bottom," Mrs. Hungerford announced, feasting her eyes eagerly on the sight of land and the welcome evidence of habitation. "There is no 'arbour there, but for a landing place at 'Ogs'ead Bay—old Dr. Margery's estate, that is. In just a minute now you'll see—ay, there it is! That is Tamarind Point, my dear." She took Marina by the arm and pointed with her other hand. "There, do you see that splash of white above the cliff?"

Marina stared, not at the great house itself, for that was mainly hidden from this angle, but at a Grecian temple set not incongruously among the rocks and cacti of this summer isle—the garden house where Julia had been used to meeting her lover not so long ago, and the cleft in the cliffs where she had plunged down to her death. How peaceful it looked now, Marina thought, in the evening calm: the white temple above, and below, in the dark green-shadowed water, a small sloop rocking quietly at anchor.

"And 'ere," said Mrs. Hungerford, " 'ere in this next bay, is Sandy 'Arbour. It was once a port, they say, but 'tis all silted up now and only these little fishing boats can use it. Do you see that great sandbar yonder? Ships are often wrecked on that—fortunately for the villagers."

"Fortunately?" repeated Miss Smith in a voice of horror.

"Why, such accidents are meat and drink to them, of course. Freed slaves, most of them are, and can barely scrape a living from their fishing and their plots of stony ground. Stands to reason a wreck would seem good luck to them."

"I have heard it is the same in Cornwall," Miss Dampier agreed. "When your children are starving, it is probably easy to forget the poor souls aboard, perishing in terror before their time."

Thinking of the *Carib Queen*'s less fortunate passengers, everyone fell silent, until Sairey pointed to a dark heap on the sandbar and asked if that had been a wreck.

"Ay," said Mrs. Hungerford with a lusty sigh. "That was the *Sally-Ann*, out of Antigua—and I chanced to be in Sandy 'Arbour the morning she went aground. She sailed in, mistaking the lights of the village for those of Charlestown, and stuck fast on the bar just where the seas are breaking. She soon began to fall apart. I was up very early, buying fish—in the dim light before dawn, it was—and 'eard the cry the villagers made when they saw the ship standing too close. I never saw Africans move so fast, before nor since—dropping fish, and the nets they were mending, launched their boats all in a flash, it seemed. They rowed out quick enough, but then—"

"Go on," Marina begged, as she hesitated.

"Well, they stood off the vessel in a semicircle, they did. Dawn was just breaking—I vow you never saw the like. They waited there like—like vultures. As you see, 'tis a fair swim from the sandbar to the shore, and very few attempted it."

"You mean," gasped Miss Smith, "that the villagers did not try to rescue those aboard the wreck?"

"Not they! Their women were waiting on the shore for the bodies to come in. But 'oo can judge them, as Miss Dampier says, 'oo 'as not known starvation?"

"What happened then?" Marina asked, for the sloop was approaching the darkening shore.

"Then I noticed 'im." Mrs. Hungerford nodded her head toward the unheeding figure of Elijah, hardening his sheets as he began to beat up to his home port.

"What did he do?"

"Do? Why, nothing—that was the worst of it. Sat with 'is back to the ship, nearer than the others,

37

oblivious to the cries and screams while 'e got up 'is fish pots—just like 'e was with us this morning. It was terrible to watch those poor wretches appealing to 'im, and 'im paying no attention, though 'e was so close . . ."

"Did they all perish?" cried Miss Smith.

"No, no—for just then there came a sudden shout, and we all looked round, me and them women on the beach—and there was Sunderland!"

"Sunderland?" repeated Marina blankly.

"Yes, my dear, the doctor. Did Miss Julia never mention 'im to you? She fair 'ero-worshipped 'im, after that day—but I daresay the excitement of going to school put 'im right out of 'er 'ead. Not that 'e'd be easy to forget—a great red-'eaded fellow, 'e is—strong as an ox. It seems 'e was returning home after 'aving been up all night attending a difficult birth in Charlestown. Mrs. Sutton, it was, she always 'as a 'ard time, poor thing. So there came Dr. Sunderland, leaping like a madman down the beach, pulling 'is clothes off as 'e ran. 'E threw 'imself upon the only boat that still lay on the sand, an old moses boat it was, with a gaping 'ole in its bottom, and 'e tore the rigging off it like a man possessed— Whoops," she exclaimed, as Elijah brought the boat about and the boom swung above Marina's head with little more than an inch to spare.

"Yes," Mrs. Hungerford went on, "tore off the rigging, 'e did, while we all stood, gaping like fools. Then 'e made one rope of it all, and tied one end to a palm tree and the other about his chest. Next—into the sea 'e plunged, and swam for the ship. 'Tis calm enough in 'ere, as you see, sheltered by the sandbar, but still there are sharks that come for the fish offal, and barracuda aplenty. You don't see many swimming 'ere, I can tell you, only the children in the shallows. Well, 'e neared the wreck—and she was 'eeling over by then and the water pouring into 'er, and men and women climbing into the rigging and 'olding on the spars and we could 'ear their screams, even upwind as we were—and the villagers be'ind me were beginning

38

to buzz like a swarm of bees, the black bees we 'ave in these islands, that sting deep when they are roused. Then—"

"Lee-o!" cried Jem, as Elijah again put across his tiller to go about.

"Then?" demanded Marina impatiently.

"Why, then we could see that Sunderland was at the end of 'is rope—it was not long enough by many feet, and swim as 'e might, 'e could not reach the wreck with it—and you could 'ear that buzzing change to a higher pitch—more of a mosquito whine of triumph—and then it fell low again when a fellow on the *Sally-Ann* slung out a rope and somehow Sunderland caught it and tied it to the one 'e 'ad with 'im. After that they swarmed ashore. Yes, every person on that ship passed down the length of that rope to the beach and safety—and the sullen looks of the villagers. To be sure, in a day or two there was nothing left of the wreck but what you see—the keel and the ribs, for the villagers 'ad took all—but the real pickings, the rings and watches and purses—all those 'ad slipped through their fingers, thanks to Sunderland. I saw 'im when 'e came ashore at last—tired, ay, for 'e'd been up all night—but alight with triumph, 'e was. I thought for a moment the women would fall on 'im like a pack of wild dogs and tear 'im limb for limb, but 'e burned them with 'is look, and they fell back before 'im. Yes, you can say what you like of Sunderland—and there are those as can't abide 'im—but no one can deny 'e is a man."

"A man indeed," breathed little Miss Smith. "Is he married?" she asked, and then blushed fearfully.

" 'E's a widower, they say," Mrs. Hungerford replied. " 'E's only lived out 'ere four years or so, and 'is wife died in England, it seems. But 'e's been courting poor Miss Winceyman for quite some time. 'Er mother was on board the *Carib Queen*, you remember, coming out to spend a few months with 'er children, poor lady. But perhaps now she's dead they can get married. I did 'ear she kept a tight 'old on the money their father left, and young Mr. Winceyman would never 'ave been

39

able to go on running a new estate on 'is income alone, if 'is sister 'ad married and took 'er share as dowry—"

A wild flapping interrupted her. Elijah had brought the *Sea Hawk* up into the wind, a boat's length from the shore. The sailors hurried to dowse the sail while he ran forward to let go the anchor, and Marina turned from Mrs. Hungerford to gaze with the keenest interest at their long-awaited landfall.

Even in the dying light, it was plain to see that Sandy Harbour was a poor straggling village of rickety old houses set on pillars of piled stones to frustrate the crabs—grey sagging wooden shacks thatched with rotting banana leaves and peopled, it seemed, exclusively by thin-legged, pot-bellied children, scrawny raw-necked chickens, and furtive swift-moving cats. A row of fishing boats was drawn up along the shore, wicker fish pots lay about in piles, and black-tarred nets were festooned along the twisted sea-grape trees.

Elijah had been first to climb overboard and let himself down into the shallow water. Now he let go of the *Sea Hawk* and began to stride away without a backward look. Mr. Hendrie hastily moved forward to detain him, bringing out his watch and presenting it to the deaf-mute, with a gesture to indicate that it was a present from them all.

Elijah took the watch. He stared at it, swung it on its chain, stroked it on both sides, and even licked it. Mr. Hendrie flicked the cover open, and Elijah started nervously. Then, swiftly understanding the mechanism, he snatched back the watch and repeated the movement over and over, his pleasure gratifyingly evident even if he showed no sign of associating it with the man whose generosity had been the cause of it.

Marina became aware of a whisper of movement beneath the sea-grape trees. Shadows flickered about the contorted trunks, and a growing murmur indicated that the adult population of Sandy Harbour not only existed, but was becoming curious. Presently an awkward figure detached itself from its darker background to come hopping down the beach—a one-legged man supported by a crutch formed from a knotted branch.

"Good night! Good night!" he cried cheerfully. "How you go do, Elijah? He no hear, dat one," he explained to Mr. Stebbings, who happened to be nearest to him. "He does be deaf, he ears stop-up—he no speak either. Now me, me Hop-Joe, me speak plain. You folk does be strangers here, I t'ink? How come you sail wid dat Elijah? Sandy Harbour no place for you, no-see-em go for to bite you at dis hour—you feel 'em, yes?"

While he was speaking Marina had indeed become conscious of small but irritating stings all over her exposed flesh, and Sairey had begun crying, jumping up and down and slapping at her arms.

Mrs. Hungerford took charge. As soon as she had explained their situation to Hop-Joe, he shouted incomprehensibly into the darkness behind him and presently a file of unhappy-looking mules and donkeys were being led down to the beach. A few minutes later several messages had been scrawled and dispatched, and Jem and Mr. Hendrie had ridden off with a guide to Fort Charles.

"Now you, my dear," said Mrs. Hungerford, turning to Marina. "Write a few words to Miss Derwent, and let one of these boys run with the letter."

"I am not staying here a moment longer, if there is a beast to carry me," Marina said. "These insects are unbearable!"

"Me have fine mule," Hop-Joe informed her. "Me have saddle."

"The no-see-ems only bite for an hour or so, around sunset," Mrs. Hungerford explained. "After that, 'tis the mosquitoes—but they are not so bad. It is the salt on you that attracts the insects, of course; but if they are plaguing you, why don't you step into the smoke of the fire over yonder?"

But Marina was insistent on making her way to Tamarind at once, and had already beckoned to Hop-Joe.

"I wish you'd wait for Mr. Flete," said Mrs. Hungerford. " 'E'd take you in the carriage, if you waited."

"But I could not be so unfeeling as to expose Mr. Flete to the ordeal of visiting Tamarind, after what you have told me about the situation between him and Mr. Granville," Marina explained. "Besides, I would rather meet him when I am more presentable." She bade Mrs. Hungerford farewell, and kissed her warmly, before walking over to the mule which Hop-Joe was holding for her beside an upturned boat. She stepped up cautiously upon the rotting hull, hitched up her skirts and mounted astride on the make-shift pad of torn blanket which served for a saddle, with stirrups of worn rope. She felt grateful for the rapidly increasing darkness, which hid her inelegant appearance from all but Hop-Joe, who had hastened to mount his donkey and was now waiting for her to follow him.

Marina called good-bye to her fellow survivors, and kicked the mule to a reluctant trot. Almost at once the stinging insects were left behind and her spirits improved accordingly.

She soon found her eyes adjusting to the dark, or rather to the starlight, for Venus shone so brightly as to cast a shadow. She saw the flash of Hop-Joe's eye as he cast her an appraising glance.

"You ride good, mistress. Plenty like boy. I take you de old road, by me charcoal pit. We make speed, den."

It was a bone-jarring journey down the old mule track, and Marina was half deafened by the insistent clamour of crickets and tree frogs. She felt too exhausted to protest when Hop-Joe pointed to a pair of gates ahead, and announced his intention of leaving her to enter them alone.

"I come for mule tomorrow," he informed her as he turned away. "Pleasant journey, mistress."

Marina rode on, up a dark avenue of stately trees. She could see scattered lights ahead from a confusing number of buildings but the drive brought her directly to the two-storied great house, and she drew rein at last before its plain white door and looming facade.

42

She sat there, strangely reluctant to dismount. She had envisaged her arrival at Tamarind so differently. . . . All at once she began to wish quite fervently that she had waited for Mr. Flete with Mrs. Hungerford. She had been so eager to get to Tamarind—but how much more comfortable it would have been to have stayed the night at Spanish Wells, arriving on the morrow in broad daylight, neatly gowned, even if in borrowed plumes, with her hair newly washed and curled and, above all, with a chaperone to lend her countenance. As it was—

But just then the white door opened, letting out a shaft of light which mercilessly revealed her sitting there astride the half-starved mule, her tangled hair flowing over the shoulders of the crumpled, ragged gown. Before she could make up her mind to dismount, the light was partially blocked by someone whom, even thought he stood in shadow, Marina had no difficulty in recognizing as the autocratic Mr. Marcus Granville, master of Tamarind.

4

Mr. Granville seemed even more formidable at close quarters than Marina remembered him, with his broad shoulders and piratical black eye-patch. His manner, when he spoke, certainly did nothing to reassure her.

"What in heaven's name—?" he demanded in a deep, impatient voice, pushing aside the portly figure of his black butler in order to allow more light to play upon the apparition in his driveway. "Who the devil—? Cudjoe!" he brusquely addressed the African, who still had one hand on the door, "see who this is and what she wants. I am late already."

And with that he stepped out onto the driveway, calling loudly for one Obed, and his horse; while Cudjoe began to make a hesitant approach toward Marina.

Marina licked her salty lips, which had become very dry. "Mr. Granville," she called after him. "I am—" It took courage, but it must be said. "I am Marina Derwent, your visitor from England."

He stopped abruptly and spun on his heel to stare at her again, while Cudjoe slunk back into the safety of the hall.

"You are Miss Marina?" echoed Mr. Granville in a tone of incredulity. "Miss Derwent's niece?"

"Yes, sir," she said wearily, and slipping her feet out of the rope stirrups, let herself slide from the makeshift saddle to the ground.

"Good God! In that case, I suppose you had better come inside."

His expression, as he came back into the light, was daunting.

"Cudjoe," said Mr. Granville stiffly, "inform Miss Derwent that Miss Marina has arrived. I must ask you to excuse me, ma'am," he added, still unsmiling. "I have an engagement elsewhere—and here comes Obed with my horse."

"This—this mule," Marina faltered, strangely breathless. "It belongs to a man named Hop-Joe, who lives at Sandy Harbour. He hired it to me—but I had no money. He is coming up for it tomorrow . . . I would be obliged if you could pay him then, for me. I will refund you, sir, the instant I have drawn out some of my allowance from Mr. Sutton's office. . . ."

The ground seemed to be behaving treacherously. Indeed, it was not only quaking beneath her feet but threatened to rise up and hit her in the face.

"Oh, dear," said Marina, and swooned into Mr. Granville's arms.

She opened her eyes to find a pleasant face close to hers, a slender black hand wielding a fan. Another woman stood with her back half turned. There was something curiously old-fashioned about her powdered hair. . . . Marina closed her eyes but she had no difficulty in understanding the ensuing conversation.

"My dear Marcus," the woman was saying impatiently, "tolerance, I beg of you! My brother Timothy's daughter could be none other than a gentlewoman. Why, her mother was a Havelock!"

"Then why, in heaven's name, should their offspring choose to dress like a beggar and look like something out of Bedlam—unless deliberately to shame me?"

"And why in the world would she wish to do that, may I ask?"

"Oh, it was no doubt some jape she got up with Julia—to punish me on her behalf for my strictness, which you know Julia resented," he said bitterly. "I told you that confounded school was to blame for much—that I saw for myself what standard of behaviour obtained—"

"I cannot believe anyone would be so cruel as to think of teasing you now."

"Oh, I do the girl the justice of supposing she never received your letter with the news of Julia's death."

"Nonsense, she wrote very prettily to condole with us upon it. No, it is obvious to me that the poor child—"

"—is a wayward, headstrong chit, of the very sort that by corrupting Julia I hold directly responsible for her untimely death!".

"Marcus! I think you had better leave. Supposing she should suspect your sentiments—"

"I intend that she shall remain in no doubt of them! Her father has chosen to deliver her into my hands. Very well: I shall do him a favour by personally seeing to it that his daughter acquires a more respectable mode of behaviour while in Antilla. I shall return her to England better fitted for whatever level of society Professor Derwent affects. Julia defied me because of the influence of such girls as this. I shall make it my business to see that this one at least learns to conform—"

"Marcus, you sound positively Roman! Have you forgotten that this girl is my niece? If anyone should be responsible for teaching her how to behave, it is I. Besides, she presents a very odd appearance now, but has it not occurred to you that she has probably been the victim of a carriage accident?"

"Niece or no niece, nothing can excuse her riding that mule astride," he said angrily. "I cannot hold you to account for her upbringing, ma'am, but I shall blame you if you make no push to overcome it. Now I suppose I must go up and change—have you seen what she has done to my best coat?"

"She could not help fainting, I daresay—and I am sure that Colonel Dawlish will excuse your late arrival, if you still mean to go to supper at the Fort."

"You may be sure I intend to do so. It would be to give this wretched hoyden rather more importance than she deserves, to allow her quite to spoil my evening."

He turned, and his single angry eye clashed with Marina's. From the swift breath he drew, and the fact that his colour rose, she was glad to deduce that he was disconcerted to find her conscious. He made no apology, however, and summoning up her strength, she attempted to embarrass him by speaking as sweetly as she could.

"Now that you *have* made your sentiments known to me, sir, you are quite at liberty to leave," she suggested amiably.

He made no answer, but his nostrils flickered and she assumed he was annoyed at her daring to dismiss him. She sat up cautiously, lowered her feet to the ground, and smiled shyly at her aunt, whose oddity, Marina was now able to observe, lay in the fact that Miss Derwent was dressed at least a quarter of a century behind the fashion, with hooped gown and lightly powdered, high-dressed hair.

"Miss Marina!" exclaimed this person, who had striking if rather bony equine looks, "allow me to bid you welcome to Tamarind—though I am sorry to see you in such a state."

"And I am sorry to be in such a one, Aunt Derwent; but the *Carib Queen* was wrecked."

It was a satisfying moment. Mr. Granville stared at her narrowly as if he suspected the truth of her statement, but he was quite silenced. Miss Derwent, on the other hand, fell back into a chair and began to fan herself, the very picture of shocked astonishment.

"Shipwrecked! My dear—where? In Sandy Harbour?"

"No—upon Damnation Reef."

At that Miss Derwent gave a smothered shriek, and glanced almost fearfully at Mr. Granville.

"My dear child! You are fortunate to be alive."

"Yes, ma'am. Only a handful of us survived, indeed."

"How perfectly dreadful! I knew there must be some

good explanation for your appearance," Miss Derwent added, unable to resist a slight air of complacency. "But when did this happen?"

"Only last night," said Marina in a tone of wonder. "It feels as if it might have been days ago."

"You must be starving, I daresay?"

Marina smiled. "Yes, ma'am, I believe I am."

"Cassia, go at once to Cotto for a bowl of soup, bread and butter, chicken—but bring the soup immediately."

The slave curtsied and, limping badly, hastened from the room.

"How were you rescued?" asked Mr. Granville, in a restricted tone.

"By one Elijah, a deaf fisherman . . ." Marina felt disinclined to go into details, nor did she feel that Mr. Granville deserved to hear them. "He brought us into Sandy Harbour, and I was able to hire a mule to ride from there."

"My dear!" Miss Derwent cried. "Surely you did not ride alone? And how could you possibly know the way?"

"I was perfectly well escorted by one Hop-Joe on his donkey. Only he mentioned curfew, and disappeared once we had reached your gate."

"Oh, the charcoal man . . . well, I shan't scold you now, my dear, but you must never run such a risk again. What do you stay for, Marcus? Are you not anxious to keep your engagement at Fort Charles?"

"Yes, I must be going . . ." But Mr. Granville lingered still. "I believe Colonel Dawlish will want some report of this shipwreck," he went on, staring at Marina. "Perhaps, before I leave, you had better inform me in greater detail of what occurred, while it is still fresh in your memory."

"No, sir," she quickly replied, "there is no need for that. Mr. Hendrie—a fellow passenger—and three members of the crew will by now have reached the Fort. The colonel can discover all he wants from them." Marina was at once aware that she had again contrived to annoy Mr. Granville, though she could not imagine why; and now, she suddenly recollected, she was going to have to put herself in the humiliating position of making a second request for money from this odious man.

"That reminds me, sir," she said quickly, feeling her colour rise, "I wonder if you would be so obliging as to give Mr. Hendrie a sovereign on my behalf, when you meet him? He gave his watch to Elijah as a reward, from us all; and I believe he is not rich. I will repay you, of course . . ."

"As soon as you have your allowance from Mr. Sutton," he concluded expressionlessly. "Very well." He bowed, leaving her wondering what he was thinking, and remarked to Miss Derwent that he would be off to the Fort the instant he had changed. Then, without another glance at Marina, he left the room as a young footman entered it, bearing a bowl of broth upon a shining salver.

"Yes, you have some colour now," Miss Derwent observed with satisfaction after Marina had taken some soup. "In fact, you are quite sunburnt, I think. When you are washed and gowned, and your hair is dressed, I should not wonder at it if you turned out to be a very well-looking girl."

"Thank you," Marina murmured, rather at a loss.

"Well, my dear, Julia did not tell us you were a beauty, you know. Taffy-haired, a bean pole, and quite untamed, was her description of you, as I remember it—but not a word as to those eyes—which, now I come to think of it, you must have had from Tim."

"I am held in general to take more after the Havelock side of the family, but my height and eyes I have from the Professor," Marina agreed.

"Do you call him that? And how is my dear brother? Ruthless as ever?"

"Ruthless?" This was a new idea to Marina.

"As all genius must be—but so charming and entertaining that one would forgive him anything, or so Tim was twenty years ago, when I last saw him."

"He was very well indeed, when we parted, ma'am."

"Good. And now, my dear, if it is not too painful a subject, how many survived the wreck with you?"

"Very few." Marina paused to reflect. She had counted ten at first, but then the sailors had rescued Daniel, and Mr. Hendrie—oh, and Mr. Stebbings, of course. "Thirteen," she said.

"Thirteen . . . was Mrs. Hungerford among them?"

"Yes, indeed; she saved our water keg."

Miss Derwent looked somewhat embarrassed. "I daresay you wondered at my requesting Mrs. Hungerford to chaperone you on the voyage, but I could not think of anyone else to ask. By the time I heard that Mrs. Winceyman was sailing on the *Carib Queen*, it was far too late to write."

"I much preferred the company of Mrs. Hungerford. Mrs. Winceyman was lost," Marina added. "Apart from myself and Mrs. Hungerford, only three sailors, two other men, a woman with a child, and another young woman all bound for Jamaica, were saved; and a Miss Smith, governess to the children of Admiral Ducheyne—oh, and a young man, a lawyer's clerk."

"That only makes twelve," Miss Derwent counted out.

Marina went through the list again. "So it does. I cannot understand it."

"Don't trouble yourself with it now, my dear. Eat your chicken. . . . So the Winceymans have lost their mother," went on Miss Derwent, sighing. "They seem to have had a good deal of ill fortune, though their estate, Spring Garden, is one of the more productive. In the hills, you know. They get more rain than we do down here. Poor Winceyman is such a good, hard-working man—though perhaps no one could be quite so good as Winceyman appears to be," she added thoughtfully, as if seriously considering the possibility of Mr. Winceyman's addiction to a secret vice.

Marina stifled a yawn.

"Yes, you are tired—though it is still early yet. The sun sets not much after half-past six, at this time

50

of year; still, I am sure you are longing for your bed. But there is something I am obliged to say to you, before you retire. It concerns Marcus Granville." Miss Derwent got up and began to pace the room with mannish strides. "He is deeply grieved over Julia's death. It followed too soon upon the loss of his dearest friend in Antilla, Alfred Singleton, in another shipwreck. That subject is still painful to him. I would be obliged if you did not go out of your way to mention it—shipwreck, I mean."

"I should be very happy *never* to mention it," Marina assured her. "As for Julia," she began, and then broke off, reflecting that she did not yet know her aunt well enough to air her theories about Julia's death.

Miss Derwent sank onto the chair lately vacated by Cassia. "How I miss that spritely child—not that I believed her to be an angel as poor Marcus did. She was far too much like her mother for that, but then I miss Juliana too, my feckless friend."

"I had a letter from Julia," said Marina impulsively. "She wrote it shortly before she died. I thought you would like to know she sounded very happy then."

"Oh! Shall you let me read it?"

"I am afraid it's in my trunk, aboard the *Carib Queen*. But I read it often after I had the news of Julia's death—I believe I know it almost by heart."

"Please tell me what she wrote, if you are not too tired?"

"Of course . . . it began with a detailed description of a gown her maid, Rosett, had sewn for her, from a sketch Julia had copied."

"Yes," sighed Miss Derwent, "Julia was clever at such work . . . and I believe every female in the house had a finger in that gown."

"She described wearing it to a reception at Government House. And then—yes, she mentioned a Miss Thurlough . . ." Marina hesitated.

"Pray don't keep anything back. She spoke of her disparagingly, I daresay? Ay, as I thought. Julia did

51

not want to see Marcus wed Miss Blanche for all the advantages such an alliance would bring. I used to agree with Julia on that," Miss Derwent went on thoughtfully, "but now I think Marcus could do worse. Miss Thurlough is a good housekeeper, after all, has some accomplishments, and would make a conscientious mother . . ."

"Is she pretty?" asked Marina, rather to her own surprise.

"She is rather short, a timorous, submissive girl, the kind he seems to like. But we digress," she added with a penetrating look. "Pray tell me exactly what Julia said in her letter, if you can."

Marina half closed her eyes, trying to conjure up the memory of that hurriedly written missive. "She said how much she was looking forward to my stay, for it seems she needed an ally—"

"Don't be afraid to tell me, child. I know she thought Marcus and I were overstrict."

"She said that her brother would not approve of the man she was to marry, though he was a king among men."

"She did not mention his name?"

Marina shook her head. "She said, as far as I recall, 'I thought I knew he was the man for me even before I went to England, and I dreamed of him the whole time I was away, though I was too young then to interest him. But as soon as I returned, one look was enough for us. We meet in the temple here at Tamarind—but I will wait to tell you all, for I hesitate to write down too much, though sometimes when I cannot bear the lack of a confidante I trust my thoughts to something like a journal which I keep well hidden—' "

Marina broke off and looked at Miss Derwent, who fiercely blew her nose. "Did you ever find that journal, ma'am?"

"No, I never heard a hint of such a thing before. I can't believe she kept it up for long. . . . I wonder where she hid it?"

Marina thought she knew the answer to that, but

for some reason she hesitated, and the moment passed.

"Go on," Miss Derwent encouraged her. "What more was there?"

"Very little, ma'am. She said, 'I am for eloping, but he is more mature than I and won't do anything so hasty. He says he has a plan in mind . . .' and then she said that I could help them if I were here, but that I must not be cross with her if she had gone by April's end, when I arrived." Marina pressed a hand to her lips. "If only I had been able to come sooner!"

"Hush, child. 'Tis all past now. I feel guilty myself, if you must know."

"You, Aunt?"

Miss Derwent sighed. "It was my decision to send Julia away. She was too like her mother, and when Juliana died I found the responsibility of chaperoning her daughter too much for me. Julia wept and stormed, and Marcus was angry, but I insisted on sending her to England. Last year, much as I loved her, I was dreading her return. My hope was to marry her off respectably as soon as possible. I knew, far better than Marcus, that Julia was capable of pulling Tamarind about our ears." She sighed. "We had had enough of that with Julia's mother. I needed a respite at least . . . but now of course Marcus blames me for that decision—and perhaps he may be right."

Miss Derwent stood up. "Here is Cassia to say your bath is ready. I hope you will enjoy your stay at Tamarind, Marina—and don't waste time on vain regrets."

Marina hesitated, longing to offer comfort, but not sure if it was her place to do so.

"Of all playthings, Julia's favourite was fire," she murmured.

Miss Derwent nodded. "She made her own destiny. . . . Good night, my dear."

Half an hour later, her hair washed and towelled, her body laved in soft rainwater and dressed in a delicate night rail that had been Julia's, Marina pushed

53

aside the shutter at her window, just as the moon swam up from the black horizon of the sea.

Marina's thoughts wandered to the sandspit, empty now. Last night there had been a huddled group of survivors on it, and three men fishing for bodies in the shallows. . . . Three men, she reflected. Later, there had been found to be three sailors who had survived the wreck. But one of those was Daniel, who had been barely saved by his mates. He had not been in any condition to stand that night. Who, then, had the third man been, the tall stooping figure at the far end of the strand, whom she had watched awhile at his gruesome task of pulling in the bodies and examining them for signs of life? Mr. Hendrie, and Mr. Stebbings too, had been among those near-corpses, and the lawyer's clerk had also lacked the strength to help the sailors in their work.

Marina turned from the open window with a shiver that the balmy air had done nothing to induce, for she knew now that the mysterious person on the beach had not been one of the survivors after all, but was that most sinister of figures—an unaccounted-for thirteenth.

5

Marina stretched herself luxuriously when she awoke the following morning. The tent bed, though by no means vast, was certainly more suited to her proportions than the cramped berth in the *Carib Queen*. It was wonderful too to be alone; she realized now that some part of her had long been thirsting for solitude—another argument against matrimony, she reflected with a smile.

Looking back, she found it hard to recall when she had last felt free to dance wildly about the room, or stand upon her head reciting poetry, if she so chose. Mrs. Hungerford had been with her all the time upon the *Carib Queen*; the fearsome journeys to the necessary-house on the orlop deck had been the only occasions of escape, and there was no pleasure to be found in those. Before that she had been helping her father prepare for his expedition at Grayling Manor, where Uncle Sir George Havelock had reluctantly allowed the Derwents to move such goods and chattels as they had not sold, after the death of Marina's mother eighteen months ago; and at Grayling Manor it was her doubtful privilege to share a bed with spiteful Serena. She would have preferred the more friendly Amelia, of course, but as the younger sister, Amelia's place was beside little Susan; and earlier still, though only six months ago, she had been still at school, Marina reflected wonderingly.

She coiled her long legs and sprang through the

filmy curtains, out of bed. The polished floor felt delightfully cool underfoot as she crossed the room to the washstand. A splash of tepid water on her sunburnt face refreshed her, and she began to brush her new-washed hair vigorously as she crossed over to the window. The shutters, closed against mosquitoes and the treacherous night air, were fastened with long hooks to the frame. Marina threw them open and leaned out, taking deep breaths of the warm air and gazing, entranced, at the bright view of the sparkling sea and the green gardens below.

The window was unglazed, a mere hole in the wall, and she leaned farther from it, forgetting that she was attired only in the thinnest of nightgowns. The wind was off the sea, there was a freedom and a wildness in it which exhilarated her, while the sun brought out the rich colours in such exotic flowers as were blooming among the shrubs below. Marina closed her eyes in ecstasy for a moment; but almost at once she heard footsteps and found herself staring down at Mr. Granville, immaculately dressed for riding in pale breeches, shining boots, and a well-cut white coat. He raised his head at the same moment, his one eye regarding her with extraordinary intensity.

Marina felt embarrassed that he had caught her thus. She ran her tongue over her lips and opened her mouth with some intention of bidding him good morning, but to her astonishment a look of fury crossed his face, and with a vicious slap of his whip against his polished boot, he turned on his heel and marched away.

How could he be so contemptuous of her behaviour when he was himself a double-dyed villain, at least by Mrs. Hungerford's account, Marina wondered indignantly. But no doubt he looked on his own actions as perfectly reasonable. He was a slave owner, of course, and must have grown accustomed to the notion that he knew best—that everyone should behave just as he expected, and that they must obey him without question. Autocracy had proved fatal to his character.

It was a pity, for he had been a hero once, captaining his little privateer only a few years ago, and still looked as if he should have been able to rise above notions of revenge and delusions of infallibility alike.

Well, thought Marina, it might not be too late to try to change him. Perhaps she owed it to Julia's memory to make some attempt to rescue him from arrogance before he became irrevocably cast in the mould of a tyrant. Yes, she thought, tossing down her brush as a knock fell on the door, she would regard his enmity as a challenge!

It was Rosett who carried in her breakfast tray. She was younger and prettier than Cassia, with a smooth chocolate face and a good deal of self-control.

"It's a very fine day," Marina offered, when they had exchanged greetings. Rosett looked at her blankly, and Marina laughed. "I was forgetting, nearly all your days are fine. In England, you know, one wakes to find it raining, or at least quite overcast, more often than not. We get a day like this perhaps ten times a year, if we are lucky. What is this fruit?" she added, staring at a slice of something juicy, orange-fleshed, green-skinned and peach-textured.

"Pawpaw, miss."

"Oh, I never heard of it. And this little green lemon—is that a lime?"

"Yes, miss. And tea."

"Tea I do recognize, and with pleasure. Thank you, Rosett."

The slave curtsied and went away. Marina sipped her tea and tried the pawpaw, cautiously at first, and then, squeezing more lime over it, with increasing enjoyment. She was still hungry when Rosett returned, but did not like to mention it.

"Oh," she exclaimed, "you have brought me something to wear!"

Rosett spread the muslin gown reverently on the daybed. "Dis my Miss Julie's," she said mournfully.

"It will be rather short for me, I fear, like this night rail."

"Me put ruffle on him, missy. He go for to fit you now."

"That was very kind of you."

"Mistress, she say Rosett must make over all Miss Julie's clothes for to fit Miss Marina."

Marina bit her lip. She put the tray aside. "Rosett," she said gently, "I was Miss Julia's friend—her best friend, at school."

Rosett slid a side glance from her dark eyes, revealing nothing.

"And you were Miss Julia's maid. She mentioned you in the last letter that she wrote to me."

"Miss Julie write me name in a scrip'?"

Rosett turned away to smooth a wide grey satin sash with her dark finger. It was impossible to tell her feelings, but Marina suspected she was interested, at least.

"Yes, she said how beautifully you had made that gown from her sketches. She wore it to Government House the day before she wrote."

Rosett sighed. "Miss Julie looked real good in that gown. Just like her mammy—like the princess in her storybook."

"Julia was like a princess, I thought. She was—very special. She could be naughty, but I loved her. It is going to be hard for me, to wear her gowns; but perhaps Miss Derwent told you, I have nothing else. I was shipwrecked, and my trunk is on the *Carib Queen* . . ."

Now Marina had her attention. "I hear so," Rosett whispered. "Cassia done tell us. You is lucky to be alive, missy."

"Yes, I'm lucky. Very lucky. Shall I get up now? Will you help me dress?"

"Mistress, she say I your maid now, long as you stay at Tamarind. Better you rise now, miss. Master, he be home soon for second breakfast."

Marina did not say she had already seen him. Relieved to hear that another meal would presently be served, she lost no time in beginning her toilette. She sat patiently before the mirror while Rosett skillfully dressed her hair with a ribbon of the same grey as her eyes and the satin sash; and was bound to own that Julia's gown, though simple in line and plain in material, was the most becoming she had ever worn. Shoes were a problem, only temporarily overcome by Rosett's replacing Julia's tiny kid slippers with a pair of her sandals, which Marina's heels still overlapped.

Marina went downstairs, feeling unusually diffident, and was met in the hall by Toney, the smiling footman. He, she noticed, had solved the problem of shoes by going without them. He led her to the dining room, where, as he informed her, second breakfast was being served, the first breakfast having been eaten by the master alone soon after gunfire—which was, Toney, explained in answer to her question, a cannon fired from the Fort at five in the morning as a signal to start the day.

He held the door, and Marina went in. Mr. Granville stared at her, then wiped his mouth with deliberation upon his napkin before rising slowly to his feet. Miss Derwent, who was just taking her place at the table, came toward Marina instead, putting her arm about her and enquiring if she had slept well.

"Excellently, thank you, ma'am. The mosquitoes hardly bit me, Rosett served me to perfection, and I learned to like pawpaw and lime for breakfast."

"I hope you will like salt fish as well," Miss Derwent said, showing Marina her chair. "Or there is goat stew, if you prefer it."

Marina chose the fish. "How did you enjoy your evening, sir?" she asked Mr. Granville, as Toney helped her from the dish. "Were you successful at the card table?"

"We were not able to play cards," he replied, somewhat distantly. "The whole evening was taken up with discussing the shipwreck. I understand the survivors would still be marooned if you had not taken it upon yourself to swim out to the *Sea Hawk* to solicit Elijah's help."

59

"Marina!" gasped her aunt. "Marcus, you told me nothing of this!"

Marina looked steadily at Mr. Granville. "From your tone, one would suppose you thought it officious of me to act as I did."

He took a draught of coffee. "Not at all, Miss Marina," he said at length. "Clearly, you are a heroine. I salute your courage."

"My dear," put in her aunt, "how could you do it? Where did you learn to swim?"

"My cousins taught me, long ago, in Grayling Lake. I had never swum in the sea before. It is much easier."

"Indeed?" said Mr. Granville coolly. "I am very surprised at your uncle—Sir George Havelock, I collect? I am surprised at his allowing you to master such an extraordinarily unladylike accomplishment."

Marina's cheeks were scarlet, but she kept her voice steady as she replied clearly, "My uncle knew nothing of it, sir. I used to slip out at night to join Rollo and Ralph at the lakeside. They taught me to sail too. It was my cousin William Crawley, of Crawley Park, who taught me to ride," she added provocatively. "Of course, he had no sidesaddle, so I can only ride astride."

She believed, but could not be sure, that Mr. Granville ground his teeth. "And what did your female cousins teach you?" he enquired.

"Serena taught me to bear her pinches without complaint," she answered seriously, "Amelia, something of a sister's love. As for Susan, I learned from her that if a child can betray you, it will. And Betty"—her face softened—"dear little Betty taught me how lovable a baby can be. My Crawley cousins, apart from William, I did not know so well, for Matty and Gussy were at boarding school most of the time we lived at Crawley Lodge. Caroline, of course, I was hardly allowed to meet. Being so much the youngest, she was sadly spoiled. She cried for the least thing, told tales on her brother when he bullied her, and for me she conceived an unaccountable admiration, so I am sure you, sir, will easily sympathize with my aunt Crawley's determination to keep us separate."

"And what did you learn at school?" demanded Mr. Granville inexorably.

She shook her head solemnly. "Very little, sir, I do assure you—apart from developing a head for heights, of course."

He put a hand up to his mouth, but whether to conceal a spasm of rage at this impertinent reply or to smother the beginning of an involuntary smile, she could not tell.

Miss Derwent said with a sort of relish, "But, my dear, do you tell us you have *no* accomplishments? Do you not play the piano?"

"Not a note, with any accuracy."

"Nor sing?"

"I am said to be tone-deaf."

"You sew, of course?"

"I have tried, very often, but my work always seems to be grubbier than anyone else's, and covered in bloodstains from my continually pricking my finger."

"You—you can make tea?" hazarded her aunt rather wildly.

Marina shook her head. "I always spill it."

Mr. Granville threw down his napkin. "There seems little profit in prolonging this conversation, Miss Derwent. Miss Marina's education is properly the Professor's care, and if he is satisfied—" He broke off, rising with an air of finality.

"I will return in time to escort you both to the funeral service at four o'clock," he said, and left the room.

Marina looked enquiringly at her aunt, who hastened to explain.

"Marcus tells me that the bodies are being brought in to Charlestown this morning, and will be buried this afternoon. A service has been arranged at St. Stephen's and there will be a small reception afterwards at Government House, for the particular comfort of the survivors. I daresay you would like to go?"

"Yes, indeed," said Marina, thinking of Mr. Peppard, Captain Burge and some others with whom she had struck up a particular acquaintance on the ship. "I hope my shoes won't seem too absurd," she added, holding out her foot and regarding it doubtfully.

"My dear! Choke will make you a pair of sandals at once. Toney, fetch Choke, and tell him to bring some leather." She turned back to Marina. "We learn to be self-sufficient here, on these small islands, you know. Choke is Marcus's valet, and can turn his hand to anything. The sandals he will make you will not be the most elegant, perhaps, but he can dye them to suit you. He made mine. I usually have them black, as the most practical."

Sandals were not in keeping with her aunt's old-fashioned dress, Marina thought; but they were certainly cool and comfortable to wear in a hot climate.

"I am an essentially practical creature," Miss Derwent remarked. "I see you wondering at my hoop. It holds my gown away from my body and allows the air to circulate. I'll wager I am cooler in my gown than you are in your skimpy muslin. But you look very nice in that dress of Julia's," she went on. "Most elegant, indeed. That frill is very well conceived. I am glad you came, child. It will certainly do Rosett good to have another young lady to think about instead of spending her time moping or slipping off to the stables, as she does."

Marina sipped her coffee, and exclaimed with pleasure when she heard that the beans had been grown on Tamarind. The light-brown man who was Mr. Granville's valet soon entered the room, holding a piece of leather and a small curved knife. He placed Marina's foot upon the hide and cut round the outline with sure strokes. She understood the reason for his name as soon as he spoke, for his voice was very hoarse and it seemed to cause him an effort to speak.

"He has a growth in his throat, poor man," said Miss Derwent when he had left the room. "Fortunately it is slowgrowing, and Dr. Sunderland gives him a few years yet before it strangles him. Now I propose to present you to the rest of the domestics."

"I would be glad to meet them," said Marina, reflecting that this courtesy had never been extended to her in England, where servants too often seemed to be treated like blocks of wood, and where they themselves seemed to despise those who "knew their place no better" than to offer them the least civility. As soon as she entered the hall, where the staff were assembled, she could see at once that these black slaves had certainly not sunk themselves in the anonymity of their calling but seemed to take pride in their individuality.

Cudjoe was the butler, tall and handsome, dignified to the point of pomposity and finely dressed but for his broad feet, which were quite bare, in striking contrast to his hands, which were elegantly gloved in white kid. Cotto, the housekeeper, was a fat smiling woman, intricately turbaned, and with a sharp bright eye. Toney, the footman, Marina had already met; he was a humorous fellow and more likable than the other footman, Ben, who had an Arab face with a hooked nose, a curling lip and a sly look. The cook, Nanny, next came forward to make her curtsy; she was as thin as a post with narrow eyes like a Chinese. Cassia, Miss Derwent's maid, was a cripple, but her pain-worn face was illuminated by a smile; and last and least came Myall the page, who bowed and grinned impudently at Marina.

"These, with Rosett and Choke, are the senior members of our domestic staff," Miss Derwent remarked, tying on her large calash as a preliminary to taking Marina for a stroll about the garden. "Obed is king of the stables; and MacTavish—" She paused. "MacTavish is in charge of all the field hands. He is Scotch, like most plantation bookkeepers." She gave a little shrug, dismissing MacTavish, and led the way outside.

"It is such a pretty garden," Marina exclaimed. The

grass was not soft and green, there were no flowers massed in borders as in England; but there was the white temple, several statues, a good deal of brick paving, and an expanse of shrubs and flowering trees, all backed by the vibrant blue of the Columbus Channel and the hazy distant islands that lay about Antilla like a necklace of jade.

"It is all so beautiful," Marina cried, raising her face to the sun's caress. "It must be the most beautiful place in the whole world."

"It is a pleasant seat, even though the glory is fading now," Miss Derwent observed. "Of course, one could not compare it with such places as Maroon, even in the great days."

"Mrs. Hungerford told me that Maroon was a house to marvel at," Marina recalled.

"It was past its best when I came to Antilla, but even then, to be invited to a banquet at Maroon was to feel oneself living in a dream. Money was no object to the Fletes in the days when the price of sugar was so high, and the house, some said, was one of the richest in the Leeward Islands. It was furnished like a palace even when I saw it, brocades from France, chairs from England, statues from Greece, Oriental china—I remember the Governor-General saying on one of his visits that it was as if Ralph Flete had been a pirate and had sacked the world to supply the great house at Maroon."

Miss Derwent paused to fan herself, as if almost overcome by the brilliance of her memories.

"The estate went down, of course, as the profits fell, though it was still one of the wonders of the islands only a few years ago. But it's all gone to ruin now, with the goats grazing over the cane gardens, and rats and jumbies having the run of that great mansion."

Miss Derwent, it was plain, had no suspicion that Mr. Flete believed Marcus Granville had driven him out of his inheritance, Marina reflected.

"I would love to see it," she murmured.

"It is very gratifying to find you such an admirer of Antilla, my dear."

"Oh, I am. Julia whetted my appetite, and now I find the half was not told me. I only hope—"

"Hope what, Marina?"

She blushed and turned away. "Only that Mr. Granville does not soon expel me from this paradise."

Miss Derwent snorted. "You have nothing to fear from Marcus," she declared. "I made an agreement with him, when his father died, that he would be master of all at Tamarind, except the indoor staff and the running of the house, so long as he remained a bachelor. My sponsorship of you falls within that category, for I look on you as my companion for the time being. Besides, he cannot overlook our blood relationship, and himself engaged to be responsible for you *in loco parentis*. I love him dearly, for I virtually had the raising of him, you know, but I don't happen to agree with him in everything."

Marina tried, and failed, to envisage Marcus Granville as a child. "How old was he when you came here, ma'am?"

"Only six. It was twenty years ago, just after that dreadful hurricane. Your father married the same year, in England."

"You never knew the first Mrs. Granville, I collect?"

"No, but she was a fine woman by all accounts. My friend Juliana Fox was quite another sort." Miss Derwent sat down on a shaded bench and stared out to sea. "That was a love match, if you like. Martin Granville met Juliana in St. Kitts, in 1785, a year or so after Marcus's mother died. I was staying with the Foxes at the time, for Peace and Plenty had been destroyed some months before. It was like a fire between Martin and Juliana. One look—and they were in flames." Miss Derwent sighed. "One might have known it would burn out soon—on her side, at least. Juliana was my dearest friend, but that did not blind me to her faults. She begged me to accompany her here to Antilla, for she knew no one here but her ardent bridegroom; and besides, she dreaded the thought of supervising a great house such as this, and of looking after her little stepson. 'I shall have children of my own,' she said to me, not knowing that Julia's birth would put a stop to all that. 'You take the boy, and run the house—I could not manage it without you.' And though at first I did not intend to stay, somehow the years slipped past—and here I am."

"I am sure you were a great help and comfort to Mrs. Granville," Marina suggested.

"I wonder. She did not realize at first that I had only agreed to come with her in the hope of being at hand to save her from herself. I failed, alas. In matters of the heart it is not merely officious but quite useless to attempt to interfere. We ended by quarrelling, I am afraid."

"But you looked after Julia, of course, when her mother died."

"Not really," Miss Derwent said despondently. "I believe I mentioned to you last night that after the dance Juliana had led me, my heart failed at the prospect of being responsible for her daughter—and with Marcus standing at my shoulder, thinking that the child was perfect and yet being so fatally strict with her. Adoring and critical—he brought out the devil in Julia, if anyone did, and yet he could not see it for she went to some lengths to hide it from him. So like her mother! No, I fear I took the easy way and insisted on her exile to school abroad. If only I had kept her here! I could certainly have done no worse by her. Suicide! It is the worst reproach. It means she thought we neither loved nor understood her."

Marina was on the point of assuring her aunt of her instinctive disbelief in Julia's suicide, but again thought better of it, and closed her lips. First she must find proof, if she could, of Julia's state of mind before reopening the painful subject. Better to find and read the journal first, before reminding her aunt that there were several forms of idolatry and that since Julia's idol was herself, the implication was that she would never have willingly destroyed it.

66

6

The carriageway to Charlestown was dusty and rut-
ted, but it struck Marina as easier driving than most
English roads, for they, in her experience, were either
a morass of mud in winter, or prone to even more
choking dust and treacherous potholes in summer.
The carriageway was, however, as winding as any
English lane. It wriggled and dipped past Sandy
Harbour, up and down the hills, and turned aside
from the grim pile of Fort Charles, isolated on a rocky
promontory, only to twist back on itself for the de-
scent to Spanish Wells.

Here Miss Derwent commanded Obed to stop. He
reined in the horse drawing the kitareen, an open
carriage shaded by an awning, in order to allow Marina to gaze her fill of the town curving along the
farther shore. The houses were mostly built of un-
painted grey wood with a silvery tone, but some long,
low buildings behind the jetty were made of brick and
Marina supposed them to be warehouses and the
customshouse. It was a busy harbour, with three ships
of considerable size at anchor and several smaller
ones; while droghers were busy lightering goods both
to and from the waterfront.

The kitareen moved on, presently overtaking Mr.
Granville, who was walking his fine bay horse down
the hill to Spanish Wells. This hamlet had its own
jetty and warehouses, Marina noticed.

"This is where Flete has his shop," Miss Derwent

remarked. "It becomes uncomfortably hot in the afternoons on this east side of the bay, so I will take you to look over his stock one morning, when his place is in the shade."

The road curved to the left, across the head of the bay. They drove by a young coconut plantation, passed through a poorer village and then entered Charlestown. By this time Obed had been obliged to slow the kitareen to a walk, and Mr. Granville had pulled in his horse behind them, for the dusty red road was thronged by a press of traffic. There were donkeys laden with greenstuff, barrels, or bulging sacks; horses sleek in their satiny summer coats which must in this climate be permanent, Marina supposed; there were mules drawing carts full of pigs or goats, with perhaps a cow tied on behind; there were shabby carriages of various designs; and a jostling crowd of pedestrians of every possible shade of complexion and style of dress.

The church was in the very center of the town, standing back from the road in its own leafy graveyard, with several carriages drawn up before it, and a more sober crowd bustling about the steps which led up off the street to the wide churchyard path.

Miss Derwent and Marina descended from the kitareen, while Mr. Granville hitched his horse to the back of it. Then he gave his arm to Miss Derwent and the three of them walked along the shady footpath among the graves, and up the second flight of steps into the church.

Inside Marina was relieved to find that St. Stephen's was high-ceilinged and cool. It was rounded at both ends, with many windows, and was thatched with palmetto leaves. Within, there were no private box pews such as she was accustomed to in England, where the gentry read or slept, or even played cards undetected through interminable sermons; but here all was light and open, and the Trade Wind blew freely over the low pews and polished benches.

A narrow-faced churchwarden, with yellowed skin and bright slits of eyes, handed out prayer books.

Marina instinctively disliked him, and was surprised when Miss Derwent whispered that he was Flete's man, Crick. The next moment her aunt had paused to pat a pale, thin gentleman sympathetically upon the arm, and was murmuring condolences to him.

"That was Mr. Winceyman," she explained to Marina, moving on to edge into a pew occupied, Marina saw, by Mrs. Roper and her daughter, Sairey, and a tiny birdlike woman with wispy hair under her dowdy bonnet, and restless fluttering hands.

"The Rector's wife, Mrs. Goodrich," whispered Miss Derwent. Mr. Granville followed Marina into the pew just as a small military band in red-and-white uniforms filed into the choir stalls and began to tune their instruments.

Marina felt a tap upon her shoulder and looked round to see Mrs. Hungerford, conspicuous in a large black hat, all nodding plumes and knots of sable satin ribbon. She bowed, winked and jerked her head sideways toward the gentleman sitting next to her, which Marina took to mean that Mrs. Hungerford wanted her to take particular note of this man, who must be Mr. Brandon Flete. He was quiet-looking and neat-featured, elegantly dressed, with slightly greying hair and an appropriately melancholy expression. His brown eyes met Marina's, to her mild confusion, before he gave her a slight bow and bent his head in order to leaf through his prayer book.

As Marina turned away, she noticed Crick looking in her direction, with a curiously speculative gaze. Then the Rector attracted his attention, and the churchwarden's manner changed again. It was, Marina noticed with surprise, almost as if their positions had been reversed, for when Crick spoke the Rector seemed to hang upon his words with extraordinary deference, and when the Rector did so, Crick paid scant attention. But they both fell back as a larger man came striding up the steps, the sun seeming to strike fire from his well-groomed auburn head as he removed his hat on entering the church; such a sense of vitality seemed to emanate from him that Marina had the oddest fancy that the shadows dwindled, and grief fled away, discouraged.

"That is Dr. Sunderland," whispered Miss Derwent, in a tone of disapproval.

Something made Marina glance once more at Mr. Crick. Like several other people, he was now staring at the doctor, but just for an instant Marina thought an incongruous expression, almost of glee, had lightened the churchwarden's bitter little face, before he controlled it and handed the newcomer a prayer book, with a servile bow.

"His Excellency and Lady Baillie," hissed Miss Derwent, and the congregation rose to its feet as the Lieutenant-Governor and his much younger wife passed to the front of the church, and Mr. Goodrich came forward to begin the service.

The familiar words of the funeral prayers reminded Marina of the bleak days following her mother's death, and when the congregation moved outside the church to attend the burial, she almost broke down at the finality of the sound of the earth striking the coffins. But Miss Derwent gripped her arm in a heartening manner, and Mr. Granville glanced speculatively in her direction, which served to stiffen her. She felt relieved when the service was concluded, and coming out again into the mellow sunlight of late afternoon, she felt a joyous gratitude at being alive, which was not mitigated by Mr. Goodrich's moist handshake and tepid welcome to Antilla, nor by Miss Derwent pointing out Julia's grave. This was set beside those of Martin Granville and his two wives, all four encircled by pink conch shells, whose function, so Miss Derwent informed Marina, it was believed in the Caribbees, was to keep the spirits in their place. About Julia's simple headstone a jasmine climbed, its frail white blossoms breathing a haunting scent.

"Julia's favourite flower," Miss Derwent murmured. "She used to splash herself with jasmine water . . . but there is Obed. Come, my dear, for he is holding up the traffic, waiting for us."

Walking down toward the gate, Marina noticed Mr. Crick lurking—there really was no other word for it—behind an ornate tomb. As she glanced at him, the churchwarden raised his hand to beckon someone—and Marina was surprised to discover that it was Mr. Granville whom Crick was summoning so furtively.

Marina was thoughtful as she accepted the help of Obed to mount into the kitareen. It was hard to envisage what sort of transaction might be taking place between the plantation owner and the churchwarden, particularly as the latter was the trusted servant of Granville's sworn enemy and victim, Mr. Flete. Or did the clue to their secret conversation lie in this very circumstance?

As the carriage moved forward, Marina glanced back in time to see Mr. Granville reappearing, ducking under a spray of Brazilian bougainvillea. As he walked down the steps toward his horse she realized the object he was pushing back into his pocket was his purse—the very same that Julia had netted for him during the long light evenings at school last summer.

After a few minutes, the carriage turned in between the gates of Government House. A moment later Mr. Granville overtook it, cantering easily past up the short incline. He was dismounting as the kitareen drew up before the steps of a handsome brick-and-wooden building with a classical portico.

A turbaned Indian butler, flamboyantly dressed in silk, received their party and led them down a long hall and through an antechamber to a partly walled garden at the back of the house, where a fountain played and several persons were strolling beneath the trees. The Indian announced them to the Lieutenant-Governor, a yellow sundried man with shrewd bright eyes, many years older than his fashionable dark-haired wife. Marina made an awkward curtsy—she had grown so fast in the last year that she had not

71

quite got used to the new length of her legs—and Sir Hugh smiled at her very kindly.

"I congratulate you on your escape, Miss Derwent," he said in a thin dry voice. "I understand that you were the heroine of the hour."

Marina, glancing away in embarrassment, found her eyes held by the sharp green ones of the Governor's wife.

"So fortunate your education was—unorthodox," drawled Lady Baillie, raising a haughty eyebrow. "Perhaps you had better teach us all to swim."

Then, from being cold and disdainful, Lady Baillie's painted face suddenly seemed to glow with warmth, her eyes widened, and she became a beauty. "Mr. Granville!" she exclaimed, holding out her hand and forcing Marina to pass farther into the garden. "How charming to see you, sir, even on this unfortunate occasion!"

It was with relief that Marina found herself face to face with Mrs. Hungerford. They embraced.

" 'Ow can I ever thank you for what you did?" Mrs. Hungerford exclaimed. "Well I reckon the lot of us would still be out there on the reef, if alive at all, if it weren't for you."

"Don't say any more," Marina begged her. "I saved myself, you know—and besides," she whispered, "Lady Baillie considers I have been sufficiently praised, for a hoyden."

"Ho! Well, I 'ave a name for 'er ladyship, but I'd best not use it 'ere. Now, my dear, I never did say a proper good-bye to you last night. 'Ow are you? Are you quite well? No fever?"

"No, it is the sunburn that makes me look hot. But where is Miss Dampier?" asked Marina, looking round.

Mrs. Hungerford looked grave. "Miss Dampier 'as took the fever, I'm afraid. Quite poorly she was, this morning. I only 'ope—ah, but 'ere's my master. Mr. Flete, 'ere is Miss Marina 'erself. I'm sure she needs no introduction from me!"

Mr. Flete, now that Marina could see him standing,

was an elegant gentleman, though not much taller than herself. He bowed and said in a slightly drawling tone with a trace of amusement, "No indeed. Mrs. Hungerford has scarcely ceased to sing Miss Marina's praises since I was reunited with her last night at Sandy Harbour. You are a very courageous young lady, ma'am, and I am honoured to make your acquaintance."

Marina blushed, and sought another subject of conversation, but to her relief Miss Derwent soon took her by the arm and removed her from Mr. Flete with the excuse that the colonel had asked to meet her.

Colonel Dawlish was a kindly-looking military man with an empty sleeve tucked into one pocket. Marina lost no time in enquiring after the fate of the livestock aboard the *Carib Queen*.

"All safely rescued, ma'am. It was a pity that the passengers did not follow their example and stay with the ship. If they had done so there would have been a great saving of life."

He took a glass of some pink mixture off a tray and offered it to her.

"Try some Planter's Punch, ma'am—a fit drink for a heroine."

"Thank you, sir. How long will your soldiers stay aboard the wreck?"

"Until everything that can be salvaged has been brought off her. We dare not leave it unguarded for a moment, ma'am, or the strip-wrecks will be all over her like wild dogs cleaning out a dustbin. The owners are entitled to their copper bottoming, just as you are entitled to your trunk—which should be restored to you shortly, by the way."

Marina thanked him, and sipped her drink, which was sweet but rather pleasant, with a touch of spice. "Colonel Dawlish—"

"Yes, ma'am?" he prompted, as she hesitated.

"I was wondering if Mr. Hendrie and the sailors had told you, sir, that our ship was decoyed into the reefs?"

"Hendrie mentioned a light," the colonel replied cautiously.

"We were led in by another vessel, somewhat smaller than the *Carib Queen*, but certainly larger than the local sloops. Did you ask Jem about it?"

"Jem? Ah, yes, the big fellow—Carter. He is of your opinion, I believe—and I have also had a message from Miss Dampier upon the subject. But these matters are best discussed in private, ma'am. Ah, Dr. Sunderland! Miss Marina, allow me to present . . ."

Marina looked round to find the doctor, who had been talking to Mr. Winceyman and Mr. Flete, and towering over both, was now beside her. It made a pleasant change, she thought, to have to tilt her head, to feel, tall as she was, quite fragile beside a man.

"So this is the famous Miss Marina Derwent," said the doctor thoughtfully. "Everyone is talking of you, ma'am—and long before today I heard Miss Julia Granville speaking of her intrepid friend, though then I dared not hope to have the chance of meeting a young lady so out of the common way."

Marina flushed, but Dr. Sunderland met her suspicious glance with a great laugh like a lion roaring.

"You've suffered for your originality, I see," he declared. "It is admiration, not censure, that I would express." He sobered quickly. "Don't let them pour you into the common mould, Miss Marina. There are enough milk-and-water young ladies about, I should have thought. And certainly there must be room for a few eccentrics in this tired old world. You ride, I have been told, like a Diana. Shall I challenge you to a race—astride by moonlight?"

Marina felt as if she were being buffeted by a great west wind. She wondered what reply she was supposed to make to such a daring suggestion, put forward under the noses not only of her aunt but of Mr. Granville himself; for he, she now saw, was watching her not many paces distant.

"It sounds exciting," she murmured, so that Dr. Sunderland had to bend his fiery head to hear her.

"And I would not have you think me a coward, after all—but I am a visitor, and must not behave too badly here."

"It won't be here," he said quickly. "I was thinking of Mount Pleasant. Admiral and Mrs. Ducheyne were saying they propose to invite you to their private racing party on Friday week, to stay until the Monday —the races are for the gentlemen, of course. As to our affair, no one need know of it—unless we choose to let them do so."

"But—but I have nothing to ride."

He laughed again, a great mad roar that startled Marina quite badly and set heads turning all about them. "Why, what's to stop you borrowing that bay horse of Marcus Granville's, ma'am? He's a rare one to go, and will know the course. You'll need a mount that is no stranger to the place, riding there at night for the first time. And on that horse you'll stand a good chance of beating me and my roan, for you'll ride pretty light, I believe. Shall we wager on it, eh?"

"I am interested, sir—extremely interested. But I can settle nothing yet. Besides," she remembered practically, "the moon is already some nights past the full."

"Confound it—perhaps we'll have to postpone it then, for you are right—there'll be no moon. I would not expose you to danger, Miss Marina, I'll assure you— only to a welcome change from your circumscribed existence at Tamarind." For an instant, his eyes narrowed. He did not like the Granvilles, Marina deduced. She found herself oddly relieved that he was no longer pressing her and wondered ruefully if she might be growing up at last, that she should hesitate to accept a challenge so exactly to her taste.

She looked around for Miss Derwent, and saw that she had been drawn aside by a small thin gentleman with an exceedingly melancholy countenance. He was murmuring lugubriously in Miss Derwent's ear and she, Marina saw with something approaching incredulity, was tossing her head in a coy manner, her

75

cheek faintly flushed, while giving little whinnies of laughing protest from time to time.

"Excuse me, sir," said Marina rather breathlessly. "There is—my aunt."

"She won't thank you for interrupting her," the doctor remarked, with his wide grin. "Miss Derwent and Mr. Cosmo Singleton have become remarkably friendly since the loss of the *Otaheite* brought them together."

"Nevertheless," Marina insisted, "I believe I should return to her."

The reception ended soon afterwards, at sunset. Farewells were made and then, to Marina's surprise, Mr. Flete came forward to help her into the kitareen, which was waiting with lit lamps. He thanked her again for saving the life of Mrs. Hungerford. "A person more precious to me, ma'am, than you could well imagine."

Marina liked him very much for saying that. She smiled warmly, and when Mr. Flete asked her to be sure to visit the shop, she immediately promised to do so.

"I also thought you would be interested to hear, if you have not already done so, that a ship is leaving with mail for England upon the morrow's evening tide," he informed her. "If you have any letters to go by her, you should bring or send them to my shop by noon, and I will see they go with mine."

Marina thanked him, Mr. Flete turned away, and Mr. Granville came up at once.

"What do you stay for, Obed?" he demanded coldly. "The mosquitoes are beginning to bite."

The coachman immediately cracked his whip, sending the horse into a long-gaited trot. He brought them to Tamarind in good time, and it was as well, for as they alighted before the front door, Cudjoe was just closing it behind two visitors.

"The Thurloughs," cried Miss Derwent in a tone of dismay. "Did we invite them?"

Mr. Granville dismounted. "No, ma'am. Harry said last night they might call this evening."

So that was why he wanted us to hurry back, Marina reflected. She found herself quite eager to see what sort of female could tame Mr. Granville to that extent, and hastened to follow her aunt into the house. She had some difficulty in suppressing a smile when she saw that Miss Thurlough was in almost every respect the very opposite to herself, being small, dark, and apparently meek, with a sallow little face and narrow black eyes. She had a gentle, pretty voice and an interesting accent, for she spoke rather as the Quakers do and her speech was sprinkled with odd mispronunciations. Apart from that she seemed strictly conventional and her manners would have passed in any provincial drawing room—Marina thought that Miss Thurlough would probably have found a London salon far too easygoing for her prim taste.

Mr. Thurlough was not unlike his sister in looks, dark and sallow, but his manner was a good deal more free, and his voice had obviously been affected by his English education. Marina set him down as a man's man, ready for any sport that might offer, and not one to think too profoundly upon any matter—until she happened to surprise an anxious look in him when he thought himself unobserved, which suggested him to be oppressed by some deep-seated trouble.

Both the Thurloughs seemed to regard Marina with suspicion. They would no doubt be displeased with any young lady staying at Tamarind just now, she supposed; and she wished she could assure them that she was far from having any designs on Mr. Granville, if that was what they feared.

"How is't, Miss Marina, that you are fray to travel so far from home?" enquired Miss Thurlough, when the subject of the shipwreck had been dealt with, and Mr. Thurlough had explained that they had not been at the funeral as it was Sir Hugh's wish that only those with some connection with the *Carib Queen* should attend it. "Lard," went on Miss Thurlough, with a glance at Mr. Granville to make sure he did not disapprove, " 'tis a strange thing, surely, for a maid to voyage alone! Are you an orphan, perhaps?"

"My father is alive, I trust; but he is travelling himself just now, and in parts where I cannot accompany him. I was chaperoned upon the voyage, however."

"Ay, by Mrs. Hungerford—a rarely malicious gossip—"

Mr. Thurlough hastened to interrupt his sister. "Now, Blanche, thee knows Miss Marina is not an orphan, for Miss Derwent told us not a week past that her brother was a—an— What the—the—what is the word, eh, Granville?"

"An archaeographer, I suppose you mean," supplied Mr. Granville without hesitation.

"An archaeographer?" repeated Miss Blanche, with a soft breath of a laugh, as if she had never heard of anything so quaint. "And what does thee mean by that, may I ask?"

Mr. Granville stared at Marina, his eyebrow raised and a mocking look in his one eye as if he doubted her ability to answer correctly.

She said carefully, "I have actually never heard my father so described before, but it is perfectly true, of course, that he practices archaeography, which can be defined, Miss Thurlough, as the systematic description of antiquities. Papa is indeed a professed student of archaeology and prefers to study it in the field, which is why he is obliged to travel continually."

Miss Blanche looked blank. Then she shrugged. "I recall now, you were in barding school with my dear friend, poor Julia. She told us many tales of you, and that you had sadly lacked a mother's consarn. Is't true your father brought you up almost as a boy?"

Her little black eyes rounded with an appearance of anxiety as she awaited Marina's reply.

Miss Derwent stirred, her feathers seeming slightly ruffled at this attack on her brother's sense of propriety, and on Marina's upbringing. Mr. Thurlough coughed uneasily, and half turned to Mr. Granville, who, Marina saw, was awaiting her reply with considerable interest.

Filled with sudden madness, due no doubt to the punch, Marina heard herself declare that her father had had little time to spare on raising her. "It is to my cousins Ralph and Rollo Havelock, and to Cousin William Crawley, that I am indebted for my wider education, for they taught me to ride astride, and to sail a boat and swim—"

"Swim!" faintly echoed Miss Blanche.

Miss Derwent said sharply, " 'Tis very fortunate that Marina can swim—and for the rest, it is no one's affair but Marina's how she behaves herself, within limits. She does not need to seek employment, and she is disenchanted with the notion of matrimony, so she lacks the usual motive to impress. She reminds me very much of her great-great-aunt Rose—a much respected, though eccentric, common ancestor of ours."

Mr. Granville made an impatient gesture. "While Miss Marina is in my house," he said coldly, "her behaviour is of very great concern to me. I do not wish to have her bringing disgrace to Tamarind. We have had enough of that, I should have thought. If I catch her playing the hoyden, be sure she will regret it."

Marina flushed angrily, but before she could speak, Miss Blanche had leaned forward and laid her little hand upon Marina's arm.

"Lard, miss, but I did not intend to cause an upset! 'Tis only that Julia said you were a tomboy. Julia," she slyly added, with a little wistful smile at Marina, "always very much admired you."

Mr. Granville sprang to his feet. His fists were clenched, Marina noticed, but he spoke in a voice of icy control.

"I hope you two will be friends," he said between his teeth. "The connection could do Miss Marina nothing but good, if you will in this oblige me, Blanche. Come,

79

Harry. I want to show you the horse I will be racing at Mount Pleasant."

"Wait," cried Marina, also rising. "I must say this, sir, although you will not thank me for it. No—it is only fair to let me speak. It seems to me, whenever your sister's name is mentioned in connection with mine, that you have formed the impression she would have been better never to have met me. In fact, I heard you say as much—that I was responsible for Julia's death."

"I don't deny my conviction that you must be held partly to blame," said Mr. Granville, his brown face yellowing. "It was not at Tamarind that Julia learned to play truant and slip out at night—"

"Julia was a spirited girl," declared Marina furiously. "Her character was formed long before I ever met her. If anyone has influenced her, it must have been someone closer to home." By chance, her gaze fell on Miss Thurlough, sitting openmouthed.

"Me?" she squeaked. "You don't accuse me, I trust?"

"Now why do you suppose I might, Miss Thurlough? You are not at all the sort of person Julia admired—I daresay you will take that as a compliment—"

"We will excuse you, Miss Marina," said Mr. Granville, holding open the door. "You are overwrought. I am sure the Thurloughs will be good enough to remember you have been under strain."

Marina flashed a sparkling glance about the room. Her eye caught Mr. Thurlough's. He looked more embarrassed than anyone, she thought; and she was suddenly quite overwhelmed by the knowledge of her bad behavior. She held her head high as she walked across the room, but her lips trembled as she passed by Mr. Granville.

"I fear she's overcome," declared Miss Thurlough. "Thou wert something cruel, Marcus—she's little more than a child, after all, great girl though she is."

"Miss Marina is a heroine, as everyone has been informing me all afternoon," he said coldly. "It would take more than a hard word from me to discommode her." And with that he slammed the door behind her.

7

Mr. Granville was quite wrong about the effect of his scorn on her, Marina thought as she climbed the stairs. She had had an exhausting day, and his disapproval was the last straw. It was not, of course, that she cared a whit for the opinion of such an odious man; it was simply that she was tired of being despised by him. And it was unforgivable of him to rake her down before that hateful Blanche! The only pleasure Marina had received from the whole evening had been her realization that the apparently meek and submissive Miss Thurlough would probably turn out to be nothing like the conformable wife Mr. Granville was hoping for. But this comfort was at best a negative one and the turmoil of her thoughts would prevent her sleeping for many hours, she feared.

Marina was unexpectedly gratified, therefore, to find that her trunk had been delivered, and now stood open in a corner of her room. Rosett had made some attempt to unpack, but finding the seawater had done much damage, she had left out a pile of ruined gowns for Marina's inspection. Some things had been already put away; Marina found several pairs of shoes in the closet, a few books sadly stained, but still readable, upon a side table with the blackly tarnished set of silver brushes which had been her mother's; and in a little pile to one side, as if Rosett accepted no responsibility for them, were the thin cotton trousers and shirts Marina had long ago begged of Cousin Rollo, and which she had been used to wearing for her illicit riding and sailing lessons. They too were stained, for the cover of the blue book had run across them, but what did that matter since no one would ever see them, thought Marina, hiding them away in the back of the clothespress. She sorted through the rest, and had a bundle of discarded clothing to present to Rosett when the maid came in to turn down the bed and close the shutters. By this time Marina was extremely hungry and was glad when Ben brought in a tray laden with conch stew, fresh bread and baked bananas for her supper.

After she had eaten, Marina pushed open the shutter again, and stayed for a long time upon the window seat, looking out at the indistinct shapes of the shrubs in the starlit garden. If only she could see Julia just once again, she thought: Julia, as she had been on that last night of her life, slipping out to meet her lover, perhaps—or else with the intention of going to her death. If only one could know what her thoughts had been as she neared the end of her short life. It must have been Mr. Brandon Flete who had caused her to despair, Marina supposed; and she recalled what she had been told of the terms of the Tancred will, whereby the money that had been left to Julia by her eccentric godmother, Lady Tancred, was tied up to prevent a fortune hunter's benefitting from it. Supposing that Mr. Flete had known only that Julia was an heiress . . . and had dreamed of marrying her to spite her brother. Supposing, when he was committed, that Julia had told him that her fortune would never be able to buy him back the lost glories of his ruined plantation, and that he then had jilted her; would that have been enough to cause that willful and romantic princess of a girl to take her life?

"No—no!" the tree frogs seemed to call. No, Marina's instincts echoed. Julia, unless love had greatly changed her, could never have destroyed the self she had worshipped so consistently. Even if her lover had

82

rejected her, she would merely have turned to her looking glass for confirmation of her beauty—and that, which was all to her, she could surely never have brought herself to mar.

But—for the first time the thought came to Marina —what if there had been a quarrel? What if Julia had refused to let him go? Might not the frustrated fortune hunter have pushed her away in the heat of his rage; and might it not be possible that Julia's death had been murder, or perhaps manslaughter?

But in that case, thought Marina, sinking down onto the bed, then Mr. Flete was guilty! Yet did she know for certain that it was he whom Julia was meeting in the summerhouse? And was that neat, gentlemanly person capable of such strong passions?

He had a temper, she remembered. He had blinded Mr. Granville in a fit of rage. . . . Now more than ever it seemed to Marina to be essential to try to discover the truth, and make it public. If Julia had been murdered, that would be a shocking tragedy for the family to bear—yet surely not so bad as the corrosive sorrow that her suicide had been to them.

Marina stood up. Somehow she would find out the truth, she vowed, though she had no notion how to go about the matter. But if she kept her eyes and ears open, an opportunity would no doubt come . . . for her father had uncovered whole cities, following no more than an awareness of the possibility of their existence beneath the desert sands. A word, a reference, a mention in the Bible—from such hints as these had sprung great discoveries to the mind attuned. And, thinking of the Professor, Marina reminded herself that the packet ship was leaving on the morrow. There was a desk in the room upon a writing table, and Marina sat at it to write to Lady Havelock to thank her for her hospitality, and to inform the family of her dramatic arrival in Antilla (Rollo would be especially pleased to hear how useful had been her ability to swim).

Reliving those frightful hours left her feeling drained,

and Marina was glad to lay down her pen at last and seal the letters. At least she was tired now, and certain she would sleep.

But when she got into bed, the thought of Mr. Granville returned to plague her. She was allowing him to assume a disproportionate place in her mind, she feared, and it was all because of those misleading looks of his. She had thought him the very figure of a hero, at that first glance: a man whom one could all too easily imagine riding in light armour, to rescue a maiden from impossible odds, throwing her upon his saddlebow and galloping off with her into undreamed-of bliss—the kind of man she should have known could not exist outside the imaginations of poets and novelists. It was not her place to blame him for his sins; certainly she could not blame him for having misled her. It was disappointing that he could not live up to his appearance; and it seemed to be as annoying for him as it was embarrassing for her that she was obliged to live beneath his roof; but since it could not be helped, there was no need to lose sleep over the situation. She must learn to ignore him as far as possible ... and thinking this, Marina put him from her mind and fell asleep.

She did not sleep well, however. She tossed and turned, dreaming fitfully of Aunt Havelock throwing a priceless vase at Sir George's head, of strange water monsters writhing in the murky depths of Grayling Lake, and at last, and most terrifyingly, of Julia plunging to her death down the cliff below the temple.

Marina awoke, gasping, to find the late-rising moon shining full upon her face. She had forgotten to latch the shutter after sitting by the window ... now, thinking of that last dream, she was wide awake. She sat up. The house was quiet; the Thurloughs must long since have departed. It was an opportunity for adventure, a night for exploration.

And suddenly the thought came to Marina of Julia's hidden journal. How could she have forgotten it? Miss Derwent had not found it—no doubt it was still where

Julia left it, and this was surely the very moment to find out.

Marina twisted her hair into a thick plait, over one shoulder. Then she dressed with pleasurable ease in the thin trousers and loose shirt. She stole to the door and opened it a crack. No sound came from beyond, though a lamp still burned upon the landing table. For all she knew it was the custom at Tamarind to leave it burning through the night. She closed the door and crossed to the window. Turning, she let herself down slowly until her bare feet rested on the pediment below. With the aid of a convenient vine, she easily descended the rest of the way. She stood a moment on the flagstones, breathing a little faster, while the warm wind lifted her loose muslin shirt and the moonlight painted the world about her in entrancing tones of silver.

Now she became aware of other sounds: the sea breaking against the foot of the rocky cliff, a horse stamping in the stables, a child crying in the slave quarters. But the house itself was silent, the windows shuttered. Her spirits rose, and she began to run across the garden, rejoicing in the freedom from her irksome petticoats.

She reached the white temple, gleaming in the moonlight, and sank down upon the stone curved seat within, to catch her breath. The scent of jasmine filled the air, bringing Julia irresistibly to mind. Here on this seat had Julia sat, only a few months ago, waiting for the man she loved . . . and now Julia lay in her West Indian grave, ringed about with conch shells to keep her spirit in its place. But could Julia's cunning spirit be so easily subdued? Was it not her essence now which breathed in the fragrant jasmine blossom, and which urged Marina on to find out the facts of her last days, and of her mysterious death?

Marina sprang to her feet and leapt down the shallow steps to stand before the statue, tall upon its pedestal. Perhaps this Venus was somebody's ideal of beauty, Marina reflected, staring at it; but in her opinion the classic face was dull, the body too heavy for perfection. What had Julia said about it? *You can't use trees for postboxes in the Caribbees, the insects would eat up your letters. I hide my secret papers in a statue we have there, an armless statue of the Venus de Milo which stands conveniently just outside the temple where I love to sit. . . .*

But how could one hide papers in a statue? Marina put her hands on the warm stone and pushed at it but it was as heavy as it looked—and if she could not move it, Julia could never have done so. She bent down to examine it more closely, running her fingers over the square pedestal. At first she thought it as solid as the rest, but then she found one corner crumbling beneath her touch. It had been filled with plaster, she discovered; a triangular piece which could be carefully lifted away, leaving a hole behind it. Cautiously she slipped in her hand, for she knew that scorpions sometimes lurked in such secret places. With a thrill she touched something tightly rolled. Could it really be a scroll of papers? Her heart beating faster, she drew it out, to discover that it was, tied with a striped ribbon which she even recognized as one of Julia's. She closed her eyes, breathing a heartfelt prayer of thanks, for she realized now that she had not really expected to find anything, after so many months.

Too excited to think of returning to her room, Marina searched the temple for a lamp. She found one with its tinderbox in a tall cupboard where oars and a parasol were stacked, and a stiff garden broom hung from a hook inside the door. She stepped into the cupboard and lit the lamp. Then, still inside with the door ajar, she spread out the pages and began eagerly to read them.

Marcus was wretchedly strict again today—how he fears the least sign that I may be my mother's daughter! I can only say, thank God I never knew *his* mother, for she sounds a dead bore to me, and tho' I am proud of my brave and handsome half-

86

brother, it is all too clear at times that he resembles her. "A very worthy woman," so my dear Miss D. describes her—not that they ever met. How glad I am no one will ever say that of me—though I do not intend an open scandal if it can be avoided, for it is more comfortable not to cause an upset—as my charming Captain says, "always get over heavy ground as light as one can," which is my whole philosophy in a nutshell.

My charming Captain? Marina paused a moment to wonder if Mr. Flete was an officer in the Militia.

"Monday." (Julia never dated anything, Marina reflected before reading on. It was almost as if she had been afraid of Time, which was to give her such short measure.)

Miss D. said today she could not like him! This is a sad blow, as I had hoped for her support in the inevitable battle with Mark. How stuffy can he be! He is so pompous sometimes, he makes me want to scream, especially when I recall how different he used to be. Who would now suppose he was the wild young man who took out his boat as a privateer, when he came home from Oxford, and even once captured some Spaniards in a periagua off one of those empty islands the nations squabble over, that are good for nothing but growing timber? But the privateering days are over now, the Court of the Vice-Admiralty is disbanded, and Marcus seems to have settled down with his two ambitions—to be both a successful plantation owner and the jailer of his half-sister! I am desperate to escape—no wonder I am driven to deceive him in a thousand ways. If we elope, Marcus will only have himself to blame. If he would only marry, perhaps it would serve to distract his mind from me—only I hope he does not choose that wretched Blanche, she is the very pattern of the sort of wife he should not have, who will but confirm him in his role of tyrant. He should marry someone like Marina ...

Marina gasped and the paper trembled in her hands. Thank heavens this journal had never been found by Marcus Granville! Hastily, she read on.

Marina, who would shock him back into humanity perhaps, and make him laugh—Marina, who would lead him a dance—and above all, who would persuade him that we should all be entitled to make our own beds and lie upon them. Yes, Marina is the ally I need now....

A few pages on, Julia wrote in triumph:

Perhaps I am a witch, as Rosett mutters sometimes—for Marina is to come to Tamarind! Her father wrote—I could see that Marcus was not pleased. I have not told him much about her, but enough for him to realize she is precisely the kind of girl with whom he would not wish me to associate. But dear Godmother Derwent is so pleased at the prospect of a visit from her niece, he will be hard put to refuse it. Well! Marina bids fair to be a beauty [Marina's eyes widened again] though she has no notion of it yet, and my Mark had ever an eye for a pretty female. I believe she may win him over in the end, with that, and her charm, and her warm heart.

In the mellow lamplight, Marina blushed. If Julia could say such things in her private journal—Julia, who never bothered to praise anyone—then, could one hope they might possibly be true? But she rebuked her winging thoughts, and forced her mind back to the words that Julia had penned, often in haste and, to judge by their appearance, on her knee.

So Marina will be a valuable ally—and, if

Marcus loses his heart to her, perhaps an *in*valuable one. I told my love of her intended visit and for a moment he said nothing, and I was afraid. Oh, yes, I fear him—fear those sudden rages that sweep him like a summer squall—but all was well. He smiled—his smile that's like the breaking dawn—and said we must wait for Marina to work her magic, then, before letting our secret out. Oh, but it is hard to wait. I'm mad for him. Sometimes I wonder if he loves me so much, that he can be so patient. I have even offered myself to him, but though he seemed excited, he refused me. I know not what to make of this. Perhaps it means that he does love me truly, and therefore respects me, and sets a value on my chastity which I fear I don't deserve. But I know I dare not tell him that I am not the innocent he supposes me to be.

Marina drew a deep shaking breath. So the demure but reckless Julia was no virgin! More than ever, it was fortunate that these papers had not fallen into Marcus Granville's hands. But another, more alarming thought occurred. What if this later lover, who valued Julia's supposed chastity so much—what if he had discovered the truth? Might that not have caused one of those "sudden rages"? Might he not in his disillusionment have murdered her?

Marina bit her lip. She was half afraid to read more, but knew she must go on.

It is as well that H. is so frightened of Marcus that he will never let it out. Not that it was my fault, to begin with at least. He took advantage of me in the storm ... later, when I agreed to meet him, it was more to spite Marcus, I believe, and because I wanted to know the things that grown-ups whisper about, than because I found much enjoyment in it then. In the end, of course, I hated him, for he became coarse and callous—seeming to despise me while still using me, so I agreed to go away to school in the hope that he would find some other interest once I had left for England. Little did Marcus ever suspect the reason why I refused so violently when he expressed his wish for a match between us! If my dear brother wants to join Prosperity and Tamarind, he will have to sacrifice himself. I will never sell myself to Harry, now that I know what love can be. Only I long to join myself in passion with this man who, I know, will make a lover beyond all my expectations. . . .

There were only a few more entries, Marina saw. Still feeling rather numb with the shock of Julia's confession, she glanced at the last of them.

He came an hour ago—he has just left me. He was different tonight—I wonder why. Perhaps someone has told him about the Trust, which I did not want him to discover before we were safely wed. And yet surely he could not be so base as only to desire me for the fortune Lady Tancred settled on me? And for my part, I noticed something that puzzled me. No, I will be truthful, and say it frightened me. Can it be the same cut-ruby fob that Marcus lost to Alfred? Yet, how could it be? Surely Mr. Cosmo Singleton would not sell his poor brother's possessions so soon after losing him, even if it had been recovered with his body? The suspicion that occurs to me is hideous, I wonder if I shall have the courage to mention it at our next meeting. Yet I could not agree to marry him with that between us.

There, abruptly, the journal finished.

Marina let out a breath. She turned back to an earlier page, but before she had read more than the first line, referring to a gown that Rosett was making, a slight sound distracted her.

Instantly, her hand shot out to turn down the lamp.

She stood in the near-dark, her heart thumping, and heard the unmistakable scrape of a boot on the flagged path. The slaves were under curfew, and mostly went barefoot. It could only be Marcus Granville walking in the garden so late at night.

Swiftly, Marina went to blow out the flame. She pushed the scroll of Julia's papers into the waistband of her trousers, and began pulling the cupboard door gently toward her by the hook on the inside.

Her fingers were still tightly gripping the hook when the door was jerked away and she fell forward, to be roughly seized by Mr. Granville and pulled into the temple.

"So it is you," Mr. Granville cried out harshly, his fingers tight about her shoulders. "I might have known it!"

Marina stared at him, her eyes dark pools, her thoughts wholly concerned with the problem of how to prevent his discovering the journal. He must never see it, she thought wildly. It would kill something in him to know what Julia was really like, and what she thought of him.

"What are you doing out here at this hour?" Mr. Granville demanded violently. "You are dressed as a boy. Where did you get those clothes?"

"They are mine—my cousin Rollo outgrew them."

"You tempt me to treat you as a boy—and give you the beating you deserve. How dare you dress like this, and wander abroad at night? What if the watchman had seen you? He might have fired his old flintlock at you."

"I did not know you had a watchman."

"Precisely. You are in alien territory here. You can know nothing of the dangers of Antilla at night—yet you should certainly know enough to beware of them!"

"But Julia told me—"

His fingers tensed, bruising her.

"Julia! What did she tell you?"

"Why, that she often came out here at night—"

"So you would blacken her name even now! Next

91

you will be telling me that it was Julia who corrupted you!"

"No—no—not that you must be thinking of her as a saint," Marina felt impelled to add.

Mr. Granville stiffened.

"Julia's reports from school were excellent," he said coldly. "I am sure you cannot say the same. She never required discipline while she was there. It was only afterwards that the pernicious influence of the place, and her associates in it, became apparent—"

"Julia was quick and neat," said Marina, stung. "These are attributes which at school are prized above originality of mind or creative force—not that she lacked in that. I would merely assure you that Julia was able to give a good impression three-quarters of the time, or for just so long as it suited her to behave."

She hesitated, wondering how much she would be justified in preparing him against the shock which might, if she could not prevent it, lie ahead of him. "Julia," she said in a low voice, "was not the innocent that you suppose."

She thought he would strike her. She fleetingly remembered something her father had told her, that men disliked above all things having their illusions shattered.

"I loved Julia," she said quickly. "There was much to love in her. Believe me, I know how you must miss her."

"How dare you?" His voice was thick with rage. "How dare you speak of her?" The moon had been shadowed by a passing cloud. Now it swam free, illuminating Marina's face, her wide eyes looking at him with pity. Mr. Granville caught in his breath. His arms went round her slender form as if he would crush her very bones. His head blotted out the light as his lips came down on hers.

It was a kiss meant to punish, and it did. Marina found herself thinking that nothing would ever be the same again. She had not known a kiss could reach into the depths of oneself. Ralph had kissed her lightly two or three times, and she had been flattered, embarrassed, and had wanted to laugh. But now, when Marcus Granville at last released her, she slipped from his hands and sank down, trembling, upon the grass, the tears pouring down her cheeks.

Mr. Granville did not speak for a few moments. When he did, his voice was harsh.

"Now you know what sort of risks you run when you play truant, miss. I hope that you have learned your lesson."

He stooped and roughly dragged her to her feet. She swayed, and he put a supporting arm around her waist.

"What's this?" he demanded, as the scroll crackled under his hand. "What are these papers in your belt?"

"Nothing to you," Marina muttered, twisting away from him.

"Are they not? But I insist on seeing them. Why, I would not put it past a girl like you to have discovered the disposition of our batteries and be intending to sell the information to the French! Be still, confound you!"

Spurred on by the remembrance of what the papers contained, Marina wriggled free of his grasp, and ran straight to the cliff top, where the new rail gleamed to guard the edge, at the very spot where Julia had fallen to her death. She heard Marcus Granville shout behind her, felt his hands reaching for her, and bending the scroll into a small compass, she flung it with all her might toward the sea.

Mr. Granville caught her, pressing her back against the fence.

"You—only meant to—to throw it away—" he panted, curiously breathless. "God! I fancied for a moment—"

He had thought she was going to throw herself over, Marina realized.

"No, no," she said soothingly. "I would never kill myself—as I am certain Julia did not."

For once, he seemed more concerned with her and with the present than with his half-sister and the past.

"It was a damnably foolish risk to take! Why did you do it? Was that your journal?" he demanded forcibly.

"No—not mine."

She longed to recall the words, or at least change the inflection, but it was too late, and her very dismay seemed to supply him with the clue. His hands fell from her and he stood upright. He was taller than she had supposed—or perhaps it was just the effect of the moonlight.

"My God," he breathed. "It was Julia's journal ... You read it! You, of all people—the one who ruined her!"

Marina felt her temper rising. "I was Julia's friend. She wanted me to read her journal, I know she did. Just as I am certain she would not have wished you to do so."

"Be quiet! How dare you come into our family like this—dividing us? I knew the first moment that I set eyes on you that you would cause trouble here—"

"I could scarcely help the manner of my arrival, after shipwreck," Marina pointed out.

"Could you not? You might have waited at Sandy Harbour for a carriage to collect you, as the others did. But no, you had to do the hoydenish thing—to ride, and astride at that!"

"You will want me to leave, I suppose. I cannot return to England, for I believe my father means to join me here eventually, but perhaps Mrs. Hungerford would allow me to stay with her. I could find work—"

"Thank you," said Mr. Granville between his teeth, "but we do not send our guests to work from Tamarind, however inimical they may be to us. You were Julia's friend—Miss Derwent is your aunt. These facts must entitle you to our hospitality as long as you remain on the island."

"Th-thank you, sir."

"You may thank me, if you wish to do so, by your behaviour for the remainder of your visit. If I am obliged to resign myself to your continuing presence here, which it seems I must, I would be grateful if you would render it as little obnoxious as possible."

"I shall endeavour to do so," promised Marina, in tones equally as stiff. "Things are not always as they appear, however. But I will make allowances for your being a little unbalanced just now—"

"What the devil do you mean?" he cried so fiercely that she shrank away from him again.

"Why—why, because I threw Julia's journal away," she faltered. "What did you think I meant?"

He did not answer, and it was only as he was grimly escorting her back into the house that it occurred to her he had supposed her to be thinking of the kiss they had exchanged.

8

During the next days Marina saw as little of Mr. Granville as she might have expected; though as master of Tamarind his hand lay over everything and she would not have been able to ignore his existence, even had she wanted to.

He seemed so remote, Marina thought, so much upon another plane, that she found herself wondering sometimes if she could have imagined both his kiss and the searing anger which had preceded it. She could detect no sign of anger in him now; his manner was distant, and he was pale, his face drawn and strained. Occasionally she caught his single eye staring at her curiously, as though she puzzled him—or perhaps it was merely that he was waiting for her to break out in some new direction to shame and confound him. He certainly bewildered her as much as he unwittingly intrigued her, and she found herself looking forward to the promised visit to Mount Pleasant, not only as a welcome distraction, but in the hope of unravelling something of the enigma of Marcus Granville. She reminded herself that even Mrs. Hungerford did not know positively that it was Mr. Granville who had caused the ruin of the Fletes. Perhaps after all he was not the villain she had feared him to be. Certainly he was a most industrious planter ... and an undeniably attractive man.

Day after day dawned in dewy beauty in Antilla, that May of 1805. Great Trade Wind clouds passed overhead continually, shielding the islands from the sun without casting them into gloom. There were dappled shadows racing across the hills, local rainstorms pouring down from time to time, but always somewhere the sunlight was visible to bring out the glory of the island-studded seascape.

Of course the climate would not seem so idyllic if one were forced to toil outdoors in the heat of the sun, as were the gardeners and field workers, Marina reflected, watching Sammy hoeing weeds after a rainstorm, when the earth was almost steaming. And from that random thought she began gradually to question the whole concept of slavery. It was remarkable how people avoided the subject here, she considered. Slavery was a fact of life, so Aunt Derwent had informed her crisply when Marina had touched upon it: the economy depended on it, for the profit margins, were so small that payment of wages would send planters to bankruptcy. "And besides, who that could choose his work would be a field hand?" Miss Derwent concluded, with the air of one having the last word.

"But wouldn't it be intolerable to be a slave?" Marina asked. "It is that very right of choice that is so precious—"

She reminded herself how she had exulted in running wild in the night—but the slaves were under curfew and without risking frightful punishment could never know that harmless joy. There were poor in England, of course, many thousands of wretched people abused by tyrannical masters, living on the verge of starvation, but no one had the right to forbid them to run out at night if they so desired—still less had anyone the right to separate them from their families by force, as she discovered to her horror was sometimes done in slave-owning societies.

When Marina had burst out with some of this to Mr. Granville, he had raised an eyebrow at her, and appeared at his most austere. But then he had said slowly, "You drag out all the thoughts we prefer to keep locked away, Miss Marina. Do you think your emotional outcry can hope to change a way of life overnight? Yet sometimes I have thought myself that a good part of the ills visited upon us planters may spring from the great wrong we should have known better than to condone. When one is born within a system, however, one looks at it differently ... but a change is coming, and I for one shall not resist it. But I must ask you not to speak upon this subject to others, whose whole dependence is upon their ownership of slaves."

With this Marina had, perforce, to be content. But by questioning Rosett, who at first would only giggle or pretend she did not understand but who gradually came to trust Marina a little more, she discovered something of the lives of the plantation slaves. From her Marina learned that the domestics were the aristocracy of slave society, at least in their own eyes—but that often even they had no place to call their own, sleeping wherever they could find a space convenient; and no slave had any real security.

Marina asked how much it would cost to buy her freedom.

"Sixty-five pounds," Rosett readily replied. "But dat going to be more, when de new law come and dey can't bring no more in from Africa."

Though Rosett had been born in Antilla, Marina thought she could detect a note of yearning as she mentioned her homeland. She began to wonder wildly how she could save up so much, to free Rosett; but then the maid confided that one day she would marry Obed, and that he would buy her from the master then, and set her up as a dressmaker in Charlestown.

Rosett was now much less suspicious of Marina, and the time came when Marina felt able to ask her to describe the events of the night when Julia died. After some initial reluctance, Rosett laid down her sewing.

"Me sleepy dat night," she owned, her manner somewhat evasive. "Miss Julie, she send me off early, to sleep."

Marina considered this, which sounded to her like one of Julia's wiles.

"Were you often sleepy in the evenings?" she asked. "I expect you might be, for you work so hard," she added quickly, lest she seem to be critical.

Rosett carefully rethreaded her needle. "Some nights," she said. "Miss Julie . . ."

Marina pressed her to finish saying what was in her mind. Eventually Rosett confessed that it was always Julia who told her she looked tired, and Julia who gave her, on those occasions, a nice drink to settle her. "If she say Rosett weary, den Rosett always sleep—so deep. Dat Miss Julie, I tell she, she like witchwoman—" Her eyes slid fearfully sideways to meet Marina's, but Marina truthfully assured her that she had often been tempted to suspect the same of Julia.

"Do you think she might have gone out, on those nights?" Marina asked bluntly. "It does not matter now, of course, but it seems to me Miss Julia might well have put laudanum in your drink to make you sleep, so that you could not prevent her. Did you ever notice if—well, if her shoes were damp, or her hem was muddy—anything of that sort that struck you the next morning?"

Slowly, Rosett nodded. "Yes, miss. She go out a lot at night. Rosett always know—Miss Julie sleep late dem morning. And if it rain, or Master sat up late, and she not able, she so cross next day dere no pleasing her." Rosett shuddered. "Dat morning—when she dead—it terrible to see her, mistress, she hand, she foot, so bruised—she poor face—"

Marina swallowed. "You laid her out? ready for burial? Did you notice—?" What? Marina wondered. A blow on the head? The fall would disguise it. "Bruises on the arms?" she asked.

Rosett stared. "She hand bruise, yes, miss."

Marina put her own hands about her upper arms. "Here, I meant."

The maid nodded. "Yes, miss. She bruised dere.

What you t'ink? You t'ink someone go for to hold she, and throw she over?"

Marina reflected. "I think it possible, Rosett. I would like to know . . . but we must not speak of it until I am sure."

"No, miss. I not speak of it." Rosett hesitated. "Me know Miss Julie not go for to kill sheself. Me know plenty slave kill heself. Me can look at one, two, three, and say, he never going to do it. Me look number four, say—he de one. He surely going to kill heself. Not Miss Julie. She white lady, but white, black—" She broke off in confusion.

"You mean that they are much the same? Yes, Rosett, that is certainly something that Antilla has taught me."

Twenty minutes later Marina was in the kitareen as it bowled westward down the carriageway. A sudden ugly squalling startled the horse, and a flight of quarrelling black birds swooped across the road.

"What were those?" Marina asked, as Obed controlled the frightened horse.

"We call them black witches," Miss Derwent replied, looking faintly put out. "They are a kind of parrot, I believe—avid for fruit. I don't hold with superstition myself, but some believe they bring bad luck."

"Perhaps Mr. Granville will not win his race at Mount Pleasant," Marina suggested lightly.

Miss Derwent pursed her lips. "I don't understand Marcus these days," she said quietly. "Something has upset him, but I have no notion what it can be."

"Well, I can't think I'm to blame—I never see him."

"No. I wondered . . ." but Marina was not to know what Miss Derwent wondered, for the kitareen had entered Spanish Wells, and now was drawing up before the waterfront building which contained Flete's shop.

A boy ran out to hold the horse, while Obed helped the ladies to alight. He was grinning irrepressibly, and Marina felt her spirits rise. They passed through the white doorway into a charming room, painted dark green, with a white moulded ceiling. Potted palms, polished boards and woven grass mats achieved a cheap but striking effect, which showed up the goods for sale to advantage. These comprised a few elegant pieces of furniture and a great many small *objets d'art* displayed in glass-topped tables and on shelves.

For the moment, the shop was empty. Marina wandered over to a kneehole walnut desk to admire its glowing patina. It was probably not for sale, she reflected, for it was in use. There was ink in the standish, an open sandbox, and a sealed letter lying on it directed to the Trinket Trading Company.

Mr. Flete suddenly emerged from an inner room. His welcome was quiet and assured, with none of a shopkeeper's servility. Circumstances may have obliged him to make his living out of trade, Marina thought, but he was still unmistakably a gentleman. And though he was extremely civil, there was yet a sense of steel in him, a pride, perhaps even a ruthlessness, which would enable him to work single-mindedly toward his goal.

She realized with a start what Mr. Flete was saying.

"I am so very sorry to have to inform you that your unfortunate acquaintance, poor Miss Dampier, died not thirty minutes ago. Dr. Sunderland was with her. He is examining the body now. That is why Mrs. Hungerford is not here. She was nursing Miss Dampier, of course. The poor woman slipped away very quietly, a painless death."

Miss Derwent put her hand beneath Marina's arm. "My niece is shocked," she murmured. "She is not used to our climate, remember. As soon as I heard that Miss Dampier had been stricken with the fever, I should have prepared her for the worst . . ."

"But it seems so terribly sudden," Marina faltered, allowing Miss Derwent to put her into a chair, while Mr. Flete busied himself with pouring brandy from a cut-glass decanter.

"Death is sudden in the tropics."

He handed Marina the glass of brandy and she began to sip it cautiously. After a few minutes Dr. Sunderland appeared, bringing his vitality into the room like a sudden shaft of sunlight.

"Well, you'll be glad to hear it wasn't yellow fever, at all events," he cheerfully announced. "Ah, excuse me, Miss Derwent, Miss Marina—I did not know you were here. No," he continued more soberly, "the poor lady never recovered from her recent exposure on the Reef. She caught a chill which turned into a fever, and developed an inflammation of the lungs. Let me give you the certificate, Flete. There is nothing to prevent a normal burial, as soon as you please. But here is Colonel Dawlish. I daresay he'll be relieved to hear my findings."

To Marina's ill-concealed indignation, the colonel was indeed relieved for, as he remarked, once the yellow fever had a hold on a community, it could be relied upon to account for more soldiers than would ever expect to die by the bullet. Mr. Flete, however, was more sympathetic.

"You will be thinking us quite barbaric," he said quietly. "You must understand that here, where friends are liable to be removed from our midst with little warning, one learns to guard against morbid depression by accepting these sudden departures in a manner which I know must seem callous and disgusting to outsiders."

His brown eyes appeared concerned. Marina was grateful to him for having taken the trouble to explain the Creole attitude. She made a determined attempt to control her feelings, recollecting an old proverb which her father much respected: when in Rome, do as the Romans do. She would not mention Miss Dampier's death again, she decided, unless someone else brought up the subject; but she wished she could have been able to attend her funeral, which the house party at Mount Pleasant would prevent her from doing.

Setting down her glass, she rose resolutely to her feet and expressed a desire to look about the shop. "You have some Persian pottery, I see. My father brought some back from his last expedition and I learned a little about it then. This is a tin-enamel glaze, is it not?"

"Yes, indeed." Mr. Flete held the object to the light. "As you see, it is so highly iridescent that the decoration is very hard to distinguish."

"I believe it is possible to paint it with some kind of oil to subdue the brightness," Marina suggested tentatively. They moved on to look at Persian rugs, while Miss Derwent bought a piece of Delft off Crick, as a present for Mrs. Ducheyne, whose guests they were to be that very afternoon; and shortly afterwards they took their leave.

"Is Mr. Flete a friend of yours, ma'am?" Marina asked as they drove away, Crick slyly observing their departure through the half-closed door.

"He is always most agreeable—but I am a little wary of him." Miss Derwent added frankly, "And I would caution you to be the same."

Marina reflected for a moment. "Is Mr. Flete in the Militia?" she enquired.

"I believe every able-bodied man is obliged to take turns of duty, in time of war."

"He is not a captain, then?"

"No, our little battalion can support no more than one, and Sam Fergus has that honour. You will meet him at Mount Pleasant."

The two ladies fell silent. Marina was vowing to herself that before she went to Mount Pleasant she would contrive to speak to Mr. Granville alone, however hard he might try to avoid her. Somehow Miss Dampier's sudden death had brought home to her the fact of Julia's, and she knew she should delay no longer in acquainting Mr. Granville of that last entry in Julia's journal.

When she had changed for the journey that afternoon, she watched from her door until she saw Mr. Granville go downstairs. She followed him then, into the book room, a pleasant chamber overlooking the garden and stocked with a rather worm-eaten collection of musty volumes.

Mr. Granville was leafing through an early edition of Mercator's atlas. He looked at her enquiringly, and slowly closed the book.

Marina greeted him somewhat incoherently and plunged into what she had to say. "I am glad to have the chance to speak to you alone," she rapidly began. "We may be interrupted at any moment, so I will quickly tell you that—" her heart was pounding suffocatingly but she forced herself to continue, "—I am now absolutely convinced that Julia—was murdered!"

She could not bring herself to look at him, but hurried on. "Rosett tells me that Julia had bruises on her upper arms when she laid out the body. And in the last entry of Julia's journal—"

"Stop! I will hear no more of this," Mr. Granville declared forcibly. "And I utterly forbid you mentioning it to anybody else."

"But—the journal—you do not know—"

He stepped toward her and then, with an obvious effort of self-control, half turned away and folded his arms.

"It is past," he said bleakly. "And even supposing what you say is true, surely you cannot be such a fool as not to realize the risks you run in making such a statement?"

"But—don't you want to know the truth?" she demanded blankly.

"I don't want *you* to concern yourself with it," he said roughly. "I forbid it, do you hear me?"

"Oh, yes, I hear you," Marina cried. "But I do not recognize your right to forbid me to do anything I please!"

His hands dropped to his sides. His fists were clenched. "A guardian," he said evenly, "has a duty to concern himself with every aspect of his ward's behaviour."

"But you are not my guardian—"

"Wrong. Your father appointed me to that position, until such time as he returns to relieve me of the responsibility."

"It is intolerable," she said in a stifled tone. "You hate me."

He moved restlessly. "You are quite mistaken. I am sorry that my reception of you that first evening should have given you such a notion. I have been meaning to apologize for it. I was guilty, I admit, of leaping to certain conclusions which were ill founded. I would like you to know that I honour you for your heroism; and by the way," he added in a warmer tone, "I was very sorry to hear from Miss Derwent that one of the persons whose lives you saved had died this morning."

"Thank you," she murmured.

"I cannot imagine, however," he continued stiffly, "why you find it so strange that your father should have appointed me to be your guardian. As one proof that his decision was a wise one, allow me to inform you that your letter of credit has failed to arrive. If it was upon the *Carib Queen*, it was in one of the mailbags that were lost. I was this morning, therefore, making arrangements in Sutton's office for you to draw upon my account, until such time as your father is able to correspond with him."

"I suppose I should thank you for that," said Marina ungraciously, determining not to touch a penny of his money.

"There is no need for you to thank me. It is no more than my duty, to see that you are adequately provided for. It is also my duty to warn you to be circumspect, especially regarding the matter we spoke of earlier."

"When it comes to a question of conscience," Marina declared, flinging up her head defiantly, "people must make their own decisions."

His fists clenched again.

"I shall not warn you twice," he informed her. "If you disobey me—in any particular—be sure you will regret it."

Marina found herself shaking with anger. She felt a mad compulsion to try his temper to the limit.

"I daresay your position as guardian has some significance when it comes to legal affairs," she said, tossing her head. "But I doubt if you can command my obedience—"

She broke off as his hands shot out to grasp her shoulders. Then he was shaking her until her hair tumbled into her eyes and she was scarlet from mortification.

"If—violence—is all you understand—" she panted, as he dropped his hands, "—try this!" and she hit him on the face with all her might—an unladylike action which, she suddenly realized, she had been longing to take since their first meeting. It felt extremely satisfying, but her satisfaction was short-lived. With the economy of movement evinced only by the very strong, Mr. Granville picked her up and put her across his knee. He gave her two smacks which hurt enough to make her wish she had put on some extra petticoats, before turning her the right way up.

"Well!" she gasped. "You—wild beast!"

"You make me feel like one," he agreed. "Never hit me again."

Instantly her hand flashed up. He caught it and bent back her arm.

"Oh!" she cried. "You're hurting me."

"You deserve it, ma'am. As you deserve this—"

He pulled her close and kissed her. It was different from the other time, Marina thought ... but then thought became impossible. Her legs felt weak, and when he lifted his head at last, he had to hold her upright.

"Do you see?" he said in a voice of—could it be amusement? Marina stared at him, but he had his head turned to the window, and only the black patch was visible. "You cannot fight me, my ward. One way or the other, I will always win."

Marina sighed. She felt in no case to dispute it; for the moment he had tamed her, and it was with a humiliating sensation of disappointment that she heard her aunt Derwent calling from the hall, that it was time to go.

9

There were two ways to travel to Mount Pleasant from Tamarind, it seemed. One was to journey east by the winding carriage road and follow it as it turned first north into the hills and then doubled back in a westerly direction along the ridge of Antilla's spine. The other route, and much the more direct, was to ride straight up the steep mountain path which led off the old mule track, for Mount Pleasant was only a mile or so to the north of Tamarind, as the crow flew, and more like four by the carriageway.

Somewhat to Marina's disappointment, though hardly to her surprise, Miss Derwent had elected to drive, escorted by Choke with Cassia riding pillion behind him on a tall mule; while Mr. Granville took his horses by the mountain path with Obed and another groom. The carriage, driven by Morgan, was heavier than the kitareen, and drawn by two strong mules. Marina watched with interest as they turned to the right out of the gates of Tamarind, for she had not been in that direction before. Presently Miss Derwent drew her attention to the entrance of the Thurloughs' estate upon their left. Even a first glance was enough to inform Marina that Prosperity was sadly run-down and far from deserving its name, despite the blessing of a well. If Mr. Granville married the daughter of the house and became part owner, no doubt he would pour his fortune into Prosperity's thirsty acres, so that in even a year from now the picture might be a very different one. But could he do that without neglecting Tamarind? Perhaps, now that he had Julia's fortune as well as his own to play with, it might be possible to cherish both estates . . . and Mrs. Hungerford had said that Mr. Granville had benefitted from Julia's death.

Suddenly Marina found herself wondering at Mr. Granville's unreasonable fury in the book room. Why had he been so insistent that she should put the thought of murder from her mind? Why had he not done her the courtesy of allowing her a hearing, even if one conceded that it was understandable of him to insist that she should keep silent elsewhere? Mr. Granville did not want the possibility of Julia's murder mentioned. That was—what? Significant? Ominous?

"Do you think this bonnet is too young for me?" Miss Derwent suddenly and quite uncharacteristically demanded.

Marina stared at the equine face, half shaded by a plain chip hat.

"I think it is—perfectly suitable," she replied. "Rather becoming—certainly not too young. And your gown"—glancing at the white printed cotton dress with its trailing yellow flower sprays and old-fashioned front lacing—"is charming. Is it new?"

"Yes—I am so glad you like it. Cassia and Rosett made it between them. You don't think I look ridiculous, in this antique style?"

"By no means. It is—you, dear Aunt. I mean, you told me the reason for preferring hooped petticoats—"

"I have discarded my hoop," confessed Miss Derwent, slightly flushed. "I hope to achieve the same coolness by wearing a false rump."

It was a concession to modernity, Marina realized; and she wondered if Mr. Singleton was expected to be visiting at Mount Pleasant.

Miss Derwent did not seem disposed to speak again. Marina returned her thoughts to Julia. She realized suddenly that Mr. Granville's attitude seemed to have had precisely the opposite effect on her from that which he had intended. She was certain that not only had his half-sister been murdered, but that Mr. Granville knew it. And yet, if that were so, why would he not want the murderer exposed and hanged? Could he possibly have any motive for protecting such a man? Very much the reverse, she told herself, especially if the villain were his old enemy, Mr. Brandon Flete, as the last entry in Julia's journal had suggested.

At least, Marina corrected herself, it suggested that it might be Julia's lover who had something to hide, for there was, she realized with something of a pleasurable shock, no proof that it was actually Mr. Flete who had been her lover, for she had nowhere mentioned his name. He had loved Julia, perhaps—but had she reciprocated? Mrs. Hungerford thought so, as did Miss Derwent and Mr. Granville. Well, probably they did know best—and yet, recalling some of Julia's more devious intrigues, Marina wondered now if she might not have used Mr. Flete's known admiration for her to conceal the identity of another and a more serious lover. Just supposing for the moment that it might be so, which of the single young men of Julia's acquaintance might it have been?

Not Harry Thurlough, at all events, Marina thought—though he had some sort of motive for disposing of her. It could have been the captain of the Militia, "my charming captain," Julia had called him—Captain Fergus. All that had been said of Flete held good for him, and in addition he might have some claim to be shielded by Mr. Granville. Captain Fergus could equally well have hoped to marry Julia for money, and been disappointed. He might—although this was pure surmise—have worn upon his watch chain a ruby fob which Julia had recognized, one that had belonged to Alfred Singleton, who drowned when the *Otaheite* was wrecked. Yes, Captain Fergus, just as well as Mr. Flete, might have been a wrecker.

Clasping her hands tightly, Marina for the first time allowed herself to dwell on Julia's "hideous possibility" that there were wreckers in Antilla, not merely strip-wrecks, sly opportunists such as Elijah and the

109

vultures of Sandy Harbour, but persons who deliberately led ships to their destruction, as she was certain the *Carib Queen* had been decoyed into the Reef; persons who hoped for no survivors, and who might even see to it that there were none; persons who must have a leader—a man who could not afford to have awkward questions asked.

Marina shivered, and Miss Derwent asked if she were cold.

"We are a good deal higher than Tamarind already," Miss Derwent pointed out, and Marina realized the carriage had wound some way up the hill. "Are you sure you would not like a shawl? Morgan will get down the cloakbag for you, if you wish."

Marina declined politely, and they returned to their own thoughts.

A leader of the wreckers, Marina was thinking. That implied a man with qualities of leadership, of organization, of daring—and no doubt with a more than superficial knowledge of the sea, and sailing. The trouble was that so many candidates came to mind, even among the few persons she had already met in Antilla. Mr. Flete—but it was hard to think of him as dangerous: his brown eyes had been so gentle this morning, when he was speaking of Miss Dampier's death. Yet he was capable of violence. . . . And there was Captain Fergus, and Mr. Granville himself—though of course it could not have been he whom Julia had suspected. But her lover might not only have been Mr. Granville's friend but his accomplice too—the bond between them strong enough to withstand the bitterness of the loss of Alfred Singleton, and the worse tragedy of Julia's death. Who else was there, attractive enough for Julia to have loved, and with a core of ruthlessness at his heart? Dr. Sunderland, she thought. He might well have swept Julia off her feet. And even Mr. Winceyman was possible, for though it seemed unlikely that Julia could have found him irresistible, yet, if he had the qualities to lead the wreckers, then those varying qualities might well have appealed to her—and he, Marina reflected, was "too good to be true," and Julia might have found that an intriguing combination.

The carriage had reached the very crest of the hill and now turned left, rocking as the force of the easterly wind struck it from behind. To the right was Dr. Sunderland's estate, Green's Fancy, where the land fell in a series of valleys to the sea, which was astonishingly blue, and dotted with islets. Miss Derwent pointed out, from right to left, the end of St. George's, with Hog Cay and Zeerovers Cay to the north of it, Little St. George's, Crab Cay, St. Joseph's, the larger Egret Island like a heaped length of crumpled sage velvet among blanched beaches, and Turtle Cay, while far on the horizon lay the long white line of Buccaneers, a flat coral island some twenty miles to the north. Between the far end of Buccaneers and Zeerovers Cay, Marina could see an endless turmoil of foaming shallows, white as cherry blossom, where the currents frothed among the coral forest of the fatal Reef.

The carriage turned left to enter a vestigial avenue of newly imported mango trees, which would grow full-shaped and beautiful in a few more years, with their dark glossy leaves giving valuable shade. The drive descended slightly through a sheltered valley which seemed quite English to Marina, scattered as it was with sleek brown cows grazing the soft guinea grass. A noble pair of Cuban royal palms marked the end of the drive. Beyond lay a rambling old house of stone approached by a flight of steps and with a wooden upper story, the wide verandahs of which commanded magnificent sea views to both north and south.

Miss Derwent and Marina climbed the steps and were announced by a grave butler into a high-ceilinged chamber overlooking the Columbus Channel. Several persons were sitting and standing about, fanning themselves and making conversation, which they broke off in order to devote their attention to the newcomers.

111

Marina felt self-conscious to attract so many stares, and was greatly relieved when a plump bustling little woman hurried forward to welcome them. Mrs. Ducheyne was the sort of woman, Marina felt sure, who loved to have people about her; and indeed it soon transpired that if her house could not always be full, at least her nurseries were.

After a warm greeting, Mrs. Ducheyne opened Miss Derwent's present, kissed her enthusiastically and professed herself delighted with the gift. Then she turned to Marina and declared that she must meet her children. "Miss Smith will introduce them to you," she said proudly.

Marina smiled at the young Ducheynes and glanced about the room to see whom else she recognized. The Thurloughs were there, Blanche simpering in a smart new gown of just the wrong shade of pink; her brother, who, perhaps in the light of Marina's new knowledge of him, looked a trifle dissipated; and also to her mild surprise, their mother, who was like a faded edition of her daughter with a puffy white face and yellowed eyes; a fussy, rather overbearing person for whom Blanche, Marina observed, obviously felt little but exasperation and contempt.

Mrs. Ducheyne now broke off her conversation with Miss Derwent and introduced Marina to a tall, dark and handsome man with striking green eyes, who she was fascinated to discover was the very Captain Fergus who had recently been exercising her thoughts. Meeting him, of course, made her surmises seem wildly melodramatic, and she put them aside for the time being.

Captain Fergus had been with a pale, freckled, somewhat pathetic-looking little lady in deep mourning, who was introduced to Marina as Miss Winceyman. Her brother was beside her, and Marina studied him with interest. He struck her as one of those mild-seeming, almost saintly people who are nevertheless endowed with a will of iron. It was very difficult to imagine him meeting Julia in secret, still less destroying her; but after some conversation with him Marina believed she could understand how such a quiet and, on the face of it, unlikely couple as this gentle brother and sister could have allowed their more forceful cousin, Lady Baillie, to persuade them to take the tremendous step of setting up as West Indian planters.

Marina turned from the Winceymans to find her attention claimed by Captain Fergus. She was glad of the opportunity to speak to him, not only because he was the best-looking man in the room but also, she told herself, because it really was her duty to be friendly with all her suspects, however unlikely, in order to find out more about them. If her conscience smote her for this attitude, she had only to think of Julia's bright young life so prematurely quenched to harden her resolve.

She was soon interested to discover that Captain Fergus was a younger son; that his parents were still living at Solitude, the estate they had built thirty-five years earlier, together with the captain's elder brother, who was married with two young sons of his own. Captain Fergus looked as if his tastes might be expensive, Marina reflected. He would be glad to marry an heiress; and since he had no great prospects of his own, it would be reasonable for Mr. Granville to have disapproved of him as a match for Julia. He also looked as if he would not relish having his plans overset, Marina thought.

Still smiling at one of the Captain's livelier sallies, Marina happened to glance at the door just as Mr. Granville entered. He stood, his tanned face hard and expressionless, jerking his gloves through his hands, his single eye intent upon her.

He was obviously displeased to see them talking together. Perhaps he did indeed suspect Captain Fergus of having dared to tamper with Julia's affections—or even of something more sinister. Or could it be that he was afraid of what Marina might be discovering from her conversation with the captain? she wondered.

Trays were brought in, and not tea but limeade was served to the ladies. Marina sipped it with appreciation, and listened with interest to the talk, which ranged from the British Government's mishandling of the West India interests, through the falling price of cotton to the possible whereabouts of the *Lady Jane,* a trading ship which was overdue, it seemed, and in whose cargo the Admiral owned an interest. Marina's thoughts at once flew to the fangs of Damnation Reef but the Admiral was thinking of Danish privateers, or even French warships. It was not long ago, Captain Fergus informed Marina, that two of these latter had been sighted in the channel, and one of them had actually fired into the town, fortunately only knocking down some unoccupied market stalls.

"How many men can you muster?" Marina asked, feeling some comment was expected of her.

"Nigh upon one hundred men, counting the drummers, of course—"

"Speaking of drummers, Fergus," said Colonel Dawlish, "we must not forget to rouse out the Militia band for some practice before our annual ball, which is to take place on Saturday week, as I am sure you have not forgotten. There is still no sign of the instruments the Governor-General promised to send over from Antigua, but I have managed to borrow two more violins from Great St. George's. . . . I hope you will do us the honour to attend, Miss Marina," he added with a gallant bow. "If you do so, I venture to predict that you will be the center of attention, for it is not often that the Fort is distinguished by the presence of a heroine of your caliber, ma'am."

Marina was not used to lavish compliments. She hardly knew where to look and was greatly relieved when a diversion was caused by the entrance at that moment of the nursery party. Marina hastened to join the circle of women admiring Baby Charles in his nurse's arms. Too late she found this move had brought her close to Mr. Granville, who bade her good afternoon in a cold voice.

114

"You have made a conquest of both colonel and captain, I see," he said dryly. "As your guardian, perhaps it is my duty to remind you that there is a great shortage of females in these parts, before you become quite overwhelmed."

Marina's feelings were divided between the hurt he plainly meant to inflict upon her, and wry amusement that she had read so much into Mr. Granville's annoyance at seeing her conversing with the officers, when he had merely been taking his duties as a guardian rather too seriously. She could see that her slight involuntary smile had further irritated him, and quickly turned away to hold out her arms for Baby Charles. The nursemaid relinquished him, and Marina buried her face in the infant's soft neck. He gave a chuckle of pleasure, and she concentrated her attention on him.

Dr. Sunderland was then announced and there was a sudden uproar as the children ran forward to swing on his hands or hug his knees. Marina, looking at him across the baby's downy head, met the doctor's green-hazel eyes with a shock which seemed almost like a clash of swords. There was a raw power in him, she reflected, which made even his casual glance seem momentous. And she was not alone in feeling his special quality, for everyone was now looking at the doctor, as he distributed gifts of guava cheese among the children, kissed the hand of his hostess, took up little Ann upon his shoulders, promised a game of cricket to Masters William and George, told Mrs. Ducheyne that he could see the physic had restored her husband; and assured the Admiral in ringing tones that he had brought his best horse with him and would give the others a run for their money, or break his neck in the attempt.

"And Miss Marina?" boomed the doctor, halting before her. "How do you find yourself, ma'am? Have you given any more thought to the subject of our conversation at Government House?"

Marina, all too conscious of Mr. Granville close

115

behind her, was saved from having to reply by the baby's getting his starfish hand into her hair and giving it a violent tug. She cried out, and the nursemaid hurried to disentangle Charles's fist. Dr. Sunderland grinned and passed on, to drop into a chair beside Miss Winceyman and engage her in a low-voiced conversation which, as Marina soon perceived, brought the colour into her cheeks and made her look quite pretty.

Dr. Sunderland, Marina thought, could well have merited Julia's description of her lover as a king among men. . . .

"He has great presence, has he not?" remarked Miss Derwent quietly, following Marina's glance. "One understands how it is that the sick feel they are drawing life from him; how he can even, it is said, revive the dying. I suppose in England a doctor would not normally be received in good society," she went on thoughtfully. "Here, of course, where society is so limited, one is grateful for his enlivening company."

"I had the impression that you did not like him," Marina remarked quietly.

Miss Derwent shrugged. "One has heard rumours. If a doctor marries a patient, who happens also to be a rich elderly widow, he is bound to attract gossip; and when the lady dies within a matter of months, he naturally becomes suspect. When he follows these events by leaving his native land and hurrying half across the world to practice, he cannot wonder at it if eyebrows are raised . . . but one must not forget that it is perfectly possible that Dr. Sunderland contracted a love match and that when he was bereaved, he was overcome by grief and could no longer endure to live where he must be continually reminded of his wife. In any event, it is plain enough that he has put the past behind him now. Ah," Miss Derwent added in a very different voice, "here is Mr. Singleton, I vow. Have you a fan, child? No matter, here is mine, after all. I thought for a moment I had left it . . . despite the wind up here, I find it curiously warm. Oh, good afternoon,

116

Mr. Singleton! You have met my niece ... we were talking of the ball. Fort Charles, you know. You will be attending it, no doubt?"

"I don't dance, I fear," returned Mr. Singleton in his gloomy voice. "It is an unhealthy exercise, in my opinion. No doubt Sunderland will bear me out. Violent motion, you know ... and the night draughts. A fatal combination."

"I was forgetting your poor sister—"

"Both my sisters."

"Oh, but surely it was the yellow fever took off poor Caroline?"

"She would have been better disposed to fight the infection if she had not already succumbed to a chill. I trust that you, my dear Miss Derwent, know better than to indulge in dancing?"

Miss Derwent seemed to Marina to be engaging in a slight unspoken struggle. Then she announced quite fiercely that of all things she enjoyed a lively cotillion.

"In that case," said Mr. Singleton resignedly, "I must overcome my natural inclination, and beg you to stand up with me for the first two dances at Fort Charles."

Marina suddenly became aware that her presence was redundant. She went to talk to the seventeen-year-old Miss Ducheyne, and presently that young lady led her through the hall, past a group of new arrivals, and conducted her upstairs to show her where she was to sleep.

"In my room, if you don't object to it," said Miss Ducheyne, leading Marina down the gallery and opening a louvered door. "There are two beds, as you see."

The room was plainly furnished, airy and cool. The overhanging roof shaded a verandah outside, which ran the length of the house, so that the sun could never enter the bedchambers.

"Your gowns have been unpacked," Miss Ducheyne remarked. "What are you wearing tonight? This one? Yes, it is very pretty—quite like one poor Julia used

117

to have. Pray tell me, Miss Marina, is that the latest style of hairdressing in England?" This last was said in an anxious tone, for Marina's thick hair was rather straight, while Sarah's fell naturally in glossy ringlets. Reassured, Miss Ducheyne rattled on until they were interrupted by the arrival of her two younger sisters, of fifteen and sixteen, who peered round their door, their blue eyes quite bulging with curiosity.

"Well, come in if that is your intention," said Miss Ducheyne quite crossly. "Though one would suppose you might know better than to interrupt a visitor who would rather be resting."

"But you wouldn't, would you?" Betsy asked, bouncing onto the bed. "Resting is no fun."

"Besides, we know what you were talking about, and we would like to join in your conversation," Susan added frankly.

Betsy nodded solemnly. "Have you made up your mind yet?" she asked Marina, adding incomprehensibly, "You'd better not, until you've met them all."

Miss Ducheyne tossed her head and declared she was ashamed to have such stupid sisters. "As if Miss Marina would tell you who she'd like to marry, at this stage. And she'd be very foolish to decide too hastily," she added thoughtfully. "When there are so many bachelors to choose among."

"I don't—" began Marina, but Susan had irrepressibly embarked upon a list of possible suitors for her hand.

"There's Dr. Longman and Colonel Dawlish and Mr. Flete—"

"He's in trade!" Betsy objected swiftly. "Mama won't even have him staying in the house."

"But he has an estate," Miss Ducheyne pointed out. "One day he will return to Maroon and be the envy of all the other planters."

"Well, Papa has asked him for the race tomorrow. We'll see how Miss Marina likes him then."

"There's Mr. Singleton—"

"He's far too old for her. Besides, everybody knows he is to marry Miss Derwent just so soon as she finds a suitable wife for Mr. Granville."

"Blanche Thurlough is to marry Mr. Granville, I thought," put in Miss Ducheyne.

"No such thing," cried Susan in her shrill voice. "I heard Mama discussing it with Dr. Margery. Blanche only wants to get away from her mother and have a house of her own to order, and Mr. Granville would never marry a girl who didn't worship him. Besides, Miss Derwent won't allow it. She must have the choosing of his bride and leave Tamarind in her own good time, not be thrown out by someone like Blanche Thurlough, who only wants his money and position." Susan turned her bright eyes upon Marina. "We thought at first that was why Miss Derwent wanted you at Tamarind, as a bride for Marcus Granville, but now I see that you wouldn't do at all—"

"Susan," gasped her elder sister.

"Oh, Miss Marina don't object. She must know that everyone is talking about her, and planning to get her married off. Besides, I only meant she wouldn't do for Mr. Granville, when his sort is more like Blanche, the submissive kind—only Blanche is no good because she doesn't love him. She's in love with Mr. Da Costa," she kindly explained to Marina, "only of course he is a married man—and quite impossible besides."

"Yes, you wouldn't do for Mr. Granville," Betsy agreed, gazing at Marina, "but—would she not do perfectly for Dr. Sunderland?"

"One doesn't marry doctors," said Susan, with a shade of doubt.

"Oh, pooh," said her elder sister, "when they are plantation owners they are perfectly acceptable. But I think he might be going to offer for Esther Winceyman."

"I am glad to hear you say so," Marina said lightly, "for I think marriage to Dr. Sunderland would be like putting one's head into a lion's mouth. If I were to think of marrying a doctor," she continued mischie-

119

vously, "I should prefer it to be the little old one we passed in the hallway as we came upstairs."

The three sisters stared at her in horror.

"Dr. Margery!" Betsy exclaimed. "But he is quite deranged!"

"Well, Father says he is only obsessed," Susan amended doubtfully, "and after all, he isn't the only person in these parts who thinks of finding treasure."

"But Dr. Margery thinks of nothing else," cried Betsy. "Have you ever been in his house? Full of old maps and charts, and he spends all his time pacing out the islands, digging pits in likely places, corresponding with people who keep old documents about galleons and so forth. Then he started that crazy company when he was last in England—and they came out here and blew holes in all the uninhabited islets. Seriously, Miss Marina," for she saw their guest was laughing, "he would have no time to be a husband."

"But I wasn't thinking of him—or of any of them—as a husband," Marina assured the sisters. "I don't want to be anybody's wife—ever. Except for babies," she added, thinking of the deliciousness of little Charles. "I would like some babies. But I don't want a man to order me about. I want to be free, to ride alone, and swim, and sail—"

They stared at her.

"You want to be like a boy," Sarah pronounced in ill-concealed disgust.

"Can you do all those things?" Betsy asked.

Belatedly, Marina recalled Mr. Granville's views on the corrupting of young ladies by such hoydens as herself.

"I can—though it is not becoming in a girl, I have been told. Young ladies must act in a seemly and dignified fashion—but there is no law which orders them to marry."

"But it is wretched to be unmarried," declared Miss Ducheyne.

"Do you think so? I believe my aunt does well
120

enough—and I know I would a great deal rather be Miss Derwent than, for example, Mrs. Thurlough, of Prosperity."

"Yes," said Miss Ducheyne slowly, "but Miss Derwent is thinking of marriage, I believe. If you remain single, you must always feel you are missing something."

"What do you think of Mr. Granville?" Susan suddenly demanded. "He is so handsome—and dashing, with that eye-patch. And so inflexible," she added appreciatively. "I do like a man who knows his mind."

Marina sighed. "Mr. Granville is a broken reed and I detest him," she said firmly. "Now, I think we ought to begin changing, do you not?"

"Yes, we'll leave you in peace now," said Susan. Betsy halted her, a finger to her lips. She listened, and then breathed in delicately.

"I can smell smoke," she whispered.

Marina sniffed. A faint fragrant scent of burning leaves hung on the air. Betsy tiptoed to the louvered wooden casement, and peeped out through the open slats. She popped her head back in with remarkable celerity.

"It's Mr. Granville," she breathed, her eyes round with horror. "He is smoking a cigar upon the verandah. Do you suppose he could hear us from there?"

"Every word," said Sarah in a voice of doom, while Susan clapped her hands to her scarlet face and ran out of the room with Betsy close behind her.

Marina and Sarah Ducheyne were left staring at each other, each mentally reviewing the recent conversation.

It was Miss Ducheyne who closed the window. "Well, now he knows," she murmured, with an attempt at lightness. "He would have found out about Da Costa sometime—better sooner than too late."

But Marina was wishing she had not called Mr. Granville a broken reed, upon no better evidence than the prejudice of Mrs. Hungerford—and though she felt she would not have minded telling him to his face

121

that she detested him, yet she was deeply sorry that he should have overheard that remark. It was in a frame of mind unusually subdued that she began to dress for dinner.

10

The horse race was to be run in the cool of the afternoon. As the day wore on, excitement mounted, the gentlemen laid wagers and, in imitation of some knightly tournament, begged favours from the women in the hope of carrying them to victory.

Marina longed to leap upon the nearest quadruped and compete in the race herself. Instead she was obliged to join the rest of the ladies, clustered under their parasols near the start, and the ancient Dr. Margery, who was too old to ride. She seated herself beside her aunt, and tried not to look at Miss Thurlough, who was tying her pink ribbon about Mr. Granville's arm with a decidedly possessive air. Mr. Flete, who had joined the party a few hours earlier, rode up on an unremarkable grey gelding.

"Miss Marina," he called out. "Am I too late to request a favour from you, ma'am?"

She had no alternative but to comply. She liked Mr. Flete well enough, she reflected, but he was as yet little more than an acquaintance and she was loath to be advertising any special connection between them. She drew the green satin ribbon from her hair, where Cassia had carefully threaded it, and gave it to Mr. Flete. As she had expected, her action was not lost on the young Misses Ducheyne.

There were two false starts. Mr. Granville's stallion began to buck as soon as it was mounted and he seemed to be finding the bay almost impossible to

123

control, but eventually the horses were brought into line for the third time, and the Admiral's bookkeeper fired his pistol. Several of the ladies shrieked; and a moment later the riders disappeared behind the young mango trees.

Marina glanced at Miss Thurlough, now demurely fanning her hot face, and recalled the previous evening, when Blanche had allowed the company to persuade her to entertain them. She had indeed played and sung most competently, but without real feeling, Marina had thought. Mr. Granville had lain back in a chair with his eye closed throughout the performance, and had not joined in the applause which concluded it; while Dr. Sunderland had obscurely gratified Marina by tiptoeing about gathering his cronies, and had disappeared to play whist before the first ballad was completed. Mr. Granville certainly did not behave as though he expected to become Miss Thurlough's husband, Marina reflected, despite the fact that he had presumably requested her favour for the race. Miss Derwent too seemed to have reverted to her original dislike of Miss Thurlough. But perhaps, like Mr. Granville, she had only lately discovered where Blanche's true affections lay. Overhearing Miss Susan's opinion of Miss Thurlough must have been at the very least a blow to Mr. Granville's pride, Marina thought. She would like to know how serious his courtship had been; but perhaps the colonel's ball would be the place to get a better idea of Mr. Granville's true feelings for Miss Thurlough.

As for herself, she continued to displease him, Marina reflected with an unconscious sigh. Last night, before Blanche's little concert, she had made a real effort to be civil to her disapproving guardian. She had asked him about his adventures in his privateering days, thinking that he would be certain to enjoy retailing exploits in which he had cut such a dashing figure. But he had only glared at her repressively, leaving Mrs. Ducheyne, who had applauded the subject with enthusiasm, to ask Marina how she had come to hear of Mr. Granville's youthful exploits.

"Julia referred to them in her journal," Marina had begun, only to falter into silence under Mr. Granville's furious stare. Too late she recalled his forbidding any mention of the journal—even Miss Derwent, fortunately now on the far side of the room, had no idea that it had been found.

"Refreshments, Miss Marina!" Susan's shrill voice broke in upon her somber thoughts. "They are laid out over there, on that table under the trees: tea or limeade, cakes and bread and butter . . ."

Marina accepted a cup of tea, and dropped a slice of lime into it. Dr. Margery hobbled up and sank into the chair beside her which Miss Derwent had vacated.

"You are a stranger to these parts, miss, I believe?" he wheezed, peering at Marina through his watery old eyes. "Wrecked on the *Carib Queen*, they tell me. Ah, many a good ship has left her bones in these treacherous waters, ma'am."

"And the waters are so beautiful," Marina observed, turning to gaze down at the southern view of the Columbus Channel.

"Ay, and so was Lucifer beautiful, miss. That channel down there was known as the Pirate's Gangway once, for there are so many islets here the pirates could play hide-and-seek among them, and slip ashore to bury their treasures when pursuit grew hot, or lurk ready to leap upon unwary vessels. Yes, there was a band of desperadoes then who knew every rock and reef, every cranny and cave—many was the vessel they holed and looted before she sank. Ay, and there are still great treasures waiting to be found, gold chalices and ruby crosses, treasures of the Church that were bound for Mother Spain, bars of silver and of gold, chests of coins . . ." His voice died away and his eyes almost closed. Marina wondered if he was falling asleep on his feet, or was merely overcome by the dazzling picture he had painted, so reminiscent of one of Julia's tales.

"Why don't you sail out to the reefs, sir?" demanded

Mrs. Thurlough, sitting down on Marina's other side and fanning herself somewhat irritably. "You still own the sloop you bought off my late husband, I believe?"

"Indeed, madam, I do. And the boat is sound enough ... I would that I could be as sure of old Neptune, my captain."

"If he is past his work, replace him," Miss Blanche suggested impatiently.

"My dear Miss Blanche, I could hardly afford to do that with the price of a good man at ninety to a hundred pounds, and rising every day. Besides, Neptune is as fine a sailor as ever he was—'tis only that he has his humours. I fear I don't entirely trust him ... and the boat," he added vaguely, "she has her humours also ... on occasion even the gift of invisibility. ..."

Marina turned toward him in surprise and would have spoken, but she caught Mrs. Ducheyne's warning glance and subsided into tactful silence.

"No, I must make my small economies," Dr. Margery was saying, "and one day perhaps I can charter some vessel with a reputable master to sail me over ... but it must be soon. Those reefs are preying on my mind. I cannot rest for thinking of them."

Mrs. Ducheyne looked concerned. She hesitated for a moment before deciding to speak.

"The *Pelican* is going out on Monday," she then remarked. "So Colonel Dawlish was telling me. They are taking the last load off the *Carib Queen,* and bringing back the soldiers. Why don't you ask if you can go out with it? You may even find some trace of the *Lady Jane,*" she added.

"Here they come," cried Betsy, before Dr. Margery could reply. She jumped up and climbed onto her chair. "A chestnut horse is in the lead! That's Dr. Sunderland. And next is Captain Fergus, I think—and then a grey ..."

"Mr. Flete," cried Marina excitedly.

"No ... it's the colonel, I believe."

Miss Smith jumped up, clasping her hands together. "Oh, dear," she gasped. "He must be riding dreadfully fast, to be in third place. And he only has one arm. I am sure it is not safe."

"Here comes William on the black," screamed Betsy. "He's gaining with every stride! Come on, William! He's carrying my colours—oh, and here comes your rider, Susan—Mr. Thurlough. And now I can see Papa, and—yes, Mr. Winceyman a long way behind—and there's poor Mr. Singleton, last of all."

"But where is Mr. Granville?" cried Miss Thurlough, echoing Marina's thoughts. "Is it possible that thee missed him, Betsy?"

"Of course not—but look at William!" Betsy was jumping up and down upon the chair. "He's catching up! Come on, William! Oh, there comes a loose horse," she cried in consternation. "It's a grey—Mr. Flete's! Oh, look, it crossed in front of Mr. Singleton and he was nearly unseated. He's pulled up. He's out of the race."

"Thank God for that," said Miss Derwent quietly, while Mrs. Ducheyne was begging her daughter to get down, and moderate her voice.

"But, Mama, they are just coming to the finish! Here's Dr. Sunderland passing the post—"

Marina found that she was standing. "Surely Mr. Granville must have fallen?" she exclaimed. "Shouldn't we set out at once to look for him, and Mr. Flete?"

Her words were lost in the drumming of hooves. Dr. Sunderland galloped by, leaning well back in the saddle, one arm raised in a victorious salute and his great horse flecked with foam. A few lengths behind him thundered Captain Fergus and young William, neck and neck, the colonel having dropped back to fourth place. The captain's arm rose and fell as he lashed his labouring horse, slowly drawing ahead. William, passing the post third, pulled his black horse to a halt as Captain Fergus slipped out of the saddle, grinning widely.

"Second place! Not bad, eh? Beat my colonel, too!

Well done, Sunderland. I fancy your chestnut is younger than my Pegasus."

"You nearly killed your brother's horse," the doctor declared in his booming voice, running a professional eye over the trembling animal. "I doubt if you'll ever get such speed out of him again."

The captain shrugged and turned away, but he had not been able to control the look of fury that had crossed his face, either at the reminder that he was beholden to his brother for the loan of the horse, or because he resented the doctor's calling attention to his cruel treatment of the beast.

"Here, what's become of Flete?" cried the doctor, looking round. "That is his horse—but where's the saddle?"

Marina opened her mouth, but Miss Derwent forestalled her.

"I would be much obliged if you would look for him, Dr. Sunderland, and for my nephew. One or both of them have obviously had a fall."

"I'll go with you," the colonel offered. "I noticed Granville was having trouble with his horse when I passed him. Perhaps he came off in that wide ditch. It was the deuce of a place, and slippery with rotting leaves."

"Well, let us go indoors," suggested Mrs. Ducheyne as the colonel turned to follow Dr. Sunderland. "There is no reason for us to be sitting out here in the heat now that the race is over." She put her hand on Blanche's arm. "Come, Miss Thurlough. Pray don't despair. I am sure Mr. Granville has not broken his neck. My sons are always having tumbles and come off little the worse. Besides, Sunderland is an excellent doctor. Mr. Granville could not be in better hands."

A slow wheezing at Marina's side indicated to her that Dr. Margery was enjoying a laugh. "Doubt if Sunderland could mend a broken neck, all the same," he gasped. "Hey, hey!"

Marina found that she was shaking with silent rage. It seemed to her that everyone was taking the possibility of an accident far too lightly—even Miss Derwent was talking now to Mr. Singleton just as if nothing had happened.

"There they are," cried sharp-eyed Betsy. "It looks as though Mr. Granville has hurt his arm—and Dr. Sunderland is half carrying Mr. Flete!"

Marina turned quickly. Mr. Granville was walking with bent head, supporting his wrist, while his hitherto fiery horse followed meekly, the reins looped over Mr. Granville's arm. The doctor was also on foot, supporting Mr. Flete, while the colonel rode behind, leading Sunderland's horse with some difficulty with his one hand.

There was a rush to offer assistance. The grooms came forward to lead the horses away. Mr. Flete was carried into the house, and Miss Thurlough, after one glance at Mr. Granville's swollen wrist, subsided gracefully into a swoon, taking care, Marina thought unkindly, that her brother was close enough to catch her as she fell.

Dr. Margery panted up beside Marina as they followed their hostess into the house.

"Very curious," he gasped. "Should have said neither of those two were likely to be thrown—not like Fergus, reckless young devil—h'm!"

Marina looked around the drawing room. Mr. Granville, his own hurt now apparently forgotten, was bending solicitously over Miss Thurlough as she regained consciousness with fluttering eyelashes and gasping sighs. Mrs. Thurlough too was fussing about her daughter. Dr. Sunderland had disappeared with Mr. Flete, leaving the other gentlemen to get down to the serious business of drinking punch and loudly discussing all aspects of the race.

A mood of wild rebellion possessed Marina, and she turned to Dr. Margery. "Why don't we ask Colonel Dawlish if he will take us both on Monday, sir?" She gripped his brittle hand excitedly. "I too would like to go out on Damnation Reef, if we can keep the expedition a secret between us."

"You, my dear? Among all those soldiers?" He sounded doubtful, but his old eyes were gleaming. "I should be glad of your company, I must own, supposing that I did decide to go."

"Oh, do let us! I shall speak to Colonel Dawlish just before we leave on Monday morning. I shall tell my aunt nothing more than that we are all going to the Fort together . . . and I shall bring my maid, of course. What an adventure it would be! Do say you will come, sir."

Dr. Margery leaned forward and patted her hand. "Very well, my dear. But not a word to anybody, eh? We don't want the world thinking that we have eloped together, what?" and he winked a faded eye.

After dinner that evening, Mr. Granville paused by Marina's chair on joining the ladies in the drawing room, in order to remark in a sarcastic tone that no doubt she was congratulating herself on her knight errant's having won the race. Marina stared, completely bewildered for a moment. Mr. Granville looked ill, she thought; but she banished her swift feeling of sympathy and prepared to do battle with him.

"You are mistaken, sir," she told him, with a haughty look. "Dr. Sunderland carried Miss Winceyman's favour to victory, not mine."

"Indeed!" said Mr. Granville, not noticeably abashed. "One would not have supposed it, from the fashion in which Sunderland was singing your praises all the time he was attending me—and, you may be interested to learn, enquiring quite precisely into your background and your prospects. Perhaps you'll live to thank me one day that I assured him you were no one in particular and had no fortune to speak of."

"I suppose your arm is hurting you very much, that you should be so disagreeable?" Marina suggested.

"You suppose correctly, Miss Marina," he replied calmly. "Tell me then who did carry your colours in the race?"

She opened her eyes innocently. "Why, sir, Mr.

130

Brandon Flete—the one gentleman on the island who I am confident would not listen if you chose to denigrate me to him."

He put up his hand to adjust his eye-patch. "Mr. Flete asked for your favour? He is on the lookout for a wife, of course. I suppose that notion was born of your shipboard acquaintance with Mrs. Hungerford. Well, you need not expect me to approve of it."

"I don't expect you to approve of anything I do," Marina snapped. She rose and dropped him the slightest of curtsies. "Good night, Mr. Granville!"

His eyebrow rose. "Are you not going to say that you are sorry about my—accident?"

Her attention was caught. "You said that as if—it was no accident?"

He shrugged slightly. "If you call a cluster of sandburs under my horse's saddle, to say nothing of Flete's half-cut saddle girth, an accidental combination . . ."

She stifled a small cry. "But were not the grooms guarding the horses?"

"It was in the saddle room that the damage was done, Miss Marina. And half the men in the race have owned to going in there at some time in the afternoon, not to mention the grooms, or Flete's man, Crick. But Miss Derwent is beckoning you. Good night, Miss Marina. Pray don't have bad dreams on my account. I can't believe murder was intended by such a clumsy method—in my case, at least."

He bowed, and she crossed the room to where Miss Derwent was sitting by Mr. Flete, who looked rather pale. He greeted Marina warmly, however; and she returned his smile, thinking that his brown eyes were a great deal more comfortable to gaze into than Mr. Granville's single one of violent blue.

"How are you, sir?" she asked.

"Perfectly recovered, except for a slight headache and a short loss of memory for the few minutes before I fell."

"Mr. Granville told me your girth was . . . unstitched."

131

"Yes. But I cannot think it anything more sinister than an unfortunate mishap. It also seems quite possible to me that Granville's burs may have been picked up quite accidentally when the saddle was being carried out of the stables. But we have been discussing a more interesting topic here," he added, glancing at Miss Derwent.

"We were just speaking of the possibility of a picnic at Maroon early next week," Miss Derwent explained. "There will be several young people, I expect. Should you like to go?"

"Yes, indeed," Marina cried, eager to explore the fabulous Maroon. "Not on Monday, however," she added. "I have a secret assignation with Dr. Margery, Aunt, which I will tell you about before we leave."

Miss Derwent smiled. "In that case, let the picnic be on Tuesday, if Mr. Flete agrees?"

"Most certainly, ma'am. I shall close the shop on Tuesday, then."

"I have a soft spot for Dr. Margery," Miss Derwent explained to Marina. "He saved Juliana's life when Julia was born. . . . Yes, I will drive up with you on Tuesday, then, and take the opportunity of calling at Indigo Hall. Mr. Singleton is anxious to discuss some scheme of decoration—and I believe I am of an age to dispense with a chaperone when I visit a bachelor establishment," she added rather mischievously; and Marina realized with relief that there were to be no further questions just then about her engagement for Monday.

Some time after Marina had gone to bed, she found herself still restless, and increasingly thirsty. She wondered if everyone else had retired, or if Miss Thurlough had been persuaded to sing again, and if Mr. Granville was lying back with his eye closed while she played, or if, since she had so convincingly betrayed her anxiety for him this afternoon, he had overcome both his disillusionment and his disability sufficiently to replace her brother and turn the pages of her music.

At length Marina could bear her thirst no longer.

She sat up. Sarah did not stir. There was no water in the room but Marina remembered seeing an earthenware pot and dipper on a stand outside the nursery. She picked up her embroidered Eastern shawl and wrapped herself in it closely. With her kid slippers and the frill of white lawn night rail barely showing below the deep black fringes of the shawl, she hoped that if she did meet someone she would not seem to be obviously undressed.

She opened the tall louvered door and stole out into the lamplit corridor. The nursery was near the head of the stairs, at the angle of the house. As she turned the corner she saw that a man stood at the window, a spyglass to his eye, peering in what she knew to be the direction of Damnation Reef.

"Tcha!" she heard him mutter. It was the Admiral, she realized. "This glass is no more use than a cat's tail! Where the deuce has the other one gone?"

Somebody else was now stumbling up the stairs and Marina hastily turned to bend over the water jar.

"Ha, Admiral, is that you?" cried the newcomer in slurred accents.

"Damme, Thurlough, you nearly made me drop my glass!"

"Dashed sorry for that, sir—put it down to your ex-excellent brandy. No, I hoped you were Granville, to tell the truth. Been looking for him everywhere—thought he might have retired early with that wrist but he's not in his room."

"I haven't seen him this past half-hour. Leave it till the morning, man. Here, let me give you an arm to your quarters."

They departed together, steering a somewhat erratic course. Marina drank a dipperful of warmish but refreshing water and moved in her turn to the window. She leaned on the sill, enjoying the cool night air upon her face. Treacherous it might be, fever-bearing as she had been warned, but it was so delicious she did not believe it could hurt her. Below, the grass ran silver in the starlight to the black-and-pewter trees

133

which edged the steeply falling ground above the sea. The water seemed from this height calm and milky grey except for the great foaming sickle of the distant reefs. There was a light out there, she noticed, faintly winking. That would be the militiamen aboard the *Carib Queen,* of course.

"Miss Marina!" exclaimed a disapproving voice.

She started, and turned to see Mr. Granville, looking even more tired than he had done earlier, with a deep shadow under his eye, and nursing his injured wrist as if it hurt him. There was something beneath his arm, a roll of music, perhaps—or could it be the Admiral's missing glass?

"What are you doing here?" he demanded sharply.

"I came to get a drink, and stayed because . . . because it is such a lovely night."

"You should not be wandering about the house alone at this hour," said Mr. Granville severely, continuing to stare at her. "It is not at all the way for a young lady to go on—though exactly what I might have expected of you, I suppose."

"Mr. Thurlough was looking for you, sir," she informed him quickly. "He said you were not downstairs, or in your room—and with your injury you would hardly have gone outside—"

She broke off. Mr. Granville had not moved, yet suddenly she felt afraid of him.

"And you," he said softly, "with your fatal curiosity, have been also wondering where I was? Better have a care, Miss Marina, for of all things, I detest a spy!"

She found her courage had deserted her and she could think only of escape. She backed away, murmuring some sort of apology, then turned and hurried to her room.

As she slid into bed beside the unconscious Miss Ducheyne, Marina found herself wondering why the notion of a spy should be quite so abhorrent to Mr. Granville—unless his conscience was not clear.

11

Dr. Margery settled himself on a coil of rope in the shade of the *Pelican*'s brown sail, and began to tell Marina about the treasure-finding company in which he had invested, and how, though this determined band had failed to find the fabled hoard for which they sought, Dr. Margery was convinced that Captain Kidd had secreted it somewhere on Freedom Island— the deserted rock which was now falling astern of their vessel.

His wheezy voice was monotonous and Marina found her thoughts wandering back to the absurd scene yesterday at Mount Pleasant, when Dr. Sunderland had again tried to persuade her to race with him. She had refused him, pleasantly and with some regret; and Mr. Granville, coming upon them obviously conspiring, had been rude to Dr. Sunderland, and unkind to her. The doctor had snorted and stalked away, and Mr. Granville was actually holding her by the arm ready to shake her when Mr. Thurlough had discovered them. Marina did not think she would ever forget the look that had been in Mr. Thurlough's dark eyes—a look of frustrated despair as if his dearest hope was being destroyed before him. He had turned on his heel and gone at once, but even if he had stayed, how could she have assured him that it was not a love scene he had interrupted? Far from being a rival to Blanche, she was the object of Marcus Granville's contempt, she feared; and if he had seemed to become indifferent to Miss Thurlough it was, no doubt, because he had just discovered that she had given her heart elsewhere.

Marina sighed, and returned to the present, a perfect sailing day in her opinion, a steady breeze, no whitecaps to be seen, and the tan sail taut above her as the *Pelican* tacked into the wind.

"People keep it quiet, you know, when they stumble on such things," Dr. Margery was mumbling now. "Don't want to go through the proper channels. A coroner's inquest and a reward, a mere percentage, when they could keep the whole. I wouldn't care for the financial gain—'tis the thrill of the discovery that lures me on. Ten percent, or five—it would be ample. The excitement would be the real reward."

"But it must be hard to keep a treasure secret," Marina mused. "There would be a crew to bribe—"

"Kill them," suggested Dr. Margery with a slanting grin.

Marina decided to believe he must be joking, and returned his smile. "And how do you sell a treasure?" she demanded.

"Little by little." He chuckled. "Little by little. Sell it to such shops as Flete's . . ."

"Then he would know," she pointed out. "He would have to be let into the secret too."

"Not if it came to him through such an agency as the Trinket Trading Company," said Dr. Margery with his rheumy sidelong glance.

Marina had heard that name before. After a moment, she remembered that there had been a letter in Flete's shop, folded and sealed, the superscription written but not the address: "Ye Trinket Trading Companye" in a crabbed old-fashioned hand—that of Crick's, she supposed. And Mrs. Hungerford had referred to the same firm, in connection with Flete's business. That was as much as she knew about the Trinket Trading Company, but now she turned her mind toward the question of how shops came by goods they sold, a consideration which had simply never occurred to her before. In the secondhand business, such as Flete's, a certain amount of the stock would come from individuals in need of money, selling their possessions directly to him; but there was no reason, Marina supposed, why a known company should not acquire stock in that way, and pass it on to retail shops for a figure which would still allow both parties to profit. And if that was how the Trinket Trading Company worked, she thought on a flash of inspiration, it was certainly possible that it could be used not only by successful treasure hunters, but far more probably by wreckers, to dispose anonymously of their ill-gotten gleanings.

"Who owns the Trinket Trading Company?" she asked now. But the only response to her question was a little snore. Dr. Margery had nodded off.

Never mind, thought Marina. Even if he did not know, very likely Mrs. Hungerford did.

A shout from the helmsman warned Marina that the *Pelican* was going about. On the new tack the sail no longer hid them from the sun. Marina raised her parasol. If she was to have any hope at all of concealing her adventure from Mr. Granville, she must not present herself to him with flushed cheeks and a peeling nose. Besides, she supposed, she should be thinking of protecting her complexion for the ball. That reminded her of the question of a gown for the occasion, and she went aft to find Rosett, who was seated happily in the stern, gossiping with a member of the crew as he spliced ropes. By the time the *Pelican* had covered the long sea miles to Damnation Reef, Marina and Rosett had planned such a gown as, Marina dared to hope, even the scornful Miss Thurlough must admire. It was to be of soft white silk, edged with gold fringe taken from a gown of Julia's, the high waist caught in with a white belt ornamented with a flat gold buckle, backfastening with flattened silver-wire hooks and drawstring, and with its short sleeves lined with a stiff muslin and delicately embroidered in gold thread. She would wear long white gloves, carry a gold-painted

fan, and her sun-streaked hair would be dressed high
... never before had she taken such interest in her
appearance, Marina reflected; and for the first time
she could sympathize with the hitherto incomprehen-
sible concentration that such young women as Julia
Granville were wont to bring to bear upon such matters.

The flapping of sails brought Marina back to the
present. The *Pelican* was coming up into the wind. As
she began to drift back, the anchor was released with
a resounding splash, and the chain rattled out into
the turquoise depths. Marina went to stand by Dr.
Margery at the rail, staring at the wreck of the *Carib
Queen*. The hulk seemed a good deal smaller than she
remembered it, crouching low in the water, settled on
the coral fangs which gnawed at the frames with
every wave. On the far side of the wreck, in the
lagoon that was too shallow even for the *Pelican,* lay a
flat-bottomed drogher, high-laden with copper sheath-
ing, spars, anchors and rigging, while a dozen or so
soldiers were occupied in bringing the last of the salvaged goods off the *Carib Queen*.

A rowing boat was lowered from the *Pelican*. Marina, Rosett and Dr. Margery made their way down the
ladder and soon were being rowed over to the sandspit,
where they were helped ashore by grinning seamen.
Marina stood on the burning sand, looking about her.
The canvas shelter which the sailor Jem had put up
was still there, though the material was torn and
flapping, worn ragged by the sun, salt air, and the
constant wind. Marina seated Rosett in the shade
with the water bottle, and then, protected by sun-
bonnet and parasol, she went out to join Dr. Margery,
who was drawing deep breaths of the clean sea wind
and gazing about him in delight.

"Well, well, let us get on with our search," he cried
at once. "We have not a great deal of time, while they
load that cargo onto the *Pelican*."

"Very well, sir—but where do you begin to look for
treasure?" Marina asked.

"You find a landmark," he replied briskly. "It would be no use burying it anywhere, you know. You might never find it again."

"But you are hoping that they never did find it again," Marina could not resist pointing out.

Dr. Margery was not amused. Shading his watering eyes with a knotted hand, he peered about him.

"I see only one landmark here," he declared with satisfaction. "That will narrow down our area of search, an inestimable advantage."

"Do you mean that little bush?" Marina queried doubtfully.

"Yes, yes, the mangrove darts. Remarkable how they spring up miles from anywhere, is it not? Birds are responsible for that, so I am told."

Marina followed as he strode eagerly toward the patch of green.

"Now," said Dr. Margery. "Supposing you had just crawled out of the sea, or stumbled ashore from a small boat, desperate to dig and hide your treasure in the nearest place ... you would come several feet above the waterline, I think."

Marina nodded. "Is it high water now?" There was so little difference in the rise and fall of the tide in these islands, she found it hard to tell.

"Dead low water," Dr. Margery replied, glancing at the coral outcrops. "The master of the *Pelican* would have timed it so. If he did touch bottom by some miscalculation, he could be sure the tide would take him off presently." He paced forward, mumbling to himself. "Somewhere in this area, I think. . . ." He began to prod delicately with the thin rod he had brought with him, plunging it deep into the damp sand in and around the mangrove roots. Marina watched with a certain skepticism.

"There!" cried Dr. Margery, making Marina start. "No, 'tis a root," he muttered. A few minutes later, when she had lost interest and was staring at the faint flat line of a low island on the north horizon, he cried out again.

"Hold! I think—fetch me my spade, miss ... this feels like something." Marina flew to do his bidding, though by the time she returned with the spade, Dr. Margery was on his knees, scratching up the sand like a terrier. Two digs with the spade unearthed a fold of cloth.

"A blue spotted handkerchief," Marina murmured, unimpressed.

Dr. Margery flung aside his spade, and reverently began to disinter the trophy.

With shaking hands he withdrew the bundle and laid it on the sand. His twisted fingers began to struggle with the knots. When he did at last undo the handkerchief and spread it open, it was to reveal a glinting heap of gold and silver to their wondering eyes.

Marina blinked.

"Dr. Margery," she said breathlessly. "You have found treasure!"

"Fobs," said Dr. Margery in an odd tone, stirring the pile with his forefinger. "Rings. Chains. Watches. Snuffboxes."

"But—aren't you pleased?"

"Look at it for yourself," commanded Dr. Margery, sounding very old. Mystified, Marina knelt down on the sand and stared at the shining pile. Her eyes fastened on a signet ring. It was chased with an unusual device, a circle and a star. She had seen it before, and she did not need to struggle to remember where.

"Mr. Peppard," she said faintly. "That is Mr. Peppard's ring!"

Dr. Margery sighed. "Was he a passenger on the *Carib Queen*?"

She nodded.

"Then, as I thought, this is some wrecker's hoard."

Marina licked her lips, which had suddenly become very dry. "But—how could it be? We were all here, upon the sand—and the soldiers came that very night after we left. You don't say that one of us was—robbing the bodies and hiding the spoils?"

Dr. Margery shrugged, but she was not looking at him. Her mind was racing. "Not Jem," she murmured. "No, I could never believe it of Jem. Nor of Jacky. Daniel? But Daniel was not fit to move that night."

Then she recalled that there had been three men pulling in the corpses in the moonlight. It must have been, of course, the thirteenth person who was the ghoulish robber.

"Elijah!" she exclaimed. "He must have swum in from his boat—"

"Elijah cannot swim," Dr. Margery remarked abstractedly.

"No? Then that was what his raft was for. He must have paddled it over from the *Sea Hawk,* in order to do his own gleaning that night."

Yet surely it could not be for this that the *Carib Queen* had been decoyed into the reefs, and fifty people drowned? No, indeed, Marina answered herself. This puny hoard must be Elijah's own. In the normal course of events he would probably have been expected to get word to his master when there were no more survivors left, and then the serious plundering would have begun. Perhaps the *Sea Hawk* would be searched by the chief wrecker as a matter of course, to ensure that Elijah had not stolen anything upon his own account, which might incriminate them both. Elijah would be rewarded for his work by other means. But Elijah had a mind of his own. He, who had been so delighted with Mr. Hendrie's gold pocket watch that he had tasted it, obviously loved the shining metals and the jewels for themselves. Like a jackdaw, he made his own collection, intending to reclaim it once his master and everyone else had lost interest in the *Carib Queen.* But both the greater plan and the smaller plan had now been foiled, the first by Marina herself, and the second by the militiamen and now finally by Dr. Margery.

"This is Elijah's work," she said slowly. "I wonder who on Antilla is Elijah's master?"

She looked at Dr. Margery, but his thoughts were running in a different direction.

"If only the *Carib Queen* had been wrecked half a century ago," he mourned, "what then would it have meant to me, to find such relics. But now—the very sight of them disgusts me!"

"Yes. But we must take them back to Charlestown, to the coroner, I suppose?"

"To Deputy Haspe, yes." Dr. Margery rose stiffly to his feet. "I daresay all treasures have blood on them," he murmured. "I have been as greedy as the men who bring about the tragedies of the sea for love of gold."

Marina could not entirely disagree with him. On the other hand she thought it was a pity that Dr. Margery should lose the harmless obsession which had until now done so much to brighten his declining years. She said carefully, "As you say, sir, the years, and the wind and the sea, do so much to wash away the stains of the past. There is no reason why the treasure itself should be blamed for the wickedness of man. The older treasures too must be of historical interest. . . ."

As Dr. Margery seemed disposed to leave the blue handkerchief and its contents on the sand, Marina forced herself to tie the knot again, and to gather it up, before following him back to the shelter.

The voyage back to Antilla was uneventful. The soldiers, hot and tired, stubble-bearded and sweating, lay about the decks as the *Pelican* rolled downwind, while Marina sat demurely in the stern between Rosett and the doctor, the blue handkerchief wrapped up in her shawl. She would have to find some way to deliver it to Mr. Haspe, she thought. She did not believe she could trust Dr. Margery to do it, and she did not want to take anyone else into her confidence.

It was late, almost sundown, when they stepped ashore off the rowing boat. Obed darted forward to meet them.

"Master send de carriage for you, mistress," he informed Marina, with a grin for Rosett, who giggled.

"Oh . . . he knows, then," said Marina faintly.

"Yes, miss—Mr. Thurlough done tell he, captain say you gone wid doc on de *Pelican*."

"How very kind of Captain Fergus, and of Mr. Thurlough," said Marina crossly.

"Well, me master, he berry worried, miss. He ask everybody where you gone. Miss Derwent, he shout at her, and she upset too."

"There's Haspe," Dr. Margery suddenly remarked. "I'd better see him and make a report, I suppose."

"Oh, if you would," cried Marina gratefully. "But how will you get home?"

"Don't worry your pretty head over me," he suggested, taking the kerchief from her. "I'll fare well enough. It sounds to me as though you are the one who is in trouble, he, he!"

Grinning, waving and chuckling, he tottered off into the dusk. Marina sank back into her seat and told herself that Marcus Granville could not actually kill her for playing truant—nor would he even beat her, in all probability. And if he tried, she reflected with a sudden surge of spirit, this time she would fight him. Cousin Rollo had taught her a trick or two. Reviewing them, her colour rose, and by the time Obed halted before the front door of Tamarind she was somewhat more prepared to confront her guardian, though she still felt quite faint with what she suddenly recognized as hunger, for she had not eaten since breakfast at Mount Pleasant.

Cudjoe opened the front door to her. He stood back, silent and correct, but his eyes rolled apprehensively as she swept past. Marina caught her breath and entered the parlour.

"Good evening, Aunt," she cried with false gaiety. "I have had such a delightful, interesting day! I hope you have not missed me?"

Miss Derwent had half risen, and now fell back into her seat. "I did, and I am extremely vexed with you, dear child," she declared. Marina was aware of Mr. Granville out of the corner of her eye but she judged it

143

prudent to pretend not to have noticed him. She hurried to throw her arms about her aunt.

"Well, please don't be cross, because here I am, quite unharmed, and all the better for an airing. Besides, I am quite tired of being scolded and I love you very much."

Mr. Granville moved out of the shadows, looking stern. "If you really meant those words, you would not wish to cause suffering to the object of your affections," he said stiffly.

Marina looked apologetically at Miss Derwent. "Did I cause you suffering? I am very sorry for it. Colonel Dawlish promised he would call on you late this afternoon, if the *Pelican* was not in sight, so that if you had any anxieties he could allay them."

"Colonel Dawlish acted very wrongly in this affair," declared Mr. Granville. "He kept his promise but long before then we had been informed as to your whereabouts." He looked at her more in reproach than anger, which she found harder to bear. "Did it not occur to you that the news of your escapade would be all about Antilla like wildfire?"

"Well, I'm sorry. I knew you would not like it, and that you would forbid me if I asked permission, so I was obliged to be somewhat underhand. The fact is that I was determined to go for Dr. Margery's sake. Everybody laughs at the poor man—"

"And you encouraged him in his foolishness!"

"It was not foolishness," she snapped, her colour high. "As it happens, sir, we did discover quite a valuable hoard buried in the sand!"

"What! I don't believe it!"

Marina sprang to her feet. "Don't call me a liar, sir, I beg!"

"Marina!" protested her aunt faintly.

Marina raised her chin. "Well?" she demanded, her colour high and her eyes sparkling.

"We-ell," echoed Mr. Granville, but in a very different tone. "Now I see what those persons mean who so repeatedly assure me you have the makings of a beauty."

Marina was momentarily silenced, as perhaps he had intended.

"So you found a treasure, did you?" he said soothingly. "I trust you delivered it intact to the coroner's office?"

"Yes," said Marina. "As it happens, we did."

"We?" he queried quickly. "Oh yes, you and Dr. Margery."

"Of course. It—oh, it was horrible." Suddenly, to her astonishment and shame, Marina found herself crying. She leaned against the wall and sobbed, trying to cover her face with her hands.

Mr. Granville raised his eyebrow, looking across at Miss Derwent, who hurried to comfort her niece.

"I'm hungry," Marina wept. "But it isn't that—it was the wreckers—"

Though her eyes were full of tears, she sensed that Mr. Granville had stiffened. He stood straight, looking like an unusually soldierly pirate with his black sling and black eye-patch.

"Wreckers?" he echoed.

Marina brushed away her tears. "The thirteenth man upon the sandpit that first night after the wreck." She glanced at Miss Derwent, who nodded, remembering the discrepancy over the number of survivors. "He—he must have been one of them. Elijah, I think. He must have got rings and watches off the bodies, and buried them in a—a b-blue handkerchief, under a mangrove bush."

"And that was the hoard which you—or Dr. Margery —found today?"

She nodded, catching her breath.

"And how do you know that is how those pieces were acquired?"

"Mr. Peppard's ring," she added. "I recognized it. When we were taking to the lifeboats, I saw it on his hand."

She shuddered, and astonishingly, Mr. Granville's arm came round her and held her tightly.

"You see, you are not so much of a tomboy as you suppose," he murmured, while Miss Derwent remarked that she would tell Cudjoe they would like dinner served at once.

"I am disappointed in you, however," added Mr. Granville gravely. "You promised me that you would behave yourself, or so I understood—the night you found my sister's journal."

"But—I was not misbehaving. I took Rosett with me—"

"What is your definition of misbehaviour, my ward?"

"Why—why, getting up to mischief, I suppose, either with the intention of causing trouble or merely for the fun of it . . ."

"Well, and does not your escapade on the *Pelican* come under that heading?"

"No, it does not," she cried indignantly. "I didn't mean to cause any trouble, and the fun I hoped to find was quite a secondary consideration. My first concern was to please Dr. Margery."

He stared at her, his single eye a bright unblinking blue, ringed with thick dark lashes.

"There was another reason too," she owned uncomfortably. "But I suppose you will not like it, and I don't wish to annoy you any more."

"You seem destined to annoy me," he assured her calmly.

She looked at him doubtfully.

"Well?" he prompted.

"I went—I thought—I was looking for signs of wreckers," she said reluctantly. "I knew you would be cross." She sighed.

He spoke evenly, but his hand went up to his eyepatch. "Does it not occur to you that the wreckers might protect their interests, if they see you are discovering too much about them?"

"You mean—they might attack me?"

"Yes, to silence you, Miss Marina."

"As one of them silenced Julia," she murmured, and he did not contradict her. The sound of Miss Derwent's returning feet came clearly to them.

146

"Please, Miss Marina, try to enjoy your time here on Antilla," he said quickly. "Behave as your father would wish you to behave ... and forget everything else that troubles you."

Marina stared at him, her eyes shadowed. She said nothing, and he turned impatiently away just as she began to shake her head.

12

Marina woke late, feeling marvellously refreshed. She
had expected to be still oppressed by the horror of
finding the wrecker's hoard; instead it was plain that
despite Mr. Granville's disapproval of it, the expedition had done her good.

After breakfast, she dressed, and took her sketchbook out into the garden. She had boasted to Mr.
Granville that she had no accomplishments, but in
fact she was a fair draughtsman and had been used to
making maps for her father from an early age. Her
thoughts turned again to Julia as she strolled down
the sun-baked paths which her friend's little feet must
have trodden so often. If she had not already found
the journal, Marina reflected, this would have been
her first daylight opportunity to do so; for though
Miss Derwent was unusually busy for a Creole lady,
settling disputes among the servants, arranging menus
with Nan the cook, overseeing the stillroom work, or
mending the fine linen that the first Mrs. Granville
had brought as a bride to Tamarind and which was
rotting now with age, she always expected Marina to
take Rosett in her place, as chaperone. Today, however, Rosett could not be spared, and Marina delighted
in her solitude.

Lifting her face to the warmth of the eastern sun,
Marina wandered to the narrow end of the garden,
just beyond the little temple, where there was a stone
seat smothered in jasmine. From there she could look

down upon Mr. Granville's little cutter, the *Dolphin*, riding peacefully at anchor in the green waters of the narrow bay beneath the cliffs. It was too much to hope that she would ever have the chance to sail in the boat, Marina supposed; but at least she could make a picture of it. She settled herself with her sketching book and began to rough in the *Dolphin*'s outlines.

It was a little while before she realized that two men were talking quite close to her, and in accents which she had no difficulty in recognizing.

"Sorry to have missed you last night ..." That, thought Marina, was undoubtedly Mr. Harry Thurlough.

"I understood it was a matter of some urgency ..."

Marina started. That, of course, was Mr. Granville. They must be sitting in the temple ... she had better make her presence known at once. She closed the sketchbook and bent to pick up her pencil, which had rolled away somewhere at her feet. Yes, it had certainly been Mr. Granville's voice, but not his usual manner where Mr. Thurlough was concerned. He sounded more as if he were conversing with Marina Derwent, she reflected ruefully: stiff, and a little wary. Now she came to think of it, he had been like that with Mr. Thurlough at Mount Pleasant too.

"Fact is," said Mr. Thurlough hoarsely, "I'm in the dickens of a fix ..."

Marina's fingers found and retrieved the pencil.

"... had this blackmailing letter, Marcus," Mr. Thurlough was saying in that strained voice, as she straightened. "The truth is—I've been a fool. Lord knows, I've regretted it a thousand times, and now—but how the deuce did the fellow find out?"

Marina sat very still. The moment had passed when she could casually have revealed her presence. Mr. Thurlough, who distrusted her already, would never forgive her having heard such an admission. What should she do now, she wondered, gazing about her in the hope of finding some way of escape. As she had feared, there was none. She was trapped, and therefore, she reflected, settling back upon the seat, she might as well listen and earn her reputation as the spy that Mr. Granville had already accused her of being.

"I haven't the money to pay him what he asks, to keep his mouth shut," Mr. Thurlough was saying. "So it's better to make a clean breast of it to you before he tells you himself, as he threatens to do . . ."

Marina's heart gave a great thump. Was Harry Thurlough about to confess his seduction of Julia?

"Come to the point, man," said Mr. Granville, in a tight voice.

"Well, well . . . the fact of the matter is that I backed you to win the other day at Mount Pleasant—backed you to the hilt—and lost my stake to Sunderland. I couldn't pay him, d'ye see? Hadn't a tithe of it—you were so sure you'd win—"

"There is always an element of risk in horse racing," Mr. Granville reminded him impatiently.

"Yes, well, there it is. I couldn't pay, and I think Sunderland guessed as much. He's a good fellow, you know, Granville. He gave me the chance of another bet—the price of the money I'd lost to him, double or quits . . ."

"You fool," said Mr. Granville unemotionally. "You mean, you now stand to lose twice as much as what you could not pay in the first place? Or have you already lost it?"

"I may yet win it," Mr. Thurlough said uncomfortably.

There was a pause. Marina could hear the sea breaking at the foot of the cliff; a man hammering a post in the distance; a donkey braying.

"Do you intend to tell me the nature of the bet?" asked Mr. Granville at length.

"It's not easy, Marcus! But, yes, I must. I certainly don't want you hearing of it from—that damned fellow! Well, the fact is that I wagered Sunderland that you would marry m'sister before the year was out."

Another silence lengthened.

"Well, it was to buy me time, d'you see? It gives me

until next January to raise the money—though God knows how I'd ever do it if it came to that. The estate is mortgaged to the hilt as you well know, and Sutton's as good as said he'll not advance me another groat." There followed an unhappy pause. "Well, I'm sorry, man. I never thought you'd get to hear of it, you see—last thing I'd want to do is make you feel you must marry Blanche before you're ready . . ."

Ah, thought Marina. So that was what all this was about. Mr. Thurlough had probably invented the whole thing precisely for the purpose of forcing Mr. Granville into this marriage, so beneficial to Prosperity. She wondered if Mr. Granville would see through him.

"Life is so curious," observed Mr. Granville in a reflective tone. "A month ago I believe I could have assured you that you would be very likely to win your wager. Now . . . I am not so sure."

Marina blinked. Her heart began to beat noisily again. Why did he say that?

Mr. Thurlough echoed her thoughts.

"Why, Marcus, what the dickens do you mean?"

"I mean," Mr. Granville continued slowly, "that I find I am not so anxious for an alliance with Prosperity as once I was."

"What?" It sounded as if Mr. Thurlough had jumped to his feet. "Who's been telling you—? Or is it the mortgage? Blanche—Blanche has done nothing foolish?"

"Your sister still believes in the alliance," Mr. Granville assured him dryly. "Even if her heart is not in it."

"Oh, her heart! You don't want to worry about that, Marcus. She'll behave herself once she's mistress of Tamarind. She's very conventional, you know—wouldn't dream of stepping out of line. That business with Da Costa, if that's what's troubling you—there was never anything more to it than him kissing her hand—you know these foreigners—picking up her fan, whispering in her ear, that sort of thing. Turned her head for a while. But she's a sensible girl, she'll soon get over it."

"Who else could have overheard this bet of yours?"

151

asked Mr. Granville, following another train of thought.

"Why—why, no one, I believe. I saw Crick earlier, but not while we were talking. We were in the stables, do you see. Plenty of grooms and so on, but none of the house party."

"And does it not occur to you that grooms and stableboys have ears?"

"Well, but, dash it, Marcus, what would they care about our conversation? How would they understand our talk of wagers?"

"You amaze me, Harry. Do you really believe the slaves don't place bets on their cockfights—or even our horse races?"

"Lord, Marcus—you think they talked about it?" Mr. Thurlough sounded abject and unhappy, but Marina suspected he was heartily rejoicing. Mr. Granville could now have no doubt that his name had been publicly linked with that of Blanche, and as a gentleman his duty must be plain.

"Have you the letter?" Mr. Granville went on. "I should like to see it."

"Oh, no—that is—I burned it. Didn't want it lying about, you know. Supposing Blanche had read it!"

"What did it say, precisely?"

"Why, it—it said that Mr. Granville might be interested to hear of my wager concerning his—his matrimonial intentions—that—that the price of forgetting it would be a hundred sovereigns—"

"A hundred?" repeated Mr. Granville. "That seems a trifle over the odds."

"So I thought," Mr. Thurlough quickly agreed. "But I would have paid it, if I had had it. I certainly did not want the fellow telling you."

"And what were you to do with the money, may I ask?"

"I am—was—to give it to Elijah at noon today."

"Elijah?"

There was another pause.

"Does it strike you that Sunderland might be involved in this?"

"Good God, no!" Mr. Thurlough was plainly shocked. "No, I know who it must be, but not how he discovered—"

"And you don't wish me to know this man's identity?"

Mr. Granville sounded thoughtful, as indeed was Marina. Mr. Thurlough might want to conceal the name of the man who was blackmailing him because such a man did not exist. This had been Marina's first impression. By now, however, she had become convinced that Mr. Thurlough was in fact being blackmailed, but for something far more discreditable than bringing his sister's name into a wager. If somebody had discovered the truth of his dealings with Julia Granville, then it might well be worth a hundred pounds to Mr. Thurlough to keep that information from coming to the ears of his prospective brother-in-law.

"Some of your worries are over, at all events," said Mr. Granville.

"Indeed?" cried Mr. Thurlough. "You mean—?"

"I mean that you now have no need to pay Elijah a hundred pounds at noon, to keep the news of your foolishness from me."

"Oh." Mr. Thurlough sounded dashed, having obviously been prepared for an assurance that the proposed marriage would inevitably take place. "You don't think—well—that if he don't get paid, the fellow will spread it about?"

"My dear Harry, even if he does get paid, there is no guarantee that he will not say what he likes. To part with a sum of money to such a rogue is only ever the least use if it is to buy a specific object, an incriminating letter, for example."

"Oh, I would never write such a letter," cried Mr. Thurlough. "I see what you mean, however. Well—you are not angry, then? My coming to you—it has made no difference to your friendship with Blanche?"

"No difference at all."

"I mean, it's not just that I—I would be ruined if—if you cried off—"

"There is no question of my crying off," said Mr. Granville coldly. "I have not committed myself to Miss Thurlough, therefore I can hardly jilt her. However, Harry, I do not forget that we have known each other all our lives. I will tell you what I will do for you. In the event of my deciding against marriage with your sister, I will undertake to give you the money to pay your wager with Sunderland—or lend it, if you prefer; since I seem to have given you—I hope not her—an erroneous impression of the certainty of my intentions."

"Well, I must own that it's very good of you, Marcus—but isn't it time you were settling down, as you said? And as for Blanche, well, I believe Blanche does expect it."

"I am sorry to hear it," said Mr. Granville thoughtfully. "I have been friendly to her, as to you, for you are my neighbours; but I have not applied to you or to Mrs. Thurlough, for permission to address her. I have made her no offer, nor declared any special interest in her. I won't deny I have considered the match—but a man likes to make such a decision for himself, and in his own good time."

"Ah, to be sure he does. Just for an instant you had me worried that you might have changed your mind about her."

"How could I change it, when I had not made it up?"

"Very well for you to say that, Marcus, but Blanche believes you have."

"If your sister is honest, she must agree that I have done nothing to compromise her reputation. I have never even danced with her more than twice in one evening. We are both as free as we have ever been. Now I must ask you to excuse me—"

"Just a moment, Marcus!"

"Yes?"

"Well, it's just—deuced awkward, this, but the fact is—I was wondering if you could make me a loan?"

"Certainly. How much do you want?"

"It's dashed good of you. I'm in temporary straits, nothing to signify, of course. Fifty? Or if that's

154

too much, thirty would do. I'll give you an I.O.U., naturally."

"I will give you a bill of exchange for fifty pounds. I don't suppose I have so many sovereigns in my whole estate, but if you will come with me to MacTavish . . ."

Their voices faded, and Marina, cramped, rose cautiously.

So Mr. Granville was not yet committed to Blanche Thurlough! She could not help wondering if the conversation would have followed the same lines if Mr. Granville had not overheard the Ducheyne girls talking at Mount Pleasant. Now she came to think of it, he had not cared to announce his presence there, within earshot of them. He too had been deliberately guilty of eavesdropping, and so she should tell him if ever he dared to accuse her of that social crime. But he had not found her out, and there was no reason now why he should ever do so.

She shook out her crumpled skirt, picked up her sketching book and pencils and returned to the house, where presently Rosett came to fit her in the white silk gown.

When the time came to leave for Maroon, Marina found herself staring at Mr. Granville from her place in the carriage. An unattached, distinctive man, he could not really be called handsome now, she supposed, marred as he was, but certainly he would have been so considered if he had not lost one of his curious bright eyes. Such a vivid blue, Marina reflected. Ultramarine? Sapphire? Deep-set, thick-lashed, yes, it was a pity . . . but his was such a vibrant, dominating personality, really it mattered very little. Lady Baillie obviously admired him. No doubt a snap of his fingers would bring most women running to his side. Perhaps that was the very reason he had been considering a match with Blanche, who was indifferent to his physical charms, of which Marina was all too well aware. She was not even sure that the black eye-patch did not enhance them . . . at least his arm was out of the

155

sling today though it seemed to her that he was sparing his left hand, holding the reins in his right as he
mounted, not the fiery bay he had ridden at Mount
Pleasant, but a quieter gelding, a brown with good
bones and a wide chest; built to stay, thought Marina.
If the racecourse had been twice as long, perhaps Mr.
Granville would have ridden this horse to victory—
though not, of course, with a bunch of sandburs under
its saddle.

"What are you thinking, dear child?" demanded her
aunt. "You have what seems a most expressive face,
which registers all manner of things, and yet I feel I
lack the essential clue to enable me to interpret them
correctly."

Marina felt herself blush.

"I—I was thinking about racing," she said vaguely.
"How very charming you look today, dear Aunt."

This was not merely a distraction. Miss Derwent
wore a printed cotton polonaise, striped in pale pink
and white with trailing floral sprays; it had a prettily
draped skirt and she wore it over a crisp white muslin
petticoat. Her hat was a rather dashing straw with
madder silk ribbons, and her gloves white kid.

Miss Derwent inclined her head. "Thank you, child.
Mr. Singleton has expressed his fondness for pink . . .
he is considered something of a judge, you know. I
must say, you look very well yourself. It suits you to
be dressed _en chemise_, and in this climate the only
harm is to your morals; but I shudder to think of such
a fashion being the rage in Europe in all weathers, as
I hear it is."

Soon after Spanish Wells the road divided. The carriage had taken the right turn and was now climbing
up into the hills a little to the northeast of Charlestown.
Marina admired the view to the right of a neatly
terraced valley, some of which was standing fallow
and the rest green with tall canes in the process of
being harvested. When she glanced down to her left,
however, she was somewhat alarmed to see a verita-
ble precipice dropping from the edge of the track down

156

into a thickly wooded ravine where a tumble of dry boulders marked an empty watercourse.

"There is Indigo Hall," Miss Derwent observed in a complacent tone, waving her arm to the left, across the ravine, to a white house, set on the hill beyond.

Marina thought it very pretty, in an excellent situation, and said as much to Mr. Singleton some minutes later when the carriage drew up before the Hall.

To her surprise, after Mr. Singleton had claimed her, Mr. Granville did not accompany Miss Derwent to the house, but hitched the gelding to the back of the carriage and took his place inside it. Suddenly the space, which had been perfectly adequate for her aunt and herself, seemed to shrink. She edged away as the carriage began to lurch over the rocks, and saw that Mr. Granville was regarding her sardonically.

"You look very maidenly, Miss Marina. Are you expecting me to take advantage of this unexpected opportunity for dalliance?"

She was naturally thrown into greater confusion by his words.

"Certainly not!" she cried. "I have not so soon forgotten your opinion of me—a 'wretched hoyden,' I believe it was— 'a wayward, headstrong chit'!"

He raised an eyebrow. "Do you remember everything I say?"

She choked. "No! How can you imply that I—that I have that degree of interest in you, sir?"

"In any case, since I have already apologized to you for my misjudging you, it would be more gracious in you to forget those earlier examples of my unwarrantable prejudice."

"Have you apologized?" she said airily. "I fear I don't recall it."

"You don't remember our conversation in the book room, before leaving for Mount Pleasant? Subsequent events erased it from your mind perhaps. Don't look so confused, my—ward; or I may find myself tempted to repeat one at least of my actions on that occasion."

Marina bit her lip. "Did you get in here to tease me?" she demanded.

"Not at all. My intention was to make a further apology. I want you to understand that I acknowledge myself to have been quite mistaken in suspecting you of—of inciting my sister to misbehave. Julia was corrupted long before you met her."

The carriage lurched again. Marina clung to the strap. In a low voice she asked, "How do you know that, sir?"

"I read it in her journal. I climbed down the cliff later the same night that you threw it over, and retrieved it."

"You might have been killed!" Marina exclaimed in horror. "I wish you had not done so," she added, recalling her own shock on reading the journal. "I hoped to spare you. Did you read it all?" she cried, suddenly remembering the passage about Julia's matchmaking plans.

"Every word, of course," he assured her with a mocking look. He took her hand. "You did your best to spare me," he added in a different tone, "and I am very grateful for your intention. Well, do you accept my apology, ma'am?"

"Yes, I do. But indeed, I am very sorry that you read the journal, even though it has helped you to think better of me."

"Don't be sorry. Would you have me live in a fool's paradise? Though it was never precisely that," he added. "I believe I always feared that Julia—" He broke off with a shrug, and Marina, forgetting her own embarrassment, turned to him with a quick gesture of sympathy. At that instant, the wheel of the kitareen heaved itself over another rock, and she was flung into Mr. Granville's arms.

For an instant, she felt them tighten round her. Then he asked calmly if she was all right, and put her back in her corner.

"I shall ride the rest of the way," he said. "I only wanted to apologize; and to remind you again not

158

to mention the content of that journal to anyone."

Marina's colour deepened. "I am very sorry my tongue ran away with me, at Mount Pleasant."

His back was toward her as he called out to Obed to halt the mules.

"I hope we shall not both regret that lapse," he murmured as he descended from the kitareen. She sighed, watching him mount his horse.

Maroon was situated on the far, or northwest, side of Antilla, on a mountain which spurred out into the sea. A tangle of abandoned cane gardens fanned out around the house, which was a stately pile of grey stone with a colonnaded portico framing a blistered front door, crossbarred with strips of wood. On either side of the front steps the guests strolled down a long terrace stretched beneath the closed and peeling window shutters, and here a fire had been lit to heat a cauldron swinging from a tripod above the flames. Mrs. Hungerford bent over it, a witchlike figure in her black robes as she stirred the steaming contents of the pot.

Marina glanced round. There was no one else near them at that moment and she swiftly took the opportunity to ask if Mrs. Hungerford knew who owned the Trinket Trading Company.

Mrs. Hungerford gazed intently into the cauldron.

" 'Oo owns it?" she repeated vaguely. "Why, I don't know, my dear—all I know is, that's the company that's 'elping us get back Maroon. But why in the world would you want to know a thing like that? Better ask Mr. Flete, I should say."

Before Marina could stop her, or make the slightest move to avert what might possibly be a disaster, Mrs. Hungerford had called out to summon her employer.

"What is that, Mrs. Hungerford?" asked Mr. Flete, apparently glad of an excuse to break off his conversation in order to greet Marina.

" 'Oo owns the Trinket Trading Company? Miss Marina wants to know," Mrs. Hungerford demanded, just

159

as Crick came forward with a pan of prepared vegetables, which he carefully tipped into the stew.

"The Trinket Trading Company," Mr. Flete repeated thoughtfully. "Why, I believe it is some group of gentlemen in St. Christopher's. But really I don't know their names—there is no need for me to do so. . . . Ah, here is Dr. Sunderland, and Miss Winceyman. You have all met, of course? Miss Smith—and Colonel Dawlish—oh, and Captain Fergus."

Marina turned. Colonel Dawlish was staring at her thoughtfully. He hurried forward now, his round face beaming with a welcoming smile. "Good day, Miss Marina! How charmingly you look. Have you seen inside the house? I would be very glad to show you around."

"Too late, Dawlish," said Mr. Flete. "I have reserved myself that pleasure. Have we time for a tour before luncheon, Mrs. Hungerford?"

"Oh, yes, sir—quite 'alf an hour 'twill be, before the vegetables are done."

"Very well then, Miss Marina. Pray take my arm. Some of the passages are quite dark."

"I'm coming too," cried Miss Susan Ducheyne.

"You've seen it all before," Mr. Flete reminded her. "You may explore where you like, of course, and later we will all be playing hide-and-seek; but I do beg you to leave me in peace to guide Miss Marina. I have been looking forward so much to seeing her first reaction to my house."

Marina hoped that Mr. Granville had not heard this rather pointed speech—and yet when she looked down the terrace and saw that he was intent upon conversing with Miss Winceyman, she was conscious of an absurdly inconsistent sense of disappointment. What was the matter with her, she wondered—spring fever? Anyone would think she was in love with Mr. Granville, so largely did he loom in all her thoughts!

A splintering sound recalled her attention. Crick had prised up the nails and now was pulling off the wooden bars that crossed the great front door. He

160

brought a large iron key out of his pocket and turned it in the lock. Then, with a satisfactory creaking of the rusted hinges, he pushed open the great door.

Mr. Flete held out his arm. Marina took it. Crick ran ahead, forcing open the shutters and sending up clouds of dust. Marina glanced back and saw Mr. Granville detach himself from Miss Winceyman and begin to cross the terrace with a purposeful tread. Sarah and Susan Ducheyne danced through the marble hall, darting among columns and statues.

"Catch us, Dr. Sunderland," Miss Susan called out. "We're going to hide!"

"It's very grand," remarked Marina, her voice echoing about the marble hall.

"This is the great drawing room," said Mr. Flete in reverent tones, opening a double door to reveal a chamber of classical proportions, with a lofty painted ceiling, from one corner of which a heap of plaster had fallen. Sticks and feathers lay scattered about the marble hearth, and one of the shutters drooped from its hinges.

"Must get Crick to see to that shutter before we leave," remarked Mr. Flete. "Can't have vagabonds getting in. There must be a window loose upstairs as well, to cause the plaster to fall—and some of these floor boards are rotting here. But before I look into that, I particularly want you to see the Green Boudoir, which was my mother's favourite room, and where she kept her miniatures." He began to turn the key in a panelled door. "The walls are hung with a green brocade woven in France—"

He broke off, his fingers biting into Marina's arm as he opened the door and saw into the room. Then he released her, and strode forward into the dimly lighted chamber.

"Vandals!" he hissed in a quiet voice more terrifying than a shout of rage. "Goths and vandals!"

His hand was shaking as he pointed to the walls, which had been half stripped of their former glory, leaving green silk hanging in limp shreds.

An exclamation of horror sounded from the doorway. Marina turned to see Dr. Sunderland standing behind her, his expression shocked.

"How—how dare anyone—" He too seemed to be almost overcome by the violence of his emotions. "Surely it would not be—? No, this must be the desecration of a madman, Flete."

Mr. Flete turned a haggard face toward him. "You thought as I did—but we must be wrong! Granville would not stoop so low."

"No, no, I should not like to think that of him." Dr. Sunderland stared at the damage. "Some slave with a grudge, or perhaps a child who thought the place abandoned . . . I wondered, when I saw that shutter. I'll tell you what it is, Flete. You should keep a watchman here. Pay a man to keep watch over the place, give him a fierce dog. In fact, I'll be glad to pay for him myself. It won't cost much—and Maroon is—well, I know what it means to you. No, sir, we must not have vandals at Maroon."

Marina went back into the drawing room. Presently Dr. Sunderland also emerged. He glanced at Marina and shook his head. He was genuinely upset, she could see.

"Some of the others were going down to the cellars, I think," he said. "Yes, I can hear them now." He half bowed toward Marina, before hurrying away. After a moment she drifted after him. She could hear voices on the air, the girls laughing, Miss Smith trying to be severe, a deeper tone—that of Colonel Dawlish?—and the lighter, apologetic voice of Mr. Winceyman, echoing a little.

At that point, Marina realized she was lost. She stared about her in the dim light at dark, unplastered walls. These must be the servant's quarters—perhaps the approaches to the kitchens. To her right an open door loomed blankly. Marina approached it. Steps led down to a greyish rectangle at the bottom. Marina reflected that Maroon was built upon a hill and that the cellars would have windows. At least one of these was obviously open. Holding her skirts out of the dust, she picked her way down the cellar stairs.

When she was near the bottom she heard an odd sound and paused, wondering what it could be. Was it human? Some kind of groan?

It came again, quite faintly, but certainly not the product of her imagination. Perhaps it was the branches of a tree rubbing against one another, or against the house; or it could be a door swinging on unoiled hinges ... and yet there was something curiously demanding about it. It seemed, she thought, to come from the room opposite the stairs.

But that room, when she entered it, was quiet and lit by a greenish light sweeping through a ventilation shaft half choked with weeds, which showed her that it was empty. There was another room beyond it, the door slightly ajar, and even as she stared at it the sound came again, unmistakably from within; and this time she was certain it was a human groan.

She pushed open the narrow door and hesitated, silhouetted on the threshold, for the room was completely dark after the first few feet. She called out, but no one answered, and yet she felt sure she was not alone. She took a breath and began to walk forward into the black room, hands outstretched before her.

"Who is it?" she asked again. "Who's there? Are you hurt?"

She wished her voice sounded steadier, more confident. She was afraid, she suddenly realized. Afraid of what she might find, down here in this dark room. Afraid that she would not be able to—

Without the slightest warning she blundered against a solid body. Unseen hands brushed over her, and she caught in her breath to scream. Before she could do so, the hands had fastened on her throat and begun to squeeze. There was a moment when the grip slackened for the hands to adjust themselves—and then they tightened in deadly earnest.

13

Marina fought like a wildcat to tear the throttling hands from about her throat.

Recalling Cousin Rollo's advice, she tried to stamp on her assailant's feet, and kick him; but she was wearing sandals and her efforts were ineffective.

The grip was tightening, and suddenly she had no more breath.

There was a hammering sound—her heartbeats thundering in her ears. Her eyes ached in agony. The tumult in her ears increased to an overwhelming drumming. She felt as if she were bursting with unendurable pain.

This was death, she thought. *Christ, have mercy on my soul* . . .

There was confused movement, a blow on the shoulder which she was almost beyond feeling. And then the hands were suddenly torn from her throat.

She was gasping for air—and she was falling.

She hit the floor, aware only of the pain in her eyes and throat, and, above all else, of her need for breath. Her mouth was open but it hurt so much to breathe that she could not gulp in air as she longed to do.

There were sounds of violent action, but she was scarcely conscious of them. All her attention was taken up with drawing tiny breaths into her aching throat.

She was aware after a while of someone bending over her. She tried to open her eyes, but it hurt to do so, even in the dim light near the threshold where she lay. She felt herself being roughly seized and formed a scream, which emerged as a tiny, agonizing croak.

"Marina!"

Whose voice was that? She did not recognize it, though she knew it was a man's, and almost as hoarse-sounding as her own would be, when it returned.

"Marina—" She knew it now for Mr. Granville's voice; but why was it so different? she wondered numbly. She felt him half raising her, felt his hand press against her heart.

"Alive, thank God!"

The next thing Marina was aware of was that she was in some carriage, jolting along. She was still in Mr. Granville's arms, she realized, and he was protecting her from the worst of the bumps. Incredibly, she slept for a few minutes, woke, and slept again. . . .

Then she heard Miss Derwent's voice, very shaken. She was being carried again. She opened her eyes, which were hurting less, and looked straight up into Mr. Granville's face. He stopped instantly.

She tried to smile, tried to speak.

"Don't," he said quickly. "You are—you will be all right. I have brought you to Indigo Hall. Your aunt will nurse you here. I expect you will be yourself in a day or two. I am going to ride to Brownacres—Dr. Longman's house. It is the next estate."

She looked a question, and he interpreted it correctly.

"I did not see Sunderland on the terrace—Miss Winceyman was also missing. I couldn't waste time in looking for him. Now, don't try to talk, lie still, and I'll get Longman as quickly as I can."

She slept badly, off and on through the following hours, continually roused by the pain in her throat, though it became easier to gasp in the air she needed. It was a long night, but by dawn she was sipping water, and the next time she woke she was able to breakfast off a few spoonfuls of tea sweetened with honey.

Miss Derwent gently smoothed lotion over the bruises on her neck and shoulder and it helped to ease them.

A later drink of warm milk revived Marina sufficiently to try to speak, and she found she could whisper.

"You saved my life!" she whispered to Mr. Granville, when he suddenly appeared in her doorway.

"What are you doing there, Granville?" cried Miss Derwent. "I thought you had gone back to Tamarind."

"I am Miss Marina's guardian," Mr. Granville reminded her. To Marina he said rather coldly, as she thought, "I was only just in time."

She licked her lips, which were persistently dry. "Who—was it?" she whispered.

He shook his head. "It was too dark to be certain. I pulled him off you. We wrestled for a moment. Then he ran—but you had fallen. I had to find out if you lived—my first duty was to you."

Duty, she thought. Of course, he is my guardian. "You had followed me downstairs?"

"Of course. Did I not say I would chaperone you? I concealed myself because I was interested to see if anyone would try to be alone with you, after your ill-advised curiosity concerning the Trinket Trading Company."

It took her a moment to understand his meaning. "The Trinket Trading Company? You think that is why—" She waved a hand toward her throat, and he nodded.

"That, and all your other indiscretions."

"Marcus!" exclaimed her aunt reproachfully.

He straightened. "You may rest easy, Miss Derwent. I am in no mood to bully Miss Marina."

"Mr. Granville—"

He bent at once. "What is it?"

"Do you have—any idea—?"

He hesitated. "I am pretty certain in my own mind—but I have no real proof. On the face of it, it could have been anyone—even the vagrant whom several people have mentioned. But I think we can discount him."

"Not—the women."

"No, I grant you that."

"Not—Colonel Dawlish."

"True, he has only one arm. But that still leaves several possible men who might have been capable of trying to silence you."

Marina stared, trying to read his mind. "I left Mr. Flete . . . my attacker—was in front of me."

"Maroon has a thousand passages. Flete could have easily got downstairs before you."

"Dr. Sunderland—"

"Ah! He was making good use of his time, it seems. Rumour has it that the reason he was missing from the terrace is that he had made an opportunity to propose to Miss Winceyman at last." Mr. Granville stared intently at Marina. Did he think this news would break her heart? she wondered. After a moment, apparently satisfied that Marina was equal to the shock of his announcement, Mr. Granville continued, "Some people consider it a trifle obvious in Sunderland to declare himself so soon after Miss Winceyman has inherited half her mother's fortune—but that is no affair of ours. Have you any other suggestions, Miss Marina?"

"Crick?" She shook her head slightly at herself, though the movement was painful. "No, too small," she said regretfully.

"But Crick is very strong for his size. Mrs. Hungerford says that he did not come out of the house until just before we did. He maintains he was looking for signs of illegal occupancy."

Marina considered the possibility of Crick as her assailant. It could be, she supposed, that an attacker in such alarming circumstances might seem larger than he actually was. But on the whole, she felt reasonably certain that the strangler was a bigger man.

"Captain—?" she whispered. Yes, he would be tall enough . . .

"Fergus? He is a possibility, though he did not have much time."

"Only a few . . ." wheezed Marina.

"You mean, it did not take long? No, well, Sam

Fergus was speaking to Miss Winceyman on the terrace while you were out of sight—and a little later he followed Miss Ducheyne and caught her in the kitchen. Between the two there are some minutes unaccounted for by another witness, during which Fergus tells me he was watching Flete behave very oddly, muttering to himself and clutching at his hair. But then Flete went out of another door, and Fergus says he wasted some further moments trying to find the girls."

"Where were they?"

"You think it relevant? Miss Smith was with Susan in the library. Miss Winceyman came in, and after a few minutes Miss Smith and Susan Ducheyne went back to the terrace, leaving Miss Winceyman in the library ready to receive Dr. Sunderland's proposal a few further minutes after that. Miss Ducheyne was in the kitchen, as I told you, when Fergus caught her there."

"Winceyman . . .?"

"Ah. Now he admits he was down in the cellar, but claims he was with Colonel Dawlish almost all the time."

"Why cellar . . .?"

"Do you mean why were so many people down in the cellar from time to time? They say they were making sure of the ground before playing hide-and-seek. Flete also admits he went down—"

A hinge creaked and Mr. Granville turned sharply. "Who's there?" he demanded.

Mr. Singleton's butler, Cato, stood in the doorway.

"Dr. Sunderland, sir," he announced.

The doctor bustled in, bringing a great breath of vitality with him—also a breath of the horse he had been riding, from his dress: biscuit-coloured coat, pale breeches, boots and cuffed leather gloves.

"My dear Miss Marina," cried Dr. Sunderland. She struggled to sit up a little, but Mr. Granville put out a lace-ruffled hand to restrain her.

"I was shocked when I heard the news of your ad-

168

venture, ma'am," the doctor went on. "But no doubt you will be glad to hear that I have been able to find a watchman already and he is now installed at Maroon with a guard dog—not that that is much use to you, my dear ma'am, but at least it will prevent any further trouble of the sort. I was so sorry too that I was not available to help you—not that there is much to be done in such a case. Bed was the best thing for you, and I am sure my estimable colleague Longman served admirably in my place."

"Do you wish to examine the throat?" asked Miss Derwent in a neutral tone.

"No, no, not for the world! Medical ethics, you know. Miss Marina is Dr. Longman's patient now, for the duration of this misfortune, at least. Lucky Longman, I have just made him the present of another patient too." He beamed at them expectantly.

It was Marina who whispered, "Miss Winceyman?"

"Now, Miss Marina, how did you guess that?"

"We were just talking of the possibility, as it happens," said Miss Derwent dryly. "Well, sir, I wish you very happy."

"Yes," whispered Marina. "When—?"

"When are we to marry?" He lowered his voice. "Not for a good while yet, I am afraid. She is still mourning her mother, of course. And Winceyman is something of an impediment. He has to be persuaded that his sister is in earnest. Young ladies do sometimes believe they have lost their hearts to their doctors, you know, when it is nothing more than a temporary infatuation due to the special nature of the relationship. But there, I mustn't tire Miss Marina. A great deal of rest, my dear, is what you require. I just looked in to wish you well."

Even as he crossed the threshold, Marina found her lids were drooping. She slept until Mrs. Ducheyne and Sarah were ushered in, hours later. Mrs. Ducheyne was warm and comforting, a little like Marina's own mother had once been long, long ago, before the Professor had begun to wander so far afield. Sarah's eyes were round with awe.

"Who *was* it?" she whispered, at the first opportunity.

"Don't know," Marina whispered back. Miss Derwent and Mrs. Ducheyne were now over by the window, talking in low tones together.

Sarah leaned forward. "Mr. Granville?" she suggested.

"No!"

"He is strong," mused Miss Ducheyne. "And he was down there in the cellar when you were, remember. You had better look at his hands, when you get the chance."

Marina looked blank. Miss Ducheyne leaned forward. "Dr. Longman says there was blood under your nails —you scratched the man, Miss Marina, probably upon his hands. Who else but Mr. Granville, who blames you for Julia's death as I have heard, would want to kill you?"

Marina felt weak and unhappy.

"If—it was he," she whispered, "why did he not finish me?"

"He must have heard someone coming. In fact, I remember now, I saw Mr. Flete going down the cellar stairs, when I was on my way to hide in the kitchen from Captain Fergus."

"Then it might as well have been Mr. Flete . . ." but Marina found herself too exhausted to pursue the matter. Miss Derwent seemed to divine her fatigue and presently banished the visitors, whereupon Marina fell thankfully into a dreamless sleep.

Dr. Longman decreed that Marina must stay where she was another day. It was on Friday morning, therefore, that Obed drove Miss Derwent and herself very carefully back to Tamarind. By then Marina's neck was a mass of colourful bruises, but though her throat was still sore, she was finding it possible to talk and eat. She looked pale, and her shoulder still ached, but when she found Rosett had finished the ball gown in her absence, she insisted on trying it on in front of her aunt.

She stared a long time at her reflection in the looking glass. The gown was beautiful, so beautiful she could not bear to think of its being wasted. She turned resolutely to Miss Derwent.

"I must wear this tomorrow! I am positive I will be well enough to go to the Militia ball, even if only for a little while."

"My dear, you must be dreaming!" her aunt exclaimed. "For one thing those bruises round your neck will be even more hideous by then."

"I have been thinking about that," Marina said, her voice still husky. "I have seen neckbands worn, of white pleated ribbon, and I believe it is a style which would suit me, as my neck is long. Please don't forbid me, Aunt! I have never been to a ball, except to look on as a poor relation, and I have been so looking forward to it."

"Well, if you are determined upon it—and 'tis true, you do deserve some amusement after your terrible experience. But you must rest, my child. Plenty of rest, that is what Dr. Longman prescribed for you. Perhaps, if you stay in bed most of tomorrow, and dine quietly at home, we may allow you to go for an hour or two."

So it was arranged.

On Saturday evening, wearing the silk gown and pleated ribbon about her throat, her hair beautifully dressed by Rosett, Marina went downstairs. Mr. Granville turned to look at her. He stood quite still, but to Marina's disappointment he did not say a word. Miss Derwent glanced at him, but forbore to comment. Marina would have more than her share of compliments this evening, she thought; and if Granville was struck dumb by her appearance, so much the better.

As the carriage drove up the winding road the Fort appeared, seeming to float in light. Every window, every rifle slit, carried its lantern, and dozens more were burning outside, below the walls.

"It's to be hoped the French don't slip down the channel tonight," said Miss Derwent dryly.

"There are none in the area," Mr. Granville assured her. "We have the assurance of the Royal Navy upon it, sent by carrier pigeon to the Governor's loft this very morning, so Sir Hugh informs me."

"Once we used to plan our evening dissipations by the phases of the moon," remarked Miss Derwent. "Now we are dependent on the disposition of French warships. *O tempora, O mores!* as Marina's grandfather used to say to us children at Peace and Plenty, when he felt like lamenting the old days, as he so often did."

The carriage halted; the colonel himself helped the ladies to alight. "You are in excellent time," he assured them. "Sir Hugh has not yet arrived, but almost everybody else is here. How seldom in this island do matters fall out so happily!"

"You contrived to assemble your band, by the sound of it," Miss Derwent put in.

"Yes, everyone has come, and none is drunk, and each has his instrument and his music. Upon my soul, I believe this ball has all the signs of being a success!"

They went into the central courtyard of the Fort, which was lively with music and bright with flowers; and here the other officers were waiting to welcome them. Captain Fergus greeted Marina warmly. He looked extremely handsome in his uniform; and his eyes made no secret of his admiration for her, and promised her more of his attention a little later in the evening.

Colonel Dawlish then introduced Lieutenant Ratcliffe to Marina. She recalled Miss Derwent's having told her that he was the adjutant of the battalion, a very capable Regular Army officer, but cursed with a quarrelsome nature which had, so Miss Derwent had informed Marina, been the reason for his having been expelled from several regiments and accounted for his present appointment. He was, it seemed, the bane of Captain Fergus's life and perhaps the cause of some of the latter's wild ways. The last officer of the little battalion was Ensign Armistead, like Captain Fergus, a local planter's son.

"Dr. Longman is our unofficial surgeon," the colonel explained. "A battalion such as ours, consisting of only one company, is not entitled to a surgeon; Dr. Longman however has volunteered to bind our wounds and forgo the four shillings a day which the post ought to bring him. And here is Mr. Da Costa, our quartermaster—again unofficial, I fear, but quite a brilliant hand with our accounts."

Marina looked with interest at Mr. Da Costa, an olive-skinned gentleman with flashing eyes and a good deal of shining dark hair. She found him rather too consciously charming for her taste and disengaged herself from him quite soon, but not before she had intercepted an acid glance from Miss Thurlough, dancing gracefully with Mr. Goodrich, the plump Rector of St. Stephen's.

Mr. Flete came up to lead Marina out for the next dance. His anxious enquiries concluded, he went on to say that he would not ask her to Maroon again until he could offer her more fitting hospitality.

Marina thought this over. "Do you mean, sir, that you are soon to move back into your house?"

Mr. Flete smiled joyously. "It was Sunderland's talk of watchmen that did it, Miss Marina. He has hired a man to guard Maroon, and suddenly I thought, Why should I not be my own watchman? Why pay a man to live in my own house when I am now in a position—not to furnish and decorate Maroon in anything approaching its former glory, to be sure, but at least to dwell there in a humble way, using only three rooms, perhaps, and shutting up the rest for the time being. Then I could employ a man to oversee a handful of slaves and plant out some provisions for them, and just one fifteen-acre plat of canes, as soon as we have any rain. . . ."

She let him rattle on, thinking that Mr. Flete was a man of many moods, swinging from suave civility to blind rage, and now showing a cheerful optimism which she had not seen in him before. Surely it could not have been his hands which had held her by the throat

173

and tried to squeeze the life out of her? Or had it been those of Samuel Fergus? she wondered a little later as the dashing captain led her out for the Sir Roger de Coverley. His were large enough, but like all the men, he was immaculately gloved so that there was no chance of seeing any scratched wrists on her partners tonight.

Dr. Sunderland next danced with her, throwing himself into the country measure with his usual abandon.

"I shall probably be called away," he told her. "Have to make the most of my hours of relaxation ... the wife of one of the sergeants is in labour, up the mountain road, Mrs. MacClennan. Had a bad time with her last, and I have more than a suspicion that this time it's twins—"

He brought her a glass of lemonade when the music stopped, and she sat by Miss Derwent, sipping it and refusing offers to dance with Admiral Ducheyne, who was celebrating the safe arrival of the missing ship, the *Lady Jane*; Mr. Goodrich, and Mr. Singleton.

"Never been so pleased to be refused in all my life," Mr. Singleton owned, sinking back onto the chair at Miss Derwent's other side. "I can't recall when I last wore these shoes, but dancing brings out the worst in them, I'm sorry to say."

"They are probably full of cockroaches," suggested Miss Derwent rather tartly. "From what I saw of your establishment, sir, it sadly needs a better housekeeper."

"I have not entirely abandoned hope of finding one," said Mr. Singleton in his mournful way. "Perhaps you could suggest a suitable person for me, ma'am?"

She darted him a swift glance, then they both slightly laughed. There was an understanding between them, Marina realized, and she was glad of it. She had not noticed Mr. Granville approaching, and now started when he remarked close in her ear that it seemed as if he too would have to be looking for another housekeeper.

"Have you finished that lemonade?" he asked. "They

are playing the waltz ... I have an unaccountable inclination to dance the waltz with you."

"But—I have never learned to dance it," said Marina, which was not quite true, for she and Amelia had whirled about the schoolroom at Grayling Manor together to those seductive strains provided by a heavily bribed Serena at the piano. But to stand up with a man, and feel his arm about one, and so dance—that was quite another matter.

"A young lady of your caliber will have no difficulty in mastering such a trivial art," he assured her. "Besides, I will guide you."

"And who taught you to dance it, sir?"

"Why, Julia—who else?"

"I—I have already refused several offers to dance—"

"But not for the waltz, I think." He took her firmly by the hand and raised her to her feet. "May I have the honour of this dance, Miss Marina?"

"Yes, sir—since you insist. But I thought we had agreed I have no accomplishments?" she went on, hoping he had not noticed how her colour had risen with the placing of his hand upon her waist.

"Oh, drawing-room talents," he said gravely. "I was not speaking of them. Your education may not have fitted you to be a lady-in-waiting to Queen Charlotte, but it is perfectly suited to one intending to live on a somewhat primitive island, remote from civilization, I think."

"You have certainly changed your opinion of me," she said breathlessly.

"Sudden revelations of beauty and virtue must be responsible for many changes of opinion," he remarked in an objective tone, spinning her about so that she felt quite giddy and had to lean against him for a moment. "Besides, you have not forgotten our last conversation alone together, as we were driving to Maroon?"

Marina shook her head, looking, she was certain, quite as confused as she felt.

"When you came to Antilla," he went on, "you were

175

determined to be a spinster all your life, I understand. Is that still your intention, ma'am?"

She took a startled breath. "I—am not sure," she said unevenly. "That is, I believe I am not so set against the state of matrimony as once I was."

"Indeed? I am not alone then, in changing my opinion?"

Was he flirting with her? It was hard to tell. Marina decided to take a chance on it. "First impressions," she said demurely, recovering her self-possession, "often are misleading."

His arm tightened a little. "Certainly they are. Shall we abandon your aunt to Mr. Singleton and take the carriage home together?"

She blinked. "Oh, but we could not do that! I mean, she is my chaperone—and," she added mischievously, "you are my guardian, sir. It is not proper for you to suggest it."

"And I thought you such a madcap girl, not caring a fig for the conventions! As your waltzing partner, I deplore your discretion. As your guardian—as you have very properly reminded me—I naturally applaud it."

He said no more, but whirled her to a halt, bowed over her hand, and went straight off to lead out a simpering Blanche Thurlough.

"What a pity Marcus did not change partners a few minutes earlier," remarked Miss Derwent. "It might have saved young Harry Thurlough from stalking off into the night looking as fierce as a Spaniard."

"I am sure he had no need to do so," said Marina, wondering why she felt so tired suddenly.

"Perhaps you are right. But Thurlough was somewhat foxed, I fear. You look pale, Marina. Would you like me to take you home?"

"I should not like to cut short Mr. Granville's enjoyment of the evening."

"Very obliging of you, my dear. But there is no necessity for self-sacrifice. I am certain Mr. Singleton will be good enough to escort us back to Tamarind, before moonset."

And so it proved. Mr. Granville, it appeared, was quite content to remain at the ball. Marina curtsied to the Governor, who excused her leaving before him in view of her convalescent state, while Lady Baillie looked quite pleased to see her go.

Once in bed, Marina was too tired to lie awake, yet too upset to sleep. She dozed and started up by turns, only to fall back on her pillow and doze again. What was wrong with her? she wondered during a more lucid interval. Could she be so foolish as to be waiting for Mr. Granville to come home, before she could compose herself to rest?

All at once she came fully awake and sat up in bed. She had heard something, she realized—some sort of clatter. Perhaps it had been Mr. Granville's footsteps on the path as he returned from the stables. She could not resist the chance of a glimpse of him, and half ashamed of her impulse, had slipped out of bed in a moment and crossed the room to peer through her slightly opened shutter.

There was no one on the path. It felt very late. The halfmoon must have set some hours earlier, but once her eyes were accustomed to the starlight, Marina was certain she could see something moving by the temple. If it was Mr. Granville, what could he be doing over there? She could only suppose that he might be getting the oars out of the temple closet—but surely he could not be contemplating taking out his boat so late? And yet, she remembered, she had seen him sail out at night before. What did it mean? Could it have some connection with the wrecking?

Marina was not aware of making any conscious decision to investigate the matter, but all at once she was pulling her boy's clothing off the shelf and dragging on the cotton trousers, scrambling into the shirt. A few minutes later, having climbed down the outside of the house, she was walking swiftly across the starlit garden between the vague shapes of the bushes. Even now, she had to own she still did not know what to

177

believe of Mr. Granville. With that eye-patch, with that cool, even voice, and with those stern features so effectively concealing his thoughts most of the time, she found she could not be sure of anything about him—except that he had affected her from the beginning, that his look, his touch, sent shivers through her.

Tonight, however, thought Marina, with a thrill between hope and fear, she might find out the truth despite him.

She passed a little way from the temple, aware of some small rhythmic sound within it. Mr. Granville must be still inside the temple, then. And if he were, in fact, preparing for a sail, she must slip down the cliff path before him, she resolved; must, in spite of her weakness, swim out to the boat, and stow away—for she had at all costs to discover the truth.

But first, Marina thought, she had better peep into the temple, to make sure that Mr. Granville was in fact preparing for a voyage. She tiptoed up two steps and paused again to listen, frowning at the repetition of that curious creaking sound.

A little squall of wind sprang up. Only now, when the stars blazed down in their tropic splendour, did she realize they had been dimmed by clouds. Their light picked out a small object four or five feet above the ground. It gleamed a little way inside the temple, dangling in midair, brushing against a column as it swung gently back and forth, in time with the rhythmic creak.

Marina stared at it until her eyes watered—and suddenly she understood.

It was a pale hand that swung white in the starlight; and the hand was attached to the gently turning body of a hanging man.

14

What should she do?

She could not scream—her throat was in no condition for it.

Marina took a deep breath. She reached up and touched the gently swinging hand. It was not warm, as she had half expected. Neither was it cold. It was slightly cool and certainly dead, though not yet stiff.

Suddenly she turned and ran toward the house. It was not from a possible assailant that she fled, for after all the man had probably hanged himself; it was perhaps from a fear of death, and a death so like the one she had herself barely escaped.

Without conscious thought, she found herself scrambling up the vine, and struggling back into her chamber. She did not stay there, however. She went out onto the open gallery, hesitating only briefly when she saw the servants lying about, all deeply sleeping. So this was where they went when their work was done! They lay across the doors of those they served, and slept as best they might. It was a shock, but she had no time to think about it now. Three doors to the left, she stepped over Choke—who was snoring, poor fellow—and entered Mr. Granville's room.

His shutter was thrown open, so she had no difficulty in making out the position of the bed. It was a great four-poster, the curtains undrawn. Naked to the waist, Mr. Granville lay upon his back and, like his slave, snored in his sleep.

179

Conscious only of her relief at seeing him, Marina bent to shake him awake. Instantly his arms closed round her, dragging her down to lie upon his chest. For perhaps half a second, Marina lay still, her cheek pressed against the throbbing of his heart, feeling an extraordinary sense of safety and comfort in his embrace.

Then Mr. Granville said in a thick, stumbling voice, "What the devil—? Is it you, my love?"

"You're drunk!" Marina cried indignantly, smelling the wine upon his breath. She struggled to rise.

Mr. Granville loosened his grip. "Marina ..." he murmured. She could sense him staring at her. Suddenly he sat up. "What the deuce do you think you are doing?" he demanded.

"There—there is a man—a man—" she stammered, shivering and clasping her arms about herself.

Mr. Granville swung his legs out of bed. He fought his way into some kind of robe, got uncertainly to his feet and stood before her, swaying.

"A man? What are you saying? A man in your room?"

"No, no." Marina shuddered. "Outside, in the temple. A—dead man. He hanged himself."

Mr. Granville still seemed to be struggling to awaken properly.

"Who was it? Did you recognize him?"

She shuddered again. "His face was in shadow. I don't know ..."

He turned and fumbled for the tinderbox. "What took you out to the temple at this hour?"

"It—I thought—I heard you come home, and just after that I saw something moving out there. I thought it might be you—"

"And what did you think I was doing there, may I ask?"

"I thought you might be going for a sail."

"So you dressed in your boys' clothes and came out to crew for me?" he said slowly, attempting to strike the flint with clumsy hands. "I should be flattered, ma'am. But since you were too proper to share a carriage with me, I confess I'm mystified!"

"Please, Mr. Granville—please wake up!"

"I am awake. In perfect poss—possession of my shenses—senses, dammit."

"Mr. Granville, you are drunk!"

"No—curse you. Yes, I am. Fact is, you are to blame. But what does that matter now you've come to me when you're in trouble? A hanged man, you say, still there, in our temple? And you're certain that he's dead?"

"His hand—was colder than mine."

Mr. Granville lit the candle, rubbed at his eyes, found the black patch and put it on.

"He would have to hang himself on the one night I'd had too much to drink. Damn that Fergus!"

He staggered over to the washstand, poured water into the basin, pushed up the eye-patch and splashed his face.

"Find me a shirt, there's a good girl," he mumbled, his face in the towel. Marina pulled out a drawer, shook out a shirt and thrust it at him.

"Now some—er, breeches."

"Can't you dress yourself?" she cried, her throat aching.

"Don't know. Never had to . . . I am obliged to you, ma'am. Shoes? Who the devil cares for shoes? Come on. Let us go to see this—this hanging man."

"I think—" She hesitated, envisaging again the swinging body.

"Well, what is it, girl?"

"It's horrible," she said in a low voice.

Mr. Granville stared at her, owlishly. Like an owl with one eye. He rocked back and forth on his bare feet. "Dashed fetching, those boys' clothes on you," he muttered. "Come here, my girl."

"No," faltered Marina, but he had put out a long arm, and pulled her to him. "Teach you to come into a gentleman's bedchamber im-improperly dressed," he murmured, and began to kiss her.

At first Marina thought that she was going to suffocate, and that she might indeed succumb to the fumes of the wine he had imbibed. Then he moved his lips and she marvelled that they should be so soft and—"delicious" was the word that occurred to her. Then he pulled her closer and she forgot everything except delight.

After what seemed hours but was probably only minutes, Granville raised his head. He stared at Marina blankly, as if, she thought in some dismay, he had never seen her before. Then he said thickly, "I'd better go and see just what is in the temple. As for you, go back to your room, get into bed and stay there. This has nothing to do with you."

"But—it has," she said numbly. "I found the body—"

"Nonsense. You were asleep. *I* found the body. Can't have you mixed up in this."

"But why not—since I am mixed up in it?"

He slid his hand, his warm hand, she thought wildly, down the front of her shirt.

"You want everyone to know you walk about at night—dressed like a boy? Like a damned provocative—" He broke off abruptly. "Go to bed," he commanded.

"Yes, sir," said Marina, suddenly finding that she wanted to do nothing else.

To her astonishment—and she had thought she was past astonishment—he pulled her to him again and dropped a light kiss on her forehead.

"I'll see you in the morning," he said absurdly, and pushed her away.

Once back in her bed, Marina relived the events of the past hour with increasing incredulity, until her exhausted body fell asleep.

She did not wake until Rosett brought in the breakfast tray.

Miss Derwent accompanied the maid. She sat on Marina's bed and gently prepared her for a shock.

Marina stared into her cup of tea and, though grateful to Mr. Granville in a way for sparing her, felt extraordinarily guilty.

"It seems, my dear," said Miss Derwent with difficulty, "that poor Mr. Crick came here last night—and hanged himself!"

Marina started. "Mr. Crick!"

"Yes, my dear. One can only suppose he had a great deal on his conscience. But why in the world he should come here—for the fact of the matter is, Marina, that he chose our little temple for the deed. There is a ceiling hook, you know—though you may not have noticed, for one seldom looks up in such places—Juliana had it put in when the temple was built, for she planned to hang a chandelier—it was much too windy for such a thing, of course . . . what I am trying to say, my dear, is that though the place was in a sense suitable for such a deed, yet how could Crick have known of it? Well, never mind that. We sent for Dr. Sunderland at once, of course—and do you know, I believe I owe the man an apology."

"Dr. Sunderland?"

"Yes, my dear. I have never liked him, as you know. I thought him vain and callous. I even cherished a suspicion he might have been the man whom Julia was meeting in the—the temple. When you were attacked at Maroon, I could not help wondering—and when he came to see you at Indigo Hall, I found myself looking to see if his hands were scratched, for there was blood in your nails, my dear, after that horrid business. But Dr. Sunderland was wearing riding gauntlets—well, he always does ride in gloves for he has to keep his hands soft and clean. In any event, this morning, when Marcus woke me—oh, before dawn it was—well, then, we sent for Dr. Sunderland. He came, not knowing why we summoned him. I broke the news to him myself, and I must own that he was quite as shocked as one could expect. He went first red, then white, and when we took him out to see the body—having left it just as it was, with Obed and

183

MacTavish in charge of it—he stared as if he'd never seen a corpse before."

"Perhaps Dr. Sunderland had never seen a hanged man before." Marina restrained herself with difficulty from remarking that it had been a horridly shocking sight.

"Perhaps you are right. Well, my dear, when he went to lift down the corpse, he pulled off his gloves and, and what do you suppose? His hands were scratched! I cried out at the sight of them, and he replied without hesitation, 'Yes, that was one of my obstetric cases—poor thing. Sometimes they become extremely violent . . .' and that of course is true. How well I remember poor Juliana quite savaging Dr. Margery . . . but never mind that. Sunderland did, as I say, examine the body—and then he said he must speak to the magistrate—Mr. O'Brien of Hope Hill—which was what one might expect but—and here comes the curious part—he insisted that he would like Dr. Longman's opinion before making out his report. Now there's not much love lost between those two—professional jealousy, I fear—Longman has the reputation for brilliance, and Sunderland has the patients—so you can understand my surprise, and—yes, my reluctant admiration for his decision."

"Sunderland gave no hint as to why he was not satisfied?"

"None, my dear. Oh, he can be discreet enough when he likes. That bluff, open manner of his can be misleading; he's as close as an oyster underneath. Sounds as if he's telling all the secrets of his practice, you know, but when you think it over he's told you nothing that you didn't know before. Well, I must go downstairs now, my dear. Mr. Flete will be here presently and the least I can do for him is to give him some refreshment. That will surprise old Cudjoe, I daresay! I wonder how many years it is since a Flete was entertained at Tamarind!"

Miss Derwent rose stiffly and left the room. Marina

toyed with her breakfast, drank her tea and then got up reluctantly.

She paused suddenly in the middle of tying her sash. Rosett looked at her enquiringly, but Marina shook her head, busy with the thought which had just struck her. A just-dead body would still be warm; Crick's body had been cooler than her own. Therefore the sound which had woken her could not have been, as she had vaguely supposed, that of the suicide kicking away the chair he had been standing on. Certainly she remembered seeing a chair lying on its side at a little distance from the pendant feet . . . but if Crick had killed himself a while earlier, what had made the sharp clatter which had roused her?

Marina slowly turned from the looking glass. Perhaps, after all, her evidence would be required. For it was not merely that she had heard that significant sound, but she had also seen some furtive movement—it now occurred to her—after the suicide had supposedly taken place.

Rosett picked up the shawl Marina had worn the previous night and dropped it round her shoulders.

"Storm coming, missy," she observed. "It plenty cold now."

Marina glanced at the window in surprise. The sky was overcast, and in one place ominously black. A chilly wind had sprung up and already she could hear the hiss of rain as a squall swept across the charcoal-coloured sea toward the Point. The temperature could have dropped only a few degrees, but after the regularity of days of warmth, the difference was noticeable.

Mr. Flete was entering the hall as Marina descended. He handed his hat to Cudjoe, who shook the rain off it. Cudjoe waited for his gloves. Mr. Flete looked down at his hands as if they did not belong to him. He made a movement to retrieve his hat, but at that moment Marina spoke to him.

He turned abruptly to stare up at her, as she hesitated on the bottom step. His face was yellow, his eyes purple-shadowed.

"Come into the dining room, Mr. Flete," she suggested. "A cup of coffee . . ."

Her aunt appeared in the doorway of the library. "Good morning, Mr. Flete. We are all so shocked—but naturally it is worse for you. Suicide is such a reproach. . . . I thought you would prefer to sit in here."

Marina coloured. Mr. Flete, she perceived, was not to be allowed to sit at the Granvilles' table.

"Cudjoe," said Miss Derwent, "take Mr. Flete's gloves; and when Mr. O'Brien arrives, show him into the library. And bring coffee."

Mr. Flete bowed. He seemed incapable of speech. He half turned his back and fumbled with his gloves. Then, handing them rather surreptitiously to Cudjoe, he followed Miss Derwent into the library.

"A terrible thing," Miss Derwent said. "I suppose you have no explanation—Crick left no note?"

Mr. Flete made some curious sound. He coughed, cleared his throat and began again.

"None," he said hoarsely.

"I expect you will find it hard to replace him?"

"Impossible."

"What could have possessed the man?"

Mr. Flete began a shrug, and then abandoned it. "Who knows?" he said flatly.

"Perhaps Mrs. Hungerford . . . ?"

"No! She knows nothing about it."

"It is very strange, his coming here. Has he ever spoken of Tamarind particularly to you?"

"Never."

"I wonder what Dr. Longman will find."

Mr. Flete sat up. "Dr. Longman?"

"Yes, did they not tell you? Dr. Sunderland has asked for him to assist with the autopsy. It seems there was something he did not understand. He wanted a second opinion on it."

Mr. Flete made a strange indecisive movement, which

he abandoned halfway through, snatching back his hands as if he wished to hide them.

"Your hands, Mr. Flete," exclaimed Miss Derwent in an odd tone. "They are dreadfully scratched."

"Yes, yes, I know—not fit for a lady's eyes. I had a fight last night. A fight with a cat. It was in my bedchamber, when I got home from the ball."

"You had better let me dress them, Mr. Flete."

"No, no—I am a quick healer, as they say."

"At least let me apply some of Cassia's ointment. You know how cat scratches can putrefy."

"No, not for the world! I assure you, ma'am, I have more upon my mind than a few paltry scratches. Alas, poor Crick! Where will they bury him, do you think? He was a churchwarden, after all."

"It will depend, no doubt, upon the coroner. There will be an inquest, I suppose, and if the verdict is suicide, then I doubt if Mr. Goodrich will allow him a place in consecrated ground."

Mr. Flete looked much struck by this. "Terrible," he murmured, "terrible."

"But something will have to be decided soon—perhaps before the inquest," Miss Derwent remarked. "I have known inquests to be postponed for as long as a year, for one reason and another—"

There was a sound of bustle in the hall. Mr. Flete looked round, then started to his feet as Mrs. Hungerford appeared in the doorway, wringing her hands. He was still comforting her when Cudjoe's deep voice announced respectfully, "Mr. O'Brien, ma'am."

Marina stood up. The magistrate was a small worried-looking man with thinning sandy hair, pale watery eyes and a freckled face.

"Good day to you, Miss Derwent, ma'am," he cried with a pronounced Irish accent. "Sure and a terrible thing it is, it is, whatever the doctors may decide. Suicide a mortal sin, and murder—"

He stopped as abruptly as if he had been gagged.

"Murder?" cried Mrs. Hungerford in a high voice.

187

"What's this? Suicide, they said—this is the first I've heard of murder!"

Mr. Flete shuddered, and Miss Derwent wrapped her arms about herself.

"Ah," cried Mr. O'Brien, advancing into the room. "And is that yourself, Mrs. Hungerford? You knew poor Crick better than anyone, I'm thinking. Would you say he was the kind of man who would be apt to kill himself, at all?"

"No," said Mrs. Hungerford, her voice hardening. "Now that you mention it, sir—no, I wouldn't. Very secret, was Mr. Crick. A wonderful secret man, 'e was, but 'e liked 'is little comforts—'ad a great respect for 'isself, 'e did, and a trick of turning everything to 'is own advantage—with respect, your honour."

"And you, Mr. Flete, what do you say to that? Is Mrs. Hungerford in the right of it, would you be thinking?"

"My opinion seems unnecessary," Mr. Flete answered coldly, sitting down and crossing his legs. "Since Crick has done away with himself, the question of his predisposition to do so is surely irrelevant."

"Ah, but you see, sir, at the risk of being considered indiscreet, all may not be what it seems in the case of Mr. Crick, deceased."

"And what the devil do you mean by that?"

"Softly, Mr. Flete, softly now. There are ladies present, are there not? And hasn't Mr. Flete the great reputation for his drawing-room manners?"

Mr. Flete sat up. "Say what you have to, sir, and be done!"

"Sure, but you're a hot one, Mr. Flete. I'm making no accusations, mind, but after what the doctors tell me, 'tis a fool I'd be not to consider the possibility of murder . . . and who should be murdering poor Crick but somebody connected with him, tell me that? And so, what with one thing and another, Mr. Flete, you'd best be keeping a civil tongue in your head, if you know what's good for you."

Cudjoe entered with the coffee tray, putting an end to the dreadful game of cat-and-mouse.

"Ah, coffee, is it?" cried Mr. O'Brien, rubbing his hands. "Just what I was after needing, and I called away before Mrs. O'Brien could have my breakfast on the table."

"In the name of pity, sir," said Miss Derwent, "what did the doctors say?"

"Ah, well now, that's evidence, ma'am. And before I'm after revealing any evidence, I'd like Mr. Granville to be joining us and the colonel, ma'am. Colonel Dawlish, and a company of his Militia—just in case there's violence in the air, and me being only a shrimp of a fellow, as you see. I'd be very grateful for my coffee, ma'am, before my throat dries up on me entirely."

Miss Derwent poured the coffee with a shaking hand, and Marina carried round the cups. Mr. Flete looked at her, when she reached him, with eyes that were curiously blank. Mrs. Hungerford wept and snuffled. Marina herself felt merely numb.

Was Mr. O'Brien amusing himself with them? Was he enjoying the exercise of a brief power, pretending that he had evidence of foul play? Or did he really know something more? Was it possible that he had irrefutable proof of murder?

"My legal adviser will be here presently," said Mr. O'Brien, draining his cup and smacking his lips over the sugary dregs in it. "Mr. Rowntree—Lawyer Rowntree, whom you all know, I think. That will leave Lawyer Sutton free to be conducting the defense—if any defense is needed—or, if I'm not after forgetting! —young Lawyer Moss, if so be Mr. Sutton will not take the case, or if he's not exactly to the liking of the defendant; if there's to be a defendant in it, that's to say."

He was not left long to savour the quality of the silence this disjointed speech produced. The regular swing of marching boots upon the gravel announced

189

the arrival of one of the two companies of the insular Militia, and Colonel Dawlish was shown in by a visibly excited Cudjoe, while a perspiring sergeant drew up his troops in the carriageway, plainly visible from the book-room window. A moment later Dr. Sunderland walked in, appearing unusually subdued, closely followed by the cadaverous Dr. Longman, taking snuff, and Mr. Granville, his eye bloodshot and heavy-lidded.

Ben hurried in with more cups, Toney followed with another coffeepot, and desultory conversation was made upon trivial topics until Mr. Rowntree bustled in, a spindly gentleman wearing steel spectacles apparently designed to be looked over, rather than through, and an air of having slept in his somewhat threadbare clothes.

"Well, now, at last we can be getting down to business," said Mr. O'Brien with satisfaction. "A table, Miss Derwent, if you would be so good."

Cudjoe, at her nod, drew forward a table, and Mr. Rowntree, who seemed somewhat inept in his movements, clumsily dropped a pile of books upon it. Mr. O'Brien fetched pen and ink from a writing desk, while Cudjoe placed two chairs behind the table.

Mr. O'Brien took his place. "This is an enquiry," he announced, "a preliminary enquiry into the death of Algernon Joshua Crick, late of Spanish Wells. Who found the body?"

Marina and Mr. Granville answered together, "I did!"

"Very interesting," Mr. O'Brien could not forbear to comment. "You were both—taking an airing, was it, at four in the morning?"

"I found the body," said Marina clearly. "I woke my guardian, and he sent me back to bed while he investigated."

Mr. Granville shook his head at her, and she quickly looked away, only to meet Miss Derwent's horrified gaze.

"And how did you come to be in the garden at such an hour, Miss—ah, Marina, is it?"

"I woke up," she said baldly. "I heard a noise. I looked out of the window. I saw something moving over by the temple—no, I don't know if it was a man. There was no moon—it could have been anything. I—decided to see for myself."

Mr. O'Brien raised his pallid brows. Then he appeared to remember something. "Of course, I'm after recollecting now—you are the heroine of the *Carib Queen*! Not many young ladies would have been so bold, I'm thinking."

Mr. Rowntree looked rather worried. After some hesitation he touched Mr. O'Brien's sleeve, and whispered to him. Mr. O'Brien looked annoyed, but nodded briskly.

"And what did you find, Miss Marina?"

She described what she had found, and her subsequent awakening of Mr. Granville.

"Are you certain Mr. Granville was asleep?"

"Oh, yes, it was hard to wake him. It could not have been he who made the noise that awoke me earlier. He would not have had time to undress and be sleeping so soundly." She hoped she sounded more convinced of that than she actually felt.

"H'm. Well, we will be leaving that for the moment, miss. Mr. Granville, will you be after telling us what you found when you went to the temple?"

Mr. Granville complied.

"Was there any doubt in your mind but that Crick had killed himself?"

"No, none."

"Dr. Sunderland, if you please."

Dr. Sunderland stood up. He too looked rather tired, his large brown face somewhat paler than usual under the sweep of chestnut hair. He had a few notes in his hand and glanced at them before he began to speak.

"I was summoned to Tamarind at twenty minutes after four this morning. I was reluctant to go out, as I had not long returned from a difficult delivery—"

"Indeed?" exclaimed Mr. O'Brien with interest. "Mrs. MacClennan, was it?"

191

"It was."

"Did she have twins?" asked Miss Derwent, and then coloured faintly as everyone looked at her.

"Ay," Dr. Sunderland sighed. "I regret to say, they did not survive. Mrs. MacClennan is doing as well as one can expect. To return to my summons from Mr. Granville, it gave no hint as to why they wanted me, and I could get no sense out of the messenger, a groom named Morgan. But I came here to Tamarind, after some delay. I was surprised to be greeted by Miss Derwent, with the news that Crick seemed to have hanged himself in the temple. She took me out there, and I found Mr. Granville and his head groom guarding the body, which was still hanging from a large hook in the ceiling. The first thing that I noticed was that the face of Mr. Crick was not that of a throttled man. The skin was not blackened, the tongue and eyes did not protrude—"

"We will take your word for it, Doctor, at this juncture," said Mr. O'Brien rather hastily, while Marina swallowed involuntarily. "Pray proceed, Dr. Sunderland."

"Very well, sir. We lifted the body down—the noose being attached to the hook by a simple loop. I found the body cool, and judged death to have taken place some three or four hours previously—"

"Hours!" exclaimed Marina. Mr. O'Brien threw her a reproving glance, and she subsided.

"I observed that Mr. Crick's body seemed in good general health—I have made several notes here on the subject. When I turned him over I noticed a plaster on his head. On removing the plaster I discovered a wound which seemed so puzzling it was at this point that I decided to send for my esteemed colleague Dr. Longman. I deferred further investigations until Dr. Longman's arrival. Perhaps you would like him to tell you what we found."

Dr. Longman was a man of few words, it seemed. In even tones, as if he were describing a visit to some dull museum, he explained that the wound was of recent origin, that it had been severe enough in itself to have caused death, that though it must have bled severely the hair had been washed and all traces of blood removed, that the surrounding hair had been shaved in order to allow a plaster to stick on to the skin and that this, and the manner in which the plaster had been applied, together with the severity of the wound, made it virtually impossible for Mr. Crick to have so treated himself.

"There were also some marks upon the body," Dr. Longman continued, "which suggested that it had been bound soon after death. Dr. Sunderland and I came to the inescapable conclusion that Mr. Crick had been stunned by a blow upon the head and had died then, or soon after; that his body had been bound for an hour or so; and that his corpse had subsequently been hanged."

"In a word," said Mr. O'Brien, looking round triumphantly and quite disregarding Mr. Rowntree's precautionary frown, "Mr. Crick was murdered! And wasn't I after hinting at it all along?"

15

It was some time before Marina could bring herself to believe that the distressing experience she was undergoing was really happening; that a justice of the peace was indeed investigating a murder here at Tamarind—a murder whose victim she herself had been the first to discover—and that he seriously did not consider it beyond the bounds of possibility that Mr. Flete or Mr. Granville might have committed this frightful crime. Mr. O'Brien made it plain too that even Colonel Dawlish and Dr. Sunderland might have been more closely questioned if it were not that, for the moment at least, he had accepted their alibis for the suspect period of the last hour or so of the Militia ball.

"But what motive are you crediting us with?" demanded Mr. Granville in sudden exasperation.

Mr. O'Brien looked uncharacteristically embarrassed. "Sure, and doesn't everybody know what the spalpeen was after?" he countered evasively.

Dr. Sunderland smothered a yawn. "Forgive me—can't conceive why I should be so tired. *Anno domini*, perhaps—usually I can lose a night's sleep and make nothing of it. About Crick, though: he was a blackmailer, which I fancy is what O'Brien has in mind—I have proof of it. In fact, as soon as I suspected foul play, that's why I brought Longman in. I have a motive myself, you see. Crick had tried to get money out of me. And I daresay I was not his only victim."

"Blackmail!" cried Mr. Flete. "So that was what the book—"

He broke off, his colour fading again to a sickly yellow.

"Book?" repeated Mr. O'Brien. "What book is this, Mr. Flete?"

"It was just—I saw him the other night in the back room—saw Crick, that is, counting over some coins. I came in quietly, came up behind him before he noticed me. He was referring to a small black book. I saw it had initials in it. Initials, and dates, and amounts of money. He started when he saw me, and closed up the book. I asked him what he was about and he said at once, 'Let us just say, sir, that fortune has been favouring me.' I thought at the time he meant he had wagered money on Dr. Sunderland at Mount Pleasant, and won. I thought the book must be some sort of betting book. But now—"

"I am surprised at you, sir," cried Mr. O'Brien. "Indeed, and I am! For you should have been the one to guess he'd not be hanging himself at all, not if fortune was favouring him by any means."

"I've only just remembered that he had that money," Mr. Flete protested. "Besides, material considerations are not everything."

"H'm! Well, that's as may be." Mr. O'Brien nodded at Mr. Rowntree. "Take a note, Rowntree, that the book is to be searched for. Ten to one, the name of the murderer will be in it."

"In that case," suggested Granville, "you would think the murderer would be sure to take the book away with him."

"Perhaps he was interrupted before he could finish searching the body. And by the way, Doctor, what in the name of all the saints could Crick find to blackmail you about?"

The doctor hesitated. Colonel Dawlish said suddenly, "In the very nature of the thing, O'Brien, you must see that Sunderland would rather not be questioned in public on such a delicate matter."

This interference seemed to be just what the doctor required to make up his mind.

"I don't mind at all, since there's not a word of truth in it. The fellow had hold of some story that I'd poisoned my first wife and that was why I had left England. He'd a notion that Miss Winceyman did not even know that I was a widower, and he threatened to tell her what he suspected. 'Pray do so, Crick, you scum,' I said to him. 'You will find, I think, that Miss Winceyman and I have no secrets from each other.' Hey, hey—" The doctor yawned again. "Wherever he got the coins he was counting, they were not from me, I promise you."

He sounded as if he were telling the truth, Marina thought; and on the face of it Dr. Sunderland seemed the last person in the world to pay a blackmailer silence money. She remembered Mr. Thurlough's ad mission in the temple, and glanced at Mr. Granville. Then, sharp as a stab, came the recollection of seeing Mr. Granville actually handing money to Crick in the churchyard of St. Stephen's.

"What is it, Marina?" asked her aunt quite sharply. "Do you wish to be excused? I am sure Mr. O'Brien can have no further need of you."

But Marina shook her head. Dr. Sunderland was remarking that he had caught a glimpse of Crick at Mount Pleasant, and had wondered then if the unfortunate Admiral Ducheyne had been another recipient of Crick's demands.

"Goodrich too," murmured Colonel Dawlish. "I have a very fair notion Goodrich was another of his victims."

All at once, Mr. O'Brien seemed in a hurry to conclude his preliminary investigation. "Sure, and we have enough now, Rowntree—don't you agree?—to justify our placing the whole affair in the hands of the coroner—or Deputy Haspe, who holds his place. It looks like murder, it smells like murder—and a deep dark plot it is, me boys, and like to draw in half the island before 'tis done." He began to wave his hands in dismissal, and Mr. Rowntree hurried to speak.

"Mr. O'Brien would remind you, ladies and gentlemen, that your evidence may be required at any time. He bids you return quietly to your homes, where you will hold yourselves in readiness to be subpoenaed. You will of course not think of leaving the island until further notice."

He stood up, gathered his books together, bowed and left the room, with Mr. O'Brien skipping along beside him.

"It is Sunday," Miss Derwent suddenly announced. "I should like to go to church."

Marina was glad to accompany her, and to find Mrs. Hungerford there, swathed in her customary black veils. Marina paused to speak to her, and caught the familiar breath of gin, which, as Marina had been long aware, was what Mrs. Hungerford kept in the black bottles to use as her sustenance and comfort.

"I 'ad to come away," she whispered, fanning herself. "Can you believe it? Them dreadful soldiers is all over the 'ouse—searching Crick's room, they are—asking impertinent questions—as if I should know what 'appened to the Persian rug any better than my master. If we should 'ave 'ad a burglary, what is that to them, may I ask? And as for little notebooks—Crick 'ad cupboards full of them. Well, 'e looked after the business side and kept the books. What would I be doing, destroying them? Now is when we need them more than ever, poor Mr. Flete and me, if we are ever to keep the business going." She glanced over her shoulder, and then grasped Marina by the hand. "Now you will take care, won't you, dear? Not that you should need warning, not after what nearly 'appened at Maroon. Just don't let 'im get you alone, guardian or no guardian."

"You mean—Mr. Granville?"

" 'Ush, my dear. Just take my word for it. Oh, I've been working it out, these last few days. And this awful business 'asn't made me change my mind. Crick

197

kept 'is eyes open, we all know that. Saw a bit more than was good for 'im, I reckon—maybe at Maroon. You be careful, dear. Stay by your aunt. I'll tell you what's at the back of it all, when we 'ave a better chance. You'd better come to the shop tomorrow, I reckon, for it may be 'ard for me to get out, now that I've twice the work to do. You'll come, won't you? And remember what I said."

She shuffled away uncertainly, and Miss Derwent took Marina's arm.

"What had Mrs. Hungerford to say to you?" Miss Derwent asked. "Poor Flete, dependent now upon one bibulous old woman for his help . . ."

"She said I was to come to the shop tomorrow. She has something to tell me."

"Better if she told O'Brien, I would think. But yes, perhaps one ought to call, in the curious circumstances." She allowed Obed to help her into the carriage. "We can't have any hint of a rift between the families, after this."

Marina shivered, and Miss Derwent pressed her hand.

"This business of Crick's," she said quickly, "you must not think it is anything to do with us. He was an odd man—extremely odd. I would not put it past him to decide to hang himself at Tamarind for no better reason than to embarrass us."

"You don't believe that it was murder, then?" Marina exclaimed.

"It certainly seems a good deal less likely than suicide," Miss Derwent said, her nostrils flaring with distaste.

"I only hope that the coroner agrees with you. It would be wonderful—poor Mr. Crick!"

"Yes, poor Crick. But now, my dear, to give your thoughts another turn, the Thurloughs have invited us to dinner tomorrow night. You have not yet visited Prosperity; it is decaying now, of course, but they have some pretty things there—very pretty. A service of French china that divers brought up from a wreck, and some charming walnut furniture old Mrs. Thurlough inherited from her mother in England. Blanche asked us at the ball, but I forgot to mention it before. They bought a turtle off Elijah, so Blanche told me—she has a way of stewing turtles in brandy which is quite ambrosial. . . ."

Miss Derwent rattled on. She was nervous, which was understandable, Marina reflected. Could it be that even Miss Derwent was not entirely certain of the innocence of Marcus Granville, whom she had reared from boyhood?

The next morning Marina found Mr. Granville alone in the dining room.

He stood up as she entered, and looked at her intently. Marina wondered what Mrs. Hungerford would have her do—ring for Toney to fetch her aunt, or turn on her heel and leave Mr. Granville to his solitary breakfast?

But he did not look dangerous this morning, she thought; for he had an unusual expression of sympathy. She remembered his flattering and unorthodox behaviour at the military ball, and wondered if he were thinking of it too—or of his even less conventional behaviour in the bedroom later in the night.

"I am afraid your father will regret his decision to send you to Antilla when he hears of your adventures," Mr. Granville remarked. "He will be thinking you would have been safer in the wilds of Turkey, after all."

"I wish I could hear from him," Marina said, suddenly aware that she was missing the Professor very much.

"I wonder how long it will take him to conclude his business in the Middle East?" Mr. Granville said, squeezing lime on his fish stew. "Two or three months more, if there's no delay? Once he has finished he will make for Gibraltar, I suppose, and there should find no difficulty in securing a passage to the West Indies."

"He could not be here before September or October

—and I cannot help but consider all that might prevent him then—disease and storms, Barbary pirates, and the French. But he did tell me once that he had the knack of survival."

"Even August would be a good deal too late for me," Mr. Granville remarked. "I am tired of being your guardian, Miss Marina," he explained, at her look of surprise.

"Oh! You—are unkind, Mr. Granville."

He stared at her in his enigmatic way. "I am honest, ma'am. It is no easy matter guarding someone as reckless as yourself, when it appears that a determined murderer is about, and one who has already assaulted you."

"You think that Crick was murdered, then, and by the same hand?"

"The doctors seem to think he was—and even on this lawless island, murder is not precisely a commonplace. We are not likely to have more than one person homicidally inclined at a time. That being so, then I expect you will have gathered from O'Brien's drift that, Crick having died upon my land, I am to be considered a prime suspect. And how can I continue to protect you, my—troublesome ward, if I am myself in prison? If I could spirit your father to Antilla this very day, be sure I would."

"Surely you are not truly expecting matters to come to such a pass?" Marina faltered.

"If the magistrates believe they have a case, Haspe is unlikely to accept bail from me. And yet—at this of all times! Only a few days more ..." Mr. Granville kept his eye steadily upon her. "Can I trust you, whenever I am not here, to keep yourself safe at home, and close at your aunt's side?"

Miss Derwent entered then, before Marina could reply.

"My dears, do you realize it is nearly eleven o'clock! Quite disgraceful, I cannot think how I came to oversleep so badly."

She poured coffee and addressed herself to a plateful of fish stew. "No news, Marcus, of any kind?" she asked, and when he shook his head remarked that Cassia had been full of nods and winks and hints so delicate that there was no understanding them. "Something is in the air," concluded Miss Derwent. "Well, perhaps we'll find out what it is, at Flete's."

Mr. Granville had risen. He paused, and Miss Derwent quickly said, "Oh, we'll be in no danger there, Marcus. Mrs. Hungerford invited us. Besides, I have a notion O'Brien won't be far away, to say nothing of the Militia."

Mr. Granville seemed to hesitate, then bowed and left the room.

Miss Derwent shot a piercing look toward her niece. "You are looking very beautiful," she declared abruptly. "Are you in love?"

Marina gasped, and choked over her coffee.

"Never mind," said Miss Derwent kindly. "I should not have asked you that, perhaps. The fact is that, extraordinary as it may seem, I begin to suspect myself of the fatal disease. Amazing, isn't it? After all these years, protesting that I had little use for men. But then I never met anyone like Cosmo Singleton before. I mean, I never really knew him, until Alfred died. Cosmo was always so quiet, and industrious. He admired his young brother and stood behind him like a shadow—but now I find he is a shadow full of parts, Marina. His wit—dry, not to everybody's taste, perhaps—his gloomy method of delivery, his intense appreciation, his intelligence, his orderly nature, his kindliness—no, my dear, he is unique. And over and above all this, of course, there is the fact that, even if I had not a particle of admiration for him, I would still want to be with him!"

Marina, on the point of declaring that she understood exactly how Miss Derwent felt, caught herself up with not a little wonder and surprise. "Has he asked you . . ." she began.

"To marry him? Not yet, but I think he is upon the point of doing so. If it had not been for this affair of

Crick—but never mind. I have invited him for dinner on Tuesday evening."

"I shall retire early," Marina promised. She rose impulsively and kissed Miss Derwent's weatherbeaten cheek. "Thank you, dear Aunt," she said softly, "for giving my thoughts a happier turn. I am sure he loves you, and that all will be well."

Morgan, the second coachman, seemed gloomy as he drove the ladies down to Spanish Wells a little later. Rosett too had been oppressed and Miss Derwent explained that the finding of Crick's corpse only a few months after Julia's death would probably appear to the slaves to presage recurring evil at Tamarind, convincing many of them that the place was under a curse.

"It is to be hoped that Crick did kill himself, despite the doctors," declared Miss Derwent. "And that he left a note avowing his intentions. But I am afraid the thing will not be so easily resolved."

The ladies found a good deal of activity at Spanish Wells, when Morgan drew rein before the shop. A dozen militiamen were in evidence; Colonel Dawlish's horse and Mr. O'Brien's gig were waiting in the shade of a clump of coconut palms; and several curious neighbours had found some excuse to gather in the vicinity of the shop.

Marina's heart was beating fast as she followed Miss Derwent inside. At first glance, however, all was as it had been on her previous visit, and somehow that reminded her of the birds of ill omen she had seen that day, and of the news that had then awaited them—of Miss Dampier's sudden death. Again, Mrs. Hungerford was not in sight, and it was Mr. Flete who came from another room to greet them.

He still looked as if he had not slept, Marina thought. He said wearily, "Good moring, Miss Derwent, Miss Marina. You find us sadly upset, I fear—no, I am not thinking of poor Crick just now, but we had an intruder here last night—and Mrs. Hungerford was involved. It was fortunate the colonel had left a guard upon the place."

He did not sound as if he really thought it fortunate, Marina reflected, but perhaps it was just that he was too tired to express his feelings. She listened intently while Miss Derwent drew further details from him.

"Mrs. Hungerford and Crick both had their rooms above the warehouse," he explained. "Last night she went home late, after working here upon the books. As she climbed the stairs she thought she heard a sound but supposed it to be one of the militiamen, who were posted in Crick's room. The next moment both she and her candle were smothered by something like a cloak, flung over her. She screamed out, certain she was to be murdered, and though her voice was muffled, Sergeant MacClennan heard it, and ran down with his men. As you may imagine, they made a good deal of noise, and by the time they had reached her, the intruder had departed. As for the cloak, it turned out to be a blanket used by one of the slaves who was accustomed to sleep upon the stairs."

"But what could an intruder want up there?" Miss Derwent asked. "If it had been the warehouse, now—but I imagine you keep that locked and bolted."

"Yes, usually we do, but—well, the explanation is a simple one. The intruder was probably hoping to find the notebook I saw, the one with the names of Crick's victims in it."

"If you know the exact time of the assault," Marina said slowly, "then you have only to find out who was away from home at that hour last night."

"That would take a long time, if we were to question everyone who might be suspect. And even if we were to discover the identity of the intruder, it is by no means certain he would prove to be the murderer—if Crick was murdered, that is to say. He may have been innocent of all but trespass—and throwing a blanket over Mrs. Hungerford. And she, I fear, is not always accurate upon the details of dramas in which she has played a central part. No, there are doubtless many names in that notebook of poor Crick's, and the owner of any one of them might have decided to try to destroy it, lest suspicion of a greater crime fall upon him."

"How is Mrs. Hungerford?" Marina asked.

"There is nothing really wrong with her but an upset to the nerves. She has taken to her bed, and desired me to ask if you would care to go upstairs to her, Miss Marina, if you should call. She is particularly desirous of the favour of a word with you, it seems."

"And I will certainly accompany my niece," Miss Derwent declared, "if you will be so good as to conduct us to Mrs. Hungerford's apartment."

This was a curiously furnished and exceedingly crowded room. All the unsalable goods of Mr. Flete's enterprise appeared to have found their way into it: all the cracked ewers, three-legged chairs and stained materials, all the bent peacock's feathers, sagging sofas, and worm-eaten books. Even a stuffed pelican was there, alive with silverfish. And in the midst of all this decaying eccentricity lay Mrs. Hungerford in flowing nightgown and lopsided turban, propped up on a quantity of soiled satin pillows, supported by smelling salts and mourning fan, with the hint of a black bottle lurking behind the stack of mildewed Bibles on her night table.

Miss Derwent, after the customary civilities had been exchanged, withdrew to examine a haphazard collection of chipped porcelain figures gathered on a table across the room. Mrs. Hungerford waited until her attention was engaged, and then leaned forward to clasp Marina by the hand.

"I'm glad you came," she whispered. "It was 'im, you know." She jerked her head toward Miss Derwent.

"Mr. Granville?" murmured Marina faintly.

"Sure of it—big—and rough. No, I never thought to be attacked on my own staircase, miss—never in my life. Safe as 'ouses, I thought I was, with the Militia up there, and all. 'Course, they didn't tell *me* they was 'oping for an intruder—not they! And didn't I give that MacClennan a piece of my mind, afterwards, for insisting on my leaving that door open. 'E—what ought to 'ave been comforting 'is poor little wife—but all 'e says is, that the other three sergeants is Regular Army and don't know the island like 'e does, so they picked 'im for the detail in the 'ope of 'im recognizing any intruder. So there it was, plain as the nose on your face—they was expecting one, and never thought to warn me of it. Lucky for them 'e didn't finish me, as I told MacClennan, for they needn't think my master would stand for 'aving 'is staff picked off one by one, as you might say. Somebody's 'ead would roll, you may be sure of that."

"But perhaps Mr. Crick did commit suicide," said Marina, clinging to her first impression of the dreadful hanging body.

"Ah! Now, that's as may be. We 'eard different from Dr. Longman, didn't we? No, my dear—'it on the 'ead, 'e was, poor Crick, and 'anged afterwards. Murder, Miss Marina, just like 'is 'onour said. And 'oo more likely to do the deed than that man, the one 'oo I've always thought pushed 'is sister over the cliff to prevent 'er runaway marriage to my master, and so 'e would inherit 'er fortune? Well! And what more natural than that Crick should nose it out and be blackmailing Granville with 'is knowledge?"

Marina found she was trembling, and yet the heat of the room was beating at her temples. She wrapped her arms about herself. "If—you are right—why should he have attacked me at Maroon?" she whispered. "Or do you think that was someone else?"

"No, no, of course it was all the one person," Mrs. Hungerford assured her. "Coincidence is all very well, but that's carrying it too far. No, 'e 'as a motive for getting rid of you, of course. Didn't you say Julia wrote to you, at the end? Perhaps 'e was afraid of what was in that letter."

"It was the journal," Marina murmured. Then she dug her nails into the soft skin of her upper arms.

205

This was Mr. Granville they were discussing, not some stranger—and murder, not the outcome of a game of chance.

A slight rattling drew her attention to Miss Derwent.

"Some of these are really very good," her aunt remarked, bent over the table. "So far I have distinguished Meissen, Sevres, and Chelsea. What a pity they are all broken!"

"There is another boxful over there, be'ind that suit of armour," Mrs. Hungerford said quickly. "Yes, indeed, ma'am, you are very welcome to inspect it. Everything up 'ere's for sale, you know, and some of them pieces want little more than an arm sticking back on."

She fanned herself vigorously. "That's better, now she's farther off," she remarked to Marina. "Now, where was I? Oh, yes, well, my dear, I wouldn't say this to you if I didn't think your life was in danger. What would I feel like if 'e did for you as 'e near enough did for me, and I'd done naught to put you on your guard? No, what I 'ave been meaning to say to you is—'ave you ever thought there might be someone be'ind all this wrecking that goes on?"

Marina bit her lip. She gazed steadily at Mrs. Hungerford.

"I see the notion's crossed your mind, and sure it is no wonder, after our experience. We was wrecked ourselves, out there on Damnation Reef, and I believe you thought, as I did at the time, that 'twas no accident. Some vessel led us in—there was lights a'ead of the *Carib Queen*, was there not? 'Twasn't just my eyes deceiving me?"

"No," Marina whispered. "There were lights—a wrecker's decoy. But—I thought—Elijah—"

"Yes," Mrs. Hungerford nodded. "For sure, 'e's in it to the 'ilt, and so I've long suspected. But it was Miss Dampier as whispered something that made me see 'ow 'e might 'ave managed it. She made me think—but one thing we both agreed, that 'e couldn't do all a wrecker's work, nor 'e couldn't 'ave thought out 'ow to go about it, not on 'is own, not 'andicapped like 'e is. And then when you asked me that about the Company, you know—the Trinket Trading Company—well, then it all fell into place, as you might say."

She glanced down the room, but Miss Derwent was on her knees and in her element, poring over a miscellany of ceramics, and setting them out around her on the bare boards of the attic floor.

"The Company, you see," whispered Mrs. Hungerford, "that's 'ow so many of these things reach us—a good deal of the jewels and trinkets that we sell."

"You mean the Company might be dealing in the cargoes of wrecked ships?" It was her own suspicion, but it was another matter to hear Mrs. Hungerford putting it into words.

"Well, you won't tell anyone I told you, miss? 'Tis for your ear alone . . . but 'tis true there are a powerful lot of wrecks about that Reef, more than you would think was likely, terrible though it is—a natural graveyard, as they say. And then it is no secret that men do go out to pick over the bones of the ships out there. It 'as come to me that a good deal of what we sell comes from that quarter, and there is a regular supply. Don't it seem possible that the Company might get tired of waiting sometimes, and might nudge a ship onto the Reef? And those pieces, what I 'as to sell in London, it 'as come to me that they might be ones what might be recognized, if we 'ad them in the shop. . . ."

"Then," Marina whispered, "surely the man, the planner, is most likely to be Mr. Flete?"

"Oh, no, it ain't—the London pieces comes from the Company, in special parcels, labelled according. Oh, I don't say 'e must suspect something, but that 'e is involved in wrecking, no, that I never could believe."

"But, Mrs. Hungerford, you must agree that on the face of it he is the most likely person to be behind the Company himself. After all, you can't deny that he does make a profit from wrecked cargoes, and that he has an overwhelming need to make his fortune. You live up here, you wouldn't know if he went out at night to sail over to the Reef—"

"Now there you are wrong," declared Mrs. Hungerford triumphantly. "Mr. Flete suffers from the seasickness, always 'as—you wouldn't find our villain risking 'is secret on calm nights when the moon and stars can shine—besides, the ships can see their landmarks then. No, stormy nights are the nights for wrecking . . . and our villain will 'ave to be a sailor born."

Marina found herself staring at a fly-spotted engraving of an appropriately terrifying storm, and remembering at the same time Mr. Granville sailing off on a wild night from Tamarind; disappearing at Mount Pleasant for a while on another night of wind—perhaps with the Admiral's missing telescope, to see if any vessel was lying helpless on the Reef . . . the *Lady Jane*?

"The man I'm thinking of," said Mrs. Hungerford, "would want the fewest people knowing that was possible . . . for one thing, a secret is no secret once three people know it, and for another, he'd be obliged to share the loot among them. No, what I think is, this man and Elijah are the only two in it together—and I 'ave 'eard as Mr. Granville 'as been seen out in suspicious circumstances, and that 'e spends a fair bit of time down at Sandy 'Arbour. Well," she concluded gloomily, "no doubt but that Crick 'ad all the proof. But it comes to me now, as if one time not long ago, I saw your precious Mr. Granville 'anding some money to Mr. Crick. After church, it was—"

She broke off with a gasp, her black eyes starting, her puffy face losing colour. "Oh, I'm not well," she cried. "Not well at all . . ." The next instant she had slumped back on her pillows with closed eyes.

Marina leaned forward. "What is it, Mrs. Hungerford? What—" Her frightened whisper died. Some quality in the silence told her that she was not alone.

She forced herself to turn her head. Far down the room the chink of china indicated Miss Derwent's serene absorption, quite unaware of Mrs. Hungerford's collapse, whether real or pretended. Out of the corner of her eye Marina saw a figure half concealed by the bed-curtain, a tall male figure. The light glinted on one shining boot. A hand moved as she stared, a gloved hand slowly clenching into a fist.

He stepped forward. His face seemed carved, his eye was narrowed, and he looked at Marina as if she were a stranger.

"Mr. Granville," she faltered; and then summoning all her courage, she stood up to confront him.

16

Marina parted her dry lips, but before she could address Mr. Granville, Miss Derwent was beckoning to him.

"Do come over here, Marcus," she cried, on her knees before a treasure trove of chipped Staffordshire. "I am sure some of these figures must be valuable, even damaged as they are, for they are made by the Woods, father and son."

"In a moment, ma'am," said Mr. Granville expressionlessly. He had a blanket in his hands, which he now dropped in a sad grey heap upon the floor.

Had he come to smother Mrs. Hungerford? Marina thought in horror. Would he have done so, and finished her as well, if Miss Derwent had not been there, hidden from his sight at first?

"What are you doing with that blanket?" Marina demanded hoarsely.

He glanced at it. "I brought it to refresh Mrs. Hungerford's memory . . . I assume it was the one the trespasser used. There is a burn in it which her candle could have made." He kicked it aside with his foot, and seemed to dismiss it as casually from his mind.

"I was sorry to hear about your alarm last night," he said to Mrs. Hungerford. "I am sure you realize your evidence on that subject is quite vital to the investigation."

Mrs. Hungerford moaned slightly, but did not open her eyes, while Marina stared at Mr. Granville, her thoughts confused.

"You were saying, ma'am," Mr. Granville calmly continued, "that you saw me giving money to Crick, after church one day. You have not heard, I daresay, that he was collecting funds toward the repair of the church roof?"

Mrs. Hungerford rolled her head slightly from side to side. Marina reflected that Mr. Granville had made no positive statement which might be disproved.

Across the room, Miss Derwent stood up stiffly. "I believe I will make Flete an offer for these pieces," she declared, brushing dust off her skirts. "It would be an amusing pastime, restoring them. What was that you were just saying, Marcus, about the church roof?" Is it leaking still?"

Mr. Granville did not hesitate. "Did you ever hear of one that did not need repair?" he parried easily. "I have come to escort you back to Tamarind, if you are ready, ma'am."

"Just carry this box down for me, will you? I have put together all the figures which interest me."

He went forward to help her, and Mrs. Hungerford beckoned Marina closer to her side.

"There!" she whispered, her ginny breath tickling Marina's ear. "Didn't I tell you to beware of 'im? A dark one, 'e is—and clever! Don't let 'im get you alone, dear, not if you value your life."

"I hope I shan't let anybody get me alone," Marina replied with feeling. "I trust you too will be especially careful, ma'am."

Mrs. Hungerford nodded. "I'll bolt the door after you've gone," she promised. "And I've Sergeant Plummer to keep an eye on me today—'e's a deal more use than poor MacClennan. No, my dear," she added, rolling her eyes toward Mr. Granville, "I believe they won't get the better of Bertha 'Ungerford so easily."

Marina hoped that she was right. But if the villain knew that Mrs. Hungerford was suspicious of the Trinket Trading Company, and if he was familiar with the building, Marina feared that neither the bolt nor Sergeant Plummer would be of much protection to such a determined murderer.

That afternoon, Marina walked in the garden under
Rosett's eye. Mr. Granville had ridden off somewhere;
Miss Derwent was busy concocting some delicacy for
Mr. Singleton's dinner on the morrow. Marina had
intended to finish her sketch but found herself too
restless to do so. She paced back and forth, while Rosett
settled herself on the temple seat with a pillowcase to
embroider, for Miss Derwent had chosen to throw the
household into a flurry of preparation, not only for
the dinner, but for the promised visit of her brother
Derwent later in the year. The guest-room linen had
been found to be unfit for the Professor, and a whole
new set was now in the making. Marina forbore to
remind her aunt that the Professor was used to resting
his head upon a saddlebag and sleeping in a tent. She
was glad of the bustle of preparation: it seemed to
make her father's arrival more probable.

Pausing by the complacent and somewhat enigmatic-
looking Venus, Marina found herself wondering if she
had really searched it properly the night she had
found the journal. Was it possible that a sheet or two
might still rest there, within the pedestal? Even a
single scrap of paper might be enough to name the
murderer. . . . But that was wishful thinking, she was
obliged to own, recalling the care with which she had
swept her hand about the hollow place after she had
taken the journal from it. But then, as she stared at
the statue, another idea occurred to her.

Supposing Crick, lured here to be murdered, or
waiting alone before committing suicide, had known
about that hiding place? Was it entirely unreasonable
to assume that, since he did delight in spying, he
might have watched Julia slipping her jottings into it,
and that he might later perhaps have thought of
concealing his own notebook there? For since it had
not been found upon his body, then it appeared that
Crick must have hidden it somewhere. Dr. Sunderland,
of course, maintained that Crick had been killed some
three to four hours before his examination of the body,

boy who had taken Mrs. Hungerford's message to Mr. Flete on the night of her arrival in the island! But the beach was empty save for one man, who ducked under a drying fish net and came striding toward her with a fish pot in his hand, a complicated structure of woven cane which he had apparently been mending.

It was Elijah. He stopped abruptly and stood staring at her, his back to the declining sun. Marina smiled nervously, and suddenly Elijah smiled back. In repose, he had a tendency to let his mouth hang open which gave him an expression at the same time foolish and sly. When he smiled, however, there was something rather disarming about his long-boned face.

His eyes fell to the packet in her hand. He moved as if to take it and Marina snatched it away. Hastily, she gestured in the direction of Hope Hill, to impress on him that the parcel belonged elsewhere. Elijah touched his chest, waved his fingers at the packet, pointed to the hill, and raised his eyebrows at Marina. Plainly he was offering himself as a messenger. Marina bit her lip, undecided. Then one of the horses whinnied, and she made up her mind. Trained by her father, she had always tablets and a pencil with her. Hurriedly she scrawled a sketch of Mr. O'Brien, with his shrimp-like eyebrows, his cockscomb of thinning hair.

Elijah nodded, and again pointed to Hope Hill. Trusting that he had understood, she gave him some money from her purse. Then, clenching her fists, she made movements with her arms like a runner, and again Elijah nodded comprehension. Marina handed him the precious notebook and he began to hurry off.

A few paces away, he turned suddenly and came back, pulling out the watch Mr. Hendrie had given him, and pointing at it with some urgency. Marina saw that it had stopped. She took it out of Elijah's hand and wound it up. He stared tensely at the minute hand, then grinned and dropped it back inside the neck of his sacking robe before loping away.

Marina returned to Obed and the waiting horses, wondering if she had been foolish in trusting the note-

217

book to Elijah, who was almost certainly a wrecker and, moreover, had some sort of connection with the Trinket Trading Company. But at least, unlike any other messenger she might have chosen, he could be relied upon not to speak of what had passed between them, she reassured herself.

Fortune favoured Marina in that her escapade appeared to have gone unremarked. Miss Derwent had been much too busy preparing for the morrow's dinner party to have noticed the absence of her niece, and Mr. Granville came in sometime after her, when Marina was already dressing to go out to Prosperity.

Rosett had put out the gown with the grey sash. Marina was obliged to wear the pleated neckband as her bruises were still visible, but once Rosett had brushed her hair, she was not displeased with her appearance. Mr. Granville certainly stared at her long enough when she joined him in the hall, though he said nothing beyond the merest commonplaces. He himself looked very well in his black coat, and once Marina was seated in the carriage beside her aunt, she was unable to resist glancing out of the window often to watch Mr. Granville riding by the light of the waxing moon.

A depressed-looking manservant announced the visitors into a square drawing room with a dark polished floor, upon which a few straw mats floated treacherously. No curtains hung at the window openings, but curtains were in any case a rarity in the West Indies, Marina had discovered. Otherwise the room seemed overfurnished in stiff chairs and little tables loaded with tarnished silver and cracked china; and every table was protected by a little crochet mat which Mrs. Thurlough, as she proudly explained, had worked herself over the long years at Prosperity.

"All the tablecloths, and all the bedcovers," she went on. "My mother believed in young women keeping busy, and as the twig is bent, you know, so the tree's inclined. Now do sit down—not there, Miss

218

Derwent, I fear you will find the draught too much—Harry, will thee move that screen a trifle? Now, the sofa—Blanche, pray adjust the cushion. Miss Marina will sit over there, and Mr. Granville will be comfortable in the wing chair—that cushion, sir, was embroidered by Miss Blanche—finished only yesterday. But perhaps you would be better on this side of the room, by me. We don't want you gossiping with Harry all evening, to be sure. Dear Dr. Sunderland is joining us presently; he is just seeing my cook, who injured her leg ... he brought me some mineral water he had sent from Bath—not Bath in England, you know, but Bath in Jamaica—the very cure for my disorder, so he tells me."

She rattled on, arranging and rearranging her guests until Dr. Sunderland entered the room like a westerly gale, threatening all the little tables and the ornaments so that Mrs. Thurlough was obliged to seat him quickly, whereupon her other guests at once disposed themselves exactly where they pleased.

"Now, Dr. Sunderland," cried Mrs. Thurlough, "pray don't keep us in suspense a minute, but tell us all how Crick was killed!"

Dr. Sunderland did not seem discomposed by this request, unlike her children, who changed colour, fidgeted, coughed and plainly wished they were a thousand miles away from their embarrassing parent.

"So that was why you invited me tonight," boomed Dr. Sunderland with a chuckle. "I wondered why your invitation was so pressing. I should have supposed you would have discovered every detail by this time."

"But there is nothing like going to the official sarce," she declared, undeterred by his mockery. "There are so many rumours going about, you know. Suicide—murder—accident—though how a man can hang himself by accident, Lard only knows. Well, sir, which was it?"

"The inquest will give you the verdict, ma'am."

"Now, Dr. Sunderland, don't be provoking, pray. We are all agog."

"Very well then, ma'am. It is the opinion of Dr. Longman and myself that Crick was stunned by a blow that soon killed him, that his hair was washed and his wound plastered, that he was then bound by ropes and carried to Tamarind; where his corpse was subsequently hanged in an attempt to make the murder look like suicide."

There was a short silence, presently broken by Mrs. Thurlough. "Well, indeed! So it was murder . . . and he was killed elsewhere. Would there not have been a quantity of blood?"

"Some, ma'am. But it was an internal hemorrhage that did the damage."

"Blood," said Harry Thurlough, his eyes rolling like a startled horse. "Is that what O'Brien was looking for, when he came here? Blood on my clothes—that must be why he questioned my valet!"

"No doubt," said Mr. Granville. "He questioned Choke also."

"As if one would be such a fool," Mr. Thurlough cried. "One would destroy the clothes, if they were stained, and wash the blood off in the sea—" He broke off abruptly.

"What is it, sir?" asked Dr. Sunderland, with his keen glance.

"Why, I remembered—but it don't signify, I daresay."

"There was no trace of blood, O'Brien said, at Tamarind," remarked Mr. Granville. "Crick was certainly killed elsewhere, presumably at his home. I imagine they have been searching pretty thoroughly at Spanish Wells."

Blanche, who had been fluttering her fan, now spoke. "If only we knew just when the dreadful deed took place—whether while we were at the ball, or later. If only we could prove that we were all together at the time, how much more comfortable it would be—not that anyone could seriously suspect one of you gentlemen, of course—"

"My dear Miss Blanche," cried Dr. Sunderland, "I fear you are sadly mistaken. O'Brien suspects each

220

and every one of us by turns. Does he not, Granville?"

"Indeed he does," Mr. Granville agreed. "And he will do so the more strongly, I imagine, once Crick's notebook comes to light—if such a thing exists at all."

Marina controlled a start and fixed her eyes upon a silhouette of the late Mr. Thurlough in an imposing wig.

"It does exist," said Miss Derwent calmly. "At least, did you not find it this morning, Marina?"

Marina gulped and sat mute, blushing guiltily.

"I thought," explained Miss Derwent, "when Rosett told me you had discovered a notebook by the temple this morning, that it might have been the one which belonged to Crick. I meant to ask you about it while we were driving here, but I forgot."

It would be useless to deny it, Marina supposed. In any case the book would be safely in O'Brien's hands by now; and though she had hoped her part in its discovery would never come to light she knew she had given herself away and that to prevaricate would make matters worse.

"Quite right, Miss Derwent," she said rather huskily. "I did find Crick's notebook. In the circumstances, I thought it wiser not to mention it."

"Did you read it?" asked Mr. Thurlough anxiously.

"I glanced through it, but it was written in a sort of cipher," she explained, taking pity on his fear. "It was mostly a list of dates and initials, which meant very little to me, of course."

"I'd give a good deal to have the chance of reading it myself," cried Dr. Sunderland, chuckling, and there was a murmur of agreement. Marina glanced at Mr. Granville. He looked rather pale and had a hand up to his eye-patch.

"Why did you not bring the book to me?" he asked, his voice ominously quiet.

"Perhaps she thought that you'd destroy it," Dr. Sunderland suggested with a grin. "Besides, she wanted to keep it for herself, and learn all our secrets, eh, Miss Marina?"

"No," she said boldly. "As I said, I could not read it—so I sent it to Mr. O'Brien."

"What?" cried Harry Thurlough, half rising from his seat. "To the magistrate?"

"It will give him something to think about," Dr. Sunderland observed. "Why, he might ride in at any time to arrest one of us, I suppose."

"In that case," said Mrs. Thurlough practically, "we had better go in to dinner at once, while we are still at liberty to do so."

She ushered the ladies ahead of her, and Mr. Thurlough did the same for the men. A little while later, over the turtle stew, the subject was resumed. Rather to Marina's surprise, it was Mr. Thurlough who reverted to it.

"Was Flote's name in that book?" he asked suddenly.

"Are his initials B. C. F.?" Marina countered "Then he was, but only with a question mark. And some date in last November. And a T."

"T for Tamarind," cried Mr. Thurlough, dropping his spoon. "Then Flete was after Julia—Miss Granville, that is to say. I wondered who she was meeting— Crick must have followed him—it all fits in! Flete, by God! So it was Flete I have to thank for coming between me and my chosen bride!"

He was quite beside himself, despite the efforts of his mother and his sister to quieten him.

"No, you must listen to this," he cried. "This is no time to be thinking of polite behavior—"

"We have long lost sight of that," murmured Mr. Granville grimly.

"This is a question of murder—and if Flete was meeting Julia then, by God, I owe him nothing! It was he who caused her death, most certainly, if he did not actually do the deed. And I know that it was he who murdered Crick."

Blanche gave a faint shriek. Everyone else was silent, until Dr. Sunderland said calmly, "Come now, Thurlough, you must substantiate such an accusation,

222

you know. What can have caused you to come to any such conclusion?"

"I saw him, dammit, saw him in the sea where it runs shallow a little way beyond his dock—I mean, toward the head of the bay—"

"When was this—on the night of the ball?"

"Yes, and he was washing his hands, over and over!"

"But why did we hear nothing of this before?" Mr. Granville demanded.

"Because—well, for one thing, I wasn't certain it was him—I mean to say, it was a man about his build—but—well, it seemed so unlikely, dash it, that it slipped my mind until just now."

"And what was thee doing down at Spanish Wells that night, might I ask?" Mrs. Thurlough demanded of her son, who flushed and looked uncomfortable.

"I had—there was—" He hesitated.

"You had an assignation, perhaps?" Mr. Granville suggested. "And that was the real reason why you did not want to incriminate yourself by mentioning what you saw in Spanish Wells?"

Mr. Thurlough looked at him sulkily.

"Harry," cried Blanche, her round eyes bright. "Thee has not been seeing that dreadful Nunney woman—not after thee promised Mother?"

"And what the dickens does thee know about it, Sis? That was between Mother and myself. Thee has been listening at doors again—"

Mrs. Thurlough, who had been fanning herself energetically, now fell back in her chair, laughing and crying hysterically while Blanche called for smelling salts.

"Had we not better leave?" asked Marina of Miss Derwent.

"By no means," her aunt replied, helping herself to syllabub. "I daresay this is the most enlivening entertainment that has ever been offered at Prosperity. I would not miss it for the world."

But the best of it was over. Blanche now left the room in tears, Harry stalked out without apology, and

223

Mrs. Thurlough was carried to a sofa, where Dr. Sunderland ministered to her with a practiced hand. Her guests meanwhile were offered tea by a thin, dispirited-looking slave, and discussed the pretty china in artificial tones until Mrs. Thurlough felt able to sit up. "Well, well," she declared, dabbing her eyes, "these men are all alike!"

Marina glanced again at the late Mr. Thurlough's prim silhouette, and raised her eyebrows at it. Then, catching Mr. Granville's bright eye on her, she blushed.

"Only to think of Mr. Flete, of all people, wickedly murdering poor Crick, who always worked so hard for him," Mrs. Thurlough went on. "Though now I come to think of it, I never do trust these quiet gentlemanly persons who have never a word of scandal laid against them I don't believe in their virtue, no, not I! An appearance of innocence don't convince me of anything more than that they must have a talent for deceit." She beamed on Mr. Granville, now plainly restored in her mind to the position of an eligible suitor for Blanche's pale hand. "Why don't you seek out Blanche, Mr. Granville? You will find her in the parlour, I believe."

"Thank you, ma'am," he said, rising decisively, "but I believe I had better be ringing for our carriage. Miss Blanche would not wish me to see her at a disadvantage, and I have not the right to comfort her."

"But you could have that right," Mrs. Thurlough eagerly assured him. "It is yours for the asking!"

He bowed over her hand. "I am honoured, ma'am— but I shall not ask it."

"Perhaps you could spare Dr. Sunderland to comfort Blanche," Miss Derwent suggested dryly, forestalling another emotional outburst from Mrs. Thurlough.

"I am grateful for your suggestion, ma'am," the doctor quickly said, "but I fear Miss Winceyman would not like it. Our engagement is not public yet but that is only because of her recent bereavement."

"Oh, go then," cried Mrs. Thurlough, losing her temper. "Go away, all of you. It has been a disastrous evening! Only to think of my Harry and that dreadful Mrs. Nunney! Oh, was ever a mother so wretched? And was ever a quiet dinner party so doomed?" she added, more reflectively.

"I have enjoyed the evening immensely," Miss Derwent truthfully assured her. "Ah, and here is dear Blanche. I am so glad you returned in time for us to bid you good-bye," she said to Blanche, who was still sniffing a little but otherwise had herself under control. "It was a most entertaining evening, a very happy note on which to sever our connection with Prosperity."

"Sever—" cried Blanche, her reddened eyes bulging a little. "What does thee mean?"

"Oh, we will always be your good neighbours, I trust—but nothing closer. Your arm, Mr. Granville, if you please. Good night," and she swept with magnificent dignity from the room.

"Why did you say that to Miss Thurlough, ma'am?" Marina felt impelled to ask, when they were swaying homeward in the carriage.

"There was no object in allowing the poor girl to keep her illusions an instant longer," Miss Derwent declared. "Marcus had made it plain that he had no further interest in Miss Blanche, but there are times when plainness is not enough—intentions must be underlined and in red ink. It is kinder in the end."

"Mr. Granville looked dreadfully angry," Marina murmured.

"Not with me, however," Miss Derwent cheerfully declared. "It is you, no doubt, on whom the vials of his wrath are shortly to be poured. How is it that you did not announce your discovery of that missing notebook, unless, as Dr. Sunderland suggested, you thought that Marcus would destroy it, which surely you could not seriously have expected of him?"

"He might have done so," said Marina in a small voice, "if he were guilty."

"But—my dear! You heard what Harry had to say about poor Flete?"

"Harry Thurlough wanted Julia to marry him—they had been lovers once. No, don't shriek at me, Aunt. Julia wrote it in her journal."

"Her journal? What journal? Why do I know nothing of this? My own goddaughter!"

"Mr. Granville asked me not to speak of it. I found it in the statue of Venus, where I found Crick's notebook. Mr. Granville read the journal too. It seems that Julia tired of Mr. Thurlough but he still wanted her—and her fortune, no doubt. So once it seemed to Mr. Thurlough that Mr. Flete had not only been Julia's favoured suitor but had—" She stopped herself on the brink of saying "killed her," and substituted, ". . . caused her death, perhaps, Mr. Thurlough would naturally like him to hang, whether or not Mr. Flete was innocent of the murder of Mr. Crick—and even if it means he has to perjure himself to implicate Mr. Flete, and give away his own clandestine appointment with Mrs. Nunney. Mr. Thurlough's evidence is prejudiced, and carries little weight with me."

Miss Derwent was silent for a while. Then she moved stiffly. "So Julia was no innocent," she murmured. "Even before she went to England . . . and Marcus knows the truth about her." She sighed, and then, as the carriage turned into the avenue at Tamarind, reached out to pat Marina's hand. "I am not cross with you, child, if Marcus told you not to tell me. But I need to talk to him tonight. Don't wait up for me, my dear. You look tired. You had better go to bed at once."

"Yes," Marina agreed meekly. "I should be glad to do so. It has been a long and tiring day. . . ."

17

Marina woke early the next morning. She did not feel very rested and remembered having listened for a long time to the hum of voices mingling with the continual tree-frog and cricket chorus in the night—Mr. Granville's voice, occasionally interrupted by that of Miss Derwent. She had slept and later still had again awoken, disturbed by a board creaking in the stairs. Then a door had shut firmly and the house was still, but Marina had lain a long while, wondering what had been said, and what the future was to hold.

Now she got up and opened her shutter, breathing in the cool morning air. She leaned out and saw that what had awoken her was the steady tramp of a quietly moving line of men with boxes on their heads, crossing the garden to the cliff in the grey dawn light. One by one they dropped out of sight down the cliff path to the sea, and one by one they returned, empty-handed.

A floor board vibrated. Marina did not turn but she knew Rosett had entered the room.

"Pigeon," said Rosett presently, staring down over Marina's shoulder. "Dat good. Dat too much work for Obed with he horse, and he fighting cock, and now he pigeon."

"But where are they taking them, Rosett?"

"Dey go for to load de master's boat, flour, salt fish, fruit and all like dat. And de pigeon-coop."

Marina's hands were trembling. Even in the warm air, she felt cold. It was as she had feared, then.

227

Marcus Granville was about to sail away, out of her life—and, by his flight, acknowledging his guilt.

"Pigeons," she repeated dully. "What pigeons are those?"

"Four-five pigeon de master bring Obed, from Solitude. Old Master Fergus, he have plenty pigeon, he sell dem to de Royal Navy, Obed say."

The garden was quiet again, empty under the sky of rose-flushed spreading gold. Marina turned from the window and sat at her dressing table.

"Pigeons from Solitude," she murmured. Captain Fergus's father bred the birds—and perhaps the naval captains were not the only ones to carry pigeons with them out to sea. There were hen coops on the *Sea Hawk*, she remembered, under the tarpaulin. The birds had made faint protesting sounds. Some of them had been chickens, but she was now sure that there had been the soft cooing of pigeons among them. And if Elijah knew enough to mark an X upon a piece of paper, he could use those pigeons to summon his master whenever a wreck was ready to be stripped.

Those pigeons, then, must be kept by the man she sought, the master wrecker, the man who attacked her at Maroon, Julia's murderer ... the man she refused to believe was Marcus Granville, however he chose to incriminate himself.

"Who else keeps pigeons on Antilla, Rosett?" she asked, holding her breath as the maid picked up the silver brush and began to sweep it through Marina's sun-streaked shining hair.

"Plenty gentlemen here, dey race pigeon one time. Not now. Dey say bad African done catched and ate dem ... freemen, like dat Hop-Joe."

"Which gentlemen, Rosett? Mr. Flete?"

Rosett shrugged. "Me know," she said, which meant that she did not. "Mount Pleasant have, Obed say. And Green's Fancy—Doc Margery too, one time, at Hogshead Bay. Prosperity ... old Master Thurlough, he give feast when he win de prize for fastest pigeon one year. And de Guvnor—when de naval ship come

228

in, de captain, he take pigeon out to sea, and den let he fly with a scrip'—news of battle, and like so." Rosett smiled. "Obed tell me dat. Plenty people tink it magic, how de Guvnor know all t'ing, but Obed say, it de pigeon bring he news."

And now Mr. Granville was taking pigeons out in the *Dolphin*, Marina reflected. When he let them fly, would they return to Tamarind, or Solitude? Or had they been trained to carry news elsewhere?

Sometime later, as she was going down to second breakfast, Marina was surprised to see Mr. Granville in the hall on his way out, as if this were just another ordinary day. She had said farewell to him in her heart and the sight of him was a shock to her. She stared as if seeing him for the first time. He was not smoothly handsome in the way of Captain Fergus, but he was inimitable, a man of presence, disturbing and, she feared, unforgettable. He was looking particularly well-turned-out today in a stylishly cut cream coat, tan breeches and shining boots, carrying his tall hat and tan gloves. He had paused to watch her descend the stairs and now raised a hand to adjust the black eye-patch, which contributed unfairly, she thought, to his air of distinction.

He smiled a little one-sidedly. "So you could not bring yourself to trust me, Miss Marina?"

"To trust you, sir," she repeated rather breathlessly. "What do you—oh, you are referring to the notebook, I collect?"

"Never mind—appearances are against me, I'll agree—but Crick was not blackmailing me; I was hiring him to help me in my investigations."

The hall clock struck the hour. Mr. Granville pulled out his pocket watch and compared it with the clock.

"I must be on my way. Wish me luck, Miss Marina."

"Very well, but where are you going, sir?"

"To the Fort," he said, unexpectedly, and bowed before turning on his heel to leave the house.

Marina went into the dining room. Miss Derwent was there, but she seemed preoccupied. Marina recollected that Mr. Singleton was expected to dinner, an occasion of more than ordinary significance, and offered to arrange some flowers as her contribution to the evening.

"Oh! Yes, how good of you, child. Forgive me, I hardly know whether I am on my head or on my heels. Marcus—but I would do better to concentrate upon my dinner, as you say. Yes. I thought, for the table, a centerpiece using some of that china which I bought from Flete. . . ."

It was high noon when Mrs. Hungerford arrived.

Marina had long since left the garden to wilt in the full heat of the day, and was contriving a charming centerpiece out of a pottery cradle and several tree-trunk candle holders. No doubt some of the flowers would die before evening, but they could always be replaced at the last minute, she told herself. The important thing was to devise the main theme and know what flowers were to be used. She heard the bustle of arrival in the hall and even while she was hoping it need not concern her, she recognized Mrs. Hungerford's unmistakable wail of despair.

Dropping her scissors, Marina hurried out into the hall to find Mrs. Hungerford sobbing in Miss Derwent's arms.

"They've taken 'im," Mrs. Hungerford was wailing. "Taken my Mr. Brandon! Oh, dear ma'am, what would 'is sainted mother 'ave said? Thank God for it that she never lived to see this day!"

"Taken Mr. Flete?" Marina cried, as Miss Derwent put her arm about Mrs. Hungerford's plump shoulders and began to lead her into the library. "Do you mean that he has been arrested, ma'am?"

"Taken 'im," wept Mrs. Hungerford, her black plumes nodding. "Taken 'im for questioning—up to Fort Charles! Taken my master—oh!"

It was strange, Marina thought, how far more terrible was the fact of Mr. Flete's arrest than her anticipation of it had seemed. It was as if she had not really believed matters could go this far. Suddenly she

230

wondered if the arrest could have anything to do with Mr. Granville's visit to the Fort.

With a little gasp, Marina remembered the feud between the two men. Was Mr. Flete a murderer? Or would circumstances (Mr. Granville's prejudice among them) combine to cause him to hang for a murder he did not commit, while the storm-defying wrecker, whom she would not believe was Mr. Granville, the mark of whose fingers was still about her throat, went free?

"Do sit down, Mrs. Hungerford," Miss Derwent was saying as she pushed her into a comfortable chair. "I am sure it is just a matter of clarifying some point and that Mr. Flete will soon be home."

"It was Colonel Dawlish 'imself, come for 'im—and very serious 'e looked. Said it was a matter of some additional evidence 'ad come up—"

The notebook, thought Marina in horror. Flete had been under suspicion before, and the mention of his name—or initials—in Crick's book must have tipped the balance against him.

But Mrs. Hungerford's next words proved her wrong.

"It seems that Mr. Thurlough bore evidence against 'im," sobbed Mrs. Hungerford. " 'E says 'e saw my master washing in the sea—as if 'e would! After 'e come back from the ball, 'e says it was—and what was 'e doing in Spanish Wells, I'd like to know? Up to no good, I'll be bound. And what if the Persian rug is missing? Someone might 'ave stolen it. And—oh, yes, then they say my master's coat was in the charcoal pit, 'alf burned, it was. Mr. Flete 'as an answer for that, of course. Spilled wine on it, 'e did, and threw it out into the yard—anyone might 'ave come along and decided to take it, and then realized it was too stained to wear, and dropped it in the pit—"

"What pit?" asked Mrs. Derwent, thoroughly bewildered. "Did you say a charcoal pit?"

"Why, yes. You know the one, ma'am—near the beginning of the old mule track—'alf open it is, and smouldering away. That 'Op-Joe, 'e makes charcoal for 'is living, but 'e don't watch over the pit night and day. 'Oo's to say 'oo might 'ave dropped it in? Someone done it to incriminate my poor master, like as not—and 'is good gloves in the pocket too," she mourned. " 'E forgot them, 'e said. Coming back from the ball—forgot they were in the pocket when 'e spilled the wine. I suppose 'e might 'ave tried to wash the wine stain off in the sea," she went on, dabbing at her tears, "for salt water is the best for that—and 'tis true the rug is missing—but that's not to say 'e murdered Crick—why, 'e owed everything to Crick. Crick and me. Just as likely to murder one as the other. And you're not going to tell me that 'e'd ever murder me, I 'ope—not my Mr. Brandon?"

Miss Derwent hastened to reassure her, but Marina, thinking hard, suddenly exclaimed, "His hands were scratched!"

She had not meant to speak aloud and would have given a good deal to retract the words once they were out, but it was too late.

"Scratched?" screamed Mrs. Hungerford. "Scratched, you say? And what if they were? What of a few scratches, then? What do you mean by it, might I ask?"

"Nothing, ma'am—"

"Ho, yes, you do! And I 'ave a right to know, if 'tis aught against my master, I believe."

Marina gestured uncomfortably. "When—when that person was trying to strangle me at Maroon, I clawed at his hands," she explained. "I drew blood. Dr. Longman told me, it was under my nails. And I just remembered that Mr. Flete had scratches on his hands ... but so did Dr. Sunderland, now that I come to think of it."

"Scratches, scratches," cried Mrs. Hungerford scornfully. "Everybody what works 'as scratches on 'is 'ands, I daresay. What about your precious Mr. Granville—don't 'e 'ave no scratches, then?"

"Not on his hands," declared Miss Derwent firmly.

"Oh! Don't 'e, then? And what about 'is wrists? 'Ave you looked there?"

Marina closed her eyes. Mr. Granville's fine linen

232

shirts boasted a neat ruffle round the wrists, short in daytime, longer for evening wear, successfully concealing them.

"I suppose—Choke would know," she faltered.

"Choke!" cried Mrs. Hungerford scornfully. " 'E'd never tell—wonderful discreet 'e can be, when 'e don't want to talk. Puts 'is 'and up to his throat, 'e does, and shakes 'is 'ead, pathetic-like. Dumb as Elijah, Choke can be, when it suits 'im. Bring tears to your eyes, it would."

"I did not know you were so well acquainted with Mr. Granville's valet," Miss Derwent remarked, rather coldly.

"Well, I asked 'im a few questions last year, I did—time your Miss Julia killed 'erself. They was suspecting my master then, you know, of driving 'er to 'er death, and I took it on myself to find out the truth. Thanks to Choke and 'is ideas of loyalty to 'is precious master, I didn't get very far. And 'ere is Choke's master," she cried, her already high colour deepening to plum. " 'Ere 'e is—talk of the devil!"

Mr. Granville halted on the threshold, eyebrow raised.

Miss Derwent turned to him. "Did you go to the Fort, Marcus, as you intended? Then I expect you will know that Colonel Dawlish has detained Mr. Flete. Mrs. Hungerford is naturally most distressed."

At this understatement, Mrs. Hungerford drew an indignant breath, but before she could let it out in a scream of rage, Mr. Granville said quietly, "They have released him."

"What?" cried Mrs. Hungerford, staggering back. "What's that you say?"

"Mr. Flete was riding down to Spanish Wells as I left the Fort."

"Lawks—coming 'ome, and I not there!" Without another word Mrs. Hungerford bustled from the room. A moment later, Cudjoe could be seen heaving her into the gig she had apparently driven up herself.

"Quite disordered, poor woman," Mr. Granville

remarked. "Ah, well, this business draws to a climax now. The suspense cannot last much longer."

Miss Derwent stared at him. "Mr. Flete is cleared, you say?"

He shrugged. "They examined him pretty thoroughly, I understand. His story is an odd one, but I think Dawlish, for one, believes it."

Miss Derwent drew him into the book room and Marina followed. "What is his story then?" Miss Derwent eagerly demanded, dropping into the nearest chair. "And how do you come to know of it?"

Mr. Granville seated Marina and strolled over to the nearest window. "I got it all out of young Armistead," he owned. "Luckily for me, he don't know the meaning of discretion. He told me there was additional evidence, and when the colonel confronted Flete with it, Flete broke down at last and confessed what seems to be the truth, or something like it. Flete admits now that when he returned from the Fort that night, he found Crick's murdered body in the shop."

"Poor Mr. Flete," Marina cried. "What a terrible shock it must have been."

"Yes, it presumably somewhat unhinged him, for a while. He says that his first thought, in fact, was to ride back to the Fort to report the murder, but then he recollected that he had just quarreled with Crick—he had occasion, it seems, to reprimand him for spying on his friends, particularly at the picnic at Maroon when Crick had annoyed Captain Fergus. The quarrel had grown heated, and Flete had threatened to dismiss Crick if he did not behave better. He says he did not mean it, for Crick is the backbone of his business, but it seems he lost his temper. Then Crick threatened him, and said he never could dismiss him because Crick knew too much about him. Flete realized that if this quarrel had been overheard—and they were shouting—then he would seem to have a motive. It was then that it occurred to him that it would suit him very much better to have the body discovered somewhere else. He had a suspicion Crick was black-

234

mailing several people and felt if the body could be placed on neutral ground there would be so many suspects the murder might never be solved. He determined to put the body on a mule and carry it into the country. At this point, he says, it occurred to him to wonder if the murder had actually been arranged to implicate himself. This notion grew on him—"

"It sounds absurd," said Miss Derwent quite crossly.

"Naturally the murderer would have had some other pressing motive for destroying Crick," Mr. Granville explained. "Flete thought that having done so, the murderer had some reason for ridding himself of Flete as well and hoped to kill his two birds with the one stone."

"Did Mr. Flete have any suggestions as to whom this amiable villain might be?" demanded Miss Derwent.

"Of course. Once he had progressed so far in his thoughts, the rest was obvious to him. He thought it was I."

"You!" Miss Derwent cried indignantly.

"None other. I had long hated him, so he thought, for his being the cause of my losing an eye. We know that he suspected me of attempting to revenge myself on him by destroying his life at Maroon. And now that he was nearing the point at which a return to Maroon would be accomplished, it seemed natural to him to suppose I would seek to throw some further rub in his way. Since Crick was rumoured to be blackmailing me—"

"Was he blackmailing you?" Miss Derwent asked bluntly. Marina bit her lip.

"No," Mr. Granville declared. "Neither was he collecting money for the church from me," he added with a side glance at Marina. "I was in fact paying him for information received. Information on a very profitable business which abounds in Antilla. Business which concerns me nearly, because it has already caused the death of my best friend, Alfred Singleton, probably that of my sister, and more recently almost

235

finished off my—ward. The business of wrecking, dear Miss Derwent, as I was telling you last night—and which Miss Marina has been hunting down since her introduction to it on the *Carib Queen*."

Marina stared at him, her thoughts in turmoil. Miss Derwent said nothing, but she had paled, and her nostrils flared.

Mr. Granville continued, "You can see that Flete had, as he thought, a convincing case against me. Suddenly it occurred to him that by bringing Crick's body here to Tamarind, he might pin the crime upon me. It was only later that he decided to make it look like a suicide. You will not wish to hear the details of the next hour, I suppose—"

"I believe I do," said Miss Derwent, and Marina nodded.

"Very well. It seems that Flete awoke to practical considerations to find that the wretched Crick had shed a certain amount of blood from his fatal wound. The Persian rug was ominously stained and so, once he had moved the corpse, was Flete's coat, and the gloves with which he had fastidiously protected his hands. He got Crick onto the back of a mule and tied him on with a rope, taking off the gloves and thrusting them into his pocket, the better to make his knots. He left the mule tied in the shed and rolled up the Persian rug while he washed the floor. Then he decided to take the rug into the sea and sink it. It was heavy enough when saturated to stay submerged. That was when Harry Thurlough saw him. He removed the traces of blood from his own person, changed his coat and bundled up the bloodstained one, ready to jettison it and the gloves in Hop-Joe's charcoal pit. It was at this point that he realized he had not the courage or, if you like, the malice to stand by his plan of bringing the murder home to me. It might be safer for himself also to arrange for Crick's death to look like suicide. He remembered the hook in the summerhouse here—he recalled a childhood party when he and I had thrown a rope over that hook and had taken it in turns to raise each other off the ground. He would hang Crick there, he thought, the body would not be discovered until daylight, and only the murderer would know that all was not what it seemed."

"Extremely cool for a man who was *not* a murderer," Miss Derwent remarked.

"He was fighting for his life, as he supposed. He had, then, to hide the signs of murder, and washed and plastered the head quite convincingly, he thought."

"The man must certainly be mad," Miss Derwent declared. "How much simpler it would have been to have dropped the body somewhere on the estate, just as it was, if he wanted to implicate you."

"I suppose he was afraid that the crime might still be brought home to him. He would not want the fact of the missing rug to become significant. No, I believe he decided to protect himself, at the risk of letting me get away with murder. After all, if Crick's suicide was accepted, then I would still be suspected of some unpleasant connection with him. The episode would serve to blacken my character. On the other hand, if I broke down under the shock, and admitted to the murder, Flete could then confess his part in the affair. Flete led the mule, then, with its gruesome burden, to the old track. He rid himself of the coat and gloves in the charcoal pit, and so brought the body to Tamarind. He was certain he had not been seen, and that everything had gone perfectly, except that since he was not wearing gloves, his hands got badly scratched by the thorny branches that overhang the path. It was while he was dealing with the body in the temple that he came across Crick's notebook, and hid it in the statue. And that," concluded Mr. Granville, "is Flete's story."

Miss Derwent looked out of the window. "There is a storm blowing up," she murmured, with apparent inconsequence. Marina instantly saw the connection.

"If Flete has been released, you will be taken next," she cried. "What is your story? Have you any good defense?"

"None, I'm afraid," he said carelessly. "I drank a

good deal after you left the ball—wandered in and out of the Fort. I daresay I had time to commit the murder during one of those interludes when I was alone, and before Flete left the ball."

"You had time—but you did not do it?"

His single eye blazed into hers. "What do you think?"

"But—the boat—I saw— Do you mean to allow them to arrest you, in the hope that your innocence will save you?"

"No, Miss Marina. As you have guessed, I mean to run away."

She stared at him in horror. "But that is the worst thing you can do! Surely that will incriminate you absolutely?"

"Perhaps. On the other hand, if Flete is right—and we must concede the possibility that he may be right, he cannot always be wrong, I daresay—then, assuming I am innocent, there is another person in this drama. A person capable of murder, who wishes to rid himself of Flete. If suspicion strongly turns to me, will not this person, if he exists, try to point it back to Flete? And since I spent the morning at the Fort talking to Lieutenant Ratcliffe—though not unfortunately to Colonel Dawlish or Mr. O'Brien—then will not Ratcliffe at least be on the lookout for the first sign of outside manipulation?"

"Let us hope so," said Marina unhappily.

"You have reservations, ma'am? Let us hear them."

"You said yourself, 'this person, if he exists,'" she pointed out. "Also—has it not struck you that it might be one of the officers themselves? And it is even possible, I suppose, that there might be a conspiracy among them."

"That is an alarming thought, indeed." He spoke solemnly enough, but she thought she caught a mocking glint in his eye.

"Then," she continued hesitantly, "it occurs to me that the murderer would be apt to bring suspicion to bear on Mr. Flete just as well if you were in prison as

238

if you escape it. And won't he suspect a plot, if you run away?"

"He will suspect nothing more than the truth, which is that I don't want to go to prison. Besides, it will look more suspicious to the authorities if I evade them." He glanced again out of the window. "That settles it! Miss Derwent is right, a storm is blowing up—and I have the oddest liking for a battle with the elements. Yes, I shall go sailing, Miss Marina. I wish I could ask you to go with me—I am sure you would enjoy it," he added with a gleaming look, "but I fear I can't allow it. You will both stay here: Miss Derwent to entertain our good friend Singleton, and you, my dear ward, to obey your aunt. I see you think that is a tame fate indeed, but so concerned am I for your safety, Miss Marina, and so little faith have I in your good sense that I have requested a special guard for you in Miss Derwent's name; and in view of your near-strangulation I am pleased to inform you that the colonel of Militia has granted our request. The guard will doubtless march up with the same company that comes to arrest me."

"One would suppose that the second act would countermand the necessity for the first, in the colonel's opinion," Miss Derwent suggested.

"Ah, but when I escape the second group, the first will be deemed more than ever essential. Hark, do I hear them now?"

He crossed to the window and leaned out. Over his shoulder Marina saw a horseman gallop into sight.

"It is Mr. Thurlough!" she cried.

"Yes, it is Harry. There must be some good in the fellow, after all. He has not forgotten our privateering days. Ho, Harry," he cried.

Mr. Thurlough reined in dramatically, his startled horse half rearing, forelegs pawing the air.

"Marcus! I came—the devil's in it, man—I overtook a company of Militia, Fergus at the head—young Armistead told me—"

"So they're on to me at last, eh?" said Mr. Granville coolly. "Thank you, Harry. You had better ride on home for it seems as if the time has come for me to take my leave, and you stand in some danger of being accused as an accessory to crime."

"There is no time to waste," cried Mr. Thurlough, brushing aside this good advice. "They are on the road —I came by the track—but they'll be here in ten or fifteen minutes."

"Long enough," said Mr. Granville, turning swiftly and catching Marina tightly in his arms before she could guess at his intention.

"Long enough," he repeated, gazing down at her. "Will you marry me, Marina, when all this is over?"

"What?" she gasped, her senses reeling. "Are you out of your mind?"

He gazed down at her, his eyelid drooping. "No, no," he murmured. "You put too low a value on yourself, my love. Well, what do you say? Are we not well suited—vagabond adventurers both?"

"But I thought you disapproved of me?" she cried.

"So I do—but already I cannot imagine myself or Tamarind without you."

His arms tightened. She felt herself drowning in his look. "You—must hurry!" she said breathlessly.

"Yes—we waste time," he agreed, and bent to press his lips on hers.

"So," he said, lifting his head at last, "is that your answer, my brave and beautiful Marina?"

"Oh, yes, I'll marry you," she cried recklessly. "Whatever you may have done!"

He caught his breath. "Soon, I hope?"

"Whenever you say—if you are not hanged!"

"Must you make conditions?" he drawled, as if he had all the time in the world. "As to when, I hope you will not insist on our waiting for your father to come, to give you away?"

"Marcus," called Mr. Thurlough from the carriage-way, "I caught a flash of steel down the road!"

"Very well," he said calmly. "Only, it is so hard to

240

part from the girl one loves. Take care of her, Miss Derwent."

With that he pressed Marina's hand extremely hard, swung his long legs over the windowsill and ran just as he was across the garden, which was bright with bougainvillea and hummingbirds in the vivid light that precedes a storm.

A moment later he disappeared down the cliff path, and the light seemed to Marina to fade a little.

The Antilla Militia came marching into sight just as the sloop dipped out into the channel. As Marina stared with watering eyes, the gaff was raised and the *Dolphin* began to run southwest before the wind, heading for freedom.

18

Marina found herself laughing and weeping in Miss Derwent's arms.

It was the neighing of Mr. Thurlough's horse that restored her to her senses. "The Militia are here," she cried, and turned to lean out of the window.

"Come in, Mr. Thurlough," she called. "Loop your rein over that post. You must act as if you are merely visiting us in the social way, or you may be arrested yourself for complicity in this affair."

"Quite right," approved her aunt, ringing the bell. "Do you sit down, Marina. Ah, Toney, bring us some Madeira and three glasses, if you please—at once!"

Mr. Thurlough hurried into the room, and the three of them were sipping at their wine with an appearance of calm when Cudjoe announced Captain Fergus.

He came to attention in the doorway, saluted smartly and announced without preamble that he had a warrant for the arrest of Marcus Henry Granville.

They all exclaimed, and Miss Derwent brought out her fan.

"I can't believe my ears," she cried. "His arrest, did you say? It is Sam Fergus, is it not? You have come to arrest Marcus? It is not just that you want to take him for questioning?"

"I fear not, ma'am. I very much regret that it is my most unwelcome duty—"

"What is the charge?" demanded Mr. Thurlough.

"The charge of murdering Algernon Joshua Crick—"

"Murder!" shrieked Miss Derwent, fanning herself.

Captain Fergus looked at her narrowly. "I am extremely sorry, as I say, to have been the one entrusted with this distasteful duty. Nevertheless, I hope that none of you has any thought of hindering me in it."

"Oh, no," said Mr. Thurlough in a shocked tone. "Not the least in the world! Dashed good Madeira, this."

"Hindering you, sir?" repeated Miss Derwent with a show of anger. "You shall see how I shall hinder you? Marina, ring the bell."

Marina did so, and Cudjoe instantly presented himself.

"Oh, Cudjoe," said Miss Derwent loftily, "pray inform Mr. Granville that Captain Fergus requires his presence here—"

"Immediately," interpolated Captain Fergus. "And you need not say that 'tis I who requires his presence."

"Tell the master to come down here at once," Miss Derwent translated for Cudjoe's benefit. "I am sure, Captain," she went on when the butler had left the room, "that Mr. Granville will be able to answer every charge without the least hesitation. We have not the slightest doubt about him ourselves, have we, Marina?"

"No, ma'am, none," replied Marina breathlessly. It was quite true; she was so wildly, insanely happy that there was no room in her for doubt at that moment, or anything else but love and wonder.

"Were you not on your way to Prosperity when I met you just now upon the road?" Captain Fergus demanded of Mr. Thurlough, looking at him with suspicion.

"Was I? Oh, ay, to be sure, I was on my way home. But passing the gates of Tamarind, I recollected that my mother had charged me with a message for Miss Derwent," Mr. Thurlough improvised easily.

"If I thought you gave Granville the nod—! Didn't I see you talking to young Armistead?"

243

"Just a word—in passing, as it were."

"Did he tell you what our mission was?"

Mr. Thurlough looked uncomfortable. "He is—inclined to be a trifle indiscreet, perhaps."

"So you rode up here at full speed to warn them—"

"Naturally, I felt it to be my duty to prepare the ladies. You need not think I enjoyed it. A sad, distasteful duty. Excellent Madeira, this, by the way."

"Did you see Granville here?"

"Now, Sam, you don't want to see poor Marcus swing, do you?"

Captain Fergus coloured hotly. "If he's guilty of murder, I do."

"Well—h'm. So do I, if he is. Only thing is, he's not."

"You had better let a jury be the best judge of that, Mr. Thurlough."

"Oh, stow it, Sam. You know you'd be delighted if Marcus got away."

"My personal feelings do not enter into it," said Captain Fergus stiffly. "What do you think my colonel would say if I came back without my prisoner? He would suppose I fell down on my duty, that I let him go."

"No such thing. We'll vouch for you, Sam. In any case," Mr. Thurlough added, so convincingly that both the ladies gazed at him openmouthed, "ten to one Marcus is upstairs. That's where he was a minute ago."

"Was he?" demanded the captain. "How do you know?"

"Why, that's what Cudjoe said when I came in," embroidered Mr. Thurlough easily. He had after all a lifetime of lying to his womenfolk behind him, Marina reflected. "I asked for the master, naturally, and Cudjoe said he was sure he would be downstairs shortly—he was just changing out of his riding dress. Ah, here is Cudjoe. He'll vouch for what I say. That's right, is it not, Cudjoe? Mr. Granville is just changing out of his riding dress."

Cudjoe did not take the hint. He stood straight, his

eyes rolling, the toes of his large bare feet curling in distress.

"No, sir!" he declared. "Massa Granville, he not changing out of he riding dress. He in he riding dress."

"Well, never mind that," cried Captain Fergus. "Where is your master? To the devil with his dress!"

Cudjoe shook his large round head with an appearance of regret. "Me know, sir. Massa Granville not in he room. Choke, he no see Massa Granville since second breakfast, sir."

"What! He's out, then?"

"No, sir. Massa Granville, he in."

"Don't bandy words with me, fellow. What the deuce do you mean?"

"Fergus, don't get so heated, man. It don't answer in this climate—"

"Quiet, Thurlough. Now, Cudjoe or whatever may be your name, again I ask you—where is your master?"

Cudjoe gazed about the room with an air of having suddenly remembered something.

"Massa in here, sir," he announced with simple certainty. "Me see Massa come in here, some while ago. He not come out."

Captain Fergus was not slow. His handsome face contorted; he cast a glance of agonized loathing at Mr. Thurlough, and strode to the window. Marina caught Cudjoe's rolling eye. He did nothing so obvious as to wink at her, but she had difficulty in controlling an urge to giggle at the expression of complicity he briefly shared with her.

Captain Fergus screamed a command at his men, and followed Mr. Granville's route, over the windowsill and across the garden. Cudjoe solemnly collected the empty glasses and removed the tray. In a few moments the captain was back, leaning furiously in the room.

"The sloop is gone!" he announced. "I suppose you'll say that's news to you? Damn you, Thurlough, how could you serve me such a turn?"

"How could you expect me not to?" murmured Mr.

245

Thurlough, draining his glass. "Well, ladies, daresay you'll wish to be alone. Best be getting home. Blanche will want to know—not that Marcus is any concern of hers, he made that clear enough last night. But she'll be interested, certainly. Might even think she's well out of it," he added, brightening.

He took his leave and rode away while Captain Fergus was dividing up his company, as Mr. Granville had predicted: one lot to return with himself and the evil tidings to Fort Charles, the rest to remain on guard duty under Sergeant Plummer in case, as he said, the wanted man returned, but also for Marina's protection.

"Oh, dear," sighed Miss Derwent as a sudden rumble of thunder presaged the arrival of the storm. "I hope the change in weather does not put off Mr. Singleton. If ever I needed the comfort of his presence, 'tis tonight!"

But Mr. Singleton, gloomy but faithful, duly presented himself at the appointed hour. Marina had already observed that he was orderly and fastidious in his dress, but now on closer inspection she could see that he lacked the care of a concerned woman in his life. The cuffs of his shirt were threadbare, there was a button almost off his coat, and his boots, though well polished, were old and cracked.

"Oh, Mr. Singleton," cried Miss Derwent as he was announced into the drawing room, "we have had such doings here as I'd swear you never would believe!"

"I've heard some of them, I think," he said in his deep, sad voice, "that Crick was murdered, and that Granville is suspected, and made off in his boat. Pray accept my condolences, ma'am."

"On what? I am delighted that Marcus escaped before he could be arrested."

"Worst thing he could have done," declared Mr. Singleton mournfully. "Makes him look guilty, you see. Just what the murderer hoped for, no doubt."

"Then you don't think he is guilty? Mr. Singleton, I knew I could rely on you."

"Fact of the matter is, ma'am, that Granville took it very personally when Alfred drowned. Swore to me that the *Otaheite* had been deliberately wrecked. Swore too he would uncover what was behind it. Then, not long ago, he discovered Julia had almost certainly been murdered by her lover because she was too near guessing the truth herself—"

"No—no!"

"Don't distress yourself, ma'am. Julia has been dead for months—the manner of it can make little difference now. And for myself"—he sighed—"I should have thought it easier to live with the notion of her having been murdered than with that of her having taken her own life in despair."

"Perhaps you are right." Miss Derwent stared down at her hands. "But are you saying she must have guessed the identity of the man behind the wrecking?"

"She recognized that fob of Alfred's on her lover's watch chain, so Granville told me—she mentioned it in her journal, it seems. She knew it because it was the one Alfred won off Granville—the one with the ruby in it. Alfred wore it always. When I received his body, there was nothing left of value on it. The wreck and all the victims had been stripped. The inference is that Miss Julia's friend was one of the wreckers, very probably their leader. And if she were rash enough to question him about the fob . . ."

"Her lover might have bought the jewel, in all good faith."

"From where? Someone like Elijah? Precious little good faith about such a transaction, ma'am."

"From Flete's shop," Marina suggested.

"At Granville's suggestion, I asked Flete about it, and he assured me it never passed through his shop."

"And can you trust Mr. Flete?" Miss Derwent quickly asked. "Everyone supposed that it was he who was meeting Julia."

"Deuced hard to know whom you can trust," Mr. Singleton agreed. "Everybody capable of everything, under provocation, so my old father used to say. Nicest fellows have been villains. Wives always being astonished by husbands' lies and deceit. Hard to say a person will never do a certain thing. Fact is, he might."

"Julia might have been so horrified at the discovery, she killed herself?" Miss Derwent suggested.

"There were bruises on her arms," Marina told her. "Rosett saw them. Rosett is certain Julia was thrown over the cliff."

"I never thought that suicide seemed like her," Miss Derwent agreed. "But that does not tell us why Crick was killed and the suspicion of it meant to rest on Flete."

"Crick was indulging in the dangerous game of blackmailing a murderer, no doubt. As for Flete being left to carry the blame, does it not occur to you that Flete is known to have an enemy here? I have never believed it was Granville who caused Flete to leave Maroon—but someone did."

"Dinner is served, mistress," Cudjoe announced.

It was an excellent dinner, of fried conch, black-crab pepper pot, mutton pies, and orange custards, with a centerpiece of shoulder of wild boar, shot on Great Mountain, with forced-meat balls and sea-grape jelly; but as the wind rattled the shutters and the rain passed by in torrents, Marina's thoughts were with Mr. Granville. How was his boat riding the storm? And what ration of hard biscuit or salt meat formed his lonely dinner tonight?

"Marcus will be as snug as you could wish," said Miss Derwent, interpreting Marina's unconscious sigh. "He has a natural talent for it. He knows all these islets and cays from his pirate-hunting days, and built huts on many of them, as a boy. Ten to one he'll be warming himself at a good fire in some cave, roasting a goat kid or a boar as fine as this; or he'll have fallen in with a band of woodcutters and be sharing their stew in a stick hut. Two things are certain: he will survive, and the Militia will never find him."

Rinsing her fingers in the bowl Toney had just placed before her, Miss Derwent explained to Mr. Singleton,

"My niece and Mr. Granville are betrothed, though we cannot of course announce it yet."

"Indeed?" he said gloomily, with no appearance of surprise. "Well, Miss Marina, I am sure I wish you very happy."

Miss Derwent rose. "And I am sure they will be happy—when all this nonsense has blown over. We will leave you to your brandy, sir. You will find us in the drawing room, when you are ready."

The drawing room felt stuffy with the shutters closed.

"Can you keep a secret?" Miss Derwent asked suddenly, while Marina was still frowning over a map of the Antillan group.

"Why, yes, I believe I can. Certainly, if it has to do with Mr. Granville."

"Then you may expect to hear from him, my dear. He told me not to speak of it, but I happen to know that he has taken pigeons with him. He promised to let me know how he went on, from time to time."

"Pigeons," repeated Marina faintly. She remembered the question she had forgotten to ask Rosett. "How long has Mr. Granville been keeping pigeons, ma'am?"

But at that very moment Mr. Singleton, having finished his glass of brandy, and availed himself of the chamber pot in the sideboard, chose to join the ladies. Miss Derwent's face lit up and Marina recollected that the visitor must be given an opportunity to propose to her. Half relieved by the interruption, she begged permission to retire as soon as she had drunk her tea.

"Oh, are you off already?" asked Mr. Singleton, pulling out his watch. "Very wise."

Marina fled before he could say he was about to leave himself. She passed Sergeant Plummer, doggedly sitting in the hall, and found another three militiamen upstairs, playing cards on a small table in the gallery. As she entered her room, Rosett stood up, and Marina could hear the tramp of marching feet below her window.

"Have those men been doing sentry duty in the

249

rain?" she asked, pushing open the shutter and staring down into the dark wet garden, illuminated only by the still-flaring torches which Cudjoe had set by the front door to welcome the visitor.

"No, sir!" replied Rosett emphatically. "Massa done sail away—why for dey goin' get wet?"

"They are supposed to be protecting me," Marina explained.

Rosett's eyes slid sideways. "It a dark night, missy. De moon, she dere, but dem cloud too much for her." She put her hand to her turban and pulled out a small screw of paper. Staring down at it, she said hesitantly, "I done hear somet'ing in de kitchen, missy. Dat Cudjoe, he say you and de massa going get yourselves married."

Marina smiled. Suddenly she felt as if she were going to explode with happiness, burst apart in a thousand directions. "Yes, Rosett," she vowed, "we will be married—one of these days."

"Dat good—you be mistress den, and Mistress Derwent, she go to Indigo, I t'ink."

"Perhaps, Rosett. Nothing is settled yet. What do you have there? Is that paper for me?"

Rosett nodded. She looked carefully about the room before handing the paper to Marina, her eyes rolling.

Marina stared at it. "Where did you get this, Rosett?"

"Dat Hop-Joe. He waiting under de man-genip tree."

Marina raised her eyebrows. She unfolded the paper, which was crumpled and very dirty. The message was brief. It read, "Come," and was signed, "M. G."

She stared at it, trying to quell the excitement which threatened to prevent her thinking clearly. Presumably Hop-Joe knew where she was to go. But could she be sure this message really came from Marcus? On the other hand, if it did, if he was in need and she ignored it—no, she could not ignore it.

She showed it to Rosett. "Does this look like Mr. Granville's writing?"

Rosett shook her head. "Me no read, missy."

"It seems to be from Mr. Granville, asking me to come."

Rosett looked puzzled. "He sailed downwind, cross channel, missy."

"I know. But he could have come back after dark, to Sandy Harbour, perhaps. I think I shall have to go and talk to Hop-Joe. But how can I get out of the house, with soldiers everywhere?"

It was strange, she thought, that Marcus should ask her to come when he had requested a guard for her. Had something happened to make him change his plans? Was it possible that he wanted her to lead the Militia to him? Or did he trust her ingenuity to throw them off the scent?

She stared thoughtfully at Rosett. "Do the soldiers leave you alone?" she asked. "If I changed clothes with you, could I get past them?"

Once her initial astonishment had been overcome, Rosett entered with some enthusiasm into the scheme. She undressed, giggling, and put on Marina's night rail, promising to take her place in the bed as soon as the door closed behind Marina. Meanwhile Marina had stripped to her shift and now began to put on Rosett's clothes. Rosett tied the turban over Marina's bright hair, and helped her concoct a vile mixture of ink and oil and blacking to dye her hands and face and her bare feet. The end result, Marina thought, might pass in a dim light, but the hall where Sergeant Plummer sat was well appointed with branching candelabra. After some thought, she took a shawl and threw it over her head. Fortunately, Cudjoe had brought refreshment to Sergeant Plummer, a tall pink glass of it, sprinkled with nutmeg; and the sergeant raised this glass in a mocking toast to Marina as she came off the last stair. She turned away, toward the passage, humping her shoulder against him, and twitching forward Rosett's shawl in a gesture of disdain. The sergeant muttered something, but he had had a long day, and did not pursue her.

Marina hurried through the side door into the night. Down between the tall chick-peas she hastened on her bare feet, and past the tania patch. The moon was still obscured by ragged clouds high overhead, and few stars were visible, but at least it was not raining. Something, probably a rat, rustled high in one of the coconut palms that, imported long since by the Spanish, were doing so well in the West Indian islands; and then she saw a man waiting with mules beyond the old bread oven, under the great genip tree, its two main limbs rearing up into a mass of foliage.

He saw her at the same time, in the faint lantern light seeping from the kitchen windows, and sprang up on his wooden crutch.

"Hop-Joe," she murmured, glad that the light was too poor for him to be able to make out the details of her disguise. "I have your message. Who sent you with it?"

"A boy, missy. Me not know he. He say, man tell he, give Miss Marina dis scrip' and bring she to Sandy Harbour. He done give me a shilling for it, and a next one promised— I glad for it, missy. Times are hard, dem."

He turned, holding his crutch, and leaned his arms across the bony spine of the nearest mule. Then with an agile leap he hopped up on its back.

Marina bit her lip, and then regretted it as she tasted the dye she and Rosett had concocted for her face. "Do you know who awaits me in Sandy Harbour?" she asked hesitantly.

Hop-Joe shrugged. "Me know, missy."

Marina wiped some of the dye off her face on the end of her shawl, took the fraying rein from Hop-Joe's hand, put her foot in the rope's end which served as a stirrup, and mounted the second mule.

Hop-Joe nudged his mount with a bare heel, and trotted off into the darkness.

Marina took a deep breath of the warm night air and followed him.

When they reached the mule track she could not

252

help but think of Mr. Flete struggling up it with Crick's body; sea-stained, sweating with the fear of discovery, scratching his bare hands among the thorns. What had possessed the usually immaculate and self-contained Mr. Flete? Had it been the thought of revenge on Mr. Granville which had spurred him on, or did he really believe he would be hanged if he had left the body where he found it? Or again, had he murdered Crick, after all, and had he hoped that the appearance of suicide would be taken at its face value?

"We here, missy. You go down by sea-grape tree, and wait."

Marina reined in, and stared at the faint pale sweep of sand before her, lapped by the sea. Only the water moved, and the feathery crabs, running lightly about the shore. Dark pools of shadow gradually revealed themselves to her as boats, drawn up out of the water for the night. No one seemed to be about. It was not late, but the inhabitants of Sandy Harbour rose before dawn, Marina reminded herself, and were accustomed to shut themselves up tightly in their homes soon after sunset.

She slipped her bare feet out of the makeshift stirrups and dismounted, handing the rein to Hop-Joe with a word of thanks. Then she began to walk with increasing reluctance toward the dark group of straggling broad-leaved sea-grape trees, which looked as if not one man but an army might be waiting there, so limblike were the swaying branches, so full of whispering shadows the trembling depths of the little copse.

She reached the nearest tree and paused under the rustling leaves, her back to the wind. A little alien scratching sound made the hairs rise on her neck, but she traced it to somewhere near her feet, and straining her eyes, she saw a hermit crab painfully dragging a whelk shell over an outcrop of dead coral. She swallowed nervously, and found her throat was still quite sore. It was, she reflected, exactly a week since the ill-fated picnic at Maroon. . . .

She stepped down onto the beach. The sand was

fine, firm under the loose drift on top, and cool to her bare feet. She bent her head to duck beneath a branch and in the same instant someone blundered into her.

At once something was forced over her head, an earthy sack, and as she struggled cords were trussed around her so tightly that she was helpless. She cried out but her cries were muffled, and Hop-Joe had long since ridden away.

Then she felt herself heaved up, lifted onto her assailant's shoulder, and hung there, dry-mouthed and breathless, while he strode away with her. The sudden splash of water startled her. He was wading into the sea, deeper and deeper. Her legs were soaked, the water must have been above his waist when he stopped and raised her with his hands, bundling her aboard some kind of small craft which rocked as her abductor followed her in over the side.

She lay immobile on the hard wooden ribs of the vessel, trying to control her gasping the better to hear what she soon recognized as the familiar sounds of a small boat being made ready for sailing.

All too soon she heard the rattle of chain, and the clanking as the anchor came aboard. Then the spars creaked, the sail flapped as it filled, the hull tipped, pressing her more painfully against the frames, and the voyage began—into the unknown.

19

Very little air was able to seep among the closely woven strands of sacking. Marina came near to losing her self-control as she gasped in what there was to breathe, until she found that she could nibble at the hessian fibers and with time and patience could hope to make a hole through which to gulp the air she craved.

Biting the earthy-tasting strands was disgusting work, however, so Marina encouraged her thoughts to roam, even though they tended to travel down disquieting paths. Could it possibly be Marcus Granville who had abducted her? she found herself wondering. Had his love been a pretense? For if he loved her, surely he would not have wanted her to suffer a moment's fear. But perhaps he had commissioned someone else to bring her to him, and that man had misinterpreted his instructions. But no, she told herself firmly. Her capture could be nothing to do with him, for he had left her under guard at Tamarind. It was a far more likely supposition, though scarcely a comforting one, that it was the murderer, the wrecker's king, who had lured her out of her place of safety with the intention presumably of killing her because, like Julia, she knew and guessed too much.

Marina wrenched her thoughts back into order. It was too dangerous after all to let herself speculate. It was better to remain strictly in the present, odious though that might be—and she bit sharply at the sacking.

After some time she had achieved a little hole, and paused to draw in some grateful but cautious breaths. The boat was heeling more steeply now, she realized. They were beating into the wind, going up channel: because she remembered that the wind had shifted to the east this evening—she could recall it blowing her hair forward when she was standing by the sea-grape trees. Up channel might mean to Great or Little St. George's—and perhaps a rendezvous with Marcus Granville after all.

Marina began to nibble again at the edges of the hole which she had made. At last it was large enough for her to get an eye to it so that she was able to see out. But the view was limited and the light at first was dim. All she was able to discern was the line of the boom above her and the dark shape of a taut mainsail. She moved her hips and shoulders cautiously, inch by inch, until she was lying on her side. From that position she could see that she was sharing the hull with a litter of boxes and crates. For an instant her hopes flared high, for she had seen just such an assorted cargo being carried to the *Dolphin* only that morning. But then she remembered that the *Dolphin* had a cutter rig and was half-decked, whereas a watery gleam of moonlight through the overcast showed her that this was a simpler, rougher boat, with one patched foresail—the *Sea Hawk* for a certainty. And if the boat was the *Sea Hawk*, then Elijah was very probably the person who had abducted her.

Lying very still, so as not to alert him by a movement, Marina shouted, "Help!" and steeled herself for a kick or a blow.

There was no response, however, not so much as the squawk of a protesting hen. Feeling remarkably foolish, Marina called out again, still half expecting a rough voice to answer her, or the toe of a boot to crash against her ribs for her presumption. But no such retribution came, so she judged she was safe in assuming that Elijah was indeed her captor, and that he was sailing single-handed. If that were so, then as

256

long as the boat was driving to windward, he would be fully occupied, Marina considered. Trusting that her assumptions were correct, she began to wriggle cautiously toward the nearest crate, some eighteen uncomfortable inches away.

As soon as she had achieved her immediate objective, she began to search for a protruding nail, and since her hands were tied, she was obliged to carry out the search with her tongue. The wood was rough, and she proceeded tentatively, careful not to pick up a splinter. The crate was clumsily built and smelled of hens, but if it was a hen coop it was certainly empty. Elijah must be planning to return by morning then, in order to feed his fowls, she reflected, if he had not troubled to take them with him ... but before she could pursue this thought, her exploring tongue had encountered a nail protruding from a plank.

Now her task was to turn herself until one of the cords which bound her was in a position to be rubbed against the nail. This was not easy. Once she had turned her back on the hen coop, it seemed impossible to find the nail. But in the middle of her struggles the *Sea Hawk* went about with a rattle of her stiff canvas and a slamming of her heavy spars, and Marina found that the sudden lurch had placed her almost exactly where she wished to be. Then began the long, tedious, tiring process of fraying the cord against the nail. She was afraid that the rhythmic movement might attract Elijah's attention, and though the sounds she made were of no consequence, yet still they served to wear her nerves faster than her bonds.

She was resting when she became aware that the night had darkened suddenly. At the same time the wind rose swiftly, first whistling, then screaming through the rigging. All at once Elijah launched himself toward the mast and began to claw down the mainsail with frantic haste, terrifying Marina by his air of desperation, helpless as she was to aid him or to save herself.

A squall struck, the boat heeled violently, the foresail tore and then ripped through with a terrifying crack. In a few moments it had flapped itself to pieces, the grey rags spinning away to be instantly swallowed by the howling darkness of the storm.

With no hand at the tiller, the *Sea Hawk* had come up into the wind. It wallowed in the heavy seas with water splashing in faster than Elijah could bail it out. Marina recalled the overturning lifeboats of the *Carib Queen*. Conscious of an overwhelming urge to live, she flung herself against the crate and sawed at her bonds with renewed energy. As she did so, she could hear a wild hissing above all the other frightening sounds. An instant later a rainstorm had engulfed the little sloop.

As suddenly as it had started, the rain stopped. The *Sea Hawk* rolled sluggishly, sending the water lapping over Marina. Elijah seemed to be bailing for a long time before he threw down the calabash with a grunt and went forward to take in the remains of the foresail. He came back to stand by the mast and paused, his hand on the halyard, staring down at Marina. She hardly dared to breathe, but when he nudged her with his toe she flinched, letting out a little gasp of fright. Elijah grunted and turned away to raise the gaff; evidently he had merely wished to assure himself she was still alive and had not drowned in the last half-hour.

With the mainsail raised, the *Sea Hawk* heeled gently and sailed on north, Marina thought, or northeast—toward Damnation Reef. But what could Elijah want with her out there? Did he suspect her of stealing his lost hoard on the sandspit, and did he hope she would lead him to it? But it was of no use to conjecture, for what went on in Elijah's mind was beyond speculation, and she could feel the bond wearing thin. Presently it snapped, and she began to work the circulation painfully back into her cramped fingers. After all, she reflected, Elijah had been brought up by a witchwoman from Martinique, whose livelihood depended, one might say, upon being mysterious; brought up in a world of superstition and fear and magic spells, no sound, no speech—what communication would there have been for Elijah? He had learned by example to fish, and to handle a boat, to look after chickens, and breed fighting cocks—and pigeons, perhaps. But someone had taken the trouble to see further into his opaque mind than this. Someone had taught him things, had widened the horizons of that inner world. Someone in a word had bribed him in some special fashion to obey. Perhaps the bribe had merely been one of interest in Elijah, whom most people either mocked or left alone. Perhaps he had basked in that person's attention, had drunk in the knowledge he was offered, finding such satisfaction in it that he would be prepared to lay down his life unquestioningly to win that man's approval.

Marina sighed. She sawed and strained against the last of her bonds, and suddenly it parted. She lay, thankful but exhausted. If it had not been for the discomfort of the timber frames beneath her, she believed she would have slept. As it was, she rested, stirring only occasionally to try with little movements to work the stiffness out of her limbs. She wondered what time it was. Ten? Eleven? And when would the moon set, three or four nights before the full? Not for several hours, she thought, catching a glimpse of it riding among the clouds high overhead. Too long to be of help to her, for if she had any chance of escaping from Elijah out there among the reefs, she would need darkness to shield her; and now that the rain had passed, the lopsided moon seemed to shine more brilliantly every minute, paling the stars. But when she moved her head to face the wind, Marina saw more clouds building up on the eastern horizon and realized with mingled feelings of relief and apprehension that they had not done with storms this night.

Conserving her energy, Marina tried to doze. She had almost succeeded when Elijah made a strange rough sound, between a cough and a grunt. Twisting carefully toward him, Marina saw that he was twisted over the tiller, looking back toward the islands. What had he seen? Another vessel? Her heart thundered in sudden hope. Perhaps it was the *Pelican*, with the Militia coming to her rescue. Or it could even be the *Dolphin*, she told herself, if Marcus had been hiding in Little St. George's, perhaps, and had chanced to see Elijah sailing past.

Unable to bear the uncertainty, she sat up and took a swift glance at the heaving sea astern of the *Sea Hawk*. There it was—a narrow triangle of sail. It was too small for the *Pelican*, certainly; but it could be the *Dolphin*, she told herself, dropping down again upon the hard ribs of the boat. It was a sloop, she thought, and of about the *Dolphin*'s size; but her speculations were interrupted by an awareness of a difference in the behaviour of the *Sea Hawk*, and in the sound and pattern of the sea. They were nearing the reefs—she could hear breaking water.

The *Sea Hawk* began to pitch awkwardly and the sound of the crashing waves became almost unbearably alarming until the boat suddenly seemed to shoot out of the turbulence into calmer waters, where Elijah turned the boat into the wind and ran forward to drop the anchor and let down the sail.

Then above the raging of the seas against the Reef and the increasing wind, Marina heard the confused sounds of another boat coming up to anchor with flapping sails and rattling chain.

Someone shouted, the words snatched away by the wind. The tone was tantalizingly familiar to Marina, but she could not place it; and Elijah, busily engaged in putting his own boat in order, did not seem to be aware of the new arrival until, whether by accident or design, it actually bumped into the *Sea Hawk*.

The other boat was right alongside, and Marina tensed herself for action, coiled beneath her sacking. She heard a voice raised in fury—suddenly she recognized it as that of Mr. Flete.

His normally cultured, measured tones barely articulate, Mr. Flete sprang into the *Sea Hawk* and grappled with Elijah, who responded quickly to the attack and began to fight with hands and feet, both men tripping over ropes and spars, up and down the rocking boat. Marina, unable to see much of what was taking place, was trodden on three times, but she bit her lip to restrain her cries, judging it safer to lie still and pray for speedy deliverance than to jump up and betray her freedom from the bonds that had so recently confined her.

Suddenly the air was rent by a ghastly and inhuman cry, immediately followed by a heavy splash.

"Marina?" shouted Mr. Flete. A light rain began to fall. Marina realized that it was now completely dark. She wondered whether to announce her presence or stay still.

"Where are you, Marina?" Flete cried, fumbling among the empty hen coops. "Elijah will be climbing back aboard at any moment," he pleaded. "Call out if you are able—"

There was a solid sickening sound, and a thumping crash.

The rain began to come down in earnest. Marina found she was shivering with cold and terror, her teeth chattering. A heavy footstep rocked the boat. Someone bent over her. Hands fumbled for her in the dark. She lay limp and felt herself roughly seized. The grip tightened, lifting her, and then she was thrown with a sudden rush of air—into the sea.

She hit the water with an agonizing crash. Gradually she realized that she was alive, winded, with a burning in her chest, and sinking like a stone. She struggled to free herself from the sacking, thinking of the inevitable and ghastly death that would have been hers if she had not previously contrived to loose her bonds.

She felt herself coming up toward the surface, and began to pull the sack over her head. As she raised her arms she started to sink again before she had completely rid herself of it, but then she kicked out more strongly, tore the last of the hated sacking off her face, and came up into the rain, gasping.

She trod water—which was surprisingly warm in contrast to the rain—forced herself to ignore the discomfort of her bruised skin, which was still stinging from the impact, and tried to marshal her thoughts in order to assess her situation.

Flete had attacked Elijah, so presumably he had come to rescue her. But he lay either dead or stunned in the *Sea Hawk,* whose bulk loomed barely visible above her. And also aboard with him was his assailant, a murderer who thought he had destroyed Marina too. No sound came from the other boat, but there might be somebody aboard it. And Flete had thrown Elijah into the sea . . . but Elijah, she remembered, could not swim.

Marina swam in a slow circle, straining her eyes to make sure that Elijah was not still struggling in the sea. But all was quiet in the lagoon, the only sound in this still center of Damnation Reef coming from the water lapping about the two sloops rocking at anchor. A calm lagoon . . . it reminded her of the dreadful night of shipwreck, and the times she had swum back and forth in similar protected waters—and how she had brushed against the body of a drowned sailor then.

As her night vision improved, Marina realized there was some large shape rearing up against the sky a good way off, where the waves surged and broke against the Reef. Could it be the hulk of the *Carib Queen?* Was she actually in the same lagoon? But it did not matter, for whatever that dark thing was, whether rock or wreck, it offered her only hope of sanctuary, Marina realized. If she could reach it unseen, while the moon was dark, then she might hide in safety there—for her unknown assailant must surely believe her to be drowned.

She began to swim steadily without splashing toward the great dark shape. Her teeth were set, for she was very tired and her body hurt in a thousand places. She tried not to think of Elijah drowning, or of the big

262

fish that might be attracted by his corpse, but concentrated her energies on swimming smoothly and as swiftly as possible while the darkness lasted, toward the hiding place ahead.

She was halfway to her objective when the rain stopped. The wind blew steadily, and then, with no more warning than a faint luminous glow in sky and sea, the flying clouds were torn apart and Damnation Reef was bathed in light from the declining moon.

Marina was almost sure in that first glance that her landfall was the *Carib Queen*, though the wreck was much lower in the water than she remembered it, had lost its masts and was somehow altered in shape, but her relief was lost in her anxiety at the prospect of being seen by the man on the *Sea Hawk*. She stopped swimming—but too late. There came a splash behind her and she turned her head to see a figure lowering himself off the sloop onto a raft, an oar in one hand. As she stared he dropped down to lie prone on the planks, pushed himself away from the *Sea Hawk*'s hull, and began to paddle in her direction.

Forcing herself into action again, Marina swam as fast as she was able, careless now of noise and movement. But her occasional backward glances showed that her pursuer was gaining on her with every stroke. If he reached her, she was certain that he would hit her with the oar until she sank. Afterwards he would return to the *Sea Hawk* to dispose of Mr. Flete before sailing away. Then, if their bodies were ever found, it would be assumed that Flete was the master wrecker, that he had killed Marina, and that he and Elijah had fought to the death.

Her only chance, she thought—and Flete's, if he were still alive—was that the man on the raft, like Elijah, presumably could not swim. When he caught up with her she would have to try to tip him into the water, for it now seemed impossible for her to reach the wreck ahead of him. She was almost exhausted and she could hear the man paddling strongly, concentrating on getting as much speed as he could out of the raft without upsetting it, intent upon overtaking her before she reached the looming hulk.

Then like a curtain sweeping across the stage at the play's end, dark clouds rushed across the moon, leaving Marina struggling in black sea, gasping black air, relieved to be invisible, but aware of a new fear. How could she tell her direction, with nothing to guide her? What if she lost her way and swam in circles until exhaustion pulled her down? It would not take much longer, she felt. Already she was swallowing water, misjudging the height of the waves; and her limbs felt so heavy it was a wonder that she did not sink. The sustained effort of undoing her bonds had tired her, and now it was only the fear of death which enabled her to struggle on, however feebly.

Timor mortis conturbat me. The phrase echoed in her head as she paddled on in time with it, toward where she thought she had last seen the *Carib Queen.* There came an instant's half-instinctive warning that something was ahead of her, but before she could pull back her flailing arm Marina's hand crashed against wood, rough splintered wood, harsh with barnacles. It must surely be the wreck, and she began to sob with thankfulness. But at any moment the moon might pierce the storm clouds to betray her presence. She could not allow herself to relax too soon. She must make her way along the hull toward the stern, which was low in the water, and where she had the best chance of being able to board the shuddering wreck.

She was trembling badly. Her hands fumbled and slipped along the planking, her clothes, light as they were, dragged and impeded her; but somehow she made her way to the vessel's stern. Her feet could find no purchase under water. The main part of the *Carib Queen* lay on the coral but the stern hung over water which was out of Marina's depth, and for the first time she began to doubt her ability to climb aboard. Her searching hand caught in a split, a vertical split running down the transom where the sternpost had pulled away. She pulled herself up with aching arms until she could get a foot into the gap, rested for a moment, and then struggled on again, driving splinters into her hands, tearing her clothes, but heaving herself out of the water inch by painful inch. She could see almost nothing, but her hand, feeling for the stern ports of the after cabin, encountered instead a gaping hole torn in the transom. Somehow she scrambled through it, slid across a fallen beam and slipped down to lie, gasping, within the ship at last.

Even here, the water lapped about her, rising and falling as the *Carib Queen* threshed and quivered, timbers squeaking and groaning, nothing staying still for a moment as though the ship and everything in her were horribly alive. But it was sanctuary, Marina reminded herself. Here was a chance to hide, here at least were weapons, pieces of wood, lengths of chain . . . but she must move while she was still able to do so, deeper into the heart of the disintegrating wreck.

She struggled to her knees, and then to her feet, hitting her head as she rose cautiously. She dashed the tears impatiently from her smarting eyes, and began to creep forward in the dark, her hands held out in front of her. She soon abandoned any idea of trying to envisage what she could recall of the design of the *Carib Queen*, for the wreck bore little relation to the ship she had once been. Fallen timbers barred the passages; cabin doors were swollen, bulging and immobile; great holes had been torn in the bulkheads; parts of the ship had subsided; water ran everywhere, now in this direction, now in that, rising sometimes to Marina's ankles, sometimes to her thighs. Blindly, Marina stumbled on, telling herself that it would have been a good deal worse if the Militia had not emptied the wreck, for then there would have been cargo scattered, barrels to stumble over, drifts of torn sails and tangled rigging to ensnare her. Yet after all she had enough to contend with, in the dark, and her own exhaustion, and the determination of the murderer who hunted her, besides the twisting and slipping of the rotting hulk as the waves continually lifted and dropped it on the grinding fangs of Damnation Reef.

Above the complaining fabric of the wreck as it released its splintered timbers to the relentless sea, above the slap and gurgle of the inner tide, Marina could now hear the sounds that she had dreaded, of inevitable pursuit. There came the splash and knock and squeak of stumbling feet, muttered curses, a body lurching, blundering, careless of the noise it made—though in truth it was impossible to tell from which direction it approached her. All was confusion in the busy nightmare darkness of the wreck, and Marina felt that she might well have been tottering in circles. . . .

Between one blink and the next, Marina saw a beam of light. It flashed and faded, then glowed again some way ahead. It was too yellow for moonlight, Marina thought, and the light was swinging; somewhere her enemy had found a lantern and tinderbox—or he had carried a tinderbox with him, more probably; and now with light he would surely be able to hunt her down unless she could find the perfect place to hide.

The beam faded, grew brighter, died, and bloomed again. It was coming closer and soon the light was bright enough to show Marina that she stood in a half-flooded cargo hold. The floor was slanting and seemed to be actually shifting underfoot where she was standing so that she had been forced to cling for support to the edge of some low-walled structure which, she now realized, was a bin to hold grain or flour. Several such bins were bolted to the sole beneath and seemed to offer the only hope of concealment in the hold. But Marina hesitated to climb into one, for there, if found, she would be trapped. She decided instead to crouch down where she was, using the bin as cover, so that she could retain her freedom of movement and creep around it as her enemy advanced.

She ducked as the sudden strengthening of the lantern glow announced his entrance. He came edging in between two fallen timbers, the lantern held low behind

266

him now and his shadow, awfully enlarged, darkening the hold ahead, rising, looming among the frames, seeming to hover like some mighty bird of prey—and then swooping as he raised the light.

Marina stared through a crack between two boards as the man hesitated, peering about him. A surge of water swelled about the bins and Marina realized there must be a hole under the water level in the ship's side, allowing every wave to enter directly into the hold, ebbing and flowing with the wind and tide. The new pressure of water caused new strains and the ship groaned.

The man turned, raising the lantern so that for the first time Marina could see his face.

He wore a black eye-patch.

20

The ship groaned.

A board creaked like a rusty hinge and a ripple of water rose along the sole until it was lapping at Marina's ankles. As it began to recede, Marcus Granville moved abruptly, sending a gleam of lantern sliding down the barrel of the pistol held in his right hand.

Then he stood still again, so still that it seemed as if he must surely hear the thundering of her heart which beat so loudly in Marina's ears.

Moments passed. Almost imperceptibly he turned his head from side to side, his single shadowed eye alert for any sign of life.

The ship sighed and shuddered. Mr. Granville began to move slowly forward, looking into each of the cargo bins as he passed, careful to keep his balance on the sloping boards, the lantern held high in his left hand, the pistol steady in his right.

Scarcely daring to breathe, Marina started to edge around the bin so that by the time he passed it, she would be crouched safely on the farther side. She became aware that the wind had strengthened again, masking the small sounds she made; and then something began to knock against the outside of the hull— Elijah's raft, perhaps. It was an eerie and distracting noise which seemed to demand investigation, like someone knocking on a door; and Marina's overtired and febrile brain plagued her with a horrifying image of all the drowned who had perished out there on Damnation Reef, craving admittance to the wreck....

And then, while Mr. Granville continued his inexorable approach, the world seemed to fall in upon Marina.

There was a crash behind her, a thunderous oath, and rough hands seized her, all in the same moment. An instant later, strong fingers were about her throat, fitting into bruises still painful from the last time those same large hands sought to strangle her.

Even as her heart leapt in shock and fear, Marina was conscious of a sense of joy that her assailant was not Mr. Granville, after all.

"Throw down that gun!" shouted a great voice above her head—the unmistakable booming tones of Dr. Sunderland.

Marina felt her head begin to spin, her knees sag under her. Dr. Sunderland! A series of pictures flashed through her mind: Dr. Sunderland, coming from Miss Dampier's deathbed with an air almost of satisfaction; Dr. Sunderland, riding his horse to victory, while others fell—and he the very man capable of training Elijah, whom he had encountered years ago in connection with wrecking at Sandy Harbour. Yes, Dr. Sunderland, a widower in suspicious circumstances, had all the qualities of the murderer she had been seeking. Ruthless, vain and powerful, he could well be Julia's idea of a king among men—and Dr. Sunderland had been badly shocked to find Crick's body hanging at Tamarind instead of lying where he left it, down at Spanish Wells.

"Throw the gun down, Granville," he cried again, "or else I kill this meddling girl at once."

Mr. Granville did not hesitate. With a gesture almost of contempt he tossed the pistol to the slanting floor, where it rattled and slid down to the edge of the lapping water.

Marina felt Dr. Sunderland relax. His fingers slightly eased their grip. She made herself breathe shallowly, instinctively trying to avoid drawing his attention to herself. But she could not repress a start when he spoke again, close to her ear.

"So this is where you chose to hide yourself, Granville," he boomed. "I thought as much when I saw you sailing in this direction some hours ago. But what have you done with your boat? I saw no sign of her when we sailed in."

"That is the *Dolphin* you can hear knocking against the hull," Mr. Granville calmly explained. "I have her warped alongside—but a fender must have slipped."

They sounded almost as if they were making conversation at a social gathering, Marina thought in wonder. Then she saw that Mr. Granville was standing tensed, his single eye roving from shadow to shadow. All at once she realized that he was trying to discover if the doctor had come alone, or if he had an accomplice with him. With Sunderland's hands about her neck, she could not speak—but if she acted, surely she could count on Granville to assist her.

She stared at the glistening slanting floor while she formulated something of a plan. Then she gathered up her strength, bending her back forward suddenly, and throwing her weight hard to the right.

For an instant she thought she had failed to undermine the doctor's balance. His fingers tightened and she was afraid he would strangle her before he fell. But then the instinct of self-preservation must have caused him to loose his grip as they tottered sideways together for a few steps before falling as one into the flooded portion of the hold.

She gasped a breath and shut her eyes as he clutched her shoulder and dragged her to him with one hand, throwing out his other arm as he splashed down into the water. She wriggled desperately, kicking at him, and felt Marcus Granville seize her hand and pull her from the doctor's grasp. He thrust her aside and she clung, dripping, to the cargo bin, shivering, her teeth chattering.

Mr. Granville set down the lantern and retrieved the gun, which he aimed at Dr. Sunderland.

"Stay in the water!" he called out. "Deeper yet—or I shoot."

Dr. Sunderland could swim, and very well, Marina noticed, for all that he had used Elijah's raft. He took two powerful strokes to the far side of the hold and turned to stare at the gun with bloodshot eyes.

"Don't shoot, for God's sake," he implored. "The blood . . ." and he threw a fearful glance over his shoulder toward the hole in the timbers that was letting in the sea.

"He's afraid of sharks," Marina cried in a hoarse, cracked voice. "Conscience has made a coward of him—and sharks could come in through that hole if they scented blood."

"Let me out of the water, Granville—"

"Not until I know all the truth. Tell me, Marina, was Elijah with him? How did you get here?"

"I had a note—I thought from you—" she answered between gasps. "It was a trick. Elijah brought me—we were alone on the *Sea Hawk*. He"—she gestured toward Sunderland—"followed in another boat with Mr. Flete. They came alongside—in the lagoon—and Flete jumped aboard. He fought Elijah—in the end he threw him overboard—Elijah cannot swim. . . . Then—it must have been the doctor who knocked Flete down. There was no one else out there, I think."

"No, no one else, I swear it, Granville. You are safe enough if you let me out. I'll tell you everything . . ."

"You will, indeed; and when your tale is done I'll let you out, but not before."

"Damn you, Granville—" Dr. Sunderland looked fearfully over his shoulder as a wave ran in through the hole, to slap echoing against the bins. "What do you want to know?"

"Let us begin with why you are here—and with my ward."

"I saw you sailing out . . . when you ran away, I had to act. There were three main objects to be accomplished." As he spoke, Dr. Sunderland turned continuously, his mind appearing to be more upon the possibility of sharks than on his narrative, which poured easily from his lips. "The destruction of yourself, since

I discovered from young Armistead this morning that you fancied you knew all the truth; the destruction of—that girl—who also knew more than I could allow; and above all, the implication of Flete."

"So that was why you brought Flete with you?"

"He had also to be destroyed, of course," the doctor explained, his eyes rolling toward the darkest corner of the hold. "At the same time, I had to make it seem as if it were he who was responsible for the wrecking, for killing your sister and the wretched Crick, and, tonight, your ward—"

"One moment," said Granville between his teeth. "Where's Flete now?"

"Unconscious, or dead, perhaps, on the *Sea Hawk*. It was a pretty plot," the doctor mused. "I devised it almost instantly, when I saw you making for the reefs."

"I hoped my action would inspire you to some further folly."

"No folly, sir! It was—almost perfect, in its way. I arranged for Elijah to abduct this girl and bring her here. I then roused up Flete and told him she'd been taken, and that I suspected you. Fired with righteous indignation, we set sail after the *Sea Hawk*, in Dr. Margery's boat, which I have often borrowed; hastening to the maiden's rescue, as Flete thought. My intention was to stun him and make it look as if the boom had hit his head by accident. I was going to leave Miss Marina's strangled body in Dr. Margery's boat with his . . . having already established Flete as a suspected strangler that day at Maroon. Then Elijah and I were going to find and finish you, young Granville, and sink your body and set the *Dolphin* adrift, before sailing back together in the *Sea Hawk*. Once at Sandy Harbour, I could slip home unnoticed by the hill paths . . . and wait in patience for Colonel Dawlish to piece it all together. He would suppose, of course, that you had fallen overboard . . . there is a risk of that when one is single-handed in foul weather, which is why I could not dispense with Flete until. I reached the lagoon. Would that I had! Unfortunately he, who had been

272

pretty well prostrated by seasickness for the better part of the voyage, became quite uncontrollable on spying the *Sea Hawk* on our arrival here, and had leapt aboard it before I could prevent him. By the time I'd finished anchoring, he had drowned Elijah. I followed him aboard the *Sea Hawk* and stunned him, thinking to continue with my plan ... but I must own that I was distracted by the loss of my henchman and impulsively tossed the girl overboard, instead of throttling her, as I had intended—"

Marina reflected that this mistake, no doubt, was the work of her guardian angel.

"I was just about to finish Flete," the doctor continued, still turning restlessly, "when I saw the wretched girl was swimming. Somehow she had contrived to get loose from her bonds. I knew I must get to her before she found you—I had guessed you were in hiding here—so I left Flete for the time being, and took the raft—"

"But why Flete?" demanded Mr. Granville. "Why take him as your scapegoat, when surely I would have done as well?"

The doctor stopped his paddling and stared. "You, Granville?" he said in a scathing tone. "Your estate was of no interest to me, sir. Oh, Tamarind is pleasant enough, and I'll not deny it had occurred to me that it would be convenient to be able to buy your slaves, when you were accounted for and the place came on the market—for slaves will soon be hard to come by, once this damnable Abolition Act's in force—but I'm insulted that you should suppose Tamarind to be the estate on which I'd set my heart. It has to be the best for me, you must understand."

"The best," Mr. Granville barely breathed the word. "You mean—"

"Maroon, of course. All that I have done these last few years has been with the object of acquiring that great house, and the fortune necessary to restore and run it."

"But your wife left you a great deal of money, so

273

I've heard. Why did you need to turn to wrecking? Above all, why did you set your mind on Julia's fortune too?"

It was a cry of agony, but the doctor smiled tolerantly. "Maroon was to be magnificent, you see. I knew the place would be insatiable, nothing would be too good for it, and I did not want to spend my life in debt like all the planters I know. The first time that I saw Maroon, I knew that it was made for me. It is the only great house in Antilla worthy of me—half a century it has been preparing to receive me—"

"It was you, then, who drove out Brandon Flete?"

"Of course. Let me out, Granville. My fingers are all wrinkled . . ."

"Not until I know it all. My God, so it was you who burned the crops, scattered the slaves, destroyed Flete's credit . . ."

"Ay, and to very little avail. Oh, I got him off the estate easily enough but he would not sell the place, which was my object. He was like a man obsessed . . . I had hoped he might kill himself, but he was stronger than I thought. He would not give way to despair but determined to work to reinstate himself, damn him. He sold off the furniture—each piece gone felt like a bitter blow to me! He sold the silver and the porcelain —I have bought back a good deal of it through the Company, of course, but I must have Maroon itself. Flete is not fit to own the place, he is letting it decay. You saw yourself how vandals had got in . . . it is intolerable! There was nothing for it but to kill him. It was difficult, it had to seem an accident, for once I bought the place I would be seen to have a motive—but he leads a charmed life, so it appears. I have set traps for him, over and over—"

"You cut the stiches of his saddle girths, at Mount Pleasant," Mr. Granville exclaimed. "And it was you, I suppose, who put the sandburs under my horse's saddle?"

"I did not want you to win the race," explained

Sunderland in a reasonable voice. "I have never liked you, sir. You always seemed to have too much."

"Was it to spite me that you set out to win Julia's heart—and her fortune, as you thought?"

"Not entirely, though that aspect of it was amusing. It was not the money either, for Esther Winceyman was due to inherit more; but when I realized young Julia had lost her heart to me, I decided to indulge her, for she would certainly have made a more gracious mistress of Maroon, and a more fitting mother for my children, than the frail Miss Winceyman, once I had tamed her. If I had known that she would lose her fortune on her marriage, however, I must confess that I would not have wasted my time upon her."

"And she would be still alive," said Mr. Granville grimly.

"I did not want to kill her," the doctor protested. "But when she saw a fob upon my watch chain that she recognized, and that could only have come from the wreck of the *Otaheite*, what else could I do? If only I had known that young Singleton had won it off you, Granville—but I thought he'd picked it up in St. Eustatius—he'd been there long enough and I'd never seen the thing before. It was a ruby—I have always had a weakness for rubies, you see. I have quite a collection of them in my private den at home. It was through buying rubies that I came to acquire the Trinket Trading Company," he added, his eyes fixed on the dark hole in the ship's side as he furtively paddled toward shallower water. "It was a useful business, once I became interested in wrecking."

"When did you begin to develop that interest?" demanded Mr. Granville.

"After the affair at Sandy Harbour. It struck me then that wrecking ships would be a way to make a quick fortune, for Maroon. I was progressing well with Elijah by that time, and shortly afterwards he took me out to explore the reefs, a storm blew up—and a wreck

275

fell right into our hands. The *Bosun Bird*—you remember it, perhaps?"

Talking easily, almost as if he was happy to share his secrets with them, Dr. Sunderland was still drifting inch by inch into the shallows.

"The pickings had to be disposed of, of course," he went on. "Flete and his shop provided the natural outlet, but unfortunately Flete is no fool. I had to acquire the Company in order to sell the goods to him. My idea was to use him until he was thoroughly implicated and let him hang for my crimes at last. Maroon would come onto the market then and I would be able to buy it and put the past behind me. I believe I would have done it too, but for that meddling Crick."

Marina edged closer to Mr. Granville. "Watch him," she murmured behind her hand.

"I am," he replied softly. "I am well aware that he has not yet given up hope of outwitting us. But I must hear as much as he will tell me." To Sunderland he said, "Crick, sir? You mean, I suppose, that he began to blackmail you?"

"Ay, together with the rest of the world. Ducheyne was his best victim, I fancy. Did you see him at Mount Pleasant t'other day? He must have had half the Admiral's prize money, I daresay, ever since he discovered Ducheyne's other, and illicit, family, down at the west end of Antilla . . ."

"And it was you, I suppose, who stole the Admiral's night telescope?"

"I borrowed it," the doctor corrected him with dignity. "I have one of my own, at home. But I needed it that night, to see if the *Lady Jane* were on the Reef. I knew Elijah was ashore, you see, so I could expect no word from him. If he had been out in his boat, he would have sent me a sign, carried by pigeon. If I received a paper marked with an X, that meant there was a wreck. If the X was circled, that signified there were no survivors and then I would make haste to join Elijah, using Margery's sloop, which he never seemed to miss. Of course, I took care to bribe old Neptune, his boat captain, to look the other way. If the weather was bad, Elijah would sail back to take me out. I don't care to sail alone except in fair conditions . . ."

"How did Crick find out about you?"

"Ah! Well, he knew that Elijah worked for the Trading Company, of course, for all the correspondence went through him, and when he saw Elijah collecting a crate of pigeons from my house the other day, when Crick was going to Mount Pleasant, it supplied him with the vital link he needed. But if I had not killed him, someone else would certainly have done so. Crick knew far too much for his own good . . ."

"Get back into the water, Sunderland!"

"You can't keep me here forever," cried the doctor. He looked cold.

"Only until I know it all, so the faster you tell me the truth, the sooner you will be able to get warm again. You decided to kill Crick, then, and let Flete swing for it?"

"Yes, but first I had to get rid of that girl." He glared across the shivering water at Marina. "Her death too had to go to Flete's account, and she knew even more than Crick. She had seen how the *Carib Queen* was wrecked, and she had been on the *Sea Hawk*. I was afraid she would have noticed not only the pigeon coops but also the sweeps and lanterns which Elijah used to lash to mast and bowsprit to make the *Sea Hawk* seem larger so that the lost ships would not hesitate to follow him—"

"So that's how it was done," exclaimed Marina.

"And a third lantern on the raft, towed behind. You did not guess it? The Dampier woman did, but she was easily disposed of—and would probably have succumbed to her fever in any case. I only hastened her end—and just in time, as Colonel Dawlish was on his way to take a statement from her when we all met in the shop that morning. You presented a harder and almost equally urgent problem, miss. Fortunately Granville's jealousy prevented the colonel from having the opportunity to begin to question you closely, as he no doubt would have liked to do, while you were at Mount Pleasant; but it was there that I made up my mind that I would have to finish you. You had the same facts as Miss Dampier to go upon; it was only a matter of time before the same conclusion occurred to you. Then you had heard from Julia just before I finished her—and you made some mention of having read her journal, that last night at Mount Pleasant. My resolution was strengthened when I heard that you had dug up Elijah's little hoard, foolish jackdaw that he is—or was. I had tried to warn him of the dangers of cupidity. . . . But it was when I heard you asking about the Trinket Trading Company that I knew I must not delay in silencing you, little as I wished to desecrate Maroon. I was within an instant of success when Granville blundered in on us." Dr. Sunderland relaxed his vigilant search of the dark waters to glance with hatred at the man who kept him there.

The *Dolphin* knocked again upon the hull. The wreck gave a long despairing shudder and Marina felt a sense of something slipping deep within the ship.

"Go on," cried Mr. Granville, "before this vessel sinks and drowns us all."

"Crick caught a glimpse of me hurrying out of the cellar," the doctor continued, staring at the widening rift in the ribs of the *Carib Queen*. "I knew he would not betray me so long as I was paying him, so I was able to arrange his end at my convenience. I killed him after the ball—but Flete came home too soon, before I had been able to find and destroy the note-book."

"You need only have searched the body," said Granville grimly. "It was in a pocket on a belt that Crick wore beneath his shirt. Flete found and hid it after he had hanged the body—so you attacked Mrs. Hungerford for nothing. Later, Miss Marina discovered it and sent it to O'Brien."

"Not before I had seen it, however," said the doctor, with an evil look. "She was fool enough to entrust it to

Elijah, whom I had trained to bring all things to me. I was able to tear out the pages which referred to me, but I did not know if she had read them. Meddlesome chit! When I threw her in tonight, bound as I thought, it was one of the sweetest moments of my life. But even there she escaped me, curse her!"

A tremendous gust of wind slammed the *Dolphin* hard against the wreck. A ripple of destruction ran through the *Carib Queen*. Beams shivered, planking gaped, and a whole symphony of new sounds struck up with water running and gurgling across the decks, loose timbers sliding, and the fabric of the hulk settling ever closer down on the coral among the turmoil of the breaking waves.

During the instant when their attention was distracted from him, Dr. Sunderland heaved himself out of the water and caught hold of a four-foot length of timber, which he raised menacingly above his head while advancing on Mr. Granville.

Marina stood petrified. Mr. Granville took careful aim, and pulled the trigger.

The gun did not fire.

21

The doctor gave a great shout of triumph at the realization that the powder had after all been damp.

He leapt forward just as Marcus Granville hurled the gun at him, grazing his temple. He stopped then, shaking his head in momentary bewilderment, giving Granville time to snatch up the lamp and seize Marina by the hand.

She forced her trembling limbs to move, hurrying with Mr. Granville the length of the sloping hold and up the splintering companionway, with Dr. Sunderland lurching behind them, impeded by his saturated clothing, snorting, swearing, and vowing vengeance in his forceful, resonant tones.

Even with Mr. Granville half dragging her, it was harder now to traverse the rapidly disintegrating wreck, Marina thought, struggling desperately to keep her feet as they splashed and slipped, crawled beneath fallen timbers, climbed and stumbled, while the doctor, rapidly recovering, began to gain on them, guided by the lantern light.

Suddenly a great blast of air buffeted the fugitives, flinging rain into their faces. Staring up in⁺o the wild night, Marina saw that the poop deck had half fallen in, blocking the way that she had come on entering the ship, and leaving a steep slide of planking open to the fury of the elements.

Marina cried out in despair, but Mr. Granville, grasping the hissing lantern with one hand, began to drag her with the other, up the slanting boards, while the rain deluged relentlessly upon them, blown almost sideways by the strength of the squall.

Dr. Sunderland was gaining on them. He was halfway up the slope behind them, still clutching the length of timber in his hand, when Mr. Granville turned and flung the lantern at him.

They heard him shout above the wind, and felt the concussion of his fall as the planking split beneath his weight. The glass of the lantern shattered as it rolled, and flames leapt out despite the rain, running over the spilled oil in wind-torn rags of light, fastening on the dry timber dropped by Dr. Sunderland, skipping the wet planks to spark along the splintered boards below, which had been sheltered from the storm. A heap of frayed tarred rope caught fire and Marina saw Dr. Sunderland stagger to his feet, circled by a ring of leaping flame, as Mr. Granville half dragged her up the last few feet of the listing poop and into the full force of the wind.

The rain beat into Marina's face, the wind lashed her with her streaming hair—but Mr. Granville's arm encircled her as he pulled her over the high stern of the ship, and she felt a resurgence of vitality at the exultant knowledge that their enemy had been outwitted, and she was protected by the man she loved.

Blinded by the storm, she found the jutting rail with her feet and edged round the transom to the starboard quarter where the stern of the *Carib Queen* still overhung the sea, and a dark heaving shape alongside revealed itself to be the little *Dolphin*.

"Feel for the lines!" cried Mr. Granville. "I have one—there should be another—"

"I've found a rope!" Marina cried above the howling of the wind in the *Dolphin*'s rigging, above the crashing of the now torrential rain which almost deafened her to the ominous roar beneath her feet as the fire caught hold below.

"Sunderland?" she screamed, fumbling with the soaking knot.

281

"His clothes are wet, he can get out. No time to be lost," Mr. Granville answered, heaving on another warp.

As Marina got her rope's end free, the wind snatched it out of her numbed grasp, and it was gone, snaking away into the night. She cried out in dismay but Granville caught her by the hand and jumped with her across a narrow gap onto the bucking half deck of the *Dolphin*.

Marina fell, but scrambled up and ran toward the mast. She found the main halyard and stood by to raise the gaff while Granville finished casting off. The gap widened and the cutter came up into the teeth of the wind. Marina heaved on the rope and slowly the mainsail began to rise, the salt-stiffened canvas cracking like a whip.

"Take the helm," cried Mr. Granville, seizing the halyard from her. Marina stumbled aft and grasped the tiller, holding the boat into the wind until the sail was up. Then Mr. Granville's hand fell on her own and the *Dolphin* heeled as he helmed her round behind the stern of the *Carib Queen*, before beginning to run down the narrow channel toward deeper water, between the two white tongues of foam which marked the passage.

Mr. Granville was preoccupied with his navigation, but Marina gazed back at the wreck, which was well alight, the flames leaping ever higher as the wind and the rain began to slacken. Suddenly a figure darted before the fire, a blackened silhouette performing a demented dance in the flickering light.

"Sunderland's on deck," she cried, dashing the streaming hair out of her eyes. "The fire is spreading. The heat must be intolerable—why does he not jump?"

"He cannot bring himself to do so yet—he fears the sharks too much."

"But he has the raft," she suddenly remembered.

Mr. Granville pulled her close.

"You let go the raft, my love," he told her.

Marina shuddered as full realization came. "You

282

mean—that was the rope I dropped? The raft was so close to the *Dolphin*? But—but if the ship's afire and he won't swim to his boat, we must go back!"

"Impossible. There is no room to beat up between those coral heads now that the wind has shifted northerly."

"But Mr. Flete," she cried, remembering. "He might be still alive!"

"I have not forgotten him. When I'm through these reefs I'll bring her up to lie off behind the sandspit. Thank God the wind's abating. As soon as it's light enough I'll cross the sandbar and swim out to the *Sea Hawk*."

Marina was silent. There seemed to be no alternative, yet she could not bear to think of Mr. Granville leaving her again. However, she had plenty to be thankful for, she reminded herself. And now the rain had stopped, the wind was falling light, and a spreading glow proclaimed the moon struggling free from a ragged layer of cloud, over to the west.

Mr. Granville jibed the *Dolphin* as they came out of the passage into the smoother swell of the open sea. The sail cracked over their heads as the boom swung across, and then for a few minutes they reached peacefully down the sparkling path toward the moon. Then, tightening his mainsheet, he steered for the sandspit, a close fetch. Once they were in the lee of the bar, Mr. Granville brought the *Dolphin* up into the wind and dropped his anchor, the chain rattling down into water streaked magically with phosphorescence. On the far side of the sandspit the two sloops were gently rocking in the wavelets of the lagoon, while beyond them the last of the *Carib Queen* flamed magnificently. Would it be a funeral pyre? Marina wondered; or would Dr. Sunderland find the courage to swim to one of the boats? Might he yet find freedom after all, and escape retribution for his crimes?

"I expect the *Pelican* at any time," remarked Mr. Granville, scanning the horizon, as if in answer to her thoughts. "I can't see her yet, but Dawlish promised me he'd send her—just in case my plan to lure out the villain worked." He began to kick off his buckled shoes. "I had best go now to Flete, while the moon's still up," he said. "If he still lives, he will have been soaked with all that rain and every minute may count with him, if we are to save him."

Marina was shaken by an unfamiliar storm of feeling. She found herself clinging to Mr. Granville as she had never clung, even to her father.

"Don't leave me!" she cried. "Don't go—I could not bear it!"

He smiled down at her, and her bones felt as if they were dissolving. "Never did I think to hear you say those words, my proud Marina. I have no wish to leave you, but you know where my duty lies."

"I'll come with you—"

"No, it would be too much for you, after all that you have done this night."

"I am a strong swimmer, and you may need help with Mr. Flete."

"I will sail the *Sea Hawk* round with him aboard. If he is still unconscious you can join us and we will leave the *Dolphin* here and sail the *Sea Hawk* back to Tamarind—" He broke off, staring over her shoulder.

"Look there, Marina, by the sandbar. Damn this eye! Tell me what you see."

She turned, brushing the wet hair off her face. Something was moving in the shallows on the far side of the sandspit, bobbing in the moon-flecked waters of the calm lagoon.

"It's—a man, I think—on some kind of box—a hen coop, perhaps."

Holding her breath, Marina watched as the strange combination reached the shore, and a man stood gradually upright, and began to stagger over the curve of sand toward them.

"It's Flete, thank God," said Mr. Granville, dropping his hands from Marina's shoulders. "It's too slight a figure to be Sunderland. I must go to him, for he looks as if he'll fall at any moment." He caught her

284

close and kissed her warmly. "Rest you, my love; and stand by to help me get him aboard."

He turned, pulling off his coat, and a moment later dived into the translucent water.

Marina watched him swim steadily toward the shore, until her eyesight blurred, and she found that tears were streaming down her face. She was very tired, she realized. More tired than she had ever been. A good deal had happened, to be sure. . . . She blinked and rubbed away the blinding tears, and saw that Mr. Granville was already on his feet, wading through the shallows. Mr. Flete lurched toward him, arms outstretched, and they embraced for the first time since they were boys. Perhaps, now that the long misunderstanding was behind them, they could be friends. . . .

The two men swam slowly, side by side. They seemed to take a long time to reach the *Dolphin*, and Marina had plenty of time to consider the problem of how to get Mr. Flete aboard. She found a stout line and knotted it at intervals, making a loop in the end. She made it fast and lowered it over the side, just as the men came up to the boat. Mr. Flete clung to the rope for a few minutes, getting back his breath. Then he began to climb slowly aboard, pushed by Mr. Granville from below and helped by Marina from above. He fell into the *Dolphin*, crawled a little way and collapsed between two pigeon coops. He lay gasping, barely conscious, while Marina hurried to cover him, and Mr. Granville swung himself aboard.

"He needs a doctor," Mr. Granville declared, hurrying forward to weigh the anchor. "We'll get him to Margery—he has a dock at Hogshead Bay—"

Marina moved toward the mast but Mr. Granville stopped her. "I'll do that—we'll drift back into deeper water. You can rest."

She turned, only to be halted, aghast. "Look at the wreck!" she cried.

The *Carib Queen*, still brightly aflame, was breaking up quickly now, as the sea dragged at her waterlogged hull and the fire devoured her topsides. Even as they watched, she heeled over and slipped into the dancing waters of the moonlit lagoon in a smouldering mess of charred and scattered timbers, a ship no more.

Mr. Granville took Marina's hand in a warm grasp. "Sunderland's gone," he said. "Flete told me that just as he was leaving the *Sea Hawk*, he saw a man silhouetted against the flames when the main deck fell in. He saw him disappear, falling back into the heart of the fire."

Marina shivered. "So that is the end of Dr. Sunderland," she murmured. "In this world, at least . . ."

Granville squeezed her hand, and then moved forward to hoist the mainsail. "Do you wish that he had lived, to come to justice?"

"No," she said thoughtfully. "It's better so—even for poor Miss Winceyman."

"She has been more fortunate than she will ever realize. How long do you think it would have been before he tired of her—and contrived a way to dispose of her and keep her fortune for himself?" Mr. Granville cleated the halyard and came aft to take the helm, pulling Marina into the curve of his free arm. "And now, my love, how do you feel? You are so wet. Promise me you will not take an inflammation of the lungs and die."

"I'm too happy to die," Marina declared. "It has been so terrible not knowing—about Julia—about the wrecking—about my feelings—and, above all, about yours!"

Mr. Granville, sailing by instinct, took some minutes to demonstrate his feelings after this. When he next looked around, he cried out, "A sail! There's the *Pelican* at last."

Marina stared at him. "Now that there's nothing left—of him—will they believe your story?"

"There's Flete's evidence, remember."

"Yes . . . but he would have been told that Elijah was obeying you when he abducted me—and Flete does not know who struck him on the head—and he heard nothing of what happened on the *Carib Queen*."

"But you heard it all, my love—and I have no doubt that Colonel Dawlish, who admires you extremely, will believe your every word." His arm tightened round her. "You are a valuable witness and I must take care of you—even though you do look very odd," he added, staring at her. "Can it be soot? Your face is very dirty."

Marina gave a little choke of laughter. "I dyed it, to look like Rosett. I am wearing her clothes. I had to disguise myself to escape the guard in response to the note I thought you'd sent me."

"Resourceful girl!"

She dabbed at her face. "But I don't want you to see me like this," she protested.

"It would take more than that to dim your beauty," he assured her seriously.

Marina stared at him, entranced. He caught his breath, and laid his cheek against hers.

"Didn't you know? I have always recognized your beauty, my love, though at first I fought against both it and you."

"Always?" she queried, rubbing the dye off onto him. "Even when I swooned into your arms, on that first night?"

"Especially then, for that was the first time I saw you properly, when I was holding you—and I must own that what most infuriated me about you was the discovery that, though I disapproved of you so strongly, you had charmed me from that moment. Then admiration began reluctantly to take the place of disapproval. And when you told me your views on slavery, I knew that I was done for. You had the courage to let light into the darkest corners of my mind. There is a lot upon that subject I wish to say to you, and serious decisions to be made. Ah, my Marina, there is no one like you—"

At that instant the *Dolphin* ran aground. There was a slow deadening of her movement through the water, followed, as they were still staggering from loss of balance, by a harsher scraping sound.

"Oh, Lord," said Mr. Granville ruefully. "No sailor ought to allow himself to become distracted while in these shoal waters, even under such provocation, I suppose."

"I hope your boat may not be damaged," exclaimed Marina.

"What if it is?" he remarked easily. "The *Dolphin* is not so important in my life since meeting you, I find. It is Flete's condition that is of more concern to me, at the moment. But—" He stared across the moonlit water. "If I am not mistaken, the *Pelican* has already altered course toward us. She should be with us in twenty minutes or so, I think."

He disengaged himself from her reluctantly and went forward to assess the situation, leaving Marina to reflect upon the difference between one shipwreck and another—and to wonder what were the chances of undergoing such an experience twice within one month.

The *Dolphin* began to list slightly to starboard, but she was not in breaking water and seemed to be in no immediate danger. Mr. Granville threw out the anchor, bent over Mr. Flete for a few moments, and then made his way back to sit beside Marina.

"What a beautiful night," he remarked, his voice deepening as he drew her into his warm embrace. "Little did I ever think, my love, that the time would come when I should find myself aground upon Damnation Reef—and think it close to paradise!"